By the Same Author

Between Sisters
Goodbye, Saigon
Maximilian's Garden
Return from Darkness
Scam

The End of Marriage

Nina Vida

SIMON & SCHUSTER

NEW YORK   LONDON   TORONTO   SYDNEY   SINGAPORE

SIMON & SCHUSTER
Rockefeller Center
1230 Avenue of the Americas
New York, NY 10020

SIMON & SCHUSTER and colophon are registered trademarks
of Simon & Schuster, Inc.

Designed by Jan Pisciotta

Manufactured in the United States of America

1   3   5   7   9   10   8   6   4   2

Library of Congress Cataloging-in-Publication Data
Vida, Nina.
The end of marriage / Nina Vida.
p. cm.
I. Title.

PS3572.I29 E53 2002
813'.54—dc21   2002017553
ISBN 0-7432-1302-5

For information regarding special discounts for bulk purchases,
please contact Simon & Schuster Special Sales:
1-800-456-6798 or business@simonandschuster.com

Acknowledgments

For the sections concerning Vietnam, my appreciation to Luis Charles of the Vietnam Counseling Center in San Antonio, Texas, who let me probe his wartime experience in Vietnam and never refused to answer my questions, even the most painful.

Special thanks to my husband, Marvin Vida, who served in Korea and has over the years told me his own war stories and what it means to live minute to minute.

Thanks to Sharon Marr for getting me into San Onofre and for taking all those goofy pictures of me in that red hard hat.

And to my agent, Susan Gleason, thank you for keeping me in the game.

For Jack and Amorena and Alexandria

The End
of
Marriage

Chapter 1

❧

*I*t was pathetic. Teo ordered a *café con leche,* and the busboy dropped his tray of dirty dishes and scrambled out the back door.

"He can come back in," Teo said to the old woman behind the counter. "I'm not from Immigration."

If he were an INS agent he wouldn't bother with small fry like the busboy. He wouldn't even pay attention to the two young men at the table near the back door, faces seared black from a three- or four-day trek through the Arizona desert, who were sipping *horchatas* with their breakfast burritos, or the girl at the counter next to him eating chorizo and eggs, a string bag stuffed with clothes at her feet, who had just asked him in Guatemalan-accented Spanish if he would, *por favor,* pass the *pimienta.*

If he were an INS agent he'd go after the men he could see through the window, fifteen or twenty of them on the corner, wearing cheap shirts, work pants, and worn-down running shoes, some of them leaning against the chain-link fence, others squatting, elbows on knees, all of them looking as if they had been born in that spot and could wait forever for someone to stop and ask them if they were interested in a few hours' work.

The café was run-down, cement floor cracked, rickety tables with names gouged into the wood, strings of paper snowflakes, thick with dust, hanging from the ceiling. Café Tacuba. Teo used to come here on Saturday mornings with his dad for *café con leche* and buttered *bolillos.* The old woman was a young one then. She wore a flowered apron wrapped like a bandanna around her slender hips and called him *m'hijo* in the same way his mother did.

He went to grade school around the corner. Nuestra Señora Sagrada Academy for Boys. Spanish archways, liquidambars ringing the playground, nuns in wimples, boys in navy pants, white shirt, striped tie, their black lace-up shoes shining as bright as their mothers' copper pans.

He should have been at work. It was almost eight o'clock. He usually was out of the barrio by five in the morning and by five-ten drinking black coffee in the Dunkin' Donuts on Bristol. He had called the station, said he'd be in around nine, that he had trouble with his car. A lie. There was nothing wrong with his car. He had had one of his bad nights. Fireworks at a church carnival a few blocks from his house that sounded like gunshots pinging off the roof, like bombs going off, like grenades tossing mangled and bloody bodies into his dreams. At four-thirty he was up and sitting in a chair, but the images lingered past daylight and left him so wound up, wired, and jumpy, so goddamn angry at himself and everyone and everything, he needed to get himself straightened out before he went to work.

Take some time off, the police shrink told him in December when he was brought up for the second time in six months for insubordination.

And do what? Teo asked.

The *café con leche* was sweet and thick and slid down his throat in a soft rush. He didn't have to swallow hard to get it down like he did with American coffee.

Café con leche smooths away worries, his mother always said.

He would sit here for another fifteen minutes and then get going. The traffic on Main would be lighter by then. He'd be in better shape.

He could see a vendor setting up his cart in the plaza across from the movie, unfurling a ratty plastic awning, trays of watermelon and pineapple glistening in the early sun. The notary across the street had his OPEN sign hanging in the front window and a line of people at the door.

You need something to ease your anxiety, the shrink said and gave Teo some pills to take. He threw them away. Pills made him lose his concentration.

Lots of traffic. An older-model Buick with a dented rear fender and a dangling taillight entering the intersection. Woman driver. Brakes behind her squealing as she stopped dead in the middle of the intersection, opened the door, and got out. Young, but not too young. Light brown hair loose and swinging, a sweater half thrown around her shoulders. Probably from a business in Costa Mesa, cruising the barrio streets looking for cheap labor. Definitely not one of the rich Newport Beach matrons needing a few undocumented workers to clear the weeds from around the boat slip. Not dressed smart enough for that. Doesn't drive the right car. And she's in a hurry, has to be somewhere. A restaurant, most likely. The last undocumented got picked up and she needs someone to peel the potatoes. Gutsy, abandoning the car in the middle of the street and ignoring the horns, not giving a damn.

She was up on the curb, had picked out her man, a sun-wrinkled, sturdy one wearing a baseball cap, and was leading him back to her car. Taking her time now, looking around. Didn't want her prize to get run over. Opening the car door. Hesitating. Looking in the direction of the café. Staring at the grease-smudged window as if she could see inside. The sun was all wrong for that, but Teo turned around, anyway, removed himself from her line of sight, and didn't see her drive away.

Chapter 2

‰

It was around nine o'clock in the morning, give or take fifteen minutes, when Alice Miller called her sister, Ellie, at her job at Mickey's Surfside Restaurant and told her she had killed her husband. Manuel had just stepped into the restaurant office to complain to Ellie about the lettuce, that it was brown, where the hell was the fresh produce delivery, it should have been here at seven, and Ellie better not pay the wholesaler one dime more until he got his act together, and right at that moment the phone rang and it was Alice, sobbing so hard that at first Ellie thought she was saying, "I thrilled Morty" (which made no sense at all), and only after about four "Calm downs" from Ellie did she understand that what Alice was saying was, "I killed Morty."

Ellie grabbed her purse, yelled through Mickey's open door that Alice was in trouble (she didn't wait for him to ask what kind of trouble or couldn't it wait or wasn't she supposed to go over the menus with Manuel and show the new boy how Manuel liked the vegetables sliced, and what price was today's soup du jour, anyway), but ran out the door, jumped into her car, and headed up Jamboree Road.

She zipped past the above-the-ocean outdoor escalators of the Fashion Island Mall, past the awninged restaurants on San Joaquin Hills Road (all of them swankier than Mickey's Surfside, which wasn't at surfside at all but down on a side street off Pacific Coast Highway), barely missing a head-on with a van on MacArthur.

Alice's house was at the top of a hill in Newport Beach, the best hill in the best part of Newport. Ellie zoomed up the drive and didn't park her car so much as abandon it, left the car door gaping open, and ran up the steps. She had a key to the house. Alice had given it to her the week before Christmas when she showed up at Mickey's, her eye bandaged, and said she thought it would be a good idea for Ellie to have a key, that anything could happen to her or Morty, that they were getting older, and Ellie should be able to get into the house in case of an emergency. As for her bandaged eye, Alice said she fainted, that she was standing on the ladder decorating the Christmas tree and suddenly everything went black, and the next thing she knew Morty was driving her to the doctor to get her eye stitched.

It had nagged at Ellie, that bandaged eye in December, but she and Eric were about to separate, and their eight-year-old son, Jamie, had died in March and it was the first Christmas without him, so it didn't register as forcefully as it should have. Then in February she happened to see Alice in Gelson's Market on Lido Isle shopping for lamb chops. Alice's upper lip was bandaged, and that should have sounded an alarm with Ellie, but it didn't. She remembered asking Alice what happened to her lip, and what was it Alice told her? That she was eating dinner and jabbed herself in the mouth with a fork?

Morty's body was on the bed in the master bedroom. He was lying on his left side, his legs curled into an S, a silver blue snub-nosed gun nestled almost lovingly in the fingers of his right hand, which was resting, as if the gun were too heavy, on the pillow next to his head. Alice, in a pink bathrobe and fuzzy white slippers, was on her knees next to the bed, her head down as if she were hunting for something she had lost.

"Is he dead, Ellie? Is he really, truly dead?" she said without looking up.

Ellie stared at Morty's bloodstained pillow, studied it actually, as if the size and shape of the stain would give her the answer to Alice's question, and the thought struck her that if she could figure out how much blood it took to make that stain, she would be able to answer Alice's question. Wasn't there an amount of blood loss that was fatal? And hadn't she spent enough time in the restaurant kitchen to know how much liquid volume of gravy it took to soak ten inches of toweling, which couldn't be too different from ten inches of percale, and wasn't there a connection there?

"Is he?" Alice said again.

He was holding the gun. He had killed himself. Alice had just been confused. She said she killed him when she meant to say he killed himself. Ellie leaned against the bedcovers and placed her hand on his arm. It was surprisingly warm. There hadn't been time for him to cool. It wasn't like Jamie, who was already glacial to the touch when she lay across his body in the hospital corridor and wouldn't get up, even when the doctor and Eric and two nurses tried pulling her away.

Aside from the small hole above Morty's bushy brow, he didn't look dead, merely relaxed. The hole, drilled as neatly as a carpenter's stud, hadn't bled much. A spray of blood on his forehead, a few drops on the collar of his white shirt, and a red circular stain on the pillow. It wasn't the gory mess Ellie would have expected. Not that her experience with dead bodies was that extensive. Dad, a peaceful expression on his face, was in his casket at the funeral home wearing his black suit and striped tie the last time she saw him. When Mom died, ravaged by cancer, Ellie was away at college. By the time she got home, the embalmers had filled Mom's mouth with cotton and put lipstick on her mouth and rouge on her cheeks, and it didn't even look like her. As for Jamie, all Ellie remembered was seeing him being rolled out into the hospital corridor with what looked like a shower cap on his curly hair and tubes sticking out of his mouth and nose and somewhere in the distance hearing the surgeon say that it had just been a routine tonsillectomy and he didn't understand what happened.

But it was Morty's face, his right eye staring absently at the mirrored dressing room wall (a fold of pillow was covering his left eye, so she couldn't tell what that one was doing), that cinched it. Yes, he was really, truly, irretrievably dead. And if he weren't, wouldn't he have sat up and said something to her, or at least twitched when she touched him?

"He is," Ellie said.

Alice's whole demeanor changed after that. Suddenly she was calm and composed, and when Ellie asked her if she'd like a cup of coffee, said quickly that she thought she would and followed her into the kitchen.

There was fresh coffee in the coffeemaker. Ellie poured a cup for Alice and one for herself.

"There's no cream in the house," Alice said. "I was going to go shopping, but I didn't get a chance. There might be some Cremora in the cupboard."

"Please, Alice, sit down, I'll drink it black."

"I know I have some Cremora somewhere."

She began opening cupboard doors. Shelf paper with a light blue border matched stacks of hand-painted Italian dishes. Canned goods were lined up neatly. Spices had a shelf to themselves and revolved on a little merry-go-round affair. Alice spun the merry-go-round, touching each one of the bottles, tipping them backward to check the labels. At one point she pulled a step stool from the service porch into the kitchen so she could examine the very top shelves. It seemed to Ellie that Alice must be in shock. How else to explain the transformation from hysteria on the telephone ten minutes before to now behaving as if her husband's death were just a random glitch in an otherwise ordinary day? If she wasn't in shock, then she certainly was behaving weirdly. The Alice that Ellie knew would have collapsed at the sight of Morty's body, would now be so traumatized she'd be unable to function. The Alice she knew was the one who came home to the artichoke ranch in Visalia after her divorce from her first husband and didn't get out of bed for a month. Ellie was barely five years old then and couldn't remember the exact details of the marriage or why they got divorced, but she remembered Dad locking himself in the bedroom and practicing the violin for hours on end and Mom sitting on the ladder-back chair in the dark kitchen reading the Bible. There was another husband after that. Ellie was away at Berkeley when Alice divorced him, but Mom wrote and said Alice didn't stop crying for a week.

"I could have sworn the Cremora was on the spice shelf," Alice said. Her hand flicked the handle of the sugar bowl, and white grains emptied out onto the floor. "I might have put it on the shelf with the olive oil and balsamic vinegar, because I sometimes do that when I'm in a hurry, but it's not there now."

That was when Ellie noticed for the first time that there was blood all up and down the front of Alice's bathrobe, long zigzaggy gooey streaks, as if painted on with a brush dipped in ketchup.

"I'm not sorry I killed him," Alice said vaguely and sat down at the table.

"You didn't kill him," Ellie replied. "He killed himself. Why do you keep saying you killed him?"

"Because I did."

"But the gun's in his hand."

Alice poured what was left of the sugar into her coffee and then stirred vigorously, the way she might have stirred cake batter, from the bottom up, dipping the spoon in shovel fashion, then letting the coffee drip back into the cup.

"I put it there. It dropped and landed on the floor, and I didn't want it to look like I was the one who had the gun and was waving it around, and I thought about the police and how I'd explain it, and it seemed just so hard to remember the details, what came first and what came second, and so I just picked it up and put it in his hand."

"You didn't."

"But I did. And I didn't faint and fall off a ladder last Christmas or jab my lip with a fork in February. It was Morty."

"Morty?"

"I didn't want to worry you."

"I don't understand. I never saw him do or say anything the least bit out of—"

"Well, he did."

"You're telling me he beat you?"

"You'd think he'd have been used to me by now and wouldn't mind that I haven't kept myself up. But I'm not blaming him for that. Lord knows, it's my fault that I look the way I do. I did get fat and I didn't keep myself up."

"You never said a word."

"I don't have any discipline. I never have had any. That's been my problem all my life, Ellie, not having any discipline, just letting myself kind of float, not knowing when to say yes or no or even understanding what was going on around me. I always feel like I'm in a fog and everyone else is in the sunshine."

Ellie was at the sink now, turning on the cold water. Paper towels to the left of the sink, press a button, the motor hums, and a large square of love-knot-patterned paper zips down, and then some contraption in the back cuts it clean and drops it on the counter. She had been virtually sleepwalking through life since Jamie died, not reading the papers or watching television, not calling old friends, not having her weekly lunches with Alice, doing nothing but going to work, coming home, eating something that didn't take more than five minutes to prepare, and then going to bed. And now it was as if a bomb had gone off and she was wide awake.

"I wish you had told me."

"I didn't want to bother you."

Ellie pressed the button for two squares, held them beneath the running water, then swiped at Alice's bloody robe with the wet paper towels, rubbing hard, first one direction and then another, pulling at the fabric as if she wanted to rip it apart, but all she did was smear blood over the entire front of the robe.

"There wasn't anything you could have done," Alice said. "There wasn't anything I could have done. I tried so hard, but it was never the same thing, it was always something else that he didn't like about me, another failing, another misstep. I know I'm not the brightest thing in the world, but I didn't need him to point it out all the time and get so mad over every little thing I did or said until I was almost afraid to breathe."

She had blood in her hair, glistening red dots staining the gray strands near her forehead. Ellie dabbed at the spots with the wet paper towel.

"He came in late last night, and this morning I asked him where he had been—it was just a question, just like you'd say is the meat cooked all right, and I didn't mean anything by it, but the minute I asked him where he'd been, I knew it was the wrong question, I knew he'd get mad, and he did.

"He said he didn't have to tell me where he went or what he did, and I said I wasn't telling him what to do, because I was trying to fix it, trying to take back the question, but there was no taking it back, it was already too late, he already had that wound-up look, and I knew I was in for it.

"I went to the bathroom, and then I made some coffee, and I came back into the bedroom and that's when I saw he was playing with the gun, and he held it out in front of him, aiming at my head, then at my chest, then at my legs, and he started telling me how my being alive polluted the air he was breathing, and I knew he was going to kill me this time, that he meant it. So I reached over and pushed the gun away. I just wanted to get it away from me, and I did it automatically, just punched his hand, and when I did that my wrist bumped against his wrist, and the gun went this way, and I heard the noise and it surprised me more than anything else, the noise, I mean, and I thought I was shot, I really did, I looked down at my chest first thing because I was sure he had shot me, and there was blood on my bathrobe, but I didn't feel a thing, and then when I looked over at him he had the strangest expression on his face, as if he wanted to say something to me but couldn't find the words, and it wasn't until he lay back against the pillow that I realized he was the one who was shot."

"I can't get the spots out of your robe," Ellie said. "I don't know, Alice, they just won't come out."

She tugged at the woolly sleeves of the bathrobe. Alice bought her clothes a size too small, as if she were sure that by the time she brought them home she would be fifteen pounds thinner. The bathrobe clung stubbornly to Alice's arms. One arm free, then the other one. Underneath was a cotton nightgown, the blousy kind that starts at the shoulders and balloons out into a loose, gauzy tent. She was plump, but without clothes on she looked smaller, as if the fat had swallowed up her bones and shrunk her down until there was nothing left but a frail, sagging heap. There were yellowish purple bruises on her chest and upper arms. Ellie asked her if Morty had done that, and Alice said yes, and a lot more, mostly where it didn't show, like cracked ribs and a bruised kidney.

"I always had an excuse to tell the doctor. One time it was an automobile accident. Another time I told him I fell down the front steps at home.

Then once I told him a door in the supermarket banged in my face, and that was a mistake, because the doctor told me I should sue the store, and I said I would, and then I worried for a whole month after that that he'd call me up and check to see if I had done it yet."

"I'm so wounded that you didn't confide in me."

"Oh, honey," Alice said.

Ellie removed Alice's blood-specked glasses and took them to the sink and held them under running water.

"Would you like a Valium?" Alice said. "You're not looking so great. I think you should sit down."

Alice stood up and Ellie sat down. This was nothing like when Jamie died. Things like burst blood vessels sometimes happened during surgery. You didn't expect them to happen, but they did. Ellie had wanted to stay in the hospital with Jamie the night before surgery, sleep on a cot in his room, but Eric said kids get their tonsils out every day, don't make a baby out of him, you'll see him in the morning. Jamie dying during a tonsillectomy was an unexpected horror. This was craziness.

"You can't take this on yourself," Alice said. "I mean personally on yourself, as if you did it, or were to blame somehow, when it was all my doing, my marrying him and putting up with him, and there was no reason before now to even tell you a thing about who he was or what he did to me, and I can see that I was right not to, just looking at your face. You look about to pass out, honey."

"I'm not."

"Your face is red."

"I'm just warm."

"Well, I think a Valium will help."

The bottle of Valium was in a cupboard to the left of the sink. Alice flipped open the lid of the bottle and shook a pill out into Ellie's palm.

"Swallow it, honey, it'll make you feel better."

"I should be comforting you." Ellie put the pill in her mouth and took a sip of coffee.

"You *are* comforting me. Just by being here you're comforting me."

"We'll have to think about what you should say to the police."

"Shouldn't I just tell them what I told you?"

"No."

"But they'll figure it out, won't they? They always do. Every movie, every book, the police always figure it out."

"There's nothing to figure out. It was an accident."

"Then why don't I just tell them that?"

"Because it's too complicated, and you'll never say it the same way twice, and they'll trip you, you know they will, so let me think, it just has to be a simple statement, no long explanations, just something easy that you can remember."

The Valium was working already. Alice and her little bottle of Valium. She had brought it with her to the cemetery in Simi Valley when Jamie was buried and handed them out like candy.

"Here's what you're going to say. You took a sleeping pill last night and you didn't wake up until eight-thirty this morning to go to the bathroom, and that's when you heard the shot. You came into the bedroom and found him, but you were groggy from the sleeping pill and—no, that's too much for you to remember. All you have to say is that you woke up, went to the bathroom, heard a shot, and when you came into the bedroom there he was. That's enough. Don't say one more thing. He shot himself. That's all you have to say is that he shot himself."

There was still the bloody bathrobe to take care of. Ellie carried it into the service porch and put it in the washing machine. Soaps were lined up on the shelf behind the dryer. She poured some Tide onto the bathrobe and set the dial for cold water soak. The service porch was spotless, floor swept, cleaning supplies, mops, brooms, vacuum in military precision in their storage space next to the back door. Alice was a cleaner. She had always been a cleaner. It could take her all day to clean a room, but when she was done, it was a work of art. She'd Q-Tip corners, take toasters apart to get at the last few crumbs, climb on ladders to pluck cobwebs from the crown moldings with her fingers.

Ellie didn't want to go into the bedroom again, but there was no other way to the dressing room. It was eerie. Just standing in the doorway looking at the bed, at the lumpy figure lying across the covers. Dead or not, Ellie wanted to hit him over the head, smash him around, smother him with his bloodstained pillow. All that smiling and glad-handing and bragging about big deals and mergers and capital gains, when all the time he was beating Alice so badly she had to make up stories to tell the doctor.

Morning shadows licked the white walls. Time to wake up, Morty, time to wake up. She crossed the room toward the bed and stood looking down at him, wondering at the finality of it, at the mystery of how he could have been arguing with Alice an hour ago and wasn't breathing now. He hadn't moved. Ellie poked at his arm with her finger. His skin was turning color, somewhere between alabaster and honey, with purple dots that looked like asterisks sprinkled here and there.

Alice has finally found the right man, Mom wrote Ellie, who was then in her second year at Berkeley, taking premed courses because Dad said to aim high. *He's from Michigan,* Mom wrote, *believes the Bible is the word of God, and loves Alice and will take care of her.*

Mom sent one more letter after that. In it she wrote that the artichoke crop was doing well, prices higher than last year, she had a black spot growing on her chest, Alice and Morty went to Lake Tahoe to get married instead of having a church wedding (in the margin Mom added that she wasn't so sure now that Morty believed that the Bible was the true word of God, and it has been giving her sleepless nights), that Dad thinks Ellie can do better than the B's and C's of last semester, and they both hope she's attending church faithfully (she wasn't). Also included was a typewritten passage from Deuteronomy, something incomprehensible about not eating too many grapes from a field that doesn't belong to you.

One morning a week later Dad woke up, got out of bed, looked out the window at the rows of artichokes, dew-damp and glistening like emeralds in the sun, said what a nice day it was, and died. Ellie met Morty for the first time at Dad's funeral. He was loud and brash. *Investing in oil wells in Texas,* he said. *Really love your sister,* he said.

Within a year Mom was dead, the black spot on her chest grown into a cancer that had wrapped its tentacles around her heart. Soon after that

Ellie met Eric, left Berkeley, and got married. There hadn't been much of Alice in her life after that. Even after Morty moved his business to Newport Beach and he and Alice bought a house there, Ellie didn't see too much of her. There were too many years' difference in their ages. They didn't have anything in common. Alice never read a book, didn't quite grasp what was going on if it was the least bit abstract. When they used to have lunch together on Wednesdays (most of the time Alice would cancel at the last minute), they'd talk about vegetables, what was in season, and fruit, what new varieties were coming to market, and exchange dessert recipes. That was one thing they had in common, they both liked to cook and were good at it. Mom always said a woman who can cook a tasty meal is beloved by the Lord and bound to go to heaven.

She leaned closer to the bed. Wasn't there supposed to be some sign of decomposition by now, the hiss of gases escaping from flaccid tissues, the creaking of limbs as they contorted in rigor mortis? And had it really happened the way Alice said it did? Her story seemed so tidy, so smooth. But the stitched eye and cut lip, Ellie had seen them, those were real. Besides, Alice didn't lie.

She went into the dressing room and pulled a bathrobe out of the closet. A yellow cotton with green piping. She would make it up to Alice. She hadn't paid attention to her this whole past year. She would pay attention now.

The bathrobe looked too fresh, too neat and unwrinkled. She rumpled it up, twisted it, pulled a side seam until threads came loose, then yanked and kneaded the material until she was satisfied that it looked as if Alice had been wearing it all morning, and might even have slept in it.

Chapter 3

*T*eo was at his desk when the call came in.

"Teodoro Domingos, Homicide," he said into the phone.

A woman's voice explaining that her brother-in-law had committed suicide. She was talking fast and sounded nervous.

"His name is Morton Miller," she said. "Was. I guess I should say was Morton Miller. Morty. *M-i-l-l-e-r.* He shot himself at eight-thirty this morning, and my sister found the—do you need her name?"

"It would help."

"Alice Miller. *A-l-i-c-e.* I didn't exactly look at the clock, but it was right around eight-thirty because I had just gotten to work. Do you want to know where I work?"

"Sure."

"Mickey's Surfside in Newport Beach."

"You are?"

"Ellie Holmgren. Eleanor. I'm the only one in the family with a nickname. There isn't that much family left, actually. I have an aunt in San Francisco. Celia. She always called me Eleanor, but she's in a nursing home and she didn't know who I was the last time I visited her, so the last person in the world to call me Eleanor is non compos mentis. I'm not usually this nervous. I practically run Mickey's Surfside, but people I know don't shoot themselves every day of the week. It's really strange how childhood nicknames stay with you even when you're grown up."

The caller's voice became inaudible, as if she were sniffling or choking, and then a dead spot, as if the phone had been disconnected or she had put her hand over the receiver. After a few seconds she was back, but her voice was weaker. He recognized the call now for what it was. A mercy mission. Without knowing one more fact, he could bet that the sister offed her husband, left a mess, and the sister was taking care of it.

"Manuel—he's the chef at Mickey's—and I don't want to get him involved in this, because he doesn't know anything about it except that I got this telephone call from Alice and ran out of the restaurant without calling the wholesaler about the brown lettuce—but that's why I'm telling you his name, because that's actually how I know what time Alice called me. Manuel had just asked me about the vegetable delivery because the lettuce was brown, and he was angry about it, and we always get lettuce between seven and eight, so it was probably, like I said, around eight-thirty when Alice called and said Morty had shot himself."

"Where's your sister now?"

"Alice?"

"Alice."

"In the kitchen. I'm at her house. With her. She's in the kitchen. I'm calling because she's too upset. Besides, she didn't know who to call, whether she was supposed to notify the police or a doctor, and to tell the truth I'm not certain myself, but to play it safe I thought I'd better call the police first, and—"

Inaudible. What were the last two words?

"—unless I'm supposed to call a doctor, in which case I'll hang up and do that, but I did want to be sure she was—I was doing the right thing."

The suicide was only about two miles from the station. Teo and George (George was Teo's new partner; Rafe, who had been his partner for ten years, retired in February) got in the car and drove over there.

The house was on a quiet street on a hill above Newport Harbor, a phalanx of towering fir trees at its back. It was the only faux Colonial on a street of angular, low-slung ranch houses. No cars parked at the curb. Junipers in white pots at the end of the long brick drive. An older model Oldsmobile, door hanging open, in the driveway behind a new silver

Lexus. Down below in the harbor a motorboat bounced along the blue water of the channel, its foamy wake rippling out toward the heavy-bottomed, flag-bedecked yachts moored at pierside.

George knocked and when no one came to the door, he opened it and went in. Teo stood on the steps for a few seconds looking down at the harbor. The victim probably owned one of the yachts moored down below, probably one with a catchy name—*Sail Aweigh* or *Sea Me Go.* Most of them never sailed anywhere, never even left the pier. Teo used to patrol the harbor before he made Homicide. Rowdy parties on yachts had been his specialty. He could break up a fight in two seconds flat, knew when to swing the baton and when to butt heads and didn't care whether he got written up for it or not. Sometimes all it took for the partyers to cool down was for Teo to show up in his cop uniform, six foot three, wild eyed and dangerous looking, raise his arm, ball his hand into a hard fist—like a swami calling to his disciples, some observers said; like an evil god about to vent his wrath, others said—and in minutes people were scrambling over the side of the yacht, onto the dock, and into their cars.

Teo followed George inside and closed the door.

There were voices coming from somewhere on the other side of the house.

"I'll do the interview," George said. "You check out the corpse. And don't give me any argument."

George had come over to Homicide three months before after twenty-three years at Missing Persons. He had seen just one dead body in his whole career at M.P., a surfer who was swept by a rogue wave into the pilings of the Huntington Beach pier, broke his neck, and was washed up four days later on the beach down in Newport. Teo had seen hundreds of bodies, not even counting the ones in Vietnam.

George headed to where the voices were coming from and left Teo in the foyer.

"I'm Detective Behrens, George Behrens, from Homicide," Teo heard George say to someone. A woman's voice murmuring something back. There was no crying or wailing.

He moved slowly through the house. A bitching place. He had been in houses like this before, rich people's houses, where the air was filtered, where the water, cold and pure, was piped in from an antediluvian stream somewhere in the mountains above Lake Arrowhead, houses with too many rooms for the amount of people living in them, put together by some decorator over on Lido Isle who was on the verge of getting a spread in *Architectural Digest* but hadn't broken out yet and still had to settle for two pictures and a paragraph in *Orange Coast Magazine*. The place was packed with furniture and knickknacks. Venetian mirrors, French tables, Oriental rugs. Every surface slick and shining.

Goddamn that George. He was skating on thin ice, on the verge, about to fall into the sinkhole. If he pulled seniority one more time, Teo wouldn't be responsible for what happened next.

Dining room down two steps to the right of the foyer. No one ate in there. No food spots on the rug, no scratches on the gleaming mahogany table. There was an odd smell in there. Furniture polish, petroleum base with lemon oil added.

What did George know about conducting a homicide investigation, anyway? What did he know about death? He hadn't even been in Vietnam. What did he say got him a deferment? Surfer knees?

The library was next to the dining room. Plush. Quiet. Leatherbound books on shelves that wound around the room. No dust on the tops of the books, the volumes carefully arranged by size, taller books separated from shorter ones (no attempt to sort by genre), everything ruler straight.

Shit. Tell the *cholos* in Santa Ana about surfer knees. Tell it to the vets in the barrio, down on Fourth and Main, drinking cheap wine, still wearing their combat jackets and jungle boots. Go on, ask them what they think about skipping Vietnam because your surfboard gave you knobby knees.

Casement windows looked out into the back garden. Fountains. A gazebo. A small putting green.

The kitchen. George was in there. Two women were with him, sitting at a big oak table while George leaned against the sink, his I'm-not-here-to-arrest-you look plastered across his face. He was wearing a gray suit that had a gravy stain on the lapel. Even if you didn't know about his surfer knees, you could just about tell who he was by that gravy stain.

A big kitchen. A family of four could live in it and have room left over. Sub-Zero, ice maker, eight-burner copper stove. Alice must be the one in the bathrobe and slippers. Late fifties. Hair freshly combed.

"I'm Ellie, Alice's sister," the other woman said. She looked right at Teo. Right straight at him. He recognized her. The woman in the Buick in front of Café Tacuba. She was better looking close up. Not a babe, but not bad either. Blond hair. Petite. Forty-two, -three. She was holding her sister's hand. Tight, it looked like from the doorway.

"Hi," Teo said and smiled. "Detective Domingos. You all right in here?"

"We're fine," George said.

"Everything in order?"

"I do the interview, you examine the corpse. Remember? When I get through here, I'll be in, we'll go over particulars. Okay?"

"Sure."

"The master bedroom's straight down the hall and to the left of the library," Ellie said. "Didn't I speak to you on the phone? I never forget voices."

"He reports to me," George said.

"Oh."

"The body's in the room down the hall?" Teo said.

"On the bed," Ellie replied. "We didn't move him. I touched his arm, but that's all. If you want, I'll go in with you, show you where he is. It's down the hall and to the left. Right past the library. You can't miss him. On the bed."

Teo didn't move. "What's upstairs?"

"A game room, two more bedrooms with adjoining baths."

"Adjoining baths," Alice murmured.

"You need a doctor or anything?"

"I'm taking care of this end," George said sharply.

Teo ignored him. "Just two people live in the house?"

"Just my sister and her husband," Ellie said.

Alice nodded.

There were cups of coffee on the table, steam circling the rims.

"Who made the coffee?" Teo asked.

"You know, this is really beginning to boil me," George said. "I outrank you. Do what I said. Get out of here."

"I made the coffee," Alice said.

"Did you hear what I said?"

"What time was that?" Teo asked.

"Oh, my," Alice replied.

Teo pulled out his blue notebook, flipped over a few pages, and jotted down, *Wife made coffee. Before or after?*

"Did you bring the newspaper in, too?"

A folded paper was lying on the kitchen table, the stained-glass skylight overhead laying pools of purple and red onto the newsprint.

"Morty did," Alice said.

"Your husband."

"I told you to check the corpse," George said.

"I'm in a daze, I think," Alice said, and put her head in her hands. "Everything's so hazy."

"You don't have to say anything," Ellie told her. "They know what they're doing, and it's all right if you just let them do it and don't say anything. Do you need a drink of water or an aspirin or anything?"

"Maybe a drink of water."

"You want to hash it out right here, right now?" George said.

Ellie was pouring water into a glass, standing right next to George. Teo stepped toward George (which squeezed Ellie up against the ice maker) and mumbled a few words to him, something on the order of wanting to break his head open.

"I can take Alice out to my car," Ellie said. "We'll just go out and sit in the car in the driveway. I don't mind taking her outside. Fresh air will do her good."

"You both stay here," George said.

Teo stepped back. "The body's where?" he asked and tugged at his shirt collar with his left hand. "Down the hall?"

"Down the hall," Ellie said.

"I'm really confused right now," Alice said. "I took a sleeping pill last night, and right now I'm not sure of anything. To tell you the truth, I'm not sure whether I made the coffee or Morty did. I usually do, but sometimes he does. He might have. I can't remember."

"It's all right," Ellie said, and gave her sister's arm a squeeze.

Teo left the kitchen and stood in the hall—an atrium, he thought some people called it, or a gallery—windows facing the garden tinted a slate blue to protect the art hanging on the inside wall. He stared at the pictures. Modern art, blobs of color. And he didn't know what happened in there. He had let the brakes slip. He looked down at his hands. His fingers were still clenched. He had almost hit him. He didn't know why he hadn't. He took a few deep breaths and wished he had a cigarette. He had quit smoking on New Year's Day. Not because he thought smoking was unhealthy but because he couldn't take it or leave it. It was the last addiction to go, the drug habit he picked up in Vietnam being the first.

He walked past the library to the bedroom. More like a suite. Sitting area, fireplace, built-in TV, stereo, refrigerator. The drapes were drawn, the only illumination a sliver of sun that striped across the jumble of covers on the bed and glinted on the shiny steel of the gun. He pulled open the drapes. Sunlight flooded the room. No sign of a struggle or a fight.

The corpse was on the bed, dressed except for his shoes. Eyes fixed and staring. Mouth slightly open. Slender, somewhere in his sixties, took good care of himself, watched what he ate, might have worked out with weights. Wearing a hairpiece. The bullet had nicked it and knocked it sideways on his head.

Suicides usually looked surprised. He didn't look surprised. He was cradling the gun against his cheek as if he were about to use the muzzle to scratch an itch. Judging from the position of the body on the bed, he could either have lain down, reached over to the end table, and grabbed the gun, or he could have had it in his hand, then sat down on the edge of the bed, both feet on the floor as if he were about to put on his shoes (he was wearing lisle socks, gray with a black stripe), then said, What the hell, put the gun to his head, pulled the trigger, and keeled over.

Teo turned and stood with his back to the carved headboard, then sat down next to the corpse and rolled to the left so that his arm was touching the corpse's back. He could have shot himself that way, but the gun would have fallen out of his hand, he wouldn't still be clutching it. Unless his finger caught in the trigger. That was possible. But do you get partially dressed and then, as an afterthought, kill yourself?

Across the hall in the library a radio was still on. Surf conditions, one- to three-foot swells. Lots of activity going on before the guy put the bullet in. Radio. Newspaper. Coffee. Or was it after?

"Tell me how it happened," he could hear George saying in the kitchen.

"She doesn't remember," Ellie said.

There wasn't much blood. A splash on his face and collar, a ring of blood in the middle of his forehead where the bullet had made a rosette-shaped hole, and a halo-shaped stain that started at the tip of the left ear and was beginning to dry into a grainy red scab on the white pillow.

"She came out of the dressing room when she heard the shot," Ellie was saying.

"Let her answer," George said.

"I did that, yes, that's what I did," Alice said.

"And the first thing you did was call your sister?"

The corpse's fingers were white, the nails manicured. Too old for Vietnam.

"What exactly are you driving at?" Ellie was saying.

Teo would have held the reins tight, wouldn't have let the sister say a word. First thing you know she'll be stopping the interview and calling a lawyer, and then the whole thing gets muddled and dragged out when it doesn't have to be, when all they have to do is say what happened.

Chapter 4

It was three-thirty in the afternoon by the time the coroner arrived and put Morty on a gurney and wheeled him out. The crime lab people had come and gone, the videographer had done his videoing and left, Detective Behrens had gone in there for a few minutes when the coroner arrived, but he was back in the kitchen now. Only Detective Domingos was still in there doing something. When Ellie went into the bedroom at four-fifteen to get Alice's purse (Behrens wanted to see her driver's license and Social Security card, as if that were connected in some way to Morty's death), Domingos was kneeling next to the empty bed checking, it looked to Ellie, the quality of the carpet.

"All I want to know is why you got up at eight-thirty, Mrs. Miller," Behrens said. He was standing with his back to the sink, his arms folded over his stomach.

"I just woke up. I don't know why. I just did."

"Give me a reason. Any reason."

"Well, I probably had to go to the bathroom."

"You probably did? You don't know if you did or not?"

"You know what I think your problem is, Detective?" Ellie said brightly. "I think you're suffering from low blood sugar. It usually hits people this time of day, especially when they haven't eaten lunch."

"We should have had lunch," Alice said, nodding her head. "A body wasn't meant to go all day on just breakfast. I hadn't even noticed that lunchtime came and went, it's all been such a blur."

"Most times you're not aware of the sugar depletion," Ellie added. "You just get cranky and start feeling out of sorts. Nine times out of ten, that's what it is."

"I made blueberry tarts yesterday," Alice said. "There are still three in the refrigerator."

"Don't go to any bother," Behrens said.

"It's no bother," Ellie said.

"No bother at all," Alice echoed.

Ellie made a fresh pot of coffee and Alice brought the three tarts out of the refrigerator and arranged them on one of her Nippon hearts-and-flowers dishes.

"Why don't you sit down and make yourself comfortable?" Ellie said. "You've been standing all day, you must be tired."

"Eating standing up is bad for the digestion," Alice added.

Behrens sat down, and Alice put a napkin in front of him (which he draped over his left knee), and Ellie poured his coffee.

"Cream and sugar?" Ellie said.

"I take it black."

"I could make some whipped cream to put on the tarts, if you'd like," Alice said. "It just takes a minute."

"No, thanks, have to watch my waistline."

He ate quickly, in a greedy, packing-the-mouth, snuffly way, as if he were afraid someone would come in and ask him what he was doing.

"I don't know why a man whose wife could bake pies like these would kill himself." He had demolished two and was now devouring the third.

"Can I talk to you a minute?" It was Domingos at the door to the kitchen.

"Can't it wait?" Behrens pulled the napkin off his lap and hastily wiped his mouth. "I'm busy here."

"No, it can't wait. I'm working and you're fucking around."

"I heard you were written up twice for insubord. You want to go for three?"

Alice had begun to shake. "I really don't know what's going on."

"It's okay, Alice," Ellie said. "It's okay, honey, it's between them, it has nothing to do with you."

The two men were out in the hall now, and Behrens was trying to calm Domingos down, telling him he ought to see someone, he really had a problem, no one wanted to work with him, he should do something about that hair-trigger temper of his. It was quiet after that. The door to the bedroom opened and closed. The bathroom door opened, a light went on in the hall, and Behrens came back into the kitchen.

"All right," Behrens said. He didn't sit down again, but took up his arms-folded position against the sink. "Now, Mrs. Miller, let's start over again. What did you say you were doing when you heard the shot?"

"She told you she was in the bathroom," Ellie said.

"*You* told me she was in the bathroom."

"I was in the bathroom," Alice said.

"You were in the bathroom."

"She was in the bathroom," Ellie repeated.

There were policemen out in front of the house, their cars parked at the curb. Ellie glanced at them through the kitchen window. Behrens was letting huge gaps of time go by between questions now, as if he had grown weary of the whole process, and the policemen out in front didn't seem to have anything to do but stand on the sidewalk. One of them was yawning.

"Did you know your husband had a gun?"

"No. Yes. I'm not sure." She looked at Ellie. "Did I ever tell you that Morty had a gun?"

"You never told me," Ellie said.

"It's something you should remember," Behrens said.

"Oh, I don't know about that," Alice replied. "I don't pay attention to lots of things that other people pay attention to."

"You wouldn't have paid attention to a gun?"

"What's so important about a gun?"

"You never mentioned a gun to me, I'm sure of it," Ellie said.

"Then I didn't know that he had one, or I'm sure I would have told you."

"And there was no note?" Behrens said.

"You mean like a letter?" Alice replied.

"All right, then, a letter. Something saying why he wanted to kill himself."

"He never wrote a letter to anyone in his whole life that I know of."

"Not a regular letter, Mrs. Miller. A suicide note. A person only has to write one suicide note. It's a onetime thing."

"I didn't see any letters or notes. He was very neat, he never left anything lying around."

"I'm not saying he wasn't neat. He could be neat and still leave a suicide note."

"I didn't see one."

"Are you going to be staying in the house? Can you at least tell me that much?"

"She's coming home with me," Ellie said.

"I can't stay here," Alice said.

"She definitely can't stay here," Ellie said firmly.

"These questions are making me very tired." Alice reached across the table for a napkin and wadded it up into a ball and pressed it against her forehead. Behrens looked as though he was about to ask her another question, but then shrugged and said he'd speak to her in a day or two, when she was feeling better. He'd call her at her sister's house and make an appointment for her to come into the Newport station.

"If you don't mind my telephoning your house," he said to Ellie. "I don't want to put you out any."

"I don't mind at all," Ellie said, and gave him her phone number, which he wrote down on the back of an envelope he took out of his pocket.

"I'm sorry I have to do any of this," he said.

"You're just doing your job," Alice said. "I wouldn't think much of the Newport Police Department if no one asked me any questions after— well, after—you know, after such a—"

He reached over and patted her shoulder. Then he walked out of the kitchen, probably to the bedroom, because it was a few minutes before Ellie heard the front door slam.

"Did I do all right?" Alice said.

"Perfect," Ellie replied. She could see Behrens through the kitchen window now. He was standing on the lawn talking to one of the other officers. "He liked your tarts. That should count for something."

"He asked a lot of questions. Why do you think he did that?"

"I think it's routine. Do you want me to help you pack a bag?"

"I can't go in there."

"Morty's not in there."

"I know he isn't. It's just—"

"That's all right. I'll do it."

Domingos was still in the bedroom, examining a dark brown spot on the wall behind the bed.

"Is it okay if I take some of my sister's things out of the drawers? I'm taking her home with me."

"Go ahead."

Alice's overnight bag was in the dressing room closet. On one side of the closet Alice's clothes—mostly pull-on slacks and boxy overblouses—hung on padded hangers. On the other side were Morty's suits, each in a see-through garment bag. Looking at those suits somehow gave Ellie more of a jar than his body had. She picked up the overnight bag and laid it on the carpet next to the bureau.

"I read an article in *JAMA* that anger can lead to heart attack and stroke," she said.

"What are you doing reading *JAMA?*" He had a tape measure out now and was measuring the distance from the dressing room door to the bed.

"Some people like romance novels. I read medical journals. They relax me."

He glanced over at her, but it was not as if he saw her. It was as if he were calculating something in his head.

"The problem is, since my son died I don't trust doctors. I suppose that means I shouldn't believe what they have to say in their journals. I haven't analyzed that dichotomy fully. I think what I'm actually doing is making a distinction between research and actual hands-on patient care, but I'm not sure."

"You sound like a doctor."

"Nowhere near a doctor. Two years premed."

He was now measuring the distance from the pillow to the headboard.

"What are you measuring?"

"I'm trying to determine the bullet's trajectory."

He let the tape roll back and stood up. He was much taller than she was and she had to tilt her head back to look at his face.

"What are you doing here?" he said.

"Helping my sister."

"Do what?"

"Well, I don't know. Get through this, I guess. She was with me when Jamie—when my son died. I couldn't have managed without her."

He was staring at the crystal jars on Alice's dressing table.

"I don't know why they call them overnight bags," she said. "I don't know anyone who goes anywhere overnight, do you? I mean, if you're going to go somewhere, you want to stay awhile. Especially if it means going on an airplane, the airfare is so expensive, I can't imagine once you got where you were going that you'd only stay overnight. Although I've heard of people who could go away for a month with nothing but what they could fit into an overnight bag. I suppose I could if I had to. I don't travel much, anyway, don't go anywhere, just to work and back home. I have an old suitcase that I bought when I went away to college. I didn't finish. I was never cut out to be a doctor, anyway. I'd never be able to harden myself enough to deal with other people's pain. It's a gift, I guess, being hard enough to deal with other people's misfortune."

He looked her full in the face now. She had the bag zipped up. It held less than she thought it would. Nightgown, socks, underpants, bras. The cloth sides were bulging.

"A man with tailor-made suits and a fancy house, and he puts on his hairpiece in the morning before he kills himself," Domingos said. He shook his head, then walked out of the room and left her standing there.

"I thought they would never leave," Alice said. Ellie had thrown the overnight bag in the trunk of the car and was now backing out of the driveway. "I thought they were planning to sleep over, not that I care if they did, it was just everyone looking at me and me not knowing what they were thinking. What do you suppose they were thinking, Ellie?"

"I'm not sure."

"Well, what would you guess they were thinking?"

"That it was strange that Morty shot himself."

"But he did. Or he did accidentally."

The other officers were gone, nothing left but the mashed-down lawn where they had been standing and some cigarette butts on the side-walk. Alice was still in her bathrobe and slippers, and what hadn't seemed strange about that in the house (who notices you haven't gotten dressed when your husband's blood is still on the bedsheets?) looked very odd in the car, and by the interested stare of the woman stopped at the signal on Jamboree Road, you might have thought Alice was sitting in the car stark naked.

"You'll need a lawyer," Ellie said.

"What for?"

"You heard the detective. He's going to question you again, and that means you need a lawyer."

"I don't have one."

"Mickey might."

"You're going to tell Mickey what happened?"

"He'll find out sooner or later."

"That is so embarrassing."

They were coming down Pacific Coast Highway. Mickey's Surfside was up ahead, the neon lights on the roof blinking.

"What was it you and Morty were fighting about?" Ellie said. She pulled up in front of the restaurant and parked.

"Oh, the usual."

"The usual what?"

"Various things. What he didn't like about me, you know, those kinds of things. You're asking me questions like the police did, acting like you don't believe me."

"I believe you."

"You don't sound as if you believe me."

"If it was the usual fight about the usual various things, why this time of all times did he get so mad that he took out his gun and pointed it at you?"

"It's hard to explain."

"Was it about money?"

"It was kind of about money."

"He always gave you whatever you wanted. You told me that over and over. What was it about money now that made him so mad, Alice?"

"That we were spending too much."

"On what? Did you buy a new car? Did he get the boat he was talking about last year?"

"No, that's not it. You don't understand how mad he could get. It didn't take much. He could start simmering and pretty soon he was at the boil, and it didn't have to be about anything in particular."

"He was threatening to shoot you, Alice. It was about something."

"I can't explain it. It's too private."

She began to cry. It was the first time since that morning on the phone that she had cried.

Ellie put her arms around her and they sat in the dark while traffic sped by and the restaurant's neon lights flashed red and yellow on the hood of the car. After a while Alice pulled some Kleenex out of her bathrobe pocket and blew her nose.

"I don't know what came over me."

"I've felt like crying a few times myself today, and I didn't even particularly like Morty."

"He wasn't very likable, was he?"

"Not very. Do you want to come inside with me? I'll just be a minute."

"I'll wait out here. Mickey will ask me what happened, and I don't want to have to talk about it."

Mickey was in his office trying to figure out the next day's menu with Manuel.

"Ah, Ellie, you come just in time," Manuel said. "You see what he want me to do? He want me to skip the veal dish tomorrow and make pizza.

Like we got a pizza joint. No one come to eat food when you start making pizza."

Manuel had a phony green card. He had come up from Mexico to visit a cousin five years ago and never went back. Ellie hired him when the last chef quit (Mickey wanted him to use cottonseed oil instead of butter because it was cheaper). There was no chef left in Orange County that Ellie could find who had real papers and would work for Mickey. Manuel had worked as a chef in the Tropicana in Cancun and knew what Americans liked to eat and how to cook it, so she hired him. The busboy was illegal, too. From Colombia. The sous-chef, Belize. The new salad man (the one she picked up in Santa Ana that morning, who said he knew all about lettuce and tomatoes and green beans and cauliflower and practically begged her for the job), El Salvador. A small restaurant like Mickey's couldn't survive without illegal aliens. The only Americans in the place were Ellie and the waitresses, most of them students at U.C. Irvine (they had no waiters; Mickey said waiters expect big tips and maybe people won't come back if the bill's too high). Ellie juggled what was legal and what was cheap and who would work for Mickey and who wouldn't, and spent a lot of time worrying that someone from Immigration would come in and haul the whole kitchen crew away.

"Where've you been?" Mickey said.

"My brother-in-law shot himself," Ellie said. "In the head. Alice is out in the car."

"Your sister? Alice?" Mickey said. He went to the window and peeked through the blinds at the rear parking lot.

"I parked in front," Ellie said.

"In the valet zone?"

"In the valet zone."

"You know I like that space empty. It looks good empty."

Mickey had had a valet sign made and had the curb painted blue, but whenever Ellie suggested actually hiring a valet to park cars, he said he didn't have the money. He was always complaining about money, that the trouble with Ellie was that she didn't know how to economize. He wouldn't let her buy new copper pots even though the tin lining on their old ones was so thin you could poke a hole through with a spatula. And they had gotten a warning from the Health Department in March because Mickey insisted on the waitresses bringing uneaten bread back into the kitchen and serving it up again, which was why, despite the fact that the restaurant was one of the oldest in Newport, it had never even had a mention in the Food section of the *Orange County Register*.

"Bring her inside," Manuel said. "I got split pea left, I give her a bowl, something hot, something for the nerves."

"She doesn't want to come in."

"Does this mean you're taking time off?" Mickey looked as if he had just come from the barber, a shower of dyed black fluff clinging to the collar of his starched white shirt. He wore his hair slicked back in the same style he had been wearing it since Ellie came to work for him, in 1980.

"Just the rest of the week."

"What am I supposed to do while you're gone?"

"I don't want to argue with you, Mickey. I only stopped in because Alice needs a lawyer. I want the name of the one who helped you out on the building code violation."

"He doesn't do criminal. His brother-in-law does criminal."

"Then give me his brother-in-law's name."

"He went south."

"You mean he went south, like a direction south, or he just took off?" Mickey shrugged. "Take your pick."

"Why is it you never come through when I need you?"

"Look, if he was here, I'd give you his name."

"The police want to talk to her again. You know how Alice is. She gets mixed up."

"You think she shot him?"

"I didn't say that."

"She shoot him?" Manuel said. "That little lady, the one come in here and like my garlic mashed potato?"

"She didn't shoot him," Ellie said emphatically.

"Then why does she need a lawyer?" Mickey asked.

"Because I'm afraid she'll get confused."

"How do you get confused?" Manuel said. "I remember when I shoot someone."

"Who'd you ever shoot?" Mickey asked him.

"I don't say I shoot someone. I say I remember when I shoot someone."

"You better learn to speak English before you get yourself in trouble."

Alice was bent over, her head nearly touching the dashboard, when Ellie got back in the car.

"I just feel so peculiar."

"Do you need a doctor?"

"Heavens, no." She sat straight up. "Did you get the name of a lawyer?"

"No. Mickey wasn't any help at all."

"Did he ask about me, you know, about all the details?"

"He was more interested in the fact that I parked in the valet parking zone. Are you hungry?"

"I'm not sure. I haven't thought about food. That's strange for me, not thinking about food. But if you're going to cook, a roast chicken would be nice."

They were in Lido Isle now, fleets of yachts in the marina a few yards from the highway. Boatyards and boat brokers and marine suppliers on the marina side of the street, restaurants and shops across the way, traffic in both directions nearly stopped. The street was being torn up, two lanes narrowing to one, commuters trying to avoid the evening freeway rush by taking the coast road now caught in a horn-honking, nerve-jangling traffic snarl. Ellie turned off at Newport Boulevard and drove a few blocks looking for a market.

Alice waited in the car while Ellie went inside. Produce was on the far wall to the left. She pushed the cart in front of her, felt hurried, rushed, as if she were late for an important appointment. But there wasn't anyone waiting for her at home. No husband, no child. And now Morty was dead, so Alice didn't have anyone waiting for her either. She picked up a head of lettuce. Flimsy. Hardly enough leaves to make a small dinner salad. All the lettuce was the same. Looking at them sideways, she could almost count the number of leaves. The hothouse tomatoes looked good, though, green leafy stems still attached. She filled a bag with tomatoes and another bag with a flimsy head of lettuce, then picked out some navel oranges and a few apples.

Alice said she felt peculiar. What did that mean? That she felt peculiar enough to forget where she was and do something drastic, like get out of the car and walk up to Coast Highway and—

Ellie left the basket in front of the potato bin and ran toward the checkout stand and looked out the window. Alice was still in the car, the market lights turning her face an ashy gray. Ellie went back and got the shopping cart, but she tried to stay within sight of the car. She hadn't paid any attention to Alice for almost a year, and now she was afraid to leave her alone in the parking lot.

"I thought you got lost," Alice said as Ellie put the bags of groceries into the backseat.

"I didn't know where the eggs were."

"They're with the butter."

"I usually shop at Von's."

"Did you look in the back of the store? Eggs and butter are in the back of the store."

"I couldn't find them."

"What about the chicken?"

"Fresh, free range, two and a half pounds."

"Delicious," Alice said.

Chapter 5

𝕂

When Eric and Ellie moved out of their apartment on Bristol in 1988 and bought the house in Costa Mesa, Ellie was six months pregnant with Jamie, and the doctor said this time there were no problems, there would be a baby, and that he could tell it was a boy and it was healthy and Ellie didn't even have to spend the last two months in bed the way she did with the four she lost. The house, a two-story, pitched-roof stucco, was indistinguishable from the other houses on the street except for the color of the wood trim. The only reason they bought it (apartment living, with no lawn to mow, had suited them fine till then) was because it had a big, safe backyard and was two blocks away from the elementary school, which, the realtor said, was the best in Orange County. It was odd, when Ellie thought about it now, that she and Eric bought the house because of Jamie, and now he was gone, and Eric was gone, and she didn't care about the house or the safe backyard or the elementary school. She had traded Eric the stocks and mutual funds for his share of the house, and lately she felt like calling him up and telling him that she had changed her mind, that giving Jamie's clothes and toys and books away hadn't helped, that seeing all the other children in the neighborhood walking to school every day was making her miserable, and did he, was there any chance, any possibility at all that he might want to buy the house from her?

In February Anita Lake, the president of the PTA, had called and asked if Ellie would make one of her raspberry-apple pound cakes for the Valentine's Day meeting. Ellie couldn't bring herself to remind Anita that Jamie was dead and that she hadn't been to a meeting in a year and didn't even belong to the PTA anymore. Instead she told her she'd be happy to bring a cake. She baked it in the restaurant kitchen the morning of the meeting, iced it in the afternoon, and at five o'clock one of the busboys dropped it off at the school. Anita had been to Jamie's funeral. Was forgetting he was dead like forgetting to pick up her clothes at the cleaner?

Ellie brought the groceries in and turned on the lights. Alice came into the kitchen, tied one of Ellie's aprons around her bathrobe, rolled up her sleeves, and said she wanted to help make dinner.

"I think you ought to lie down and rest," Ellie said.

"I don't want to lie down. I'm perfectly fine. I need to keep busy. My mind is going a hundred miles an hour."

Eric had been planning to remodel the kitchen before Jamie died, make it more like a den, with a fireplace and a picture window and room for Jamie's train set. He had drawn up the plans and there were still big holes in the wall where he had punched through to see if there was a bearing beam where he planned to add a door leading out to the side yard (there wasn't). Rain had come in through the holes in January and warped the cupboards, and now they didn't close.

"I don't know what I'll do about the house," Alice said. "It's ruined for me. I can't live in it. There's no way I could ever walk in that front door again. Do you think the police will make me go back there and show them where—you know—how it all—and where he was and where I was and—I just won't do it."

"There's no use in worrying about that now."

Ellie made the salad and peeled two small potatoes while Alice prepared the chicken.

"You'll think I'm crazy, but every once in a while I dream about artichokes," Alice said, "that I'm back in Visalia and Dad says, Why don't you go and count the rows, Alice, and I put on my boots and go out in the fields and start counting, and I count and count and count and never get through counting, and pretty soon I get so tired of walking the rows and counting that my legs give out and I lose count, and then I wake up." She set the chicken on a rack in the roasting pan and slid it into the oven. "What kind of questions could they want to ask me?"

"The same as today, I suppose," Ellie said and beat the dough for the biscuits.

"Did you happen to see any artichokes in the market?" Alice said.

"Not any that I'd buy."

"No one knows how to cook artichokes. They either cook them too long or not long enough, and they end up tasting like the bark of a tree or like mushy grass."

"I wish you hadn't said you took a sleeping pill."

"Did I?"

"You said you did."

"I don't remember if I did or not."

The chicken and biscuits came out of the oven at six-thirty, the chicken crisp and brown, the biscuits so high some of them toppled over and broke in half. The potatoes had boiled for twenty minutes and pierced easily with a fork. Alice set the table while Ellie whipped the potatoes with butter and hot milk.

"I thought I was hungry, but suddenly I'm not," Alice said. She had put a dollop of potatoes on her plate along with a slice of chicken and a biscuit, and had eaten a forkful of potatoes and one bite of chicken and then shoved her plate away and sat with her hands folded in her lap.

"Do you notice how no one bothers to cook much anymore?" she said after a while. "Just the quickest, easiest way to do things is what everyone wants."

"Eat a few bites more of chicken," Ellie said.

"No one has any taste buds left. Bad food has pushed out the good, and no one, from the littlest child on up, even knows the difference."

"You'll need your strength. Today wasn't the end of it."

"I don't know what more I can tell them."

"About the gun."

"What about it?"

"It's just not clear, Alice. How exactly did you push Morty's hand?"

"With my wrist."

"But if your wrist hit his hand, wouldn't the shot have gone wild?"

"You don't believe me."

"No, no, I do believe you. I'm just trying to get it straight in my mind."

"Well, stop trying."

Ellie made up the bed in Jamie's room. It wasn't Jamie's room anymore. It was now the spare room, the room with nothing in it but a bed. And it wasn't Jamie's bed. Ellie gave that to Goodwill along with the Mickey Mouse lamp and the toy chest and the bookshelves and children's books and the collection of airplanes and cars and trucks. The bed in what was now the spare room was the one Eric slept on those last few months before he moved out. A mattress and box spring.

"If you need more pillows . . ."

"One is fine."

Jamie was buried in a cemetery in Simi Valley, an hour and a half away by freeway, two hours or more if there was an accident or freeway construction going on or holiday traffic or if it was a Monday or Friday (for some reason the freeways were always more jammed up on Mondays and Fridays). Eric had wanted Jamie buried at Fairview, which was ten minutes away by surface streets, no freeway necessary.

"No," Ellie said, "I don't want him buried anywhere near the house."

"But Fairview's convenient," Eric said.

"I wouldn't be able to breathe if I knew he was lying in the ground that close. I want him buried far away, so I can't get there easily. Otherwise I'll want to be with him all the time, I'll be sitting at the gate of the cemetery in the mornings waiting to go in. I won't be able to stand it. I won't be able to think of anything else."

"You're just not facing the fact that he's dead. The only reason you want him buried far away is so you can pretend he's still alive."

"And you have no heart," Ellie told him, "no soul, no feelings."

She sat on the side of the bed now. Alice's head was in the middle of the pillow, her gray hair a frazzly mop on the white pillowcase. Her face had no lines in it, lying down. They had all fallen away, sunk into the pillow.

"I probably should have told you before," Alice said.

There used to be a bureau in Jamie's room, the drawers filled with size eight pajamas and sweaters and T-shirts. All given away.

"The problem is, I was afraid to tell you, I didn't know how you'd take it."

The only sign of Jamie and Eric in the house was the pictures on the dresser in Ellie's bedroom, their faces smiling at her the last thing when she closed her eyes at night and the first thing when she opened them in the morning. They were old photos from happy times. Eric on his motor-cycle. Jamie holding the beagle puppy that ran away, like some evil omen, the week before Jamie died.

"Will you be warm enough with one blanket?" Ellie said.

"I've thought and thought——," Alice said.

"I can bring you another one, if you think you'll be cold."

"——and there's just no point."

"No point in what?"

"No point in not telling you, since you're about to figure it out anyway."

"Are you talking about Morty and the gun and how it happened?"

"I would have told you right away, but it just seemed easier to make up a story, because I thought if I told you the truth then you might hate me for it. I've been so afraid you'd hate me, Ellie."

The room was cold. Ellie stood up and closed the window, and her warm breath fogged the glass.

"It was an argument about something that happened a long time ago, and it—well, we never did get it resolved—it just festered and grew and got uglier."

Jamie used to be able to see the moon from this room, and on dark nights a flicker of stars.

"But I didn't know how different it would be this time. He had never waved a gun in my face before. He liked to use his fists, and I was used to that, but this was something so different, so scary, so I asked him—and I said it very nicely, too, because I didn't want to get him any madder than he already was—you see, I knew his limits exactly. He was like a ther-mometer. I could tell just how hot he was getting, how close to boiling, and when I'd see it happening I'd try to run, if I could, and get out of his way. I locked myself in the bathroom once for three hours until he cooled down, but today was different, it was a strange day, and I didn't run, and then he was sliding the bureau drawer open, and I said, Morty, please put the gun down and let's talk. Please, honey, we can talk this over, can't we? So he did. He put the gun down. That surprised me no end, Ellie, it really did. He actually listened to me and put the gun down. And I don't know what came over me. I think I went into a trance. Do you think there is such a thing as a trance, Ellie?"

In the summer Ellie would leave the window open so Jamie could hear the crickets in the azalea bed. She looked out now but couldn't see the moon or a flicker of stars, and the azaleas had died of neglect, and the crickets had run away, to some other house, some other azalea bed.

"Whether there is such a thing as a trance or not, I was in one, I'm certain of it. There's no other explanation. I've tried to think of one. I've racked my brain, tried one way and another, and it always comes out the same. He put the gun down. I looked at the gun. It was on the bedside table, shining in the light, an oily shine, like a mirror or a piece of crystal. I remember thinking how pretty it was the way it caught the light. I don't know what I thought after that. I don't think I thought anything. It was as if a door opened and my brains flew out. There's no other way to explain it, Ellie. I just couldn't have been thinking. I've never hurt anyone in my whole life. I hate to swat flies. I won't step on a snail. I once rear-ended a car because I thought a piece of paper in the street was a dog. And I've been thinking all day about it, wondering if someone else was in the room, someone besides me, someone who picked up the gun when Morty laid it down. But I know there was no one else there. Just Morty. Just me. And no matter how much I'd like to blame someone else, I know I was the only other person in the room and that I'm the one who picked up the gun and shot him."

Chapter 6

Teo lives alone in the wood-shingled, tree-shaded house in Santa Ana that he was born in, forty-eight years ago. When his mother was alive there were flowers in the front yard, petunias and pansies and ring-leaved geraniums that popped out of old gasoline cans and rusted pots and cracked bowls, even out of wooden egg crates from the supermarket. Butterflies swooped over the riotously bright jungle of plants then, and a pair of yellow canaries chirped in a cage hung from the wood beam right in front of the door. His mother said the birds wouldn't have been happy anywhere else. So what if you have to duck your head when you step inside? Now the flowers are gone—dead, trampled, dried up—just a bare cement path from the house to the sidewalk; so are the butterflies, and someone stole the canaries, cage and all.

Ma's voice still echoes throughout the house, her words bouncing excitedly off the slick green walls of the kitchen—*Get up, muchachos, time for school*—or calling to her children from the back porch, telling them not to forget to take their lunch. She spent a lot of time on the back porch. That's where the washing machine was, an old Bendix with a glass porthole that could make you seasick if you watched the clothes sloshing and slapping and spinning in it for too long. She sang when she washed clothes, and Teo imagines he hears her songs at night when he can't sleep, a ghostly blend of whispery voices and off-kilter tunes that sound like 78s piled on the turntable of an old phonograph.

Teo has two brothers—Raul and Jose—and three sisters—Luci, Estella, and Roxana. Raul lives on a ranch in Texas with his wife, Cindy (the last time Teo talked to Raul was in 1973, but don't get him started on that). Jose, the youngest of the boys, won a track scholarship to Claremont College and went on to dental school and is living in a shack up in Santa Rosa, taking care of the teeth of migrant farmworkers because some professor filled his head with a load of idealistic bullshit. Luci, the one who wanted to be a singer and got married instead at eighteen, lives in Portland with her husband, Kenny (a diesel mechanic), and three kids. Estella (she teaches sixth grade at a Santa Ana middle school) and her husband, Oscar (a cop in Lakewood), live in Pasadena (one hour away by freeway) with Estella and Oscar's eleven-year-old son, Derek, and Estella's seventeen-year-old daughter, Angela (fathered by someone Estella met when she was at Columbia working on her doctorate). No one knows exactly where Roxana (the youngest of them all) lives. She has a four-year-old son named Troy and changes men and addresses so often it's nearly impossible to keep track of her.

Teo's father died in 1981 of something to do with the asbestos he breathed into his lungs working at the Long Beach Naval Shipyard during the war (the Second World War, not the one Teo still has nightmares about), and Ma had a stroke in 1988. She didn't die right away, although she couldn't see or hear or speak and might as well have. Teo drove her up to Portland to live with Luci and her family, and she died there a year later. Ma believed that if she was good, life would go easy on her, when she should have known right from the start that it wouldn't, that she should have got ready, hardened herself, quit singing.

As for Teo, he is without hope. Bereft is a better way of putting it. Hollow at the core. Empty. Blame it on Vietnam, if you like. He does. He went from listening to Mom singing on the back porch to signing his name on a government-printed form in a recruiting station in Del Rio, Texas, in '68 (Del Rio, because that's where Raul enlisted) to blowing people away in Vietnam.

He had never heard of Vietnam before he went there. The plan was to enlist, do his hitch, get out, go to school on the GI Bill, learn a trade, and get a job. He was supposed to be going to Panama after basic, and at the last minute he heard there had been a change of plans and his unit was going to Vietnam. *Where's that at?* he asked. *In the East,* someone told him.

To Vietnam and back, Teo carrying himself and everything he was and knew and had experienced in life with him, pictures in his wallet, fudge brownies from Luci and scented soap from Estella in his mess kit. Went off to war a green kid and came home an old man, his nerves raw and his head unraveling.

"Listen," the VA doc told him, "you have to make the best of things, have to get on with your life. Why don't you get yourself a hobby, take up beekeeping or bowling or archery?"

He went hang gliding, soaring off the cliffs near Temecula, the wind rushing by, the sky a cold blue hiss in his ears, and it didn't do a damn thing for him. He couldn't figure it out, what it was for, what the purpose was, what it meant, what he was supposed to feel.

Some guy in the record store said he was taking engineering courses at night. That sounded like something to do. Teo enrolled at Cal State Fullerton, put in four years, and walked out without taking his finals. He didn't want to engineer anything, didn't want to measure anything or calculate anything.

Pa said, "What about police work, why don't you try it, what have you got to lose, maybe you'll like it." He did and it stuck.

Then he met Bonnie. She was dancing in a topless bar in Hawthorne. Teo told everyone she was a stewardess, just to make it easier. She liked playing the part of a stewardess. She used to tell Pa about the famous people she met on her flights.

Ma wanted the wedding to be in church at Mass with the ceremony in Spanish, but Bonnie (who didn't understand a word of Spanish and had no religion) said she wasn't going to let Teo's mother plan her life, so they got married in Cabrillo Park, a few blocks from the house, with an English-speaking minister that Jose found in the yellow pages. It was 1978 and Bonnie wore a billowy white gown, daisies in her blond hair, and flip-flops on her bare feet. Teo was in jeans and combat boots and had pinned his Vietnam medals to his khaki shirt. Everyone said what a great couple they were, which they were for about two years, although the marriage lasted another ten.

The way Teo lives now is by sticking close to a plan, a schedule, a routine. It takes time and concentration. One slipup can bring the whole thing down. The energy it takes to stick to the routine and get through every day without lashing out at someone drains him. He doesn't always make it. Still, he owes his sanity to routine. Anything might happen if he fucked around with his routine. It could bring on flashbacks. Flashbacks make him crazy. No one wants a crazy cop on their hands. So he follows his routine and manages to keep himself together. He could be worse off. He could be like one of those guys who came back so rattled they ended up in shacks in the desert, unable to stand the sound of another human being's footstep.

His routine is simple and basic. The mornings are easy. A shower and shave, check the house to see that no one got in during the night, get dressed, then out the door, past the day laborers leaning against the fence on the corner waiting to snag a few hours' work, to where he parks his car a block away in the last row near the Dumpster in the Fiesta Market parking lot. (When he moved into the house, three of the street vendors were using the garage in the alley to store sacks of beans and jars of chiles and spare parts for their carts, and he didn't have the heart to throw them out.) Then he drives over to Dunkin' Donuts for coffee, sits at a table facing the window, drinks the coffee, leaves a dollar tip for the girl behind the counter, and goes to work.

It's when he gets home that the routine becomes serious and a little more complicated. The first thing he does when he walks in the door is head for the bathroom to wash up. Homicide clings to you, hangs around, sticks to your skin. He doesn't really notice it until he hits the house, and then he feels like ripping his skin off.

There was only one bathroom in the house when Roxana was born. Then Pa built one onto the back porch. Pa could do things like that. Rebuild a car engine, rewire a house, add a bathroom. Two bathrooms in a house with five kids, someone always waiting to get in, to take a shower, a piss, a crap. The girls leaving their makeup on the sink and underpants on the shower rods. The bathroom Pa built is the one Teo uses.

He eats alone every night. He picks up something on the way home. Hamburgers and fries. Fried chicken. Maybe a pizza. He used to love Ma's cooking. Mexican with a touch of Peru thrown in (Ma's mother was Peruvian). Green tamales, tortillas patted out by hand, shrimp (shell on and legs still dangling) fried with chopped garlic to a crusty brown. *M'ijo, have some more to eat. How are you going to grow up big and strong if you eat like a pajaro?*

He eats in the living room, sitting on the green couch while he reads homicide reports and checks crime-scene photos. At eleven o'clock he turns on the local news and, if he doesn't get beeped, at eleven-thirty gets ready for bed.

Getting ready for bed is the same every night. He walks from room to room checking to see if anything has been disturbed. He examines windows to make sure shades are in the same spot they were the night before and that the dust on the sills hasn't been disturbed. He peers into closets with a flashlight. All those empty closets where his brothers and sisters once kept their clothes. He checks the pantry, where his desk is. His mother once kept cornmeal and dried fruits and all the used wrapping paper from Christmases and birthdays in the pantry, along with tangled satin bows and old clothes she had mended and sorted for the church bazaar. When Teo moved back into the house the first thing he did was call the church to come and get the clothes, and then he threw everything else away and closed off one of the doors to the pantry, just put up boards and sealed it off, so there was no surprising him from behind, no way anyone could jump him.

The last thing he does is check the two outside doors. First the front, then the back. He twists knobs and flicks dead bolts back and forth, and finally, when his checking and reconnoitering is done, lies down on his bed in a pair of jeans (he doesn't bother with blankets; since Vietnam he is always warm), and if he's tired enough, falls asleep.

He isn't tired tonight. Not much excites him, but today's suicide did. Did she kill him? He drove over to the Orange County Courthouse before he headed home and did some checking. According to the records there were no restraining orders, no records of any police calls from the

Miller house, no complaints of domestic abuse. There was a notation that the same Morton Miller had been arrested in Carpinteria, with no details. Otherwise a solid citizen. Described himself on a jury duty form as a businessman. In a sloppy scrawl he wrote, *I buy sick companies, heal them, then unload.*

At around midnight Teo does his checking and locking routine and gets into bed. He doesn't think about Vietnam at night as much as he used to. The images aren't as sharp. More like quick, nasty little snapshots. The main thing is he doesn't wake up anymore thinking he's back there. He finally got rid of that.

All right, so he's not always in control of his temper, so sometimes he thinks fireworks are gunshots and it pushes him over the edge, or a wise-ass like George says one wrong thing too many to him and he loses it. The bottom line is it isn't easy being alive. When he was in Vietnam, in the middle of it, he thought he wouldn't make it, wouldn't come back, so he wouldn't have to worry about it. But he came back. Unless you're dead, you always come back.

So here's how it goes. A guy gets up in the morning—a business-man—gets dressed (except for his shoes), puts on his hairpiece (like he's going somewhere to cinch a deal), and shoots himself. And why doesn't the wife have any blood on her bathrobe? Don't you, when you've heard what you think is a gunshot, run to where you think the shot came from, see the body of your husband, and at least lean over him? *Hey, are you okay?* or, *What was that noise I just heard?* Don't you do that and get blood on the front of your bathrobe? Maybe on a sleeve? Across the chest? Somewhere? George should have pinned her down, shouldn't have let her get away with telling him she couldn't remember anything, should have stopped the sister from giving her all those cues and sideways looks.

Teo looked through the window of the interview room. George was in there. And the widow and her sister. They had an attorney with them, a tanned guy in an Italian suit. Teo knew him. Kenneth Singleton, a vulture perched in a chrome-plated office in a high-rise building in Fashion Island. Teo had gone up there to sign the divorce papers. He remembered

Singleton saying he was always sad when the time came to sign the final papers, it didn't give him any pleasure, it was such a dashing of hopes, such a destruction of dreams. Bonnie cried. Teo was glad to get it over with. Singleton had a mural painted on the wall of his waiting room, the whole wall, of himself in a blue suit and gold tie, like an angel, like Jesus Christ, like God himself, arms outstretched and bloodred rays shooting like goddamn lightning bolts out of his head.

Teo went in and sat down next to George.

"What are you doing here?" George said.

"The same thing you are."

"Are we going to be taped?" Singleton asked.

"It's procedure," George replied.

Singleton stood up and shook Teo's hand. "Ken Singleton. Your wife. Bonita. Bonnie. I handled the divorce."

"Sure."

Bonnie worked for Singleton before the divorce. Maybe she still did. Maybe she was still sleeping with him, too. Teo hadn't even bothered to get an attorney. Take whatever you want, he told her. Everything except the house. She cried through the whole thing. He didn't know what she was so unhappy about, when she was the one fucking around on him, not the other way around.

"You're not sitting in," George said to Teo. "St. John wants to see you."

"I'm here and I'm staying."

"There'll be some guidelines, if it's going to be taped," Singleton said.

"Like what?" George asked him.

"About questions I don't want her to answer. I'll let you know what they are."

"If there are guidelines, set them out now," Teo said. "You can't wait until the question is asked and then tell us we've violated your guidelines."

"St. John wants to see you," George said again.

St. John was the station commander, the one who said who went where.

Teo tilted his chair back against the wall. The conference table and eight chairs ate up the whole room, and every time someone squeezed in to sit down or get up, or leaned back, like he was doing now, there would be another dark brown streak on the wall. The streaks made a solid line around the room, wall to wall to wall to wall, at the same exact height as the tops of the wooden chairs. It looked as if some kid had taken a key, stuck out his arm, and marked it off.

"I'll want a copy of the tape," Singleton said.

"I left a call on your machine last night," George said to Teo.

"I didn't play it back."

"I don't remember anything," Alice said. "How am I supposed to answer questions when I don't remember anything?"

"Don't talk now," Singleton said. "I'll tell you when to talk."

The sister was avoiding Teo's gaze, kept turning her head when he looked at her. She looked paler than she had the day before, as if she might have had a rough night.

"I don't think Mrs. Holmgren ought to be here," Teo said. "I've never heard of an interview where there's a friend or a relative in the room."

"She needs her for emotional support," Singleton said.

"Then this is a waste of time."

"Fine. Let's end the session right now."

Teo had known it wouldn't work the minute he looked into the room and saw Singleton sitting there. He could have predicted exactly how far into the toilet it would go.

"St. John wants to see you, Teo," George said.

"Is this going to take long?" Ellie said.

"Ask them about the body," Alice murmured.

"What about it?" Singleton said.

"We need to know when it will be released," Ellie said. "My sister needs to make arrangements, needs to know what's going to happen, where to go, what to do, who to talk to. Not having any idea what's going on, where he is, what you guys have done with him is very upsetting."

"Can't she talk for herself?" Teo said.

"Wait, wait," Singleton said. "I object to that question."

"There's no question," George said. "Let's all get settled here."

"The coroner's not through with the body," Teo said. "He'll be doing some tests on it."

"What kind of tests?" Ellie said.

"He shot himself," Alice said.

"Why does he need to do tests?"

"There aren't going to be any tests," George said. "Detective Domingos is mistaken."

"I don't remember anything," Alice said. "You can ask me anything you want, but I just don't remember a thing."

"She doesn't remember anything," Ellie said.

George told Teo again that St. John wanted to see him. Teo said he hadn't heard anything about St. John wanting to see him; it was just another one of George's tricks to get rid of him, push him out of the picture, and he wasn't going to fall for it, he was going to hold his ground, not get shoved around by some surfer-kneed asshole.

The door to the interview opened, and it was St. John himself, motioning for Teo to come into his office, he wanted to talk to him.

"You've seen it coming, Teo, don't pretend you haven't seen it coming," St. John said. "Take six months off and pull yourself together. Full pay. Go somewhere and relax. You haven't taken a vacation in five years. It'll do you good."

"So are you going to listen to my side of it, or not?" Teo said.

St. John got up and shut his office door. Anyone out in the hall, anyone walking past, knew he was canning someone when he did that, or at least putting them on the shelf.

"He's pulling seniority on me," Teo said. "I've got ten years in Homicide, he's here three months, and he's telling me what to do and how to do it. He's been trying to get me since he took Rafe's place."

"It's not just George. You can't get along with anyone. Everybody's been talking. Anyone looking at you or listening to you knows you're someone to steer clear of."

"Did you pull my file?"

"I pulled it."

"Did you read my last two reviews? Two commendations for bravery in the last year. One for risking my life jumping into the L.A. River and pulling out that Chavez kid."

"You were off duty."

"How about when I disarmed that perp, saved the clerk's life in the liquor store on Grand Avenue, when was it—February—near Valentine's Day—hearts strung over the front of the store, I could hardly see the guy with the gun. What about that? Did the clerk complain about that?"

St. John began reading from a sheet of paper. "'Threatened bodily harm to a witness at the scene of a homicide.'"

"He wouldn't stay where I told him to stay."

"'Used profanity and demonstrated menacing behavior to the coroner while he was examining a body.'"

"He was tearing up the evidence. I could see the hole in the guy's chest. Anyone could see the hole. He didn't need to poke around in it and lose fibers and gunpowder residue and whatever shit you can name, he didn't have to do it."

"He said you pulled your gun."

"All I did was tell him to get the hell out of the lab, I'd find someone else to sign off."

"That isn't what he said. And there were witnesses."

"You know what you can do with witnesses."

"What about punching a suspect in the interrogation room?"

"He spit at me."

"You shouldn't have punched him and you know it."

"Ask Rafe about that one. He was in the room."

"You broke the suspect's jaw and he's suing the department. And Rafe won't answer questions about you."

"Did you ask him?"

"He says he's retired."

"George is an asshole."

"He does his job."

"And I don't?"

"Not if there's friction when you're working, not if witnesses say you act like an unexploded grenade when you're on a scene. Even when you don't do anything but show up, you scare people."

"Some people need scaring."

"Give it a rest, Teo, take the leave."

"The guy didn't commit suicide. Tell George to fuck off, and I'll give the widow to you. She was too calm yesterday. Husband dead down the hall and she wasn't even crying. You were in Pleiku?"

"Da Nang."

"Go out and stand in the hall and look through the window at them, see what I mean. George is fucking the whole thing up."

"Nineteen sixty-two. I reupped in sixty-eight."

"Then you know what's eating me."

"Sure. I took small grenade shrapnel, four or five small pieces. Wouldn't call that wounded."

"I was a medic, Special Forces," Teo said, "but I carried a carbine and ammo and grenades. I wasn't going to pay attention to no Geneva Convention. I was sure as hell going to kill them before they killed me."

"No one's citing you for breaking the rules of the Geneva Convention, Teo."

"The sister knows something. Yesterday she was a little nervous, but holding her own. Today she's stumbling around, not so sure of herself, maybe heard something last night she can't digest, I don't know, but I sure as hell can find out. If I'd have been handling it yesterday I would have gotten an admission."

There were pictures on the walls of the early days in Newport Beach. Model T Fords on narrow streets. Men in three-piece suits, women in long white dresses, floppy hats on their heads, all of them lined up, standing on the beach, squinching their eyes in the bright sun. Teo had seen St. John in the hall a half hour before, laughing at a joke one of the telephone operators was telling him, his rough-featured face crinkled up. Some people said he didn't know how to handle personnel, he wasn't tough enough, was too quick to see the other side of any story. He coached Little League, had twin boys who wanted to play baseball more than eat. The pictures on the wall blurred. Trying to bring them into focus made Teo's head hurt.

"No one's blaming you," St. John said. "You need a rest."

"I can't rest. I keep remembering how horrific it was. Eight or ten hours of constant fire, killing, explosions, getting so disoriented you didn't know if you were standing or sitting or lying down—the unbeliev-able stress, unbelievable—then it was over." He snapped his fingers. "Just like that. Over. Just as fast as it started, it was over, then nothing for maybe three, four, five days, nothing. Quiet. So quiet. And no one wants to hear about it. They never wanted to hear about it. The VA docs didn't want to hear about it."

"What does that have to do with anything, Teo?"

"It has everything to do with everything."

"It was a suicide."

"It wasn't. I know it. I feel it in my bones. I smell it."

"I read George's report. I don't think so. And the widow looks all right to me."

"Where in hell did you learn that you could tell a murderer by the way they look?"

"Calm down, Teo. I'm not the enemy."

"George screwed it up royally, got her suspicious, and now she has an attorney in there with her and he'll keep her quiet. George won't get anything out of her. And she did it. She shot him."

He stared at his shoes and suddenly everything came into focus and he wasn't sure, but he thought he might have said more than he should have. St. John was to the right of him now, his hand on his shoulder. Teo couldn't remember seeing him get up, hadn't heard his footsteps, had no idea how he got there.

Chapter 7

✍

"**I**t's hard to believe there are bodies right on the other side of that wall," Alice said.

"Hard to believe," Ellie replied.

They were in the Coroner's Office, a gleaming white building across the street from the marina, parking in back (one-hour limit for passenger cars, two for hearses), bright blue flowers out front (salvia, Ellie noted, not the delicate variety but the desert type that thrived on neglect), and a lobby that reminded her more of a travel agency than a morgue (a map of Orange County on the wall, travel brochures in a rack next to the plastic couch). There was a counter in the lobby but no one manning it when they came in, so they had wandered down a long dark hall until they came to a door that said *Enter,* and now they were sitting on metal chairs in a square room (white tile walls and a faint whiff of formaldehyde), waiting for the clerk (he might have been the coroner's assistant or a lab technician; he was about nineteen, with spiky hair and a gold earring, and was wearing a doctor's white coat with *Kevin* on its pocket name tag) to get some papers for Alice to sign.

"Morty's probably in a drawer," Alice said.

"Probably."

"It's so cold in here. Are you cold?"

"No."

"But you're upset and angry."

"I'm fine."

"You don't act fine."

"I didn't sleep well last night."

Ellie hadn't been sleeping very well since Alice told her she shot Morty. She'd go to bed, lie there for a while, then sit up and start smoothing the pillows where they had bunched up under her jaw, turning them over, fluffing them up, crunching them together. She'd finally give up and jam them up against the brass headboard, lean back, and stare into the dark, listening to Alice's rhythmic, slightly wheezy snores in the adjoining bedroom.

She used to think about Jamie on nights when she couldn't sleep, reliving the doctor's words, seeing his face, his sharp eyes, his dimpled chin as he told her Jamie was dead. Now she thought about Alice. It wasn't the same as trading one misery for another (what could compare to Jamie's death?). It was more like a stomachache that wouldn't go away. Had Alice held the gun with both hands? Did she tremble? How did she manage to shoot such a neat hole in Morty's forehead? Had she ever fired a gun before? What had she felt at that moment when she pulled the trigger and heard the explosion and saw him fall backward onto the bed? How could she sleep so soundly?

On the way over to the coroner's Alice had prattled on about what they ought to make for supper. A lamb roast would be particularly nice, she said. Not the frozen variety from New Zealand. American lamb, cooked to pink perfection, with salt-and-peppered potatoes sautéed over high heat and then stuck in the oven until they were tender. And asparagus, she said, was plentiful now. Maybe they'd have asparagus. She had made some last week with a light hollandaise that Morty had really enjoyed.

"If you really want to know what's bothering me," Ellie said suddenly, "it's the way you're acting now. It's unnatural."

"I don't know how you want me to act. This is me. I don't know any other way."

"Why didn't you run when Morty put the gun down? Why did you have to shoot him?"

"Because I had to end it sometime or other. It couldn't go on the way it was going."

"And how can you talk about him eating asparagus last week? When you talk about him that way it sounds as if you liked him."

"I did. Sometimes. He wasn't mean all the time. No one's mean all the time. There were times when he was nice to be around."

"Why didn't you just divorce him?"

"I didn't want a divorce. I wanted him to leave me alone and not to hurt me anymore. I didn't do it on purpose, it just happened, one of those things that you never dream will ever happen, and then it did, and now it's over, and the thing that bothers me the most is that you won't stop talking about it."

The steel chair had a screw or spoke or burr that jabbed into Ellie's back every time she moved. She stood up and tried to find the offending part, ran her hand across the back of the chair and over the top.

"I can't feel anything," she said.

"You feel too much, is your problem."

"Something in the chair is stabbing me."

"I'll give you my chair."

"I don't want your chair."

She began to walk around the room. The floor was concrete and had stains on it that looked like coffee. There was a wad of chewing gum in one corner and a stubbed-out cigarette under the steel-topped desk along with a balled-up piece of paper, a small wrinkly globe of continents and oceans of handwritten words lurking in its folds. She was tempted for a moment to pick it up, smooth it out, and read what was written on it. Maybe a confession: I did it. How did that work, anyhow? If Alice wanted to confess right now, right this minute, did she confess to the coroner or Kevin? Or did she have to go to the police station? And did she have to make an appointment with Domingos or Behrens, or could she confess to anyone who happened to be on duty?

"I just don't see how you can shoot someone and then act as if he's been dead for years instead of days. That's all I'm trying to say."

"There are lots of people who could do what I did," Alice said quietly. "Lots. They just haven't had the opportunity. And he has been dead for years. To me, anyway. You can tell the police what I did, if you want to, if that will make you feel better."

"You see, that's what I mean. It's not natural, Alice. You shot him and now you've shifted the burden to me, and you know I can't tell the police anything, because you're all I have left, and I couldn't do that, and you know it, and I think that's why you can say that, and I'm so torn I can't think what to do."

"Then don't do anything."

Kevin came in and put a stack of papers down on the metal desk.

"Just sign your name at the *X*s and your address."

Alice began glancing through the forms, licking her index finger and flipping the pages.

"At every *X?*"

"Every *X*. And then you can have him. We give you your choice. Option one, we deliver him to any mortuary you pick out, as long as it's within a fifteen-mile radius. Option two, you take him with you. And I'm supposed to tell you that we haven't prepared him in any way."

Alice wrote in longhand in tiny letters with none of her loops open and never crossed her *t*s or capitalized anything.

"Prepared?" she said, looking up.

"No cosmetic enhancement or embalming or cremating. We ship in the same condition we find them."

"Oh, we'll take him ourselves. Actually, not now, not right this minute. Dickey's Funeral Home will pick him up. Are there any special times, you know, like closed for lunch or—"

"There's always someone here. Just give us a time."

"Is eleven o'clock all right?"

"That's fine."

"I'm not supposed to pay you anything, am I? I mean, this service, what you did, it's all—I mean I don't have to—there isn't . . ."

"No charge. If Dickey's brings a casket and fresh clothes, we'll dress him and put him in it."

"Dress him?"

"For the funeral."

Alice shook her head. "No funeral. I don't believe in funerals. Let someone who wants the space have it. I suppose if Morty were famous or had a big family and lots of friends, I'd have to have a funeral, but it would be embarrassing, having a funeral with no one there but me and Ellie. And as far as a minister, Morty didn't believe in anything that I know of. Of course, I never asked him, but he never made religious remarks, you know, about praying that something would turn out the way he wanted it to, or about going to church when he was a boy. I think he was born in Ohio. He never wanted to talk about where he came from. I sometimes thought he was an orphan and was ashamed of it. Some people are, although I don't know why they would be. So it's just me deciding whether to have him dressed and put in the ground, and I know how I am, I'll never visit him if he's in a grave somewhere. He'll just take up space unnecessarily. He's going to be cremated."

"We'll still dress him and put him in a casket."

"To cremate him?"

"They don't just throw him in the oven." Kevin was becoming impatient, his eyes wandering to the door where the bodies were stored.

Alice resumed writing. "My, there are a lot of forms," she said.

Dickey's grief consultant greeted Alice and Ellie when they arrived. He reminded Ellie of Dad, a slight belly protruding over the belt of his suit pants, thinning gray hair, and light blue eyes that never looked straight at you. He offered Alice a packet of Kleenex, which she took and put in her purse, and then he led them from the airy reception area (windows looking out onto the cemetery; Ellie was glad Jamie wasn't buried here, it looked too much like a golf course), down a set of carpeted stairs to a rectangular basement chapel. Three rows of wooden pews, a carpeted aisle, flowers in baskets, but instead of an altar there was a floor-length wall-to-wall dark brown velvet drape.

"It will be just a few more moments," the consultant said. He was seated in the pew behind them, leaning forward, his hand resting comfortingly on Alice's shoulder. "Don't be frightened. It's very clean, very sanitary."

Alice had chosen a Model B casket, which the mortician's salesperson assured her was the most popular model, burned quickly, and left no splinters in the remains.

Something exploded behind the drape.

"They're just starting the oven now," the consultant said. "That's the pilot light catching fire."

The drape slid smoothly away to reveal the oven. It looked no more ominous than a stainless steel refrigerator except for the loud roaring noise, which was partly obscured by the music that was now flowing through speakers in the ceiling.

"Good-bye, Morty," Alice said, and she nodded her head as if someone had said something with which she agreed.

Dickey's Funeral Home told Alice they'd take care of Morty's ashes if she wanted them to, that they would scatter them in the rose garden at Fairview Cemetery for a nominal fee.

"Morty would have wanted me to personally take custody of his ashes," she said, "and I don't think he'd be happy in a rose garden. He never spent much time outdoors, he was mostly the indoor type, on the telephone or going to meetings with bankers and investors. Anyway, I think he'd prefer the ocean."

Ellie drove her down the coast looking for a likely spot, pulling off the freeway at the exits to quaint beachside towns. Each time they got out of the car, Alice would exclaim excitedly that this was the location, the ideal place, but then she would begin finding fault—it was too windy, the waves were too high, the surf too rocky, the sand too coarse—and they would get in the car and be on their way again.

"I don't know what you're looking for," Ellie said.

"I'll know it when I see it," Alice replied. "First, it has to have a long stretch of beach, and it should have a few trees or shrubs between the beach and the highway. Nothing but sand to look at can become very depressing. And a view of Catalina would be nice, if possible."

"He's dead, Alice."

"I know that, but what's the difference between finding the perfect beach to scatter Morty's ashes or you buying a cemetery plot for Jamie that had a tree and a bench and a flower bed that he'd never see? Oh, honey, I'm sorry, I take it back, I didn't mean what I said."

Cardiff by the Sea was the next town.

"I think we've found the perfect place," Alice said as they drove down the frontage road. "The name alone is enough to give me goose bumps."

The beach was narrow, a short slog through hillocks of soft sand to the water's edge. Alice held the metal box with Morty's ashes in it tight to her bosom.

"I don't know why I feel as if I was the one who shot him instead of you," Ellie said.

"Because you like feeling guilty," Alice replied.

Alice was wearing running shoes with her blue jogging suit. Ellie couldn't remember her ever wearing anything but running shoes, even with a dress, even at Jamie's funeral. She claimed that her arches had been ruined by wearing high heels when she was a young girl, and now there were tender spots all up and down the soles of her feet.

"What I want to know is if it really happened the way you said it did."

"Would it make you feel better to think I planned the whole thing? You know I'm not good at planning anything more complicated than what to cook for dinner."

Alice took off her shoes and socks and waded slowly into the surf. Wavelets lapped at the ribbed bottoms of the jogging suit, pulling at the legs until the material drooped around her thick ankles.

"I do love the smell of salt air," she said.

"Are you going to do it here?"

Two seabirds, perched on the toe of one of Alice's shoes, pecked at each other and made squawking noises. The birds scattered as she reached for her shoes and started back toward the car.

"I don't think so. I can see the road and part of the freeway, which spoils it entirely."

The sun was in Ellie's eyes as they drove back north, little shards of fiery brilliance shimmering against the windshield and sinking deep into the centers of her eyes. She leaned to her left against the door window, feeling glum and put upon and helpless.

"You could have run. You could have screamed and run. That's the mystery of it, the thing I'm having the hardest time understanding, that you didn't do that."

When they reached Dana Point, Ellie said she thought they were being followed, that she had seen the same brown Chevrolet in her rearview mirror earlier that morning when they turned onto Pacific Coast Highway, and there it was again, idling in an alley behind an abandoned lifeguard tower.

"It's that policeman, Domingos," Ellie said. She hadn't been sure earlier when she saw the car, but she had gotten a good look at him as they pulled onto the freeway from Cardiff by the Sea. "He's not even trying to hide what he's doing."

"Oh, well, he can follow us all he wants," Alice said. "Are we going to stop at Dana Point?"

"I think we'll go a little farther."

"Laguna Beach would be nice."

They stayed to the narrow coast road, the brown Chevrolet traveling at a respectful distance behind them. Alice said to turn off at Heisler Park in Laguna, that there was no point in driving around all day, that she could tell that having a policeman following them was making Ellie nervous, and it was silly worrying about being able to see Catalina, when most days the fog blocked it out, and besides, ocean was ocean and dead was dead, and if she remembered right, Heisler Park had a pretty gazebo on a cliff above the water and would be just the place to scatter Morty.

Ellie found a space at the curb near the grass and pulled in. Domingos parked behind them and came over to the car.

"Beautiful day," he said. He was wearing jeans and a white T-shirt under his windbreaker and looked as if he hadn't shaved in a while. "Great day for a drive. The ocean's something this time of year. Not many people on the beach. You practically have the whole Pacific to yourselves."

"We've come out to scatter my brother-in-law's ashes," Ellie said, squinting into the shifting sun.

Alice held up the metal container for Domingos to see.

"Amazing how little room a body needs," he said.

"He wasn't a very big man," Ellie told him.

"Thirty-eight medium," Alice chimed in.

"It might not be the best time of day to scatter ashes. Earlier would have been better, before the wind came up. The mornings are the best, actually. Mind if I tag along?"

"If you like," Ellie said.

"I don't mind," Alice said.

There were skateboarders on the path, and beyond that a thicket of flowering shrubs leading to the gazebo, which was situated on the very edge of the bluff, so close to the rim it appeared from a few feet away as if it were suspended by wires over the ocean. The gazebo had garlands of roses wound around its frame and a banner hanging from the roof that read *Rob and Cathy*. Below, Jet Skiers, their bodies like sails, skipped over the foam-mottled water. Teo and Ellie stood in the middle of the path, skateboarders scooting around them while Alice walked ahead.

"You're not in uniform," Ellie said.

"I'm off for a while. Disability."

"Oh."

"She shot him."

"She never told you that."

"She didn't have to."

Alice had reached the gazebo and was inside, leaning out over the rail.

"My sister is the gentlest soul alive," Ellie said.

"Gentle souls commit murder, too."

"I wish you wouldn't keep saying that."

Not only had he not shaved in a while, but his eyes were dark rimmed.

"My son died last year," she said. "I haven't gotten over it. I don't sleep well. Do you?"

"It's spotty."

"Is that why you're on disability?"

He was watching Alice, who was holding the metal box out over the water as if offering it to the seabirds.

"Posttraumatic stress. Vietnam. She's making you an accessory. The interesting thing is how she's sucked you into it. I checked with your boss and he said you weren't working and they don't know when you'll be back. It's like a jigsaw puzzle and all the pieces are there, they're just scattered around, and the game is to gather up the pieces. I like gathering up pieces. I like making order out of mess more than catching bad guys. There were no powder burns on her husband's body. The shot came from a few feet away. I don't know whether her fingerprints are on the gun or not. George let it go to Property without dusting it first, and so that's all fucked up."

"That means you don't have any evidence."

"Right. I don't have anything. But I know she shot him and I'm trying to figure out a way to prove it. You could say I'm just amusing myself because I don't have much to do. The days are long. I don't know how to spend them. I don't enjoy anything about them. The nights are even longer. I'm short-tempered and nasty, and no one wants me around."

She put her hand on his arm.

"Do you live alone?"

"What?"

"Alone. You know, alone. Does anyone cook for you?"

"No."

"Do you eat meat?"

"Sure."

"Then come to dinner."

He laughed.

"I mean it. I'd like to make dinner for you. Do you take anything?"

He couldn't stop laughing.

"I don't either," she said. "I did at first. I was zonked out of my mind for six months. I hardly remember what happened during that time. I know I went back to work and I think I ate some food here and there, but I know I took a lot of pills. I don't remember what the weather was like, if it rained or was cold or hot. I don't remember what anyone said to me.

I must have said something back to them, but I can't remember it. I'm still in a deep pit, trying to crawl out, and I feel sorry for anyone who feels the way I do, and I don't know what's so funny about asking you to dinner. You look as if no one's ever asked you over for dinner before. It's not that strange. I used to ask people over all the time before my son died. Maybe this is the right time and maybe you're just the one who needs an invitation. I can tell that you don't like being alone, that it's making you miserable, but that you don't know what to do about it."

He had turned away, was looking in the direction of Catalina, and she still had her hand on his arm. The wind was blowing briskly now, and Ellie heard Alice calling her. It sounded as if she were a long way off, her words were so splintered and torn.

Alice said since they had company it should be a little more festive, and Ellie said she thought that was a good idea. Glass candlesticks and linen tablecloth were in a box on a shelf in the garage, and Ellie asked Teo if he didn't mind going out there and getting them while she and Alice finished preparing dinner.

"He's very strange, isn't he?" Alice said when Teo had gone out the back door. "He stares a lot and doesn't say too much."

"He's depressed."

"I don't know how you could know that. You've hardly spoken two words to him."

"I can just tell."

"Do you want me to do the biscuits?"

"I think a crusty bread would go better with meat."

Alice had the Anjou pears peeled and cored and sliced in half.

"Ten minutes for the pears?" Alice said, and she drizzled clarified butter over them, sprinkled fresh cinnamon on top, and slid the pan into the oven.

"I'd give them fifteen," Ellie replied. "There's nothing more unappetizing than a half-cooked pear."

Alice had made a prime rib roast the night before, and Ellie sautéed the remaining slices in herbed olive oil while Alice boiled the noodles and prepared the Parmesan cheese topping. A loaf of yeasty sour dough bread went into the oven at the last minute, and by that time Teo had found the box and brought the candlesticks and tablecloth into the kitchen.

He was very polite, but he had no small talk at all. He stationed himself next to the refrigerator and watched Alice and Ellie work. Once he did say that his mother did a lot of cooking, but when Ellie asked him what his favorite dish of hers was, he didn't answer. He did comment on the fact that he had never seen two women spend time in a kitchen without fighting, that his sisters fought all the time. Ellie asked him how many sisters he had, and he didn't answer that either.

Alice lit the candles and they sat down at the table, Teo in the chair next to the refrigerator, Alice in the corner between the sink and the back door, Ellie with her back to the stove. They ate dinner as if they were old friends, as if they had so many experiences in common that there was no need to talk, and so they just ate, companionably, with the oven still warm, the candles burning down, and Teo staring silently as Alice chattered on.

"I don't know why everyone is so afraid of butter," she said. "It's so tiresome to hear people talk about the lengths they'll go to avoid eating it, when everyone knows that a cook who doesn't use butter is no cook at all, although I admit you can overdo even a good thing, and too much butter can ruin a perfectly fine dish as well as too little. The trouble is you just can't keep people from going to extremes."

Sometimes there were mysteries in life that no amount of examining could unravel. This was one of them. Ellie didn't know why, couldn't for the life of her figure out what they were doing, but she felt happy for the first time in months.

"As for funerals," Alice said between bites of meat, "everyone in Visalia loved them when I was a little girl growing up on my parents' artichoke ranch. I could never have had Morty cremated if they were still alive. Neighboring farmers would have talked about it for years. The only way to handle a corpse in Visalia was to bury it in the ground. Anyway, there was so little to do that everyone looked forward to a good funeral. I'm not sure that Morty wouldn't have preferred to be buried—he never actually told me what he wanted." She held her fork suspended in front of her mouth as she gazed contemplatively at the refrigerator. "I don't think he ever thought he was going to die." She put the fork in her mouth, chewed what was on it, and buttered another chunk of warm bread. "He was one of those people who thought he was going to live forever."

"And then he went and killed himself?" Teo said.

"Well, of course, circumstances change. I'm talking about years ago. I have no idea what was in his mind when he pulled out that gun."

"No idea at all?"

"None."

Teo ate steadily after that. He seemed to be listening intently to what Alice was saying, but he made no more comments, other than to say when she paused for a moment that he had never eaten baked pears. Ellie took that to mean that he wanted seconds, and she spooned two more halves into his plate.

"I hope his ashes actually went into the ocean and didn't fly down the coast and land in someone's hair," Alice said.

Ellie liked watching him eat. He was neat, didn't dribble gravy down his chin or stuff his mouth or chew noisily. He was an unobtrusive eater, someone you could imagine feeding long-stringed spaghetti to without embarrassment.

"Many times I asked him, I said, Morty, what do you want me to do with you when you die? And he'd get angry at that."

"Did he get angry a lot?" Teo asked and put his fork down.

"I think what Alice means is that he wasn't happy about the idea of dying, not that he was particularly angry at her for bringing it up," Ellie said.

"I told him," Alice went on, "I said, Morty, if something happens to me, I want you to scatter my ashes in the ocean, and he didn't say he thought it was a bad idea, so I just went with that. I think he would have been happy if he had been there today and seen all the care we took in picking out the location."

After dinner Teo said he wanted to help clean up, that he had washed a lot of dishes in his time and could make short work of it, but Alice said she never allowed company to clean up, and Ellie said she never did either, and gave him a glass of brandy and sat him down in the living room in Eric's easy chair and turned on the television.

"I think that went very nicely," Alice said when Ellie came back into the kitchen. She was scouring the pan the pears had baked in, scraping the crusty bits of buttered cinnamon into the garbage disposal.

"I'm not sure how it went," Ellie said.

The dishwasher motor had ground to a halt in January and the dishwasher was good now only for storing bread and rolls. Alice finished scouring the pan and washed the rest of the dishes while Ellie dried them and put them into the warped cupboards. Then Alice said she thought the pears had splattered the inside of the oven and did Ellie have any oven cleaner. Ellie said she did but tried to talk Alice out of cleaning the oven, and Alice said she wanted to, that it relaxed her to get inside a dirty oven and make it shine.

Ellie went into the living room and sat down on the couch.

"You look so familiar," she said. "All through dinner I kept thinking how familiar you looked."

He didn't answer.

"I think it's one of those phenomena. I know I've never met you before last week, but I feel as if I have. If you're cold, I can get some wood in and start a fire."

"How old was he?" He was staring at Jamie's photograph on the bookcase next to the fireplace.

"Eight."

"Then you know how it is."

"I have nightmares that he's calling me and I can't save him."

"Don't patronize me."

"You don't think I have nightmares?"

"I don't think you tell that to anyone. Personal shit is personal shit. No one cares."

"I suppose everything we say you're going to go and write down in that blue notebook of yours?"

"I'm on disability."

"But you were following us."

"I happened to be where you were."

He sat up straight in the chair, feet flat on the floor, which made his knees come up nearly to his waist.

"So Morty had money," he said. "Cars, big house. She's set, fixed for life, no worries."

"We haven't talked about it."

"I don't believe it."

"We haven't. I've never talked about money with her. I don't know what Morty had or what he left her. I have no idea."

Alice was humming in the kitchen. "If I were a rich man . . . ta-da-da-da-da-da-da-da."

"Has she always been this way?"

"You mean has she always been slightly distracted and pleasant and unchanging, no matter what happens?"

"I mean, has she always been on the slow side?"

"She isn't slow. Don't say that. People underestimate her."

"I was watching the two of you. You think you're leading, but she really is."

"Not true."

"She calls the shots."

"It only looks that way. I don't like to make her unhappy."

"But it's okay if you're unhappy."

"That's not what I said." She got up from the couch and sat down in front of the cold fireplace. The bulb was out on the table lamp, and the crackly light of the television danced along the living room walls.

"I can't tell if you're sympathetic or not," she said, "if you're going to do Alice harm or not. You're behaving decently now, you listened politely to everything she said about butter and funerals, as if you cared, as if you were interested, and I keep wondering if it's just an act, if you're just going to turn around and act like a shit."

"I am the way I appear."

"That isn't a good enough answer."

"It's the only answer I've got."

Chapter 8

꒰

It was the annual Easter Sunday barbecue at Estella and Oscar's house. Sirloin steaks, twice-baked potatoes, tossed salad (field greens and arugula), spinach quiche, Brie cheese and imported Belgian crackers, chocolate mousse pie, and a backyard full of noisy kids looking under bushes for the Easter eggs Estella had spent a week coloring (natural plant dyes, of course, no synthetics; Estella was against, in deadly principle, chemicals of any kind).

"No, no, over there, over there!" she shouted as children scampered across the lawn.

"How do you want your steak, Teo?" Oscar speared a magenta hunk of raw meat with a fork and threw it onto the barbecue grill. Oscar was a beefy guy with a small mustache and a full head of straight black hair.

"Rare," Teo said.

Estella had kissed Teo when he arrived (late, of course, when there were only a few uncooked steaks left), told him she thought he wasn't coming—didn't he say he wasn't?—and that he really looked terrible, he could at least have shaved, and she had told Oscar that this was the last time she'd go all the way out to Santa Ana to see if her brother was dead or alive, and she didn't understand what the significance was of not answering his telephone, anything could happen to anyone in the family and he'd never know about it, and if she had to go to Santa Ana every time she wanted to get in touch with him, she might just give up.

"The yard looks good," Teo said.

"Did the patio myself," Oscar said. "Dug up the old one and put in the new. Your sister doesn't like it. How rare?"

"Bloody."

The house, a well-kept Victorian built in the twenties, wasn't far from downtown Pasadena. It reminded Teo of the house in Santa Ana, except that this one wasn't in the barrio, the wood shingles were freshly painted, the roof was in good repair, and the yard, flowered and shrubbed, was as neat as the inside of Estella's house.

Oscar leaned back out of the way of the sizzling fat. His family was from Mexico, but he was born in East Los Angeles, went to college in San Jose, and was now a police sergeant in an all-Anglo precinct in Lakewood.

"She says it's crooked. I said show me where it's crooked, go on, get out a tape measure and show me, and what the fuck difference does it make if it's crooked or not?"

Estella was kneeling down now, stern faced, her fingers tight around the arm of one of the boys, talking into his face, telling him if he pushed Shelley (or was it Selby?) one more time she'd tell his mother to take him home. Watching her, Teo imagined this was the way she handled her sixth-graders when one of them got out of line.

There wasn't anything about Easter at Estella and Oscar's that was anything like what Teo remembered growing up, nothing Mexican about it. Ma making tortillas, rolling pinches of *masa* between her fingers, patting them flat, and laying them gently on the hot stone. At four o'clock the neighbors arriving carrying dishes of tamales, pots of beans, platters of corn cakes. By four-thirty, five or six women in the kitchen, cooking and gossiping and opening the refrigerator so often all the cold air seeped out, three or four men in the living room watching television, a few more out on the front porch, sitting on the wood railing, flicking their cigarette ashes into the pots of geraniums (the railing broke once under the weight of three husky men and everyone tumbled over the porch into the rose-bushes; it was just a miracle, Ma said, that no one was killed). And there was always music. Pa's two brothers had a mariachi band, and they'd play old ranchero music, and Luci would sing (Teo rigged a microphone for her, hooked it up to the washing machine in the garage, and she'd sing and sing and sing; you couldn't stop Luci once she started singing), and when it got dark there'd be dancing on the lawn. By midnight the grass would be shaved bald, and Teo and Raul and Jose would have to spend the next two Saturdays rototilling and reseeding and fertilizing.

"You been working out?" Teo now said.

Oscar patted his stomach. "Feel. Go ahead, feel that, hard as a board."

Teo put his hand out.

"Not bad."

"Weight work. It's the best. Abs of steel. I'm working on my buns now."

Angela, the daughter Estella had when she was at Columbia working on her doctorate in early childhood education seventeen years before, was counting the eggs in each child's basket. Estella had never told anyone the identity of Angela's father, not even Ma or Pa, who refused to see Angela until she was a year old and only then because their parish priest said the child couldn't be blamed for Estella's sins, and also because Pa was dying.

Angela didn't resemble Estella at all. She was golden haired and blue eyed and had eyelashes that were so light you didn't think they were there until she turned a certain way, and then they looked like a transparent stubby brush. Estella was the exotic bird in the family. Thick eyebrows above dark brown eyes, a strong nose, full lips, her hair a mass of frizzy curls. When she was a teenager she had her hair straightened and wore it long and hair-sprayed so it wouldn't move. When she got her doctorate, she let her hair frizz out again and since then always looked as if she had washed it and let it do what it wanted.

"Whoom, whoom, watch out, everyone, I'm coming through." That was Derek, Estella's eleven-year-old by Oscar, riding his bicycle back and forth over the lawn and into the flower beds. Derek looked exactly like Oscar, even down to the way his earlobes were shaped, like two thin dimes.

"Roxana's here with her kid," Oscar said. "She asked if you were coming. Probably needs money. I'm not giving her another cent. She doesn't spend it on Troy, anyway. The kid needs shoes. He's needed shoes since the last time she was here with him. I think she's spending her welfare checks on drugs again, and I told Estella not to call her, but you know how Estella is about family." The steak had curled up at the edges and looked like a blackened cereal bowl.

"So I told Estella to get out the tape measure, go ahead, get it, and we'll see if the damn patio's crooked or not. Goddammit, Teo, I used to shit bricks trying to please her. You know what? I don't give a fuck anymore. I can't relax around her, can't put my feet up, can't say 'hell' or 'damn' or 'shit' or 'fuck.' She corrects my English, tells me to wipe my shoes off, to take a shower before I come to bed, to stop sweating, stop stinking, stop farting. She never used to care about any of that. She used to like everything about me."

Teo didn't know half the people at the party or their children or who belonged to whom. For instance, the red-haired little girl obviously belonged to the auburn-haired woman in the pink cotton dress. The little Chinese boy was easy, since there was only one Chinese couple. And the black child's mother had to be the woman with the cornrowed hair. They were all probably teacher friends of Estella's. They looked familiar. He had probably seen them the Easter before, looking as out of place then as they did now, standing in a straight line up against the eugenia bushes on the far side of the yard, holding drinks in their hands, and talking stiffly to one another.

"I feel like saluting her," Oscar said. "Yes, ma'am, no, ma'am. And now she's out to ruin Derek. She took him to some quack of a doctor who told her some shit about him being hyperactive and gave her pills to put in his milk, and I told her Derek just needed someone to listen to what he was trying to say, and she said I wasn't a psychiatrist, what did I know about it, did I have a degree or some such shit. I know this much, Derek's just a normal kid, but she's made him crazy, and now she doesn't want to have anything to do with it. So I take care of him. I put him to bed, I get him up and ready for school. There's nothing wrong with him. Look at him. So he rides his bike on the lawn. Is that a crime?"

"I guess you heard I'm on the shelf," Teo said.

"Did you hear what I just said?"

"I heard you."

It was a cool day. The sun had come out late, and only for an hour, but Oscar was perspiring, streams of water running down his sideburns and dampening the collar of his shirt.

"So how long you going to be out?"

"Indefinite."

"I'd just quit and try for a full pension. I'd sure know what to do with a full pension right about now. Boy, I sure would."

He had turned the steak over and was brushing a gooey red sauce on top of it.

"I can't do a thing right. She looks at me like I'm a goddamn worm. She's got her way of doing things and God help you if you disagree."

"I don't want to hear about it," Teo said.

Oscar grunted and screwed his mouth tight over his teeth.

"That's why I don't like to come over," Teo said. "You two have been going over the same ground now for the last ten years. Give it a rest. No one cares. I don't care. It doesn't mean anything to me. Don't tell me about it."

Oscar wiped his face with the towel he had hung over his shoulder.

"So why'd you come over? Estella said you weren't coming. You were never one to show up at a party after you said you weren't coming."

"I need a favor."

Oscar took a sharp knife and cut all along the fatty edge of the steak until it flattened itself out on the hot grill again.

"A suicide in Newport Beach. My case before I went on disability. I'm supposed to stay away from the Records Department, supposed to be getting counseling, going to the police shrink, so I don't want to let anyone know I'm still fooling around with it. I think the wife did it to him, but she's a stone, I can't make any headway with her."

"What do you mean you can't make headway?"

"She's living with her sister, they're out tossing the guy's ashes in Laguna, and I follow them, walk over, say hello, and they invite me to dinner."

"No shit."

"So I go over there, I listen, I ask a few questions, I don't get many answers. The widow's too dumb to know when I'm trying to trip her up.

Or too smart. I'm not sure which. The dead guy was arrested in Carpinteria a couple years back, and I can't get at the records. I think there's something in there. I don't know. I'm just spinning wheels, trying to make something out of nothing, probably. Tell me now if you don't want to do it. No hard feelings if you don't want to."

"Maybe the wife didn't kill him."

"Maybe she didn't."

Oscar turned the steak around on the grill, then lifted up one edge to check the underside. He had poked so many holes in it all the juice had run out.

"So?" Teo said.

Oscar hesitated. "Sure. Why not." He pulled the steak off the grill, plopped it onto a plate, and told Teo there were cold beers in the ice chest next to the steps.

Roxana was sitting on the steps smoking a cigarette. She was wearing her usual getup. Indian sari, Moroccan head wrap, and she had twisted loops of orange-tinted seashells around her neck. She looked thinner than the last time Teo saw her.

"Hi, sweetie," she said, and made room for him to sit down next to her with his plate and can of beer. "Give me a smooch." Teo leaned toward her and she puckered her lips and planted a kiss on his cheek. "You look tired," she said. "I'll bet you're not taking the vitamins I sent you, and I spent good money for them, too." She wiped her lipstick off his cheek with her fingers. "Did you see how tall Troy is now? Four years old two weeks ago." She pointed her cigarette in the direction of the play yard. The egg hunt was over and Angela was handing out bags of cookies to the children while Estella went over to the picnic table where the food was spread out and tied up the four corners of the gingham cloth so they would stop flapping.

"Which one is he?"

"Oh, you, not recognizing your own nephew. The little kid standing in front of the tree looking like he's going to pee in his pants if anyone comes near him. He's got asthma, and he's pretty clingy, so I try not to coddle him. I swear, he's like an old man, like Pa. I swear he reminds me of Pa. I always thought I'd have a boy like Derek, you know, wild and rough and tough. I'd know what to do with a boy like that. I didn't see your birthday present anywheres around. He doesn't even know he has an uncle Teo. You're just a hermit, Teo, just an old hermit. So how's Bonnie?"

"How would I know how she is?"

"Don't take my head off."

"Well, it's a dumb question, how's Bonnie, like I'd know."

"I really liked her."

"You did not."

No one liked Bonnie when Teo was married to her.

Did you have to go and marry a blond Anglo when there are nice Mexican girls waiting in line for you to call them? Estella said the first time she saw her.

Luci was more diplomatic. *She doesn't look like your type.*

Roxana was blunt. *She's a bigger whore than I am, and I don't know why you'd want to marry her.*

"Didn't she work for a lawyer?" Roxana said now.

"What do you want to know that for?"

"My, aren't you the grumpy old fart." She took another drag of her cigarette. "If you wanted to marry a whore, at least you should have married a smart whore. She wasn't smart enough for you, Teo, you know that?"

"She was smart enough."

"No, she wasn't. You're the best thing that ever fell into her lap and she didn't know how to keep you. I'd say she was pretty stupid."

Roxana was thin but looked all right otherwise, no sores on her arms. Her eyes were clear, her skin free of blemishes. Oscar was mistaken. No drugs. And Troy had climbed up the rope ladder to the tree house and was sitting on the platform, his legs half hidden by quavering branches and gleaming leaves. His shoes looked all right. High-topped tennis shoes, no holes. Teo didn't know what Oscar was talking about.

"Know what? I've got this new boyfriend," Roxana said. "He's an artist, Teo, a really good guy, doesn't do drugs or drink, doesn't even smoke. He keeps me on the right road, you know? We went to church last week. Honest to God, I'm not shitting you, to church, Teo. He's twelve steps, too. Alcohol. He knows what it is to fight the fight, and he says he loves me, can you imagine that, Teo, someone who doesn't want me for my pussy but actually takes me to church and says he loves me? So he says, let's get married, and I go, no way, uh-uh, I'm not marrying anyone, the sure kiss of death is you say 'I do' and the next thing you know it's all over. So we're living in L.A. now. I drove over here in this crappy Mustang he's got, stop and start, stop and start, it scared Troy to death, he was afraid we wouldn't make it to the Easter egg hunt. Can you believe it? Estella's still having her stupid Easter egg hunts. So, anyway, my boyfriend—did I tell you his name?"

"No. What's his name?"

"Gordon. He's an artist. You really should see the stuff he does, it'd blow you away. So I said, hell, I won't marry you, but there's nothing wrong with moving in together. So he moved me and Troy into his loft on Sixth Street. You should see how it is downtown, everyone living in those old office buildings, only they call them lofts. You ever hear of a loft, Teo?"

"I've heard of them, Roxie."

"You know the streets, then, down there where they are?"

"Sure, I know the streets."

"Well, he's got this loft, it's really a bitchin' place, Teo, he does these big wire sculpture things, using welding torches, all that shit—I have a hell of a time keeping Troy from picking one up and burning himself alive; you've really got to watch him, he's at that age when he wants to know how everything works. Isn't that the way Jose was? Taking radios apart and toasters? Anyway, Gordon does these big, big sculpture pieces that take up nearly the whole loft. He's got this commission coming, they're going to put one of his pieces on the lawn in front of City Hall. Do you believe it, Teo, I got a guy who's going to have a piece of art shit on the lawn in front of City Hall?"

"Sounds good, Roxie."

"Damn right it sounds good. Thing is, we're a little short this month, you know how it is, you do your work on commission, and you don't figure right, and it runs out before the next one comes in, and I'd sure like to get Troy in camp this summer, you know, get him outside to play with other kids."

Teo looked over at the play yard again. Troy had climbed down the rope ladder and was standing by himself, not part of the chasing game the other boys were playing near the swing set. Teo wasn't sure how big a four-year-old should be, but he looked small for his age, delicate, and was wearing glasses and a hearing aid (Roxana did drugs the whole time she was pregnant with him).

Teo looked away.

"So how much to tide you over till the art shit goes on the lawn in front of City Hall?"

"How much can you go?"

"I just got my first disability check. I'm pretty flush. How's three hundred?"

"Oh, God, Teo, you're saving my life!" She put her arms around his neck and whispered, "Thank you, thank you, thank you," into his ear.

"What's the big secret?" Estella said. She had crossed the yard toward them, a tray of dirty glasses in her hands.

"There's no secret," Roxana told her. "Why do you always think there's a secret? I'm talking to Teo. Can't I have a nice conversation with someone without you asking if it's a secret."

"Your problem is . . .," Estella started.

"Your problem is you have to know what everyone in the world is saying and doing."

Teo put his plate down on the ground and took the tray of glasses out of Estella's hands, and the two of them went up the stairs, through the back porch, and into the kitchen.

"In the sink is fine," Estella said. "I have a special way of loading the dishwasher. Was your steak all right? You didn't finish it. I can make you a sandwich. There's cold chicken, some tuna salad."

"I don't want anything."

She plugged in the coffeemaker, then opened the refrigerator and took out a carton of cream. The refrigerator was covered with calendars and reminders and coupons and children's drawings, all of them fastened to the white box with vegetable magnets. She poured some cream into a pitcher, then stood in the middle of the kitchen holding the pitcher of cream out in front of her, as if she were bewildered or confused or thinking hard about something.

"I'm not hungry, anyway," Teo said.

"You're just saying that. You'll probably leave here and stop and get a pizza." She opened the refrigerator again and stared into it, still holding the pitcher of cream.

"I've got ham and sliced turkey," she said.

"I don't want anything."

She shut the refrigerator and stood in the middle of the kitchen clutching the pitcher of cream with both hands and staring at Teo.

She was forty-two and didn't look any different to Teo than she had at fifteen. Maybe her arms were a little heavier, maybe a few gray hairs were mixed in with the black. He didn't know the girl Oscar was talking about. The girl Teo knew used to laugh all the time. Giggly. She was a giggly girl. She'd put her hand in front of her mouth to hide the one canine tooth that stuck out farther than the other one, and giggle.

"Do you need me to do anything for you?" she said.

"Why would I need you to do anything for me?"

"The disability. I know how you get when you're depressed. You forget to eat or sleep. I was talking to Bonnie last week . . ."

"Great."

"No, no. It isn't what you think. She called me just to talk and I told her you were on disability. Now, don't look at me that way. Everything I do for you, Teo, I do for love, because you're my brother and I worry about you . . . See, you make a face the minute I start talking about how much I care about you."

"I don't need anything, Estella. I don't want anything. I just want to be left alone."

"No, you don't. You say you do, but I know you, Teo. Remember, I'm your sister and I saw you before you went to Vietnam and I know this isn't you, this is someone else, someone we've got to get rid of. Now, can I tell you about Bonnie without you biting my head off?"

"Go on."

"Well, she said say hello to Teo for me, and I said Teo's on disability, and she said she thought you never really should have stopped seeing that doctor you were going to, that she thought he was doing you some good, and she knew you'd relapse one of these days, that you always looked like you were on the verge of it the whole time she was with you. She really cares about you, Teo, she really does."

"Jesus, Estella, don't start that."

She put up her hand as if to silence him. "No, no, now listen, I'm not starting anything, I'm only saying what's right is right, you didn't give her a chance to explain, you were so far removed, so out of it, she wasn't getting what she needed from you, and I know how that is, it makes a woman feel—well, I don't know how to explain it, but she had her reasons for doing what she did."

"She screwed around because she wanted to screw around."

"That may be true, I won't dispute it, I don't know what was in her head. All I know is that she wants to see you again. She said she'd do anything in the world if she could make it up to you, start over, and I asked her where she was living and she gave me her address, and she said she isn't with anyone, and she's sorry as she can be for what she did, but that when she did it she was just so unhappy and didn't know what to do, because she thought you didn't want her anymore. I told her to just tell you that herself, and she said she might just do that, but she was afraid you'd shut the door in her face or say something mean, and she wanted me to pave the way, you know, see how you felt about it."

"I don't like it."

"But the way you live isn't right. You need a wife. Every normal man needs a wife."

"Who said so, Estella? Where did you read that?"

"Well, it's a known fact, Teo, that a man isn't complete without a woman, and a woman isn't complete without a man. It's just the way it is, the law of nature. Are you seeing anyone?"

"No."

"You see, that's the way you get the minute I try to tell you anything. You get mad and look like you're going to poke a hole in the wall with your fist. You don't let me talk to you. You just shut me off when all I want to do is help you."

"Don't help me, Estella."

"But I have to. I don't want you to die alone, without anyone caring about you or loving you or touching you. That's the most horrible thing I could imagine. Do you know what I pray for when I go to church? I pray that you'll find peace and love and you and Bonnie will get back together again."

"Jesus."

"Don't swear."

"Then don't preach."

"But how can I get to you, how can I make you see?"

Her eyes filled with tears, which caught him off guard.

"What are we talking about here?" he said.

She was sobbing now, tears rolling off the tip of her nose and into the pitcher of cream and onto the floor.

"Oscar doesn't want me anymore, Teo. There's someone else. Someone he carpools with."

"What?"

"She came to see me, said she and Oscar were in love and he wanted a divorce. I don't know what to do. I want him to leave, get out, but what about Derek? He'll leave me with Derek, and I don't know how to handle him. Derek is so different. He isn't the same as other boys, and Oscar says it's my fault, and maybe it is. I can't manage him. He won't do what I say, he's obstinate and stubborn, and when I talk to him, tell him to do something or stop doing something, he gets a glazed look in his eyes and I could just scream when he does that, and it's all I can do to keep myself from hitting him. I've never told that to a living soul but you, Teo, that I want to hit Derek. And how will I live without Oscar? He looks at me as if he hates me. There's this big gap that's between us, and I want to say the right things to him, and I want to tell him I love him, but then when he's around all I can do is yell and criticize, and he isn't exactly pure, you know, he's had his flings, not just in the carpool. He's probably told you everything, hasn't he? Weren't you just talking about it with him outside?"

"He didn't say a word about it."

"I know he tells everyone. I'm the only one who's not supposed to know. He doesn't tell me anything, and he doesn't think I have eyes and ears and can figure it out for myself. This one, the carpool one, is a clerk in the Lakewood station, and he sees her every day, and I don't know what they do together, and how can I let him stay here when she told me he loves her? There's this hole inside me ever since she told me that, Teo, and it's dripping blood, I swear to you it is."

She stepped toward him and put her head against his chest, tears and cream pouring down the front of his shirt.

"Tell me what to do, Teo," she whispered, "just tell me what to do."

He felt awkward, holding her, knowing she expected him to say something to make her feel better when he had no words of comfort, didn't know any, and didn't want to know any.

"I'm not the one to tell anyone anything," he said.

Chapter 9

The idea of putting Alice under surveillance came to Teo in the middle of one of his sleepless nights and had him sitting at his desk outlining strategy until the sun came up. It was beautiful. Simple. He'd follow her everywhere she went, make her nervous, make her anxious, make her beg him to let her confess.

Two shifts, six-thirty in the morning to six-thirty in the evening, an hour to grab some dinner, then on duty again from seven-forty-five until Ellie turned out the lights and she and Alice went to bed. Grueling, but no worse than some tough cases he had worked before he went out on disability, the main differences being he didn't put on a uniform and didn't make out a report and shouldn't have been doing it.

That was three weeks ago. It might have worked out exactly as he had planned, out on his own like some wild-eyed vigilante, except for the fact that somewhere along the line he realized it wasn't only Alice or her confession that interested him. It was Ellie.

At his last visit with Aaron, the police shrink, he told him he had met a woman. Another Anglo like Bonnie, he said, but not like Bonnie. This one doesn't have Bonnie's flash. And she isn't beautiful. Bonnie was beautiful. Ellie is merely all right. And I don't know why, but I feel like turning myself inside out for her. Aaron listened, stroked his salt-and-pepper beard, wrote something down in his notebook, and said he was glad Teo was starting to think about sex again, that it was a healthy sign, some-

thing to be nurtured, and that if the woman didn't turn out to be someone he could be serious about, not to worry, it didn't mean the attraction
or affair or relationship was a failure, because just starting down that road
was a success. Teo didn't tell him that it wasn't an affair or relationship of
any kind, didn't tell him he had only spoken to her a few times, didn't tell
him that he was tailing her.

Anyway, here he was, twenty-one days and twenty nights later, at
seven-thirty in the evening, heading back to Costa Mesa for the second
time that day just to get a glimpse of her.

It wasn't quite dark yet. The days were getting longer, heading toward
summer, although you'd never know it by the fogged-in mornings, the
windy afternoons, and the chill that descended the second the sun went
down. He was wearing his windbreaker over his T-shirt and had turned
on the car heater, but still felt cold. He stopped at the Burger King on
Bristol, bought a cup of coffee, then sat in the car in the parking lot and
drank it. Some kids were skateboarding on the cement delivery ramp
behind the supermarket, climbing up the ramp, whipsawing down its
face, then climbing up again. He watched the single-minded way they did
it, the careful positioning of their feet, the precise tilt of the body, then
the loud whoop as they flipped the board and headed down. He used to
feel that joy playing baseball, fingers tight around the ball, the windup,
then the exhilaration when the ball skipped across his fingers and
corkscrewed into orbit. It was all he ever wanted to do. Before he went
to Vietnam he had even played a few games in the minors. A great arm,
everyone said. He came back from Vietnam with the arm shot through
with shrapnel fragments. For years the VA doctors kept busy fishing sliv-
ers of metal out of his flesh.

He opened his car window and tossed the crumpled paper cup into
a trash can about four car lengths away. One of the kids rolled over to
the car.

"Bet you can't do that again."

"Give me a paper cup."

It was easy, a sideways throw, plop, a clean drop into the trash can, no
effort at all. He waved at the kid and was on his way again.

Costa Mesa was off the 405 Freeway, between Santa Ana and Newport Beach. No fancy houses or view lots or ocean frontage, just one ordinary housing development after another, each one with a similar square patch of lawn in front and a basketball hoop hanging over the garage.

Teo had a special place to park around the corner from Ellie's house, with just enough of the nose of his car sticking out so he had a perfect view of the front door and bay window plus a partial view, no more, really, than a pie-shaped wedge, of the side yard.

Parking a car every night in the same location nearly always drew attention from neighbors. The week before, one of them, an elderly woman in a pink housedress, had come out of her house and asked him what he was doing sitting in his car every night, was he a pervert, was he a peeping Tom, was he a thief casing the neighborhood? He had shown her his badge and told her the city was thinking about putting in a stop sign at the corner and that he was counting cars.

Sometimes Ellie would drive Alice somewhere, and he'd follow. He was more careful now about keeping a safe distance than he was that first day, when he followed them down the coast and watched Morty Miller's ashes drift gray and silty in the air, then settle briefly on the surface of the ocean before they disappeared.

His spot was waiting for him. He pulled up to the curb and stopped. The light was on in Ellie's living room. She didn't leave lights on when she went out or when she went to bed. No small lamp in a corner of the living room. No light timed to come on at dusk and shut off at dawn.

He had a copy of the Carpinteria file on Morty with him in the car. Oscar had delivered it to Teo in person. He didn't trust the mails, he said, but Teo knew it was because he wanted to talk about Estella, tell his side of it. Teo wouldn't let him. He told him he thought he and Estella were mismatched, they had always been mismatched, and they ought to cut their losses right now while there was still some life left in them.

"I don't want to cut my losses," Oscar told him. "I still love Estella, I just can't live with her the way she is and I don't know what to do about it."

There was a flashlight on the seat. Teo flicked it on and read the file again. Something had been eating at him about the arrest in Carpinteria.

It made no sense. Morty had no other arrests, no criminal record, no complaints of shoddy business practices, no pyramid schemes, no strong-arm tactics, no links to drug trafficking. Just an ordinary, moneymaking businessman.

He looked up at the house. He didn't want to miss anything. The drape was half open in the front window. There was no light on in the den, no wavery television images flitting across the window.

The arrest report was skimpy, not many details besides date and time. Cops called to a residence in a condo in the Carpinteria Keys to break up a fight between Morty and another man. The Carpinteria arresting officer said there were no drugs or alcohol in evidence. Philip Brookner was the name of the other guy. He and Morty were charged with disorderly conduct, assault, and destroying public property (a lamppost rammed by a car belonging to Brookner). Morty was charged separately with unlawful possession of a firearm (no description of the firearm, no way to know whether or not it was the same firearm that later killed him). They were both booked, fingerprinted, photographed, and then released on their own recognizance. Both paid fines. Charges later dropped. Photographs of Brookner and Morty attached to the arrest sheet. Brookner was a lot younger than Morty. He had hair. Morty hadn't gotten his hairpiece yet. The camera caught the shine on his bald head.

The problem was that he had gotten off on the wrong foot with Ellie. He had shown her his cop face, come on too strong and opinionated, argued with her when he should have kept his mouth shut. He had played right into the picture of the ugly cop. When she looked at him she was probably thinking about all those stories in the newspapers about cops roughing up suspects, beating confessions out of them, fabricating evidence. She probably followed the trial of the cop who stopped a young girl on the Newport overpass, raped her, shot her, threw her over the railing into a gully, and then joined in the hunt for her killer. Teo knew the guy. Forty-one or -two, a wife and two kids, member of the police liaison to local high schools, lectured to seventeen-year-olds about driver safety. Ellie reads the newspaper. He sees her go outside every morning, pick it up off the lawn, and carry it into the house.

He leaned back against the seat, made himself more comfortable, let his eyes roam down the line of jacaranda trees in the parkway. Fine-veined leaves drooping over the hood of the car filtered the lights from the houses along the street and traced lacy webs on the windshield. A cat meowed on the roof of a nearby house. He knew everyone's habits on the street, who worked and who stayed home, what cars came out of what driveways, who got a newspaper delivered and who didn't, what day the trash was picked up, which house had rusted, crumpled garbage cans without lids and which had shiny polystyrene barrels with hinged covers, and what time the automatic sprinklers were set for on the six houses that had automatic sprinklers. The rest watered their lawns by hand or with the little rotating gizmos that ran water onto the sidewalks and into the gutters.

Ellie still hadn't gone back to work at the restaurant. She and Alice went to the market nearly every day, they went to the cleaner's once a week, to the drugstore every few days. They met with a realtor out on Lido Isle exactly three times and with an agent at Accurate Insurance twice. They went to the movies once. The bargain matinee.

The house in Newport was on the market. Teo had checked the multiples. Nine hundred eighty-seven thousand dollars. Priced for quick sale, it said. It looked as if the house was the only asset Alice Miller was going to get out of Morty. He had a life insurance policy (Teo had an informant at Accurate who gave him a copy), double indemnity for accidental death, but the suicide clause said no payoff if the insured kills himself before two years. It had been eighteen months.

He sat up. A light gray BMW had pulled up in front of Ellie's house. Ellie's boss had dropped off what looked like accounting books that afternoon, but he drove a black Mercedes.

A man got out of the car and walked up the sidewalk, stood a few moments between Ellie's house and her neighbor's, then turned and gazed across the street as if he were looking for a house number. Medium height, mid-forties, wearing what looked like a Pendleton shirt over his khaki slacks. He hesitated a moment, then walked up the steps to Ellie's house and knocked on the door. Hard, it looked like from where Teo was. He wasn't bothering with the doorbell, but was pounding on the door now with his fist.

Ellie opened the door. She didn't seem to know him, was asking him something. Teo started the motor and moved slowly down the street. He could see now in the yellow porch light that it was Brookner, the guy in the arrest report. Ellie looked out at the street once. Teo caught her glance. She was uncertain about Brookner, was wavering, and then Alice was at the door, and she said something to Ellie, the door opened wider, and Brookner stepped into the house.

Teo got out of the car. It was quiet. No shouts or screams. He walked quickly around the side of the house to the back.

The yard was overgrown with weeds, the patio nothing but chunks of cracked cement. There were a few trees dying against the back fence. A redwood picnic table was weathering to a pearly gray. There was a sand-box in the corner of the yard and a swing set. Devil grass had grown up to the leather seats of the swings, and a chain on one of the swings was broken. It was plain that no one came back here, not even the teenager down the street who mowed the front lawn on Wednesdays.

There was a light on in the back porch and one on in the kitchen, but the window was too high. All he saw was cupboards. He thought he heard footsteps in the kitchen, but wasn't sure.

His watch said five minutes had passed. Anything could be happening inside. Brookner and Morty had gone at it hard enough to get arrested in Carpinteria.

He walked around to the front again, up the cement path, up the first step, his palm swiping up and down against the revolver in his waist-band. When he got to the top step, the door opened, Brookner stepped out, looked at Teo in surprise, and then ran past him, got in his car, and drove away.

Ellie grabbed Teo's arm and pulled him into the house. "Alice fainted."

The oak hat stand to the right of the door had Ellie's nylon jacket hanging on a hook, there was a pile of books on a table, the fireplace was the same, Jamie's picture on a shelf, and Alice was lying on the rug in front of the cold fireplace flat on her back with her eyes closed, her right arm twisted beneath her as if she had fallen and hadn't been able to move it out of the way in time.

Teo knelt down next to her. No signs of trauma. Her respirations were slow, her pulse faint.

"I've never known her to faint before," Ellie said.

"It looks like a stroke,"Teo said.

Alice clutched Teo's shirt with her right hand, and moved her head from side to side, and said, as clearly and distinctly as she would have if she were conscious, "Don't, don't, don't."

Teo knew where the emergency entrance at Hoag Hospital was. He had pulled up to that door a thousand times in the past. He took the ambulance parking spot, and the minute he stopped the car Ellie got out, opened the back door, and leaned in toward Alice, who was lying curled on the backseat, her eyes closed.

"Alice, honey, it's me, it's Ellie. Can you hear me?"

Alice moaned but didn't answer.

"I'll go get someone,"Teo said.

Everything went by rapidly after that. An IV hooked up while Alice was still in the car, then a quick ride on a gurney to a side door, the doctor asking Ellie if Alice had a history of heart, blood pressure, stroke, cancer, "No, no, no, no," all while they were running along the deserted halls of the hospital, the IV bottle held high in a nurse's hand, the doctor pushing the gurney, Ellie trying to grab hold of Alice's hand, trying to talk to her, trying to wake her up. And then a door that the doctor said they couldn't come past.

"The lounge is down the hall."

The lounge was empty, tattered magazines strewn across a glass-topped coffee table, a jigsaw puzzle on a card table, the outer pieces all put together, only the center missing. A floral arrangement in the corner of the room had shed its leaves on the carpet, a wiry shag that looked as if it had been woven out of iron filings.

Ellie sat down in one of the steel-framed chairs that lined the white wall. She had Teo's windbreaker around her shoulders. She had started to shiver in the car and he had pulled it off and given it to her. She was still shivering.

"Did she know him?" Teo said.

"Who?"

"The guy, Brookner, the one in the house."

"Don't talk to me that way."

"I'm sorry, but there was only one other person in the house besides you and your sister."

"You don't have to interrogate me."

"I don't mean to interrogate you."

"Then don't do it. And yes, she did know him. She didn't say who he was, though, or what he wanted, but there are lots of things she didn't tell me. She didn't tell me Morty was beating her either. I shouldn't have said that. I don't know why I said that."

"She never reported it."

"No."

"Had he beaten her the day she shot him?"

"Stop it. I won't talk to you at all if you keep asking questions like that."

He was sitting across from her, leaning forward, his arms on his knees, the muscles in his legs wound tight.

"You really do attack people, you know," she said. "You'd get a lot more out of them if you'd relax and think before you speak."

There were beeping sounds from the nursing station, and the wail of an ambulance a few blocks away, everything magnified by the emptiness of the corridors. It was black outside the waiting room windows. Inside, the lights were dim. A nurse walked past the waiting room door and her rubber-soled shoes made a slight squeaking noise on the tile floor.

"You don't have to sit here with me," she said. "I'll find my way home."

"I want to sit here with you."

"I didn't mean—"

"I'm trying to—"

"I know you don't mean to—"

"Not with you I don't."

She got up and went into the hall and Teo heard her ask the nurse at the desk if Alice was all right. The nurse said she didn't know and sent Ellie back to the lounge.

She folded herself into the chair again, body bent at the waist, arms hugging her chest.

"Why don't they tell you anything? They send you to a cold room and let you sit and don't give you any information."

"Look, I'm not attacking, but when Brookner came into the house did he say what he wanted?"

"No, but I didn't like the way he was looking at Alice. I didn't like the way he was looking at me, as if he knew me, when I had never seen him before in my life, but Alice said it was all right, she knew him, to let him in. She called him by name. 'Philip,' she said. 'I didn't expect to see you.' And I asked her what was going on, and she said, 'Oh, it's nothing, I'll take care of it, we have some business to talk over,' and then they went into the kitchen. I couldn't hear what they were saying in there, but I didn't think she was in trouble, there was no arguing or loud voices, so I didn't go in there, and I should have, I should have said what's going on, why do you have to go into the kitchen to talk? And I thought it was strange that she had never mentioned him to me before. And what kind of business could they have to talk over? I thought maybe it had something to do with Morty, maybe Morty died owing him money, and now he wants Alice to pay him off, but she always said Morty never talked about his business with her. And I was about to get up, about to go and ask her about that, and then they came out, the two of them together, and he walked slowly toward the front door, and then he stopped and turned around and said to Alice, 'I'll be in touch.' She nodded her head and then told me she was dizzy and fell down, and then you were there."

"Do you want me to get you something to drink? There's a Coke machine down the hall."

She shook her head.

"She was fine all day. She's been fine all week. There was an offer on the house, and it wasn't what she wanted, but she was thinking about taking it anyway, and using the money to go on a trip. How did you know his name was Brookner?"

"A name and photo in an arrest file."

"What kind of arrest?"

"In Carpinteria. He and Morty had a fight and they were both arrested."

"A fight? What about?"

"I don't know."

Someone with a stethoscope around his neck was in the hall talking to a nurse. It wasn't the doctor that had taken Alice away. That one was red haired and pink cheeked. This one looked Indian.

"I hate hospitals," Ellie said.

"Was this the one your boy—"

"No. That was in Oceanside. We were at Sea World in San Diego when he got sick. He was eating pink cotton candy, and he said, 'My throat hurts,' and I said, 'Oh, honey, when did that start?'"

"Well, she's not going anywhere tonight." It was the doctor, the pink-cheeked one, standing in the doorway. He had tucked his stethoscope into the pocket of his white smock and was looking at Ellie benevolently. "You go on home, there's no use losing sleep. I'll have a cardiologist look at her in the morning. She's on an IV and a monitor, and in no danger of dying, as far as I can tell."

Chapter 10

✃

They had left in such a hurry that Ellie had forgotten to lock her front door. The glass of water she had held to Alice's lips was overturned on the living room rug. And the small plant Teo had knocked off the top of the television with his elbow when he picked Alice up off the floor had landed on the couch. Philodendron, fibrous roots, and soil covered two cushions. Pieces of the clay pot were scattered next to the empty water glass.

The light was still on in the kitchen. Account books and a spreadsheet on the table, along with a calculator, pencils, erasers.

"Alice made a lemon pound cake with raspberry sauce today," Ellie said. "We bought the raspberries this morning, they couldn't have been any fresher. She made the sauce first and put it on ice, then made the cake. The whole thing was ready by one o'clock. You should have knocked on the door and she would have given you a slice. I saw you watching the house. I saw you yesterday, too, and the day before and the day before that. You didn't have to stay outside alone, I would have let you in."

"I wasn't stalking you," Teo said and waited for her to object, to argue with him, but she merely took a plate out of the cupboard and put a slice of lemon pound cake on it and covered it with raspberry sauce.

"Alice's cakes aren't like the cakes you buy in the market. Store-bought cakes have preservatives that make your tongue tingle and probably destroy your liver and kidneys. Alice's cakes are like spun honey. She would have gladly offered you a slice."

She put the plate down on the table in front of him.

"There's a difference between surveillance and stalking," he said stubbornly.

"Alice thought she might have put too much lemon in the batter."

"See, in surveillance you keep your distance, you try not to be observed, and don't approach. I don't want you getting the idea I was stalking you."

"Actually, the cake and sauce would taste better with whipped cream, but I don't have any. I could make some, though. I don't like the kind that comes in a can that you spray on. I think the air pressure in the can does something to the lactose molecules. Manuel, the cook at Mickey's, makes fresh whipped cream a couple times a day."

"The problem was," Teo said, "I had no way to tell day from night, if you want to know the truth. A person has to be able to distinguish the two. I was on disability and my hours and days got stuck in one place, wouldn't move, couldn't be lived through, made me crazy."

"Hmm," she said, and took a carton of heavy cream from the refrigerator.

"I was in Vietnam. I didn't die there, but I've wished sometimes that I had. For years I've eaten rage every day for breakfast, lunch, and dinner. And then you asked me if I liked meat. I thought it was crazy that you would do that, that you would think of feeding me when I was nothing to you, when I was trying to hurt you, trying to make a case against your sister. It made no sense. And I thought about that, it not making sense, and I thought about you, and then my days and nights got screwed up thinking about you, because I had a hunch you were the same as I am, you know, damaged, deep down damaged, and that the things that ordinary people think are weird aren't weird to us, that our wires have gotten rearranged, shorted out."

The eggbeater whirred and clicked. She added some sugar and vanilla and beat until the cream made little peaks when she lifted the beater. He couldn't tell if she was listening or not. At least she wasn't giving him what he used to call Bonnie's sympathy stare, the I-can-wait-this-out-if-you-don't-go-on-too-long look.

"I don't have any kids," he said. "Bonnie—my ex—didn't want any. She wanted to be an actress. Her father was a propman and got her some bit parts in a few movies. She worked in a topless bar when I met her, all the men pawing her, and she'd bend down just far enough so they thought they could grab one of her breasts, and then she'd dance out of the way. I told everyone she was a stewardess, just to get them off my back. I didn't care that men wanted to touch her breasts, what the hell difference did it make to me as long as she danced out of the way? She used to get on me about the war, that I shouldn't have gone, no one with any brains went. She said smart guys knew what to do to stay out, what good did my going do, that I was a fool for going.

"I was working for the LAPD, so we moved from an apartment in Santa Ana to one in Hollywood and she got some small parts in a few movies no one ever heard of. She was really into the Hollywood scene, was always telling me what some movie star said to her on the set. If they had farted in her face, I think she'd have tried to catch it in a bottle. She was working for your friend Singleton when we got divorced. She can't type, so you figure it out. She's forty-six now and I don't know what she's doing. I haven't seen her in a movie or on TV in a long time, so I guess it didn't work out for her. As for me, I came back from Vietnam with my arm screwed up, and now it's fine, but I'm not, and you can ask me anything you want about anything you want."

She took a spoon out of a drawer and dipped it into the bowl of whipped cream, then shook her wrist delicately over the lemon pound cake and raspberry sauce in Teo's plate. Teo watched how she did it. Practiced. Deft. She liked doing it.

"Eric said he thought I babied Jamie too much." She wrapped the bowl of whipped cream with a sheet of plastic wrap and put it in the refrigerator, and then sat down at the table. Her hair curled away from her face in long silky strands. She pulled it up now, held it against her head, curls crushed, then let it drop. He loved looking at her, at the roundness of her cheeks, the sharp angle of her jaw in profile, the smooth sweep of neck, the hollow where the small pulse fluttered.

"He said Jamie was always having sore throats, that this one was no different. So we went back to the hotel—a small hotel on Mission Bay, near the playground—and Eric said, 'Come on, Jamie, let's go outside and watch the sailboats,' and Jamie said he didn't feel good enough to do that, he just wanted to go to bed, and so Eric went down to the beach by himself, and I lay down on the bed with Jamie—I remember the room had a picture of dolphins on the wall next to the bed—and we turned on the television and watched cartoons, and every few minutes I'd put my lips to his forehead, and he got hotter and hotter, and by the time Eric got back he was burning up."

The kitchen light cast shadows on her hair, changed it from blond to chestnut. In sunlight it always seemed to him that tiny red threads, coiled and shining, had been brushed through it.

"The hotel clerk said there was a small hospital nearby. 'Everybody goes there,' he said, 'really good doctors,' so we put Jamie in the car and drove over. A nice doctor came in and took Jamie's temperature and blood pressure, and Jamie laughed and said the blood pressure cuff made his arm itch, and a nurse came in and gave him a lollipop, and he said he was feeling better, so Eric and I left him there and went back to the hotel. We could have taken him home right then, right that minute, but the doctor said his tonsils were enlarged, why did we want him to suffer another attack of tonsillitis when he could just snip them out. 'We'll do it in the morning,' he said, 'and he'll be eating ice cream by ten o'clock and ready to go home at noon.' He died in the operating room.

"My husband wanted to sue the hospital and the doctors and the nurses and the building and I don't know what all. He didn't understand that I couldn't take money for Jamie's death. He said I was being babyish, that we should sue everyone in sight, and I usually let him do what he wanted, but I couldn't let him do that. He tried to cheer me up, bought me a fur jacket—I just hated that jacket; I gave it to Goodwill, I didn't want to look at it. Eric said, 'It isn't the end of the world, you can get pregnant again, we can replace Jamie with another child, maybe a girl this time.' He just didn't get it at all. We couldn't make it together after that. He'd go to work and come home and talk about thermalization and radiation and I don't know what else he said, because I had stopped listening to him."

Her mouth was slightly open, the lower lip fuller than the upper, and he bent forward and put his mouth against one corner of it.

"I'm glad you were watching the house," she said.

There were flowery curtains on the windows and fluffy slippers on the floor next to the bed, and a brush and comb on the dresser. Teo had run across Vietnamese paddies with guns going off around him and not felt the fear he had now, that she would turn him away, change her mind.

The sheets were white, no pattern, no flowers, and he wondered briefly if this was the bed and the sheets and pillows and quilt she and her husband had shared.

There was no delicate dance between them. No *Should I open the window?* No *Do you want the left side of the bed, or the right?* No kittenish glances from her or macho poses from him. She undressed in front of him while he watched. She had a small scar across her belly. She took his hand and pressed it against the scar.

"Cesarean," she said.

Then she lay down on the bed and he took off his clothes. Not many people saw him naked. He didn't like anyone to see the mangled muscle, didn't want any remarks or stares or comments. She didn't make any. She just threw back the quilt and opened her arms in the same generous way she did everything.

Teo was gone. How could he have left and she didn't hear him? She reached her arm across the bed where he had been. The sheet felt cool, no trace of warmth, and his clothes weren't on the chair next to the dresser. She brought her arm back and laid it across her eyes. It was her fault. She did that every time with people she liked, gave too much too soon too fast. Telling him about Jamie, showing him how needy she was, was a mistake. She should have pulled back a little. It was all right to let him talk about Vietnam, tell her what it was like, and about his family, about Roxana and her damaged little boy, about Estella and Oscar, she just didn't have to tell him every single detail about herself, that she hadn't been with a man since Eric left, that she had really loved Eric and thought she couldn't live without him, but that she had gotten over that and hardly thought about him anymore. She especially didn't have to tell him about Jamie.

She stood up and picked the pillows and quilt up off the floor and put them back on the bed. Well, she wasn't the one who had wanted to share confidences. He said he had all these thoughts stored up in his head that he hadn't told anyone, and he wanted to tell them to her. He could have kept quiet, he didn't have to talk at all, but he hadn't shut up, telling her about Vietnam and his family, and then asking her all those questions about Jamie, did he like to play ball, was he tall for his age, was his name really Jamie, or was that short for James? Just Jamie, she told him. And why did he have to ask her that and then leave without saying one single thing? Not, *I changed my mind*, or, *It won't work out*, or, *I hate the scar on your belly*, or, *You're just too used for me, I'm looking for something fresher and younger*. It made her head ache thinking of all the excuses he must have given himself.

She sat up on the side of the bed and stared at the flowers in the curtains. Maybe it was that thing about Eric not going to Vietnam because the doctor said his knees were bad. Teo was quiet for a while when she told him that, and then he said he separated men into two categories, the ones his age who had been in Vietnam and the ones who hadn't, and that there were doctors during the Vietnam War who made a living writing notes to the draft board, and he was still trying to get past the bitterness over healthy guys who didn't go because some doctor said they had a few knobs on their knees. Damn, why did she have to tell him anything at all about Eric?

She walked to the closet and got her bathrobe and slipped it on. And how could she have stripped herself bare the way she had? Asking him to stay, as if she did that all the time, as if she slept with everyone, and telling him there were condoms in the medicine chest in the bathroom and then putting one on him, smoothing the tip, and guiding his hand. She couldn't believe she had done that.

She sighed and went into the kitchen. What was it about the dark, about nighttime, that made you do and say things you wouldn't when the sun was up? Like now, bright sun streaming through the window over the sink, no clouds in sight, the vines bristling against the screen as the breeze shook the dew from their leaves, and she couldn't imagine behaving the way she had just a few hours before. She had wanted to give him pleasure, to see his excitement, had wanted pleasure for herself, but she shouldn't have abandoned all her modesty so soon, she should have held some in reserve, restrained herself. She had scared him, and now he was gone, and she was mortified.

He had made coffee. She hadn't heard water running in the sink or coffee beans being ground. He had even wiped the sink down and folded the dish towel and rinsed out the mug he drank the coffee in. She sat down at the table. She was so gullible. She had no experience with men. There had only been Eric. And she had loved him to death. *I need space, Ellie,* was his favorite refrain. *A man doesn't like to be crowded, doesn't like to have to tell all his thoughts, explain where he's going every time he leaves the house. Jesus, why are you always asking me what I'm thinking, when half the time I'm not thinking anything at all?*

And was she so desperate for affection, for attention, for someone to caress her, that she didn't even care he had been following her and Alice around for three weeks?

She had almost forgotten about Alice.

She went into the living room and sat down on the couch and dialed the hospital's number.

"I'd like to speak to a nurse or a doctor about Alice Miller. Her condition. How she is. A nurse would be fine. If a doctor is available, that would be better."

He had cleaned the living room before he left. The water glass was gone, the water spot on the rug blotted dry. He had put the philodendron in one of her kitchen bowls and set it on top of the television.

"Connecting," the operator said.

"Ellie?"

"Alice?"

"Oh, honey, the food is terrible. When are you coming?"

"You scared me to death. Are you all right?"

"I think so. You know what I'd like, some of your French toast. Do you think it would hold if you made some and brought it with you?"

"Did the doctor say you could have French toast?"

"I don't have to ask a doctor what I can eat. They brought me a tray that you wouldn't give to a convict."

"That man last night, Alice, what did he say to you, what happened?"

"There was some kind of mush in a dish with two raisins on top. The toast was cold. I asked for butter, and the nurse said my food order said bland diet, and I told her never mind that, just bring me some butter, and she walked out right while I was talking."

"He came in and did or said something to you and now you're in the hospital."

"I'm not sure, but I think if you put the French toast into a plastic bag the minute you take it out of the pan and then bring it straight to the hospital, it should hold very nicely. As for what's wrong with me, I have no idea. The doctor here is trying to find my doctor, and I told him that was a waste of time, because my doctor died a long time ago and I don't have a doctor, and he said everyone has a doctor, especially women my age. 'What do you do to keep well?' and I said, 'I don't go to the doctor, that's what I do to keep well.' I told him doctors always find something wrong with you if you let them get a hold of you. I think I insulted him. There was a different doctor came in a few minutes ago, and if he comes back I'm going to try to be more careful with him, not just blurt out what I really think. I don't remember what happened last night. Did I do something awful? Did I say anything?"

"You said, 'Don't, don't, don't.' Are you sure you can have French toast? You know I use heavy cream in my French toast. You're not dying, are you?"

"Not today. But they do want to find out what's wrong with me. Maybe I did have a little stroke. My cheek in one spot is a little numb, although it could be that bad tooth I had last December, the one the dentist said was sure to act up again. It might be my tooth and not a stroke at all. I do feel tired, though, and I don't remember how I got here."

"Teo."

"Who's that?"

"The policeman, the angry one."

"That's strange. I don't remember a thing."

When Ellie hung up, she went into the kitchen. She'd get the French toast started, and then finish it when she had taken her shower and gotten dressed. She took out a mixing bowl, put it on the sink, and stared at it. She had no idea what was happening. Her life and everything in it was shifting around her. She wasn't sure of anything. She liked to be sure, liked to have an idea, liked to know what to expect. At least reasonably expect. She liked to know the people in her life, really know them. She didn't know Teo, but she had thought she knew Alice.

She cracked two eggs, added three tablespoons of sugar, a teaspoon of vanilla, a half teaspoon of cinnamon, and a pinch of baking powder, whisked a cup of cream into the mixture until it began to froth, then put two thick slices of French bread in a pie dish, poured the whisked egg mixture over the bread, covered it with a dish, and went into the bathroom to take a shower.

The sun wasn't up yet, the cars coming out of the Valley and heading toward downtown L.A. still had their headlights on. Traffic was light heading toward Carpinteria, but it wouldn't be in another half hour. Teo didn't know what happened the night before between him and Ellie. What he thought was a small spark between them turned out to be a bonfire, and it had thrown him off his stride, made him lose control, made him think he could tell her anything. And he had, and now he was sorry he had. Well, he had left without saying good-bye and without leaving a note and was back on track now, doing what was familiar, what he knew best how to do, chase down some cop in Carpinteria and find out what really happened two years ago when Morty Miller was arrested.

There it was, the commuter crush, brake lights going on, everyone slowing to a stop. Too many cars for too little freeway. He swerved to the right, crossed two lanes, and hopped onto the shoulder. In a few minutes he was back up to seventy and passing all those cars to his left. When he used to work traffic, he would ticket anyone driving on the shoulder, unless the driver was taking a pregnant wife to the hospital or having a heart attack.

He couldn't get it out of his head. He had actually spent the night with her. Or most of the night. She said she knew he had been following her and Alice and he didn't deny it and she didn't care.

There was a cop on the other side of the freeway giving someone a ticket. He looked up as Teo drove by. If Teo were that cop he would have put in a call for a patrol car going north to pick up a 1992 brown Chevrolet driving on the shoulder. He glanced in his rearview mirror. No cops in sight.

He shouldn't have left the way he did. He could have stayed. And he had wanted to. He hadn't wanted to leave. But how could he explain to her that he still had all this garbage in his head about Bonnie? It felt too serious with Ellie, not the light attraction he thought it would turn out to be, and he was just too tired to go through the pain of loving her, too old to worry, the way he had with Bonnie, about whether he was making her happy. He didn't want to have to wonder when he walked in the door at night if she'd be glad to see him or would ignore him or not be there at all.

Chapter 11

It wasn't hard to find Officer Ketterman. Mobil Oil was blowing up a seventy-year-old pier north of Ventura, the dispatcher told Teo, and Officer Ketterman was on safety patrol there until noon.

An unpaved access road angled off the highway, past a sign that said, DO NOT ENTER, DEMOLITION WORK IN PROGRESS. Then a dirt lot with two trucks (one with crane attached), a semi, and a patrol car parked up against the ramp leading to the pier. Explosions came at thirty-second intervals. With each one a puff of acrid yellow smoke belched upward and another piece of timber leaned sideways, splintered in two, and slid into the water.

Teo parked and started up the ramp. Officer Ketterman, the only one of the men on the pier not wearing a hard hat, spotted him and came running (loping, Teo thought as he watched him, like some thick-necked graying lion), waving him back and hollering something that was sucked away by the ragged screech and boom of packed dynamite.

"Detective Domingos, Newport Beach P.D.," Teo said when Ketterman reached him. "We spoke on the telephone a few days ago."

Ketterman was out of breath, his face flushed pink all the way to the tips of his ears.

"Refresh my mind."

"Carpinteria, an altercation between two men, March thirteenth, nineteen ninety-six."

Ketterman shook his head. "I'm near retirement and there have been a lot of arrest reports."

"A man named Miller shot off his gun on the balcony of a condo during a fight with someone named Brookner. Police chase, Brookner's car wrapped around a telephone pole. Arrests made, charges dropped."

"Okay, sure, I remember it. So which one's the homicide?"

"Miller."

"Did Brookner kill him?"

"My partner wrote it up as a suicide. I don't know where Brookner fits in, or if he does. I'm just running down possibilities to make sure, to satisfy myself."

"Drove all the way up here on a suicide?"

"All the way. So why are they blowing up a perfectly good pier?"

"It's not perfectly good. Stinks from creosote. The oil's all played out on this part of the coast. Seventy years, thirteen million barrels of crude, forty wells down ten thousand feet. They're going to put in an RV park. How did he die?"

"With his own gun in his own bed in his own house."

Ketterman laughed. "You think Brookner climbed down the chimney like Santa Claus? A guy shoots himself and you drive all the way up here like some goddamned superdetective. Because why? To prove what? How long you been a cop, anyway?"

"How long have you been an asshole?"

Temper is nothing more than unbridled egotism, Aaron told him.

Teo pinched his lips together and looked toward the end of the pier. Half of it was already gone, inverted V-shaped timbers sticking up out of the water like broken teeth.

"Twenty years," Teo said with effort. "I've been a cop twenty years."

You want to be disliked and left alone. If you didn't, you'd behave yourself, you'd say the right thing, you'd be pleasant even if it hurt, even if your cheeks melted and your teeth fell out. What would it cost you to be nice and smile whether you wanted to or not? Think about it, Teo. You're the enemy.

Ketterman stared at Teo for a few seconds, then wiped his mouth with the back of his hand, and said, "I'll bet you don't get along with many people, do you?"

"Not many. Look, I can't breathe up here, and I'm sorry I called you an asshole. Can we get off the damn pier and talk for a few minutes?"

They went down to the dirt lot and sat in Ketterman's patrol car.

"Okay," Ketterman said. "Got a call from a neighbor that two guys were out on a balcony of one of the condos in the Carpinteria Keys Lagoon beating each other up, and one of them had a gun and had already shot off one round, and the neighbor had a baby and the shot could have gone through the wall into her apartment, and she calls nine-one-one and says get someone out here pronto. So me and my partner hop in the car and go over there. It's upstairs, and these two guys are fighting on the balcony. Looked like a knife fight, they were so cut up and there was so much blood, but it was just their fists. I figure right off it's something personal, like they know each other pretty well and hate each other's guts.

"So my partner says, Break it up, break it up, and they don't even look at him, and the neighbor lady is out on her balcony right next door holding her kid, looked to be about nine months old, and I see the older guy, Miller, has got hold of a gun and is waving it around, so I tell my partner to hold the fort, I'm taking the neighbor lady and the kid downstairs out of the line of fire.

"I get downstairs with her and she wants to go back over to the foot of the stairs to see what's going on, and I tell her, hey, lady, you want to get killed, and then her boyfriend comes running from somewhere across the street because he saw it on television, and—"

"They had a television crew out there?"

"Someone reported a hostage situation, so there's the SWAT team on its way, and channel eight's doing an on-the-spot newscast, and I'm waiting for the army to show up. So I tell the neighbor lady's boyfriend to get her the hell out of there, and she puts up a fuss, doesn't want to go, but he finally gets her out of there and across the street and the last thing I seen she's talking to Chet Walker from *Action News*.

"Meanwhile my partner is upstairs trying to talk this Miller guy into putting down his gun, and while he's doing that the other guy—"

"Brookner."

"Yeah, Brookner—hightails it out of there, down the stairs and into his car. I see him run by and I get into the patrol car and chase after him. You ever been down to the Keys?"

"Once or twice."

"Then you know the streets are like strings of spaghetti, winding and narrow, and I'm chasing him around and around, up one street and down another. He's going, I swear, sixty miles an hour, and I'm just waiting for the crash. Sure enough. I'm following right behind him, and someone pulls out of a driveway, and Brookner swerves to miss him and hits a lamppost. I end up on a lawn and take down a trellis and a fence and miss hitting a three-year-old kid by a few feet. So I arrest him and my partner arrests Miller, and we take them down to the station and book them."

"That was it?"

"That was it."

The explosions had stopped. The half-destroyed pier swayed, gray and sickly in a shroud of yellow smoke, the only sound now the squawk of seagulls swooping over the broken pilings. It had been a dumb idea coming up here. Sometimes it seemed to Teo as if every idea he ever had in his life had been a dumb idea, from enlisting in the army to marrying Bonnie to fixing his eye on a dead guy's forehead and deciding he hadn't killed himself.

"So what's eating you?" Ketterman said.

"Nothing in particular. Vietnam in general."

"My son Eddie was in Vietnam. He used to fly off the handle like that. I haven't seen him in eighteen years."

Workmen knelt at the blunt edge of the pier and stared down at the broken pieces of timber. It felt to Teo the way it had when a battle was over and the bombardment had stopped. Quiet, but not devoid of noise. A seagull's screech could be mistaken for a cry of pain. The clunk of heavy equipment being dragged across a sinking pier wasn't unlike the distant sound of tanks lumbering down rutted dirt roads. He looked out over the water to the Channel Islands, a low curve of land nearly lost in the mist, and listened for the engines of unseen planes and the twang of hidden snipers. Ketterman was talking to him about the pier now, about it being a shame to blow up something that had been standing that long. He wasn't saying anything of any importance, but it was the comforting way he said it that pushed Teo to the verge of tears.

There were five three-story buildings in the Carpinteria Keys Lagoon condominiums, all of them exactly alike: white with green trim, shake roofs, and one bougainvillea per patch of front lawn. Mrs. Lipman, the condominium association president, lived in building one. Teo knocked, and she opened her door partway.

"We don't allow solicitors," she said. "Can't you read signs?"

She was in her sixties, a heavyset red-haired woman wearing a silvery caftan and rubber flip-flops.

"Newport Beach Police Department," Teo said, and showed her his badge.

"Just a minute." She closed the door. When the door opened again, she was wearing glasses with half-moons in the lenses. "Let me see that again."

Teo handed her the badge, and she studied it.

"Newport Beach," she said, handing it back. "I have a cousin who lives in Newport Beach. Esther Bianco. Married an Italian man."

"I'd like to look at one of the units," Teo said. "Number thirty."

"If this is about that fight, I don't want you traipsing over there and scaring the wits out of the neighbors. That unit finally sold last week and the new owners might back out of the sale if they find out there were policemen swarming all over the place."

"I just want to take a look at it."

"Let me see your driver's license."

"I don't know what—"

"Just let me see it."

He handed her the license.

"Hmm, the picture doesn't look like you. What else have you got?"

He gave her his Police Association membership card.

"Easily faked," she said.

He had no credit cards. He never bought anything he didn't pay cash for. The only thing left in his wallet was a library card from the Santa Ana Public Library. He handed it to her, she read it over, told him it was about to expire, he had two months left, then said she couldn't imagine why anyone would want to fake a library card, and he could come in and she'd take him over to the unit he was interested in, but she had a few things to do first.

He sat on the sheet-covered couch in the living room while she finished her breakfast (a bagel, scrambled eggs, bran muffin, and orange juice) in the adjoining dinette. After breakfast she went to the bathroom (she was in there for almost half an hour). When she came out she put a row of ant traps along the baseboards in the kitchen (she said it had been a terrible year for ants, there must be a nest under the building), and then she made a telephone call (a ranting one about a garbage can lid being left off and cats eating the remains of a roast chicken and strewing the bones on the grass). She finally opened a drawer in the dinette and took out a bunch of keys, sorted through them, found the one she wanted, put it in the pocket of her caftan, and told Teo she didn't have all day, that she'd let him look at the unit, but he'd better look fast.

Number thirty was in building five on the second floor. Mrs. Lipman's flip-flops slapped dully on the cement steps going up, and then she walked swiftly down the hall ahead of Teo, the full skirt of her caftan whipping in and out between her heavy legs.

"I shouldn't even let you in without a court order," she said and unlocked the door.

There was no furniture in number thirty, no carpets. The walls were freshly painted, a mint green color that hadn't quite covered the yellow underneath. Teo glanced around the empty living room, then headed toward the bedroom.

"Don't go in there," Mrs. Lipman called after him, her arm upraised as if she were directing traffic. "They might have boxes in there." She paused. "I'm responsible, you know. If anything's missing, I'll be held liable."

There was nothing in the bedroom, no boxes, no personal possessions.

"You didn't touch anything in there, did you?" she said when he came back into the living room.

"There was nothing to touch," he said, and tried a smile.

A sliding door opened onto a narrow balcony, which was nothing more than a ledge ribbed with wrought iron. A sailboat, its red sail unfurled and rising to catch the breeze, slipped through the sheer green water a few yards off a narrow strip of beach, where a young girl was playing with her dog.

"No dogs, no dogs," Mrs. Lipman hollered at the girl, who looked up at the balcony in confusion and then called the dog to her and disappeared into one of the downstairs units.

"There aren't supposed to be any dogs on the beach," Mrs. Lipman said to Teo. "The rules specifically state that you walk out on the sidewalk and keep the animal on a leash. They defecate on the sand, and you step in it. The rules are posted. No one reads them."

Teo knelt down and looked at the stains on the cement floor. Oil, food, green paint, a few rust circles where potted plants had stood. Mrs. Lipman was leaning over him, her plump hands on her knees, as if she were afraid he was going to lift one of the stains and take it with him.

Teo stood up and examined the outside wall. The stucco had been spackled and repainted a chalky white, but there were three distinct indentations, two on one side of the sliding glass door and one above the door. Wild shots.

"Mr. Brookner owned the condo?" Teo asked.

"His mother owned it. She made the mortgage payments, but he lived here."

"What was his mother's name?"

"Rita. Rita Brookner. She spoiled him rotten. He didn't work, was forty if he was a day, and had no occupation. A very nice woman, very stylish, wore hats and suits. She's in some kind of business in Los Angeles. Antiques, I believe she said. I don't think Phil's father liked him very much, although I never met the man. It was always the mother who came and saw to things, brought him groceries, hired the cleaning service, replaced the television when it broke. You think Phil Brookner appreciated what she did for him? I had to come up here once and tell him that if the neighbors complained about him screaming at her one more time he'd be in violation of the covenants and would have to sell. I see it all. You run a condo board and you find out that human beings are just animals."

"The neighbor with the baby, does she still live here?"

"They moved to Fresno. Her boyfriend was transferred. I was glad to see her go. She collected newspapers and magazines and when she left her drapes open it looked like a warehouse in there. I don't think she read any of the papers, but it was a fire hazard, and I told her so. Still, I wouldn't have wanted to see the baby get hurt, and it isn't as if the man with the gun didn't know there was a baby living next door. He had been here enough times to know that."

Teo hit the evening traffic on the way back from Carpinteria. Stop and go, cars jockeying around him, horns honking. He didn't even care, didn't do his usual aggressive maneuvers, didn't hop onto the shoulder or ride anyone's bumper. He felt oddly detached and tired out. He had thought if he dug up something significant in Carpinteria, he'd feel better, his mood would change, he'd see that there was, after all, some symmetry and purpose to life, that there were, as Pa always said, no random acts, no accidental outcomes. Life is a mystery to be solved by diligence and determination. Selfless effort as a pathway to enlightenment. All bullshit. Pa did his wartime stint as a boilermaker in a shipyard and died of asbestosis. There was no mystery in that. Teo went to Vietnam and got his head screwed up. So much for enlightenment. And seven hours in Carpinteria trying to make sense out of senseless information hadn't brought him any closer to understanding the secret of the universe or lifting his depression.

He didn't intend to, he didn't think he was even going to, but he swung off the freeway in Santa Ana and headed toward Costa Mesa. He should have at least called Ellie on the telephone. A telephone call didn't mean anything. He had thought about calling her when he left Carpinteria and had even thought of a few things he might say to her. First he'd ask about her sister, how she was, is she all right, is she out of the hospital, what was it, anyway, a stroke? a heart attack? But it didn't make sense to ask about her sister. And he couldn't think of anything else he could have said that wouldn't trap him, wouldn't put him in a spot he couldn't get out of. So he didn't call her.

And now he was standing in front of her door, and it was dark inside, and he knew she wasn't home because he knocked and rang the bell and called her name and went around to the back and knocked on the back door and called her name again, and all he got was someone two yards over telling him to shut up.

He went back around to the front and sat down on the steps. He was seriously pathetic, a creature without a brain, making himself crazy trying to turn a suicide into a murder when he should be figuring out how to be someone Ellie could love.

When he opened his front door he knew in an instant that someone had been there. The air felt different. Thick, used, unfamiliar. He stepped inside and listened. This was what he had always thought would happen, the break-in he couldn't protect against by any amount of vigilance or checking and rechecking, the break-in that anyone determined enough could pull off.

He turned on the lamp next to his easy chair. He had made enough noise opening the door that anyone in the house would have heard him. That was the only advantage on the intruder's side. Everything else belonged to Teo. It was his house and he knew it down to the studs, knew every inch of floor and wall, every light socket, every piece of furniture, every closet, every hiding place.

He walked down the hall, the floor creaking under his feet. The bedrooms were empty, curtains in the same position as when he left, windows locked, closets empty. The door to the bathroom off the living room was closed. It was always closed. He twisted the knob and went in. The window above the tub was still locked. The toilet hadn't been flushed recently (there was the same gray-brown ring beneath the rim of the bowl). The faucets that he had torqued shut with a wrench wouldn't budge.

There was a light on in the hall, a forty-watt bulb casting shadows on the walls. He hadn't left it on. He took a few steps into the kitchen and looked around him, at the corner where the stove was, across the room at the refrigerator, then a half turn to the right, where the sink and countertops and cupboards were.

Nothing on the sink. No trash in the basket next to the pantry. The papers on his desk still piled the way they had been. There was only the back bathroom left.

"Anyone in there?" His voice echoed against the tile walls. No one hiding in the shower, but the towel on the rack next to the sink had been moved, rearranged. He stared at it awhile, then went back into the kitchen, opened the refrigerator, and thought about that towel while he ate a piece of cold pizza.

At nine o'clock he heard a car pull into the driveway on the side of the house, and then footsteps on the porch and the rasp of a key in the lock.

"Where have you been?" Estella said. She was carrying a suitcase and juggling a bag of groceries.

"Carpinteria."

She walked across the living room to the second bedroom, left her suitcase in there, and then went into the kitchen and put the bag of groceries on the sink. He could see her through the open kitchen door, the yellow overhead light catching the gray strands in her mop of dark hair. She busied herself with the bag of groceries, her high heels clacking on the linoleum floor as she walked from sink to refrigerator to cupboards.

He got out of the chair and stood in the kitchen doorway. She was washing apples, taking them one by one out of a plastic bag, running them under cold water, then drying them with a towel and laying them on the counter. She opened the cupboard above the sink.

"Where's Ma's fruit bowl, the one she bought in Chiapas?"

"I don't know. What did it look like?"

"It had purple chickens painted on the side. You know the one, Teo. She kept it on the table with fruit in it. The fruit bowl."

"It must have got broken. So what are you doing here?"

"I'm moving in." She had found a small pot in the cupboard next to the stove and was putting the apples in that. "I tried to call and tell you that last night, but of course you don't answer the phone, so I just came over. I slept in the front bedroom. I'll bet you didn't see the quilt moved one inch from where you had it."

"The towel in the bathroom was different."

"It was not. It was exactly the way it was."

"I could have shot you if I came in last night."

"Oh, Teo, you would not."

She was like the sea, like the ocean, unstoppable.

"Are you bringing Derek and Angela with you?"

"No, just me. They won't miss me. And I've had it with Oscar. Angela sides with him, and I can't understand it, he isn't even her father, and so I said, fine, you stay here and take care of your brother, I'm leaving. Oscar hasn't even called me once today at school and wasn't home when I went over to get some clothes. Derek is glad I'm leaving, I could see it in his face when I told him I was going to go live with Uncle Teo. Well, I'm through with the whole bunch. They don't want me, then I don't want them. Oscar didn't say a damn word to me when I told him I was going to leave. I don't think he believed I'd do it. Well, I did, and I'm here to take care of you now, Teo, to turn your life around and do whatever needs doing to help you get over this depression of yours."

He pulled out a chair and sat down at the table. His initials were carved in one corner of the wooden surface, and Raul's were in another. Jose had hammered a nail into the center of the table right next to the charred hole made by one of Roxana's cigarettes. The table was a map of carelessness.

Estella put the pot of apples on top of the burn hole. One of the apples fell onto the table, and she picked it up and balanced it on top of the others. That was another thing he remembered about her, the attention she gave to every goddamn detail.

She turned and looked at Teo. "I can stay here, can't I, Teo? I know we all said you could have the house, but an apartment would be so expensive, and I don't know whether I'll get any money out of Oscar right away, and I just thought to myself, Teo needs me, and there are all those bedrooms going to waste. It's okay, Teo, isn't it, if I stay here?"

It was one of those moments that required him to tell the truth, tell her no, he didn't want her there, he'd give her the money and she could look for another place to live, that his life was arranged the way he wanted it, that he needed to own every waking hour and not have to think of anyone or anything else.

"Well, Teo, it is all right, isn't it?"

Her brown eyes were red rimmed and slightly swollen, and she nibbled now on the nail of her right index finger.

He nodded. "Sure, it's all right."

It was the wrong move. Teo knew it, and he did it anyway. One crack in the dike can flood a whole town, a whole state, a whole country.

"I'll do the shopping, Teo, but I'll need help with the cleaning. This place is a mess. The smell of dust hit me in the face when I opened the door last night, and I thought to myself, how does he live in this place?"

She was happy now, bustling around the kitchen, inspecting the drawers and the cupboards.

"We'll need to reline the shelves," she said. "I don't think they've been relined since Ma was alive, the gunk on them must be at least two inches thick."

Chapter 12

"You haven't eaten a single bite, and you always liked the way I made lasagna."

Ellie had gotten up at six to make the bolognese sauce (most people used marinara sauce in their lasagna, but Alice preferred Ellie's bolognese) and sauté the sausage and grate the Parmesan cheese and season the ricotta so she could get the lasagna assembled and baked and at the hospital in time for Alice's lunch. And now Alice was poking at it with her fork, lifting up one layer, peering at the filling, smooshing it onto the plate, then staring at the azaleas Mickey had sent. Florist's azaleas, trained to a lollipop shape, the short stem (wrapped in white satin) holding a ball of once bright orange flowers now turned to dusky brown and as crinkly as a bad perm.

"I bought some apples for a pie," Ellie said. "I'll roll out the dough tonight."

Friday it had been panfried veal chop that Alice hadn't eaten. On Saturday a platter of sweet potato chips, warm and crisp and lightly sprinkled with salt, that Alice said gave her a headache just to look at. On Sunday she wouldn't eat the baked squab with herbed rice stuffing because she said she thought the garlic in it might give her gas. She didn't eat the casserole of linguine with ham and peas in cream that Ellie brought on Monday either. The night nurse took it home to her kids.

"I've washed your nightgowns." Ellie plumped up the pillows behind Alice's back. "I'll bring them with me tomorrow when I bring the pie."

"It's freezing in here," Alice said.

"Do you want me to buy you a bed jacket?"

"No. Are you going to use pippins, or Romes, for the pie?"

"Pippins. Romes are too flat tasting."

"Not if you add lemon."

"Then they're tart, but still flat. Has the doctor been in yet?"

"No. He's avoiding me, because he doesn't know what he's doing, and he knows I know it. He says I need a pacemaker, but I don't need anything but to get unhooked from all this machinery and out of this bed. I told him his heart would beat as fast as a hummingbird's, too, if he had to stay in one place and endure all these tests. I get so tired of people poking me that sometimes I don't have enough energy to even blink my eyes. I hate this place, I really do. If you want to do something for me, call the doctor up and tell him I want to get unplugged from all these tubes so I can go home."

"You know I can't do that."

"You can if you want to."

Alice had not only lost her appetite in the hospital, she had grown testy and unreasonable. She was being held against her will in a drafty room, was one complaint. The doctor being unqualified was another. Lesser ones were that the sheets were scratchy, the lumps of foam in the pillows matted her hair and made her neck ache, the night nurse had bad breath, and the aide used the same dirty mop every day to wash the floor.

"What's the point of my being here? No one will give me an answer on how long they plan on keeping me. It's a prison, not a hospital, and stop hovering over me like I'm an invalid. The next thing you know you'll be bringing pictures to hang on the wall, and a portable stove so you can heat up the food you bring me. And maybe a small refrigerator. I half expect to wake up one morning and find you asleep beside me."

"Well, then, I'll leave you alone, if that's what you want."

It was tempting. Just walk down that long expanse of corridor, past all the little signs—X RAY, PATHOLOGY, NUCLEAR MEDICINE—and march right out the hospital door and leave her flat.

"You're not really going, are you?" Alice said as Ellie stared at the door.

"I should. Maybe you'll do fine by yourself without me hovering. You'll stay in this room by yourself and count your heartbeats and check to see how bad the nurse's breath is and look at dirty mops and not have to put up with me at all."

She was sorry she had said that. She didn't know what was happening to her lately. Alice had changed, and so had she. She hardly recognized herself, snapping like that. Alice's heart rate probably went up twenty beats because of it. She bent over and kissed Alice's cheek. The skin was as cool and moist as bread dough and gave slightly under the pressure of her lips.

"You do feel cold."

"I told you."

She had brought a small blanket to the hospital the day before, one that Ma had knitted years before out of odds and ends of yarn, a garish mix of purples and reds and blues and yellows. She draped it around Alice's shoulders and then picked up the magazines that Alice had tossed unread onto the floor and put them in the closet next to the door. Everything was jammed in there. Two folding chairs, rolls of plastic tubing, boxes of cotton balls, a step stool, the cotton dress and house slippers Alice was wearing when she was admitted to the hospital. A scrap of paper with writing on it was on the floor of the closet. Ellie picked it up and put it in her jacket pocket.

"Was it something that that man Brookner said or did that made you sick?" Ellie asked.

"I think the only reason you come to see me is to ask me questions. I've never known you to be so nosy, poking into my business, wanting to know things, to find out about me and who I know and who comes to visit me. You were always such a quiet little girl, never asked questions, were always reading a book. The house could come down around your ears and I think you would have just crawled out from under the rubble, gone outside, and started reading again. All this questioning and curiosity isn't like you at all, and it wears me out." She laid her head back against the pillow. "Did I tell you I sold the house? Yesterday. Full price, all cash. A man and his wife and four children from Arizona. Mr. Diamond was here this morning with the escrow papers. I said, 'I want the house sold, but I don't feel like signing forty pieces of paper,' and he actually scolded me. I said, 'In case you hadn't noticed, I am in the hospital with tubes running in both arms,' and he didn't even apologize. I told him you'd meet him at the house tomorrow morning and give the papers to him. Ten o'clock. Call the Chevron storage people tonight to take the furniture, and I don't even know what I left in the closets. Morty's suits. My Lord, Morty's suits. I can't believe he's gone. An architect bought the house. He wants all my things out by tomorrow. Give Morty's suits and the rest of my clothes and any food that's left in the cupboards to the Santa Ana Rescue Mission. Morty's file cabinets are locked. Just store the desk the way it is. And try to get me out of here. This is the worst place I've ever been in in my life."

The nurse was in the room now, fiddling with the machinery at the side of the bed, twirling knobs, unkinking tubing. Ellie sat in the straight-back chair and stared at her sister while a bright streaming sun slipped through the window and beat down on the shriveling azaleas. The nurse went into the bathroom to refill Alice's water pitcher, and white-coated figures walked by in the hall, pagers beeping. In the next room a doctor was telling someone about the results of a test. A little problem with it, he said, and then the rest was muffled. The important parts of overheard conversations, it seemed to Ellie, were always muffled.

"Ah, she's sleeping," the nurse said when she came out of the bathroom.

She wasn't sleeping. She had let the thermometer slide out of her mouth onto her chest and her eyes were closed, but Ellie saw her lashes flutter. Gray lashes. Gray eyebrows. Pinched, bony cheeks. An old woman's face. Ellie had never thought of her sister as an old woman. She was just Alice. Baking, cooking, cleaning Alice.

The nurse pulled the blinds shut and the room darkened. Suddenly Ellie felt as if she had wandered into the wrong room, that her sister was in another room down the hall, chattering away about Visalia and how to clean lamp shades and the best way to barbecue artichokes.

At ten in the morning Ellie met Mr. Diamond, a tall, middle-aged, wispy-haired man (each wisp carefully combed to his scalp), at the Newport Beach house and gave him the signed escrow papers. At ten-thirty two men from the storage company arrived and began carrying furniture out of the house and into the moving van in the drive. The carpets had already been pulled up the day before (the new owners had allergies to carpet dust, Mr. Diamond said), and a workman was on his knees in the living room grinding away at the hardwood floors with an electric sander.

At eleven-thirty Mr. Diamond came into the kitchen, where Ellie was sorting through the items in the cupboards.

"I thought you left," she said.

"Still here, still here."

Canned goods and staples went into a box. Rotted fruit and vegetables into a garbage bag.

"I hope your sister is feeling better soon and on the mend."

There was no end to the kitchen equipment. Pots and pans and measuring cups and silverware, along with three mixers and two blenders, a meat grinder, knife sharpener, four electric can openers, two bread makers, four Crock-Pots, three pressure cookers, an electronic food scale, an ice cream maker, three sets of spice mills, a Swedish egg slicer, and the small birchwood chest where Alice kept her recipes. They took up eight cardboard storage boxes.

"Illness, of course, creates its own space and time and relevance, and it might seem never-ending, but end it does, and I trust happily for her. Do you care that the movers aren't wrapping the case goods in blankets? My experience, if I may, has been that if one speaks first, then there are relatively few mishaps later. Scratches, et cetera."

"I can't worry about scratches now, Mr. Diamond. There isn't time. When did you say the painters were coming?"

"Oh, no, no, don't rush. A moment more or less, the painters can mix colors, prepare brushes, mask and drape, while you continue removing objects."

One of the moving men came into the kitchen and said he was going to empty out the master bedroom next, did Ellie want to leave everything in the drawers, or take them out, or did she want them to do it, because they were on a schedule, another house that afternoon, and if she wanted them to do it, they couldn't do it today, they'd have to come back.

"No, to come back, there isn't time in the plan," Mr. Diamond said. "Mrs. Demarco's decorator, I promised the woman an empty house, tomorrow is taken with that, so it isn't possible."

"I'll empty the drawers out," Ellie said.

She had avoided going into the bedroom until now. She hadn't seen it since the day Morty died. Mr. Diamond had shown the Demarcos the house the way it was, not cleaned up, he said, except for what the police took away. He said the Demarcos had been anxious to buy the house, and he wasn't sure they had noticed the condition of the bedroom, and Ellie wondered how they couldn't have noticed a bloodstained bed.

The bedroom looked exactly the same, Alice's slippers on the floor in the dressing room, the clothes she didn't take still hanging in the closet, the bloody pillow and spattered sheets and quilt still jumbled up on the king-size bed.

"Houses of this vintage, six outlets in this room, the builder was generous." Mr. Diamond was strolling around the room counting the number of electrical outlets. "The house, while old, is well built and well cared for. One would think, if forced to give an opinion, that at the least, and without considering, as well we might not consider at first glance, the pipes, it shows a love of hearth, which in this case may not mean home necessarily, but 'hearth' is the word I'm concerned with here, love of it, which manifests itself—"

"Do you need me for anything, Mr. Diamond?" Ellie said. "You're following me around as if you do."

She was at the bed now, contemplating the blood, trying to figure out what to do with the sheets and pillow and quilt.

"The Demarcos are of the very finest, lovely people, have said they would permit me to do the walk-through, not due to disinterest, for what more interest than a large purchase such as this, but businesswise, an architect, Mr. Demarco is one, I think I neglected to mention, and plans on remodeling. Certainly in his capacity the idea of remodeling would to our eyes be de minimus in such a well-kept, not to speak of elegant, home, but he will do what he will."

The movers came into the bedroom.

"I don't know what to do with the bedclothes," Ellie said to the one who called himself Dusty.

"Regulations are we don't touch anything bloody," Dusty said.

Mr. Diamond stood back out of the way while Ellie made a bundle of the sheets and pillow, then wrapped the bundle in the quilt.

"I would hesitate," he said, "to place what you have in your hands in any receptacle that will remain behind when you leave. Might I suggest your car. When you leave, of course. In that corner for now, out of the way of feet and traffic and observation, and I do feel it behooves us not to mention this, do you understand? I have alluded to an accident, shall we say, a sorry, unfortunate, unplanned, unanticipated, tragic, but innocent, demise."

Dusty and his men had taken the bed apart and were tussling the headboard through the door.

Mr. Diamond continued talking. "Mrs. Demarco, a sensitive soul, paints portraits, children and dogs, and is quite innocent of worldly matters. A position of trust, I have that with my clients."

The painters had arrived and were in the living room talking to the floor sander about where to store their paint buckets and brushes, their voices echoing through the half-empty rooms.

Dusty was back. He followed Ellie into Morty's office. "Is the desk ready to go?"

"Not yet."

"The point of disclosure, by law, signifies a level of honesty," Mr. Diamond said, "which I have in abundance, but as you can see, bloody sheets, and the police not permitting removal at the time of showing, there were the yellow tapes encircling, keeping us back, but Mr. Demarco said he understood there was an innocent explanation, and I didn't lie to him about the suicide, it wasn't mentioned, the point being if you don't say a thing, that doesn't constitute a lie, it is merely, to some, and to me as well, an omission that can be rectified if need be, if pressed, and I admit I fostered the idea that an accident had occurred."

A pen and pencil were on a malachite stand on Morty's desk. A dead ivy in a pottery elephant on a corner of the desk. Bank statements piled to one side next to a folded *Wall Street Journal*. Cigars in a carved wooden box. A calendar clock in the shape of a ship's wheel.

"My point being, if you, as a fine, and I know you are, woman, of what use is it to you to mention blood or sheets or pillows as being from a suicide rather than an accident? Do you see what I mean?"

"Not exactly."

"Let me clarify."

She put everything but the bank statements in a storage box, and started on the drawers. Pencils and Wite-Out and Post-it tabs and postage stamps, a ruler, a Mickey Mouse watch. She held the watch in her hand. It was ticking, but it was four hours off.

"For now, the question is moot, of course, as to who would volunteer, let alone let slip, because for what reason does one slip, as Freud has written, except for some underlying desire to sabotage oneself, for which I see no earthly, or heavenly, for that matter, purpose. Fines to be paid, if found out, but certainly not jail time. Have you ever heard of such, that is, jail time over bloody sheets not disclosed as to reason?"

It was in the third drawer on the right-hand side of the desk. A picture. That's all it was. A picture. And it took Ellie's breath away. It was in a park or a garden somewhere, with umbrellas in the background and kites flying. Three people standing together looking into the camera. Morty and Alice and Philip Brookner.

"What?" Ellie looked up at him.

"Sheets," Mr. Diamond said. "Bloody sheets. You aren't going to say anything to Mr. and Mrs. Demarco about the reason for the bloody sheets, are you?"

Ellie called the number on the piece of paper.

A woman answered. "Brookner's Antiques."

"Pardon me?" Ellie said.

"Brookner's Antiques."

"Well, I thought—is Philip Brookner there?"

"Who is this?"

"A friend. Not exactly a friend. He knows my sister, Alice. Is he there?"

The woman had walked away from the telephone and was now talking to someone. Classical music—Bach, or was it Brahms?—quavered in the background. The music had a tinny, insubstantial quality, as if it were coming from a long way off, or the space it was being piped into was too large for the sound to fill completely. Ellie could make out a man's voice now inquiring about a French vitrine and a woman answering.

"Is the mirror original to the piece?" the man asked.

"Fuck, yes, darling, everything in this store is original, including me," and then there was only music and what sounded like the scraping of furniture or sliding of drawers and overlapping voices where nothing made any sense.

"This is Philip," someone said into the phone. "Who's this?"

"Eleanor Holmgren—Ellie. Alice's sister."

It was definitely Brahms.

"Okay."

"You came to my house to talk to Alice."

"Okay."

"It's really hard on the phone."

"What is?"

"To talk. Can you meet me?"

"I don't know. What for?"

"Alice is in the hospital."

"Okay."

"I just want to talk to you."

"Okay."

"Can't you say anything besides okay?"

"What do you want me to say?"

"Can you meet me at Lenny's on Harbor Boulevard in Costa Mesa this afternoon?"

"Okay."

"I'm late, aren't I?" Brookner said. He was wearing open-toed fisherman's sandals without socks and had a slight body odor.

"A half hour," Ellie replied.

He looked different. Ellie had thought she remembered him as being taller, that his voice was lower, deeper, that he had a large head, that his eyes were mean, suspicious, frightening. He was none of those things. He was ordinary looking. Not tall at all. Average height. A plain face with nothing special about his voice, nothing frightening in his eyes.

"Weatherman says rain," he remarked.

Ellie was seated in a booth, but he was standing in the aisle as if he didn't intend to sit down. When he said the word "rain" he leaned over the booth and peered out the window.

"Oh?" Ellie said, and she looked out the window, too. The sun had come out late, but it had come out, and there was no sign of rain, no gray overcast or mist or drizzle, not even any clouds in the sky.

"I must listen to the wrong weatherman," she said and smiled at him. "I don't want to tell you what to do, Mr. Brookner, but it's awkward talking to you when I'm sitting down and you're standing. It makes my neck hurt."

"I like to stand."

The waitress came by. "You're blocking the aisle," she said, so he sat down, but he didn't look happy about it, and he wasn't completely seated. He hovered over the seat, legs bent, feet on the floor, his weight on his thighs. Like a jockey. But he was too heavy and soft and flabby for a jockey.

She hadn't been sure he would show up. She had sat in the back of the restaurant looking out the window for him, watching people come out of the movie across the street, some of them going to their cars in the adjoining parking lot, some of them crossing the street and coming into the restaurant.

"So where's the rest room?" he said.

"Excuse me?"

"The rest room."

"Well"—she looked around—"it's in the corner. The sign. REST ROOMS."

He nodded and didn't get up.

"I always like to know where the rest rooms are," he said.

They ordered coffee. He put three spoonfuls of sugar in his and stirred and stirred, but didn't drink it.

"How is Alice?" he asked.

"We don't know yet. Something's wrong with her heart, it beats too fast."

He cleared his throat and squirmed around on the seat.

"I hope it wasn't because of anything I said to her."

"Well, I don't know. I mean, what exactly did you say to her?"

"I can't say."

He poured some more sugar in his coffee, put his index finger in it as if to test how hot it was, and then took a large swallow of water instead.

"So she didn't tell you anything?" he said.

"No. No, she didn't."

"Nothing at all?"

"No, nothing."

"Okay." He took a deep breath. "Okay," he said again. He looked around the restaurant, and shook his head and grinned, then rolled his eyes ceilingward and shoved at the table with the palms of his hands.

"This is going to sound terrible," Ellie said, "and I don't mean in any way to accuse you of anything, but were you present when Morty died?"

"Me?"

"That morning. It was early, I know, but were you there? Did you by any chance see what happened?"

"Wait a minute now, wait a minute."

"I'm just asking if you were there."

"No. I wasn't. I wasn't there." He looked toward the rest room sign again and drank some more water. He was sitting full on the seat now, arms hugging the back of the booth, legs sprawled as if he were on a couch in someone's living room.

"I have a picture, an old picture," she said. "I don't know how old it is or where it was taken. It's a picture of you and Morty and Alice, the three of you are together in a park or somewhere. Outside. There are trees and bushes. Does it ring a bell?"

"Uh-huh."

"So you did know Morty?"

"Uh-huh."

"And you had business dealings with him? Was that the connection?"

"That was the connection."

"Alice never mentioned you to me, and I never heard your name, but I have Morty's bank statements. I didn't know what to do with them. They were on his desk, and the drawers were locked, and I couldn't very well put the statements in a drawer, so I picked them up and took them home. I'm a bookkeeper, I work for a restaurant, maybe you've heard of it, Mickey's Surfside, off Pacific Coast Highway. It's not actually on Pacific Coast, but around the corner, which is probably why it doesn't do more business than it does, and so I'm always used to looking at bank statements. I probably shouldn't have, they weren't mine, but I did, and that's when I noticed all those checks, monthly checks, that he made out to you."

"So you want to know what again?"

"How you knew Morty, what you had to do with him and Alice."

"Okay, so here's the deal." He looked up at the ceiling light, a trio of grease-encrusted bulbs. "Well, it's hard to explain." He took a sip of water and put the glass down precisely in the same watery ring he had picked it up from. "It wasn't the usual arrangement. You know what they say, you had to be there? Well, you had to be there. Really, it was a long story, and so now he's dead, so that's that, and she's in the hospital, and I don't know that much about real estate, but it was a land deal, I think is how we got started—or maybe it was some acreage." He looked up at the ceiling light again, then rubbed his eyes and gave his nose a swipe with the back of his hand. "No, that's not right. How did that go? Jesus, I forgot how that went now. What the hell did Morty say it was? A building. Christ, how do you forget a building? It was—I think he said it was a— what do you call those?"

"A limited partnership?"

"Maybe that was it. You know, it was like a corporation or a syndicate. That's it, it was a syndicate. It's been such a long time ago that I forgot the details. What he was giving me was a payout on my investment, or a buyback." He took another gulp of water. "I'm not sure what you call it."

"You know what? I think I've given you the wrong impression," Ellie said. "You were nice enough to meet me here and I'm practically accusing you of murder. I want to make it perfectly clear that that's not what I'm doing. Definitely not doing that. I'm just floundering around, trying to connect the dots, and I didn't intend to put you on the spot. I haven't paid much attention to Alice the past year, because my son died and I was out of it for a long time, and things were happening between Alice and Morty that I didn't know a thing about. I guess you could say I woke up with a bang when Morty was—when Morty—well, when Morty died. And Alice is acting so strangely. I've thought more than once I'd just leave her alone, that it's none of my business, but it is my business, because she's all the family I've got left. I'm really not trying to pry into how you knew Morty or what your business was with him—not exactly, any-how—it's just that I don't have any information, and there's something terribly wrong going on, and I certainly appreciate you driving over here to talk to me when you didn't have to. It's really out of character for me to do this, but I did want to ask you a few more questions, because you've got to admit it seems strange and more than just a coincidence that you knocked on my door and went into my kitchen to talk to my sister and an hour later she ends up in the hospital."

He stood up and bent his sour-smelling body toward her. It was a sudden gesture, a downward motion of his head toward her eyebrows. It was almost intimate in nature, as if he were going to kiss her or sniff her hair.

"Don't try to get in touch with me again," he said.

Chapter 13

ᠺ

"Come in through the alley and park in back," Mrs. Brookner told Teo on the phone. "Do you know where the Chateau Marmont is?"

"Sure."

"My shop's down the hill from there."

That was a laugh, did Teo know where the Chateau Marmont was. He had lost count of the times the clerk at the Marmont called Teo to come and get Bonnie, she was passed out on the couch in the lobby. But that was when they were still married. It had been a long time since Teo had had any reason to come up to West L.A., to drive down this part of Sunset Boulevard. Tiny's Coffee Shop was still on the corner across from the bookstore. All the movie biz wanna-bes—struggling screenwriters, broke producers, *Star Search* contestants—used to hang out at Tiny's in the 1980s. He and Bonnie lived in the apartment on Fountain Avenue in Hollywood then. Teo had just made detective in the Beverly Hills Police Department, and Bonnie was waitressing at Tiny's, still thinking she was going to be a movie star. He glanced in the plate-glass window as he drove by. No thick haze of cigarette smoke obscuring the window. No one hanging around the glass door or sitting under the umbrellas in the patio. The wanna-bes had moved on, were no doubt sitting in some other coffee shop with their tattered scripts and five-dollar options.

Brookner's Antique Gallery. There it was. Two large windows, a heavily carved door, and a green awning. He pulled into the alley behind the shop and parked. His shirt was wet under the arms and sticking to his back when he got out of the car. The drive up from Santa Ana, even with the windows open, had been hot. Fiddling with the air-conditioning controls had squeezed out a few bursts of tepid air at first, and then nothing but steam.

He reached into the backseat for his blue blazer (it was worn at the elbows and had a few threads dangling from the lapels), put it on over his damp shirt, then gave the driver's door a shove. Instead of closing, it rattled once and then hung half locked on its hinges. He leaned into it with his shoulder, and when it wouldn't budge he fished his keys out of his pocket, unlocked the door, then held the handle tight and eased the door in until the latch clicked and sank into position. The car was as obstinate and broken down as everything else in his life. Besides the dead air conditioner and the sprung driver's door, the rear right window wouldn't open, the shocks were shot, not all the pistons were firing, and the carburetor (he was lucky if he got ten miles to a gallon) was on its last legs.

A cool breeze slapped at the back of his shirt. No matter how hot it got, there was always enough air stirring on this part of Sunset to blow away the smog that floated over from the Los Angeles Basin. Somewhere west of where he was standing, over the Palisades, beyond the lush gardens and walled estates of Bel-Air, the boulevard twisted around like a cat chasing its tail before it dead-ended in the blue chill of the Pacific Ocean.

He had enough money to fix his car. He had enough money to move out of the house in Santa Ana, buy a condo in Anaheim Hills or a small house in Sunset Beach. He could afford to take a trip somewhere if he wanted to. His disability check went into the bank, and except for giving Estella some money for groceries, most of it stayed there. But he had no appetite for buying anything or going anywhere, no desire for possessions, no interest in fixing his car.

The back of the store looked even fancier than the front. Another green awning. Two tall ficus trees in stone urns. A wrought-iron bench on a slab of white concrete that looked as if it had been scrubbed that morning. A small garden with a burbling fountain. And right above the fence on the top of the hill behind the parking lot, the Chateau Marmont. Portions of it, anyway. A teasing glimpse of roof, a few windows cloaked in trees and shrubs. The same old stone guardian of mystery and misfortune.

"I open the shop at ten-thirty," Mrs. Brookner told him on the phone. "I have designers coming in by appointment, so if you want to talk to me, I'll be in my office at nine. If you're late, you're out of luck. I mean it. I do not fucking stand up my paying clients."

He walked toward the rear entrance of the shop, past the burbling fountain, and rang the bell. A reenforced steel door opened and a young black man, head shaved and four gold hoops in his left ear, peered at Teo through a set of iron gates.

"I had an appointment with Mrs. Brookner. Detective Teo Domingos, Newport Beach Police Department."

"Miz B. isn't in." He was wearing white cotton pants and had tied the tails of his orange shirt into a knot at his waist, leaving about six inches of bare midriff.

"And you are?"

"Paolo, with two *os*."

"I'll wait inside."

"I can't let you in till Miz B. comes back." He opened the gates far enough to step out and take a look at Teo's car. "That car isn't leaking oil, is it?" he asked, sunlight dancing on his bare scalp. "You'll have to move it to some other location if it does, because Miz B.'s very particular about not letting cars leak oil on her property."

"Sometimes it leaks and sometimes it doesn't."

"That's not good."

"Look, I'm trying to learn to curb my hostile impulses, and waiting makes me very hostile. She said come at nine, and it's nine. So is she coming back today, or are you just shitting me?"

"Oh, no, no, no, she's coming back pretty soon. She had to meet a set designer at Universal Studios, and it might take her a while, but she's coming back. Miz B. always does what she says."

"So are you going to let me in?"

"Miz B. doesn't allow anyone in her office when she's gone."

Teo could have pushed his way in, he knew how to do it without pre-cipitating a police brutality report. Instead he asked for a glass of water, then sat in his car with the windows and doors open and drank it (ice water with a twist of lemon in what Paolo said was an eighteenth-century Venetian glass), and stared up the hill at the Chateau Marmont. He had been on duty the night John Belushi overdosed in one of the hotel bunga-lows. KTLA had interviewed him a few minutes after the coroner got there. Did you see needle marks in his arms? Was he in bed, or in a chair, or on a couch, or on the floor? Who was the woman with him? What is she being arrested for? No comment, no comment, no comment, no comment. Bonnie missed her big chance that night. If she hadn't been fucking a casting director in one of the hotel suites, she could have run down and gotten her picture taken with John Belushi's body.

Paolo came outside at ten-thirty.

"Miz B. is here."

"Good for her."

"She said to come into her office and be quick, because she's got another appointment coming in fifteen minutes."

Teo followed him through the shop. Gold leaf on glossy furniture, ornately framed portraits, bronze statues on marble pedestals, floor-to-ceiling tapestries, shelves lined with leather-bound books, painted plates, colored glass. Not like the antique shop Ma's cousin Pocho owned in downtown Santa Ana. Pocho's had old fans and broken chairs in the front window next to a sign that said, NOTARY PUBLIC, IMMIGRATION, TAX PREPARATION, PASSPORT PHOTOS.

Mrs. Brookner, a tall, slim woman with a sixty-year-old neck and a forty-year-old face, was on the telephone.

"You dress the set the way you want, darling, and don't let Sheldon tell you it'll break the budget to have real Louis Quinze furniture. Did you tell him thirty-five thousand was a bargain?"

Teo sat down in a delicate-looking honey-colored bamboo chair.

"Eighteen fifty," Mrs. Brookner said. "No, I'm not talking to you, dar-ling. There's a man sitting in one of my Indian chairs. You didn't see it? It was here in my office when you were in last. He's sitting in it now, but if you want to buy it, for you, darling, seventeen ninety-five." She winked at Teo. "I know, I know, darling, he's upset you, but I absolutely can't go below thirty-five thousand."

She held out a silver cigarette case, and Teo shook his head.

"Don't smoke," he said.

"But, darling, now listen to me, darling, I've been in this business long enough to know that budgets are made to be broken. The studio is just fucking with you, they've got the money."

Pictures of movie stars hung on the walls. Some were of a younger Mrs. Brookner with various movie stars. Arm in arm with Clark Gable. At a nightclub table with Gary Cooper. At poolside with Marilyn Monroe. Affectionate inscriptions were preserved beneath glinting glass.

"Did you check their grosses for last weekend? Shit, darling, they can afford to buy carloads of Rembrandts to put on the set of the goddamn picture. Tell Sheldon to come down and talk to me. No, I mean it. I'm not afraid of him. I'll talk to him. I'll explain the facts of life to him. No free lunches, darling. If he's setting the goddamn picture in Louis Quinze period, then it better goddamn well be authentic Louis Quinze furniture. You can't fool the public, they notice things like that. This isn't some fucking indie film he has to nickel-and-dime me on. No, no, don't say that. I won't listen to that bullshit. I'm in business here just the way you are, just the way the studio is."

She was vaguely familiar. Teo hadn't known the young woman in the photographs, but somewhere in between, when Mrs. Brookner was in her early forties probably, he might have known her.

"It's Louis Quinze, darling, and they're for fucking real—a bureau plat, the sofa, the tables—no, I won't break the set. Do you understand what I had to go through to get this shit? Four five-star dinners for my French picker, then money under the table to avoid the tax, a bonus to the trustee of the estate—a goddamned nightmare."

Her large teeth were exposed in each smiling photograph.

Dear Rita, the best time in the world, Deepest Love, Elvis.

Darling Rita, you're the one, Clint.

Rita Sweetheart, thanks for everything. I'll never forget you, Jack. Teo got up out of the chair and examined that one. Jack Kennedy and an unlined Rita Lemoyne (Teo remembered her name now) together on a small yacht on some large body of water.

"Of course you have to take the sofa with it. What the hell good's the rest of the grouping if you don't have the sofa? It's silk and damask. Of course, the cushions are down. One hundred percent, darling. The French wouldn't have it any other way. No, no, don't start that shit again, or I'll hang up."

She took a cigarette out of the silver case and lit it.

"I know you do, darling, and if you want me to take care of it for you, I will. No, no, I won't antagonize him. I'll be the soul of sweetness. No, I won't say 'fuck' when I talk to him. I know he's genteel and sensitive, and I promise I won't say 'fuck.' Reproductions? Are you out of your mind? Where do reproductions come to the real thing? They don't have the feel or the smell. I know you can't smell anything in a movie. It's just a figure of speech, darling. Go with me on this, Jerry. I won't say 'fuck' or 'shit' when I talk to Sheldon, but I've got to know that you're behind me on this, that you're not going to go behind my back and end up with some whore at Pacific Design."

She blew smoke out of the side of her mouth and pushed a ceramic ashtray back and forth on her desk, back and forth, back and forth. Her fingernails were perfect pink ovals, a diamond solitaire on her right hand, no wedding ring on her left.

"Look, you're squeezing me too hard on this deal. I'm busting my ass here for a lousy thirty-five thousand. You can look at Swan Gallery, but I'm telling you I'm the only one that's got what you need, and I'm firm on this, so piss or get off the pot."

She slammed the phone down.

"Business," she said and smiled at Teo.

He smiled back.

"So what is the new alarm system you're recommending?"

"Laser."

"Cut to the chase. How much?"

"It's really funny, but I know you."

"I have that kind of face, darling. What police department did you say you were with?"

"Newport Beach."

"What are you doing this far north, darling? Don't we have our own moonlighting policemen in Beverly Hills? I wouldn't think we'd have to import them. Duke Wayne had a yacht in Newport Beach. Did you know Duke Wayne?"

"Not to speak to."

"I used to play poker with him."

She began going through her mail, as if he weren't there. She didn't remember him.

"I'm not really selling alarm systems," Teo said. "I want to ask you some questions about your son."

She wore glasses on a chain that was studded with bright blue stones. She took the glasses off and they dropped down the length of the chain, caught on the middle button of her green silk blouse, and hung there.

"You fucking fraud," she said.

"He was arrested in Carpinteria in nineteen ninety-six, April. He and a man named Morty Miller."

"If you want to know how to decorate your house, I'll start the meter running. I get two hundred fifty dollars an hour."

"Did you know Morty Miller?"

"Of course I knew him."

"How?"

"You're making me a little angry, darling. My time is valuable. You're wasting it."

Teo stretched his legs out in front of him and the bamboo chair made an ominous screech.

"I don't bluff as easily as the guy on the phone."

She smoothed one plucked brow with an oval pink nail.

"I know you, too," she said.

"All right."

"I have a thing for faces. Club Med, nineteen eighty-four."

"Nope."

"Ojai. The tennis pro. You helped me with my backhand. April, nineteen ninety-one."

"Nope."

"Sun Valley. The ski instructor, married to a Swedish model. Thanksgiving, nineteen ninety-three."

He shook his head. "Hollywood, the parking lot of the Playboy Club. You offered to set up a threesome for an undercover cop and I busted you. Christmas Eve, nineteen eighty-one."

You can lift the skin of a sixty-year-old's face and staple it behind her ears, and redo the chin and fill the lip creases with injected fat, but the eyes don't change. Hers were blue agates, narrow and suspicious, and not a bit afraid. She buzzed Paolo on the intercom and he brought coffee in on a silver tray. Tiny napkins, bite-sized cookies, a blooming orchid in a gilded pot. He shut the door behind him.

"I haven't been in the business for a long time," she said and poured the coffee.

She was relaxed now, her taut face slack over the wrinkled neck. She sat in the back of his patrol car that foggy Christmas Eve fifteen years before and gave him all the reasons why he should let her go. She had started out a working prostitute, she said, married one of her johns, and when he started beating her she ran. She had no college degrees, she said, no connections, no family money, her son was in trouble, and she needed money to put him in rehab. *Let me go and I'll pay you back in pretty girls.* He remembered that she knew how to talk, could twist her way around any subject. He had almost let her go that night. He would have if there hadn't been another policeman involved. He was a lot looser in those days about right and wrong, wasn't sure he even knew the difference. An exec at Fox picked her up before the fingerprint ink was dry on the arrest sheet, and that was the last Teo heard of her.

"Morty's dead, poor thing, shuffled off to Buffalo, left this vale of tears, went off to the great beyond," she said. "Philip's upset about it, naturally. Shit, darling, anyone would be upset. Even the worst father in the world is still a father. You were in Vietnam. I remember you now. The angry look."

"His father?"

"My second husband adopted Philip, but he was Morty's." She took a cookie, bit into it, and chewed. "I'm very protective of my son, and I have all sorts of friends. Newport Beach Police Department? I'm sure I know someone who knows someone there. One thing I don't do anymore is buckle around policemen. I've found that a well-aimed phone call does wonders. It's simple mathematics, so many favors here, so many there, and when you need something you know where to go. You can frighten Paolo, darling, but not me. I'm unfrightenable. Oh, look at that cold stare. It's quite sexy, darling, but I'm too old for you. Plastic surgery goes only so deep. Everything else dries up or falls off or disappears."

She put the nibbled cookie down on a napkin and wadded it into a ball.

"I remember that you told me your wife was sleeping around, and I told you everyone sleeps around, some just do it more discreetly than others. She wanted to be in the movies and you were having trouble controlling her, and I said maybe she should work for me. You didn't like that very much. Did she finally make it in the movies? Have I seen her in anything? Are you still with her?"

She lit another cigarette. The other one was still burning in a ceramic ashtray on the credenza in back of her.

"We're divorced."

"Too bad. I've always said that divorce is overrated as an end to marriage. Marriage shouldn't have to end at all. Respect can keep it going indefinitely. It's not sex that keeps it going, for chrissakes. I've been thinking about writing a book about how to stay married and still fuck around. It will be all of two pages long. Absolutely no contempt allowed between husband and wife. Contempt is the killer of marriage, not extracurricular fucking. Banish contempt, that's the first page. Freedom, unconditional, is the second page. Beyond that I don't care. Don't look so dismissive, darling. I'm serious."

"Maybe it was the drive up here," he said. "Maybe it was listening to your bullshit on the telephone. Maybe it's just me. I don't know, I don't drink anymore, but I feel as if I'm hungover, and it doesn't leave me with a whole lot of patience for this kind of crap."

She put her cup down, pulled her chair away from her desk, and stood up.

"Listen to me, darling," she said. "Morty shot himself. Blew his brains out. Finis. Done. Over with. You want to find a murderer, is that it? Well, there isn't one. Save your energy. Go home. Forget about it. It's a family matter."

"Whose family?"

She walked across the room and opened the office door.

"Go home," she said.

Chapter 14

"Here's the way it works, Ellie. You don't pay a bill the minute you get it." Mickey had been in and out of Ellie's office all morning, whining and complaining. It was now one-thirty and he was back again, pointing a cream-cheesed bagel at the stack of bills on her desk. "You wait a month or two, then you pay it. See, if I pay my money out to someone else, I don't have it anymore."

He sat down on the edge of her desk, his left leg crossed over his right. "You make them wait. They expect to wait. They like waiting. They like sending late notices. It gives the bookkeepers something to do. I saw how it went while you were gone. I didn't pay the bills and I had more money in my pocket." He now crossed his right leg over his left and waved the bagel around in a circle. "I figured out what you were doing wrong. You were paying when you should have been putting off, and now you're back ruining the delicate balance I created between bill, past due bill, and final notice. Get my drift?"

"You don't want to keep getting deliveries of meat and eggs and milk?"

"I didn't say that. Did I say that? I said don't pay them so fast." He took a bite of bagel. "Manuel bought premium eggs again last month instead of commercial grade. I won't pay for premium. Don't send the egg guy a check. Call him up and tell him he made a mistake, we didn't order expensive eggs, we won't pay for them. We've got to economize. Fire the busboy. Let the waitresses bus their own tables."

"The restaurant goes down one more notch without a busboy."

"And no coffee refills. We pour gallons of coffee down the sewer. The customer doesn't drink what he's got and the waitress comes by and fills it up. They want a refill, make them pay for it."

"Chintzy. Can't do it, Mickey. You might as well close up."

He was now examining his face in the beveled mirror on the wall next to the door. "There's a guy wants to talk to you, out in front, last booth."

"A guy? What guy?"

"I didn't ask his name. What does the Health Department inspector look like?"

"Tall, thin, serious."

"It might be him." He pinched the loose flesh at the corners of his eyes with his fingers. "I've been thinking of going in for an eye lift. I look sleepy all the time. Did you ever notice that I look sleepy all the time?"

"I never noticed that you looked sleepy. Did he say anything about inspecting the kitchen? I promised we'd get the kitchen fumigated. Did you call the fumigators while I was gone? How are the bugs? Are the bugs gone?"

"Which ones?"

"You didn't do it."

"Manuel wouldn't let me. He said poison gets in the air and stays there for months and lands on the food and gives it a bad taste. I'm not going to fight with him over a few lousy cockroaches."

When mail came, Mickey had a habit of holding envelopes from creditors up to the light trying to read what they said, and then, as if that were sufficient, not opening them. He not only avoided paying bills, he avoided fumigating the kitchen (he blamed it on Manuel, but Ellie knew he didn't want to close the restaurant for the time the fumigation would take), avoided dealing with the Health Department inspector (he hid in his office when the inspector was there), avoided just about anything that cost money or was unpleasant.

Finished with the mirror, he sat down in the chair across from Ellie's desk and ate the rest of the bagel, talked a little about plastic surgery (he

wanted to know if there was enough in the checking to make a down pay-
ment on a complete face-lift or if he had to make do with an eye lift; Ellie
told him there wasn't enough for either), and then went back to his office.

They weren't due for another Health Department inspection until
November, but sometimes the inspector pulled surprise visits, just
turned up when you weren't expecting him. Like in February, a month
after the yearly, he showed up and wanted to see the kitchen and toilets
again. Like that. Without any warning. Four o'clock on a Friday, with
Manuel getting ready for the dinner crowd and Ellie making salads
(Solomon, the new salad man, had cut his finger) and Mickey at the race-
track (not that it would have mattered if he was in his office, he was perfectly useless in an emergency). Anyway, there had been no time to clean
out the ants under the sink or get rid of the weevils in the flour or the
cockroaches in the lettuce bin or to scrub bathroom floors and put disin-
fectant in the toilet tanks.

Manuel was at the stove now finishing up the last of the lunch orders.
He was still fuming and sputtering over the fight he and Mickey had had
that morning. Mickey said he didn't want him putting ketchup bottles on
the tables anymore, that it cost too much money. A few spoonfuls in a
custard cup is enough, Mickey told him. Manuel had nearly quit in the
middle of breakfast.

"He thinks he runs the place," Manuel muttered now. "He tells me I cut
roast beef too thick and I put too much gravy on the mashed potatoes."

"He grew up during the Depression," Ellie said. "He keeps expecting
it to come back."

"I tell him to stay the hell out of my kitchen, but he keeps coming in
every time I'm not looking. He thinks I don't keep my word that I'm
leaving. I keep my word. I told him I'm going to the Marriott, they don't
scream at the Marriott. They don't tell me there I give too big a piece of
meat to the customers."

It was a compact kitchen, smaller than most restaurant kitchens. It
needed painting. The appliances were aging. The stove sometimes
belched up thick black smoke. Mickey needed to gut the place and redo

it, but didn't want to spend the money. It wasn't Manuel's fault that there were ants and cockroaches. Vermin loved old appliances and rotting insulation.

Ellie opened the double doors to the storage cabinet and a dark object—she couldn't be sure what it was, a fly, a gnat, a mouse, a cockroach—flew past her cheek. She shut the doors and went over to the stove.

"You've really got to clean out the pantry, Manuel."

"Tell Solomon. That's not my job."

Solomon was standing in the door to the alley, trying to see around the corner of the building to the restaurant parking lot. When he wasn't chopping onions and tomatoes and julienning carrots, he spent his time standing in the kitchen door checking the parking lot for Immigration agents.

She didn't want to talk to the Health Department inspector. She didn't want him coming into the kitchen and opening the pantry. She had promised him the place would be cleaned up and vermin-free the next time he showed up, and it wasn't.

"I run a whole kitchen in that hotel in Cancun, twenty-five people in the kitchen, fifteen in the dining room," Manuel said. "No one tell me what to cook, how to cook, what to put on the plate. I'm my own boss in Cancun. I don't listen to no crazy person like Mickey, who don't know good food if he choke on it."

Well, there was no use dodging him. He'd just keep coming back until he caught her, and then he might decide there were a few more things wrong with Mickey's Surfside than he thought.

She looked into the restaurant through the kitchen pass-through. There were two rows of booths in the coffee shop section. The fake plants in the window had turned a watery purple where the morning sun hit them, and the stuffed marlin that Mickey caught in Cabo San Lucas was falling off its mounting. The whole tail section had already split away from the wood, and a customer sliding into a booth the year before had scratched her cheek and sued Mickey for $750 (she settled for $250). What was left of the marlin was still hanging on the wall. The dining room section needed refurbishing, too. The tables were always set with cloths and silverware, but almost no one ate in there. Customers would walk under the trellis archway, look in at the four white walls and the metal-framed chairs, and then ask for a booth in the coffee shop. Mickey had been talking lately about turning the dining room into a doughnut shop.

The restaurant was nearly empty. A woman finishing a slice of pie, an elderly man eating a plate of crab cakes and doing a crossword puzzle, and the man Mickey thought was the Health Department inspector still sitting by himself in the booth near the door. Even though his back was turned and Ellie didn't recognize the shirt, and the dark hair was longer than she remembered, she knew it was Teo.

"I never fight with anyone before Mickey," Manuel said. "He bring out the bad side of me. I think maybe I'm going to get an ulcer, maybe I have one already, every time I see his face it makes my stomach hurt. He tells me I can't buy premium eggs. He says, what's the difference? I tell him, taste it, go on, taste it, and he won't even taste it, so what can I do with such a stubborn man?"

She pushed open the kitchen door.

He was studying the menu, had it open to the breakfast items, and was looking at the glossy pictures of pancakes and bacon and waffles.

"The cook stopped making breakfast at eleven-thirty," she said.

He looked up at her. "I like the pictures."

"They're sleazy looking. Mickey ordered them anyway because they were cheap. If you want breakfast, Manuel turns off the griddle at eleven, oils it, and won't turn it on until morning comes around again."

"Estella left her husband and moved in with me. It's a long story."

"I might coax Manuel into making breakfast for you. No pancakes, but we've got eggs. I haven't paid the egg bill yet, and they might have stopped delivery, but I'm fairly sure I saw eggs coming out of the kitchen. There might be some hollandaise left, if you want eggs Benedict, but hollandaise curdles so fast I wouldn't recommend it, you might get sick, and the ham looked a little green to me, very unappetizing."

"She makes breakfast for me every day. I don't like breakfast food. She makes it and acts hurt if I don't eat it, so I do."

"If you've come here to tell me you still think Alice shot Morty, I don't want to hear about it."

"I just had an urge to see you."

She sat down on the leatherette seat and her knee brushed against his. "I thought you were the inspector from the Health Department. We only got a provisional approval in February, so I was sure that's who you were."

She was fiddling with a paper napkin, folding it in half and then quarters, and then tearing it into strips.

"You look really good," he said. "I forgot how good you look. I didn't know whether you were back to work or not."

"If you don't want breakfast, the turkey hash is good for lunch. Guaranteed not to make you sick. Don't worry about the provisional we got from the Health Department. All restaurant kitchens have a few vermin in them, and it's pretty rare when something falls into the food. 'Rare' isn't even the word. I don't remember it ever happening. The hash isn't bad. I was in the kitchen when Manuel made it. Absolutely no bugs in it at all. He won't be putting it away for another half hour. That's when he starts prepping for dinner. Dinner's at five. We don't serve anything between lunch and dinner. Manuel's pretty rigid about serving times. He doesn't have enough help to keep serving all day long, although there's Solomon, who does the salads, and I come in when there's a rush, and do some cooking. You never called me. You just disappeared."

There was nothing left of the napkin but a pile of cellulose. The overhead fan tugged gently at the soft strands, lifting up the stray bits at the periphery of the pile and teasing them closer and closer to the edge of the table.

"But I can certainly recommend the hash. It's not the premade hash that you unwrap and fry up. Manuel makes his own. Fresh turkey, chopped with potatoes and onions, browned in seasoned oil, with a little cajun spice added for color and heat. I threw myself at you and I'm so embarrassed about it. I don't do things like that. I'm careful about people. I thought you liked me, and then you were gone."

Someone opened the front door and velvety bits of napkin blew like snow out onto the sidewalk.

"I came back to work last week. Mickey messed up the bills and the bank says we're overdrawn and Mickey insists that they're wrong, and he has strange ideas how a business should be run. I've been writing checks all morning. He hates it when I write checks. Frankly, I don't know how he's kept the business going as long as he has. He thinks he's lucky. He goes to the track, gambles and loses, and he thinks he's lucky. I shouldn't even talk to you."

Her right hand was trembling.

"Alice had a pacemaker put in," she said.

A blob of gravy had congealed in a corner of the faux wood table. Atrophied. Turned to stone. Like a tree stump that's been left to rot for a thousand years. The busboy probably thought it was part of the table.

"She's still in the hospital. The doctor can't seem to get the speed of the pacemaker right."

"I don't want you to think that I stayed away because I wanted to. I thought about you. I just couldn't seem to move. I got used to not seeing you, it seemed to be all right, no big deal, life went on, things were okay, I went to the shrink and he said I was making progress, so why change the way things were?"

"She said it doesn't feel like her own heart. You wonder about that, if when your heart isn't beating on its own, whether you even have one."

He had hold of her hand and was pressing his knee hard against hers.

"Help me, Ellie," he said.

They had hardly come in Ellie's front door when they were on the floor, on each other, Teo's shoulders pushing against the couch, bumping it along the carpet, couch legs snagging the shaggy loops, then breaking free and bumping along some more. Afterward she put her white silk (or was it satin?) panties back on, but her bra was still hanging from the knob of the television set, and she and Teo were eating pea soup, the bowls on the carpet, their clothes strewn around them.

"Sometimes Manuel just waves a grizzled, bare ham bone over the top of the soup pot and thinks no one can tell the difference," Ellie said. "He put the whole bone in, meat and all, this time, so I brought some home."

They had been half crazed, on the floor, sliding slowly toward the wall, oblivious to the burn of the carpet against their skin. His arm ached now, but he hadn't felt any pain when Ellie laid her weight against it.

"Estella's taken over the house," he said. He was naked, his pants somewhere under the couch. "The first thing she did was wash the windows and hose off the screens. Then she threw all the rugs outside and beat the hell out of them. One of these days I expect to find her on the roof, scrubbing the shingles."

"The soup needs something," she said.

He watched her get up and walk toward the kitchen, the slightly round hips in the white silky pants swaying, her brown-tipped breasts moving up and down. He could still feel them in his mouth, the taste of the skin, slightly tart from the bath salts she used.

She was back, bending over, offering him more warm bread, shaking cayenne flakes into their bowls of soup. He had made the wrong move, grabbing her the way he did, as if he had been just waiting to get her alone, as if he were a love-starved kid. Sure, something was happening between them, he'd admit that much. He had already admitted it, just by being here and eating pea soup with real ham in it, when he hated peas and couldn't taste the ham, but he wasn't sure he was ready for anything like what he could see shaping up in her mind.

"Then she went to Sears and bought a refrigerator with an ice maker and a butter dish and egg keeper and separate bins for meat and vegetables. She moved my desk into a corner of the living room and put a bookcase where the desk used to be."

"Maybe Estella's not trying to take over," Ellie said. "Maybe she just wants to make you more comfortable, wants to do things for you. I understand that perfectly."

"She throws things away. It drives me crazy. Ma's old clothes that were in a box in one of the bedrooms. And the suit Pa wore the day he got his citizenship papers."

"Maybe she thought you wouldn't mind."

She liked the word "maybe." *Maybe Estella meant well. Maybe Estella will go back to Oscar and leave Teo alone. Maybe the moon is made of green cheese.*

"Do you think contempt ruins marriages?" he asked abruptly.

"If you mean do you need respect for one another, is that what you—"

"I'm not sure what it means."

He had a thing for blond Anglo women. After Bonnie left, Estella fixed him up with one of her girlfriends from high school, a bilingual teacher in the Valley. She was a pretty girl from Guanajuato, black curly hair and smoked-almond eyes, but there were no sparks when he was with her. Estella rubbed it in about sticking to his own, that marriage is hard enough without going looking for trouble. But what could he do if there were no sparks? His last date before Ellie was six years ago, a witness in a homicide, a Swedish girl named Ingrid. When he told her the DA was planning on arresting her as an accomplice, she threw a stapler at Teo and called him a dumb Mexican. And here he was with another blond. This one wasn't cool like Bonnie or Ingrid. She wasn't hot either. She was somewhere in the middle. Warm. She sat across from him, bare tits jiggling as she sipped her soup.

"You never said what you think about Mexicans," he said.

"Think? What am I supposed to think? What kind of question is that?"

"Just your average question. So what do you think?"

"I don't even understand the question."

"Then skip it."

"No, I won't skip it. It's obviously important to you. What is it you want to know?"

"I can't explain it."

"You asked it, so now you have to explain it."

"Some people don't like Mexicans."

"I don't know how to respond to that. I don't see anyone but you when I look at you. I like you."

"So where do you stand on name-calling?"

"Name-calling?"

"You know, like 'you dumb Mexican.' Have you ever said that to anyone?"

"How can you even ask me that?" she said, moist little droplets beading in the corners of her eyes.

"Forget it then."

Who said tears didn't lie? What was that last lie Bonnie told him, tears in her eyes? *I've got to go to Santa Maria, my sister's very sick,* when all the time she had airplane tickets to meet some over-the-hill actor in Aspen.

"The floor's hard, let's go in the bedroom," he said.

"I'm more hurt about what you just said than I am about your not calling me for two months."

She wasn't too hurt to go into the bedroom with him, but she kept crying, and that unnerved him, and finally he just held her until they both fell asleep.

Alice was afraid of the dark. Dark nights. Dark closets. Even dark roads, where no cars drove, where the lights of houses were too far away to flicker any brighter than the weakest star. But daylight had its problems, too. You were exposed in daylight, open to questions by anyone who came along, anyone who stopped and asked you what you were doing, asked you if you needed help, asked you if there was anything they could do.

The nurse came in at midnight and shined her flashlight on Alice's closed eyelids, a shock of orange light, then a shivery beam that squirreled around the bed and the floor and finally disappeared.

It was time to leave. She had put it off long enough. Dark or no dark, she'd put on her clothes and walk down the hall and just leave.

She pulled the monitor leads out of her chest with little quick yanks, then looked down at her chest. Wireless, and nothing awful had happened. Her heart didn't rebel, the pacemaker kept its pace. She swung her feet over the side of the bed and stood up. She had been secretly practicing walking, not merely to the bathroom, but back and forth across the hospital room, bed to window, window to bed. She sat down for a second to let the pacemaker catch up, then stood again, walked to the closet, and felt for her clothes. She had the dress she was admitted in, but no shoes. Slippers would have to do. Purse, glasses. The light from the nurses' station glowed outside her room. Not enough for her to see if she had forgotten anything.

It was like a movie. You walk slowly, but with authority. Past the shower room, then the laundry. BIOHAZARDS, the sign on the door said. Two nurses were charting at the other end of the hall, shoulders forward, dim yellow light like a halo around their heads. They didn't look up. She walked more quickly now, waiting for her heart to explode or shatter or, like a worn-out car, sputter a little and then die. Out the hospital door and down the steps, and her heart kept beating.

Chapter 15

Teo wasn't sure what was going on. Ellie wasn't answering her phone. Maybe his asking her whether she ever called anyone a dumb Mexican had hit a nerve.

And what was it he said to her when he was putting his clothes back on and she was still stretched out on the bed? Something along the lines of, *Things are really heating up between us; maybe we ought to cool it a little?* He had just been testing her, had expected her to say she was glad things were heating up between them and she didn't want to cool it. Instead she said, "All right, if that's the way you feel." It wasn't the answer he was looking for, but it didn't seem to him anything as drastic as dumping him was in the offing. That was three weeks ago. So he cooled it himself, just let her hang out to dry, didn't call her, didn't drop by the restaurant. The best thing was to end it bloodlessly, before they both got in too deep.

And now she wasn't answering her phone.

He wasn't trying to spy on her, but at about eleven o'clock Friday evening he took a drive down to Costa Mesa and rode past her house. There were no lights on, and a pile of newspapers were lying on the grass in front. That was no big deal. It didn't mean that she had left the country and was never coming back.

On Saturday she still wasn't answering her phone, and when Teo tried calling her at work, Mickey got on the line and said he didn't know what the hell was going on, but she hadn't been in for two weeks.

*   *   *

Sunday morning. Teo had fallen asleep on the couch in his clothes the night before, and now it was daylight and Estella was straightening the sofa cushions around him and telling him to hurry up and get his shower or they'd miss the nine o'clock Mass.

She picked up the beer bottles on the floor next to the couch, and then opened the drape that he had closed the night before. He sat up and lowered his head against the sudden brightness.

"I told you I'm not going," he said.

She was now wiping off the end tables with a soft white cloth (one of his old T-shirts?), scraping at a recalcitrant spot on the coffee table with her fingernail, bending down and examining more closely some old chocolate stains on the carpet.

"What time is it?" he said.

"Seven o'clock." She leaned against the coffee table and pulled herself up. "When were you last in church?"

"I can't remember."

His shoes were under the couch. He was still wearing his socks, new ones that Estella bought him. "I can't let my brother go around with holes in his socks," she said, and came home from Nordstrom with ten pairs.

"Who was on the phone?" he said.

"It was a wrong number. I made breakfast. Go eat it before it gets cold. Eggs taste terrible cold."

"I don't want any eggs. All I want is a cup of coffee, Estella. Just a lousy cup of coffee."

"You don't have to lose your temper over a plate of eggs, Teo."

"Losing my temper would be if I got up from the couch, went into the kitchen, threw the eggs in the sink, and smashed the breakfast dishes. I'm just explaining to you that it doesn't matter whether the eggs get cold or not, because I'm not going to eat them."

Her lower lip quivered.

"I'll have some toast, how's that?"

"White or rye?"

"Either one."

She went into the kitchen, and he could hear the crinkle of the bread's plastic wrap and then the metallic slide of the toaster handle.

He was trying to get the hang of this, how to say what he wanted in a halfway sane manner. Actually, he had lost his temper with Estella only once since she moved in. Semi lost it, anyway. She wouldn't still be living here if he had entirely lost it. It had been about the backyard. She wanted to clean it up—chop down the trees, clear out the shrubs, and put a lawn in to replace the scrawny-looking devil grass. He told her to leave the yard exactly the way it was. The overgrown, leggy hibiscus that Raul had dumped fourteen-year-old Luci's dime-store cologne on that afterward sprouted flowers that smelled like Chantilly. And the pit at the side of the garage that was part of the tunnel Raul and Teo dug when they were still in grammar school (Pa pulled them out, half suffocated, when the sides caved in). And the rope swing that still hung on the walnut tree, and the clotheslines that Ma used to hang the wash on, and the cot (the canvas rotted away) where Pa would snooze on Saturday afternoons. "Don't touch any of it," he told her.

"You're just being sentimental," Estella said, and the next thing he knew she had hired three Salvadoran laborers to demolish the yard, just wipe out everything in it. They had begun to tear out the honeysuckle vines that were holding up the grape-stake fence, machetes biting into the blossoms that Teo and Raul used to suck the juice out of to disguise the smell of cigarette smoke, when Teo lost it, got so mad he started shouting at the Salvadorans in Spanish to get the hell off his property, then just rammed their asses through the rusty gate and told Estella he knew now why Oscar ran around with other women. She had been pretty careful around him since then. Although every once in a while she'd slip and try to boss him around, tell him what to eat or what to wear, or say something contemptuous (*You just don't understand plain English* was her favorite remark), and he'd have to pull her up short. He had come to the conclusion that Estella, like a dog that wouldn't stop jumping up and knocking people over, could be trained.

"We'll go to Mass at Saint Joseph's today," she said. She had buttered Teo's toast and sliced it into quarters.

"Saint Alban's is closer."

"I know, but I want to go to Saint Joseph's."

Saint Joseph's was in Newport Beach. It was where Oscar and Estella had been married and where Angela had been confirmed and where Derek was baptized. All the Masses were in English at Saint Joseph's. Estella had spent every Sunday when she was growing up sitting in a pew at Saint Alban's in Santa Ana alongside Ma and Pa and Raul and Luci and Roxana and Jose and Teo, listening to the Dominican priest celebrate the Mass in Spanish. And now she said it had always made her feel like an alien, like a misfit, like she wasn't even an American. Teo couldn't remember hearing her speak Spanish after she left home (except when she was hiring day laborers from out in front of the movie in downtown Santa Ana), had never heard her use Spanish with Angela and Derek, and whenever Teo would throw a few Spanish words into a sentence she'd give him a dirty look, which made it all the more curious why when she left Oscar she came running back to the old house in the old neighborhood, where all the shop signs were in Spanish and people on the street looked at you blankly when you spoke English to them.

She had the vacuum plugged in now and was pulling it back and forth over the rug. She didn't talk about Oscar at all. But in the evening after dinner she'd go out and sit on the swing on the front porch. *I think I'll just go and get a little air,* she'd say. But Teo knew she was watching for Oscar's car, waiting for him to pull up to the curb, jump over the gate, run up the path into the house, and beg her to come home. When the phone rang she'd answer it on the first ring, and then look disappointed when it wasn't Oscar's voice on the other end.

"You don't have to eat breakfast," she said. "I didn't mean to boss you about eating breakfast. I didn't boss you, did I, Teo? Did I boss you?"

"You were okay."

He went into the bathroom and peed while he stared at himself in the mirror. He looked haggard. He had had only three beers before he fell asleep. He used to be able to drink and smoke pot and sniff coke and hardly feel it. Now he was wasted with three beers.

Estella was talking to him through the bathroom door, rapping softly against the scarred wood with her knuckles.

"Teo, are you in there?"

"I'm in here, Estella."

"I was thinking, that gun in the laundry room on top of the washing machine?"

"What about it?"

"I think you ought to put it somewhere else. What if Derek came over? You know how Derek is, always wanting to pick up things and look them over. He could shoot himself."

"Is Derek coming over?"

"I'm just saying, in case he does."

"I'll take care of it."

She was still at the door.

"You're not sorry I'm here, are you, Teo? You're not sorry you let me move in, are you? Because I'd be heartsick if I thought you were sorry about that."

"I'm not sorry about it, Estella."

"I was reading an article," she said.

He usually shaved in silence. Not even a radio on. Windows closed so he couldn't hear anything but the rasp of honed steel scraping across his skin. Estella's voice wasn't unpleasant. It was just that she was there, talking, wanting conversation from him, pulling him where she wanted him to go. And his mind wasn't on anything she had to say. He didn't want to go to church. He wanted to get dressed and go looking for Ellie.

"The article was about paranoia," she said, "people thinking that other people are going to get them, you know, checking doors and locking up and checking doors again and windows, and, well, you know what I'm talking about. Anyway, the article said not to give in to it, to fight it. You wake me up when you walk around in the middle of the night. Maybe you could do your checking earlier, before I go to bed. I'm a light sleeper, and I hear you moving around, and the floors creak—that's one thing that's wrong with this house, is the creaky floors—so if you could check the house earlier, before I go to bed, I'd appreciate it. I know we all said this was your house and you could live in it and do what you want in it, but it's just a suggestion, because I'm having a little trouble sleeping, and every little noise wakes me up."

"I'll try to be quiet."

"But the floors creak, and it doesn't matter how quiet you try to be. If you could check on the windows earlier, that's what I'm getting at, an earlier checking on the windows. Teo, are you in there? Did you hear what I just said?"

"I heard you."

"You aren't mad, are you? Did I say something to make you mad?"

"Not yet."

"I'm glad, because I do love you, Teo, and I appreciate you letting me stay here, and could you wear that nice striped tie to Mass, the red and blue one, the one I got you for Christmas? And the white shirt. And do you have any other jacket except the blue one? It's so shabby."

"It's all I've got."

"Well, all I have to say is I got here just in time. Another year, and God knows what shape you'd be in."

He took a shower, letting the water run and run. No use getting excited just because Ellie doesn't answer her telephone and hasn't gone to work for a couple days. No use acting as if she had to account for what she did when he wasn't around.

Estella was transparent. Of all the kids, Pa said he could always read Estella's mind. As hard as she tried she could never keep a secret. In the car on the way to church, Teo could tell she had one and was dying to tell it to him. *What if you,* she began, and, *What would you think,* and, *What if I told you that,* and, *Would it surprise you to know that,* and, *What would you say if*—he lost count of how many sentences she started and didn't finish.

When they got to Saint Joseph's, she hardly waited for him to stop the car before she opened the door and ran up the steps into the church.

"So, has Estella driven you crazy yet?" Oscar said. He was standing in the church parking lot, next to the chain-link fence, with Angela and Derek.

"Not yet," Teo replied. "You look nice, Ang." She was wearing a short black dress, white fishnet stockings, and high-heeled shoes, her ponytail secured with a glittery pink Barbie barrette.

"The kids haven't been to church in a while," Oscar said. "I was going to go fishing, but Angie said she wanted to go to church."

"I didn't say that, Daddy. I said maybe Mom's at church, and if we go we'll get to see her. I didn't say I wanted to go to church."

"She's a lot like her mother," Oscar said to Teo. "I say one thing and she contradicts me."

"I was only saying—," Angela began.

"I'm hungry," Derek said.

"The trouble is they miss their mother," Oscar said to Teo. "Does she say anything about coming home?"

"No," Teo replied. "She goes to work, comes home, fixes dinner, cleans the kitchen, and when I ask her what she's got in mind to do about you and the kids, she says she hasn't got anything in mind."

"Will she be home by June second, at least?" Angela asked. "She was going to help me shop for my prom dress."

Derek said, "I don't want her to come home. She messes up my room, she puts everything away, I don't know where anything is when she puts everything away, she loses pieces, I don't want her to come home." He started to cry, and Angela took a Kleenex out of her purse, bent down, and wiped his nose.

"You all seem pretty happy," Teo said.

Oscar looked glum. "So she hasn't said a word about me?"

"Doesn't mention you."

"Well, like you said, we're plenty happy. So she's fixing the house?"

"Top to bottom."

"Well, okay, so that's it, okay, so come on, kids, let's go inside."

"I won't sit next to her," Angela said. "If she doesn't want to come home, then I won't sit next to her."

"She breaks up all my toys," Derek said, and started to cry again.

"We're better off without her," Oscar said, and he and his children walked across the parking lot toward the church.

Teo wasn't going inside. He was once an altar boy, but he didn't believe in God anymore. He sat on the hood of his car and watched the cars pull up on the hard-packed gravel. He could have stayed home and let Estella go to church by herself, but she had been too anxious for him to come, and so he had, if for no other reason than to find out what she was up to.

People did dress up to go to church. He had forgotten how they trotted out their best clothes and got their kids cleaned up. No ripped jeans today or turned-around baseball caps or too large T-shirts over baggy drawers and unlaced sneakers. No short-short skirts with panties showing. Church was for turning back the clock to the seventies and looking like you stepped out of a rerun of *Father Knows Best*. Boys in slacks and ironed shirts, their hair watered down and combed flat against their scalps. Girls wearing demure dresses and not too much makeup.

And there was Bonnie, getting out of her car and running toward him in her backless sandals, skintight slacks, and armload of gold bracelets, her chin tilted downward and her shoulders going from side to side as if she were doing the hoochie-koochie. So this was what Estella wanted him to dress up for.

"Oh, God, I thought maybe you wouldn't come," she said. Just that little run and she was out of breath. "I thought maybe you'd change your mind at the last minute."

She didn't look bad. Not bad at all. Eight years since he had seen her or heard her voice, and it felt as if no time had gone by. That same flashy prettiness that had tripped him up in the beginning was still there. Maybe a little puffiness under the eyes. A few wrinkles around her mouth. But the gorgeous blue gaze was as sparkly as ever, the pouty mouth still looking as sweet as ripe berries. The body needed a little tightening up. He remembered her as being able to eat anything without gaining weight. She never did like to exercise, though, and at forty-six there was definitely a little thickening around the waist and hips. But at a glance, and if you didn't stand and take her apart feature by feature, she was still a babe.

She tried to kiss him, puckered her lips and stood on her tiptoes, but he didn't give her any help, and she settled for taking hold of his right hand with both of hers.

"It's been eight years, nine months, and fifteen days since I saw you last," she said. "I got out my calendar last night and figured it out."

"A long time," Teo said. "How've you been?"

"Oh, all right, I suppose. So many things have happened." She had his arm locked up against her breast. Soft. He remembered that her breasts were soft. Not mushy. More pillowy than mushy.

"One thing after another, one disappointment after another," she said. Her voice was the same, maybe a little lower. Too many cigarettes. She always smelled of cigarette smoke. In her hair and her clothes. When she would open her purse, it smelled as if something had been smoldering in it for days.

"Estella said you were sorry about us, that you wished we never got that divorce," she said.

"When did she say that?"

"Yesterday, I think. Yes, yesterday. I really have wanted to call you every day for years, and I thought to myself, what's Teo doing—it could be the middle of the night or an afternoon, or even in the morning, and I'd think about you and wonder where you were. Estella said you aren't married. I'm not either. Not even the least bit attached. I live in Anaheim near Disneyland. I can see the Matterhorn from my kitchen window. It looks like a Sno-Kone. I'm not going on auditions anymore. I gave all that up. Well, mostly, anyway. I had this agent who was sending me out on commercials, and that didn't work, so I told him I wanted to do voice-overs because I heard that voice-overs make a lot more money, but then everyone said my voice was too thin, so I told him to forget it, I didn't need Hollywood, and not to call me unless something really good came up. Meanwhile I'm hostessing in the Monkey Bar on Westminster. It's not a dive. It's just got a funny name. It's really a nice bar. Food, snacks, pool in the back room, sports night, karaoke on the weekends. I get up and sing on karaoke nights. Everyone says they can't understand how come I didn't make it in Hollywood. I'm getting along all right, I guess, but I keep thinking about you and wondering how it all went so wrong, and then I start feeling so blue, because I know it was because of my screwing around, and if you could only see into my heart to know how sorry, how awfully sorry I am that I ever thought about Hollywood or the movies or those horrible people that don't do anything but take advantage of a girl. No one's like you, Teo. No one." She took a breath. "I don't know why I ever left you."

"I told you to get out."

"Well, I mean why did I do what I did so you'd tell me to get out? You know what I mean."

Right about then Estella came out the church door. Teo could see her standing on the steps looking over the parking lot, and when she spotted him with Bonnie, she waved at them both and went back inside.

Chapter 16

✿

"**Y**ou could really do something with this place," Bonnie said. Estella had invited her to come back to the house after church and have lunch, but hadn't done anything about preparing it except to go into the kitchen with Oscar and shut the door. Teo didn't know what had gone on inside the church, but when the Mass was over, Estella and Oscar and the two kids walked out together, laughing and talking as if nothing was wrong.

"Knock out that wall and put in an atrium," Bonnie said. "Everyone in Beverly Hills has an atrium. It's called indoor-outdoor living. You can't tell whether you're in or out. Of course, you have to water the plants, and that's a drag, and people are always banging into the windows thinking they're outside when they're really inside. Have you got anything to drink?"

"What do you want?" Teo said.

"Surprise me."

Angela was on the telephone talking to her boyfriend. She had been talking to him for almost an hour, murmuring into the mouthpiece. Derek had run through every room in the house, opening drawers and closets, slamming doors, and was now standing in the middle of the living room, legs spread like a commando, his round face flushed and perspiring.

"This is a dumb house with nothing to do," he said to Teo.

"Go out in back and swing on the swing," Teo said.

"I don't know where it is."

"Out in back."

"You used to drink Johnny Walker," Bonnie said. She had kicked off her sandals and curled herself up on the living room couch. "I sure remember all the drinking we used to do, Teo. Do you remember that night out in Hermosa Beach when the two of us came out of that bar on the pier and couldn't find the car? And the 92nd Street Corral? Do you remember that place? All those shit kickers in cowboy hats and high-heeled boots? *I get tears in my ears just a-lyin' on my back in my bed just a-cryin' over you.* Remember that song, Teo? My God, when I think of the things we did in the parking lot of the 92nd Street Corral in that yellow convertible of ours. Whatever happened to that yellow convertible, anyways?"

"I don't want to swing," Derek said. "I want my bicycle."

"Tough. Your bicycle isn't here," Teo said.

"But I want it."

"You don't want to see me get angry, do you?"

"I don't like this house."

"Go out in the back and stay there."

"I don't have to."

"Yes, you have to."

"Show him your badge," Bonnie said with a laugh. "That always used to work, Teo, showing people your badge when you wanted your way. Remember when we got stopped that time in Lomita, and you didn't want to take a Breathalyzer, and I told you to show the cop your badge, and you didn't want to, but you finally did, and he turned out to be someone you went to high school with? Do you remember that?"

"Do you have a badge?" Derek said.

"I'll get it and show it to you if you go out in back and play on the swing and don't come back in until I tell you to."

"I sure am thirsty, Teo," Bonnie said. "It's hotter than hell in Santa Ana. I don't know how you stand it, it's so hot."

Derek climbed up on the arm of the couch and then jumped off. The plant Estella had bought for the top of the television rocked back and forth. He climbed up onto the arm of the couch and jumped again.

"I said go outside," Teo told him.

"I don't want to."

Two steps forward and Teo had him tucked under his arm and was carrying him out the side door to the yard, Derek crying and kicking, and Teo telling him he didn't think he had anything to cry about, and to stop it, that if he wanted to be a brat, he'd have to be a brat somewhere else. He sat him down on the swing, gave him a shove, and went back into the house. He used the kitchen door this time.

Estella was sitting on the kitchen table, and Oscar had his hand down the front of her dress.

"Come on, Estella, don't be that way, honey," Oscar said. He was easing her back across the table with his left hand and unbuttoning his pants with his right.

"You think sex can fix everything," Estella said.

"I missed you."

"Your middle name is sex, Oscar."

"Come on, Estella, you can't tell me you didn't miss me."

The bottle was on the shelf over the refrigerator. Teo didn't drink hard liquor anymore, and it was still at the same mark as it was three years before, when he took his last drink out of it.

"What about that tramp in Lakewood?" Estella said. Oscar had her dress up over her knees and his hands up somewhere underneath it. "What do you tell her? Do you tell her your wife doesn't understand you, doesn't have sex with you? All those mornings, douching before I went to work, and by twelve o'clock you were probably screwing her in the lunchroom."

"That's crazy talk, honey. I haven't even talked to her since you left me."

Teo couldn't find the water glasses. Estella had rearranged the cupboards. Where drinking glasses and coffee cups used to be there were now measuring cups and small serving dishes.

"The kids will hear us," Estella said.

Teo glanced over at them. Sex was a pretty funny thing to watch other people do, bodies all contorted, legs up in the air, bare bottoms wiggling.

The water glasses were on the shelf next to the vitamin supplements Estella took by the handfuls. Oscar had Estella flat on the table now and they had both stopped talking. Teo went back into the living room.

"I'm drinking alone?" Bonnie said when he put the bottle and glass down on the coffee table.

"I don't drink whiskey anymore."

She filled the glass and settled back into the couch cushions with it.

"I was telling you about the part I had on television last year. I played a schoolteacher on a Lifetime drama."

"What's Lifetime?"

"You don't know what Lifetime is? The cable channel Lifetime?"

"I don't watch much television."

"Anyway, I've got a tape of the part I was in. It's only about a minute and a half. Four of us—we're all teachers who work in the same school—are having lunch together for the last time, because the heroine is getting married and moving to Canada, and my part is— What's that look for? You don't think I had a part in a Lifetime drama?"

"I didn't say anything."

"You looked funny."

"I don't think I looked funny."

"I know when you look funny, Teo. Anyhow, I had five whole words, and I said them really slow, so everyone could hear me. I got this little sad sound in my voice while I was saying them. 'We're all going to miss you,' I said. I even managed to squeeze out a tear. I'll bring it over next time I come. There was a producer on the set who said he could tell I had some real talent. I don't pay attention to that kind of talk anymore, but it was nice to hear him say it, anyways. He came into the bar once after that and kidded me about playing a schoolteacher. He said he didn't think it was typecasting, because I look like I've done a few things a schoolteacher wouldn't think of doing, which made me laugh. I do love to laugh, Teo. Remember how we used to laugh and laugh?"

"Can you hold that thought for a second, Bonnie?"

"Sure, I can hold any thoughts you want me to hold, Teo. I'm yours, you know that, I always have been, always will be, till death us do part."

Angela was still on the phone.

"Hey, Ang," Teo said. She looked up at him. Just that second it could have been Estella looking up at him, asking him if he wanted the phone, she was sorry she was hogging it, it was just that she and her boyfriend, Oscar, had a fight and she was trying to straighten it out.

"Here," Angela said, and handed the phone to Teo. "I've got to go to the bathroom, anyway."

He had the number of the hospital on the corner of his ink pad, heard the voice mail operator come on and recite all the options, then pressed the number for patients' rooms and asked for Alice Miller.

The table in the kitchen was rocking back and forth, making a hollow knocking sound on the living room wall.

"Sounds like someone's having fun," Bonnie said. She got up from the couch and stood behind Teo, her arms around his waist, her head resting against his spine.

"Have you been helped?" the operator said.

"I'm waiting to be put through to Alice Miller's room," Teo told her.

"I'm so happy just to be with you again," Bonnie said. "If you knew what was in my heart, how I've thought about you, over and over, so many times I can't even count them, and just kept saying to myself, if only I could explain to Teo how I feel, make it up to him, make it all better. I'll come over tomorrow with the tape. I only had a few lines, but everyone said I did it like a pro. I'd have you come to my place, but it's such a mess, I've been there eight months and I'm still living out of boxes. Do you remember our apartment on Fountain in L.A., the one where the landlord wore a red toupee and pancake makeup and locked us out that time when we were just a few days late with the rent?"

"Sure, the guy who was in all the Buster Keaton silent movies."

"No, you're thinking of Dave, the neighbor downstairs, who had a part in a movie with W. C. Fields."

The operator was back on the line.

"I'll put you through to the cardiac floor."

"The one I'm talking about," Bonnie said, "was the landlord. His name was Charlie, I think. Yes. Charlie. And he had a girlfriend who dressed like Mae West, even to the feather boa and the big hats, and they were always sitting out on the bench in front of the apartment house holding hands and watching traffic go by. I'll never forget those days, Teo, they were the best days, weren't they?"

"I don't think they were all that great, Bonnie."

"Cardiology," a voice said.

"Alice Miller, please," Teo said.

"Is Alice your girlfriend?" Bonnie whispered. "I hope she's not your girlfriend, I hope I'm not too late, Teo. Am I too late? Do you remember all those nights, Teo, just screwing our brains out? Do you remember that?"

"Can't forget any of it, Bonnie."

Derek was back in the house screaming that he wanted to go home. Angela came out of the bathroom and told him they couldn't go home yet, and would he stop crying if she turned the television on.

"I wanted Alice Miller's room," Teo said into the phone.

"I'll transfer you. Please hold."

Angela had found the cartoon station, and Derek was sitting on the floor, quiet for once, watching a bear chase a raccoon up a tree.

"They've been in the kitchen a long time," Angela said to Teo. "Have they made up yet?"

"I think they're working on it," Teo said.

"I thought she was going to make lunch. I don't smell any food cooking in the kitchen." She sat down on the couch and began flipping through the pages of one of Teo's *Police Digest* magazines. "This whole thing's a drag, I mean it, Uncle Teo, they are so stupid. They might be my parents, but they are the stupidest."

"Hello?" a voice on the phone said.

"Alice?"

"No, Mrs. Miller isn't here. She left. The doctor still had some tests to do on her, and we turned around and she was gone. She pulled out her monitor leads and walked out in the middle of the night. We've been concerned about her. Are you a relative?"

Bonnie's weight was spread across Teo's back, and she was kissing his neck.

"No one saw her leave?" he said into the phone.

"That's right, no one saw her."

Estella came out of the kitchen, her hair matted down in back and her skirt wrinkled.

"Who wants fried potatoes with their hamburgers?" she said.

"Cemeteries and bright mornings don't go together," Alice said as they drove through the iron gates and up the hill.

Ellie didn't answer.

"I can't imagine being stuck somewhere underground on a day like this," Alice said. "I don't mean that Jamie's stuck, I didn't mean that. I was speaking for myself, how when I'm dead I want to be gone, zapped, fried. I don't want any part of me left hanging around with the sun shining like it is and me not being able to see it. Of course, if I believed in spirits, I suppose I could hover, kind of fly around—when the weather's nice, of course. I suppose there's no law against that. Hovering. I'm not saying you shouldn't come and put flowers on Jamie's grave, I'm not saying that at all. I'm only saying that if a person believed in spirits, Jamie's wouldn't be here, it would probably be hovering over the Grand Canyon enjoying the view."

They had reached the children's section. There were cherubs on pedestals in this part of the cemetery, and fountains and a reflecting pool flanked by miniature chairs made out of stone.

"I'm surprised they don't put in a playground," Alice said.

Ellie had stopped the car at the flower shop down the hill and bought a bouquet of pink carnations. They were on the floor next to Alice's feet, the soft petals tickling her ankles.

"I think the flowers are wilting," Alice said. "They should have put them in a container like they did yesterday. Flowers wilt without water on hot days. I suppose they don't care. I always used to buy my cut flowers on Lido Isle. They really care about flowers on Lido Isle, wrap the stems in soaked cotton, put plastic wrap over them, and give you a cup of water to douse them with if you're going to be going a long distance. It's the difference between just running a business and caring about what you do. Swanson's Flowers on Lido Isle."

You'd have thought that angry as Ellie was, she'd have at least asked how Alice felt, if her chest hurt where she had pulled out the wires or if she could breathe all right or if she thought she ought to see a doctor, but it was as if Ellie hated her. Alice had explained over and over what happened and why she had been quiet about it all these years. It was no use. Ellie turned against her at the first sentence. "I don't want to hear any more," she said.

None of this had been Alice's idea. She couldn't see the point in staying in a motel for three weeks when there was a perfectly good house waiting for them in Visalia. And Ellie visiting Jamie's grave every day, putting fresh flowers out—pink carnations today, yellow mums yesterday, tiger lilies the day before—clipping the weeds with a manicure scissors. When was it going to end?

Well, she was just trying to do what Ellie wanted. She hadn't even complained about the motel room bed (even though the bed was the lumpiest she had ever slept in and the pillow slips the scratchiest), hadn't said one word about the food in the coffee shop next to the motel (even though she had asked for five-minute eggs at breakfast that morning and gotten scrambled), hadn't made a single comment about the bacon (limp and tasteless as shoelaces).

"At least they keep the grass trimmed," Alice said.

Ellie stopped the car and got out. She didn't ask Alice if she felt up to walking today or if she wanted to wait in the car.

"We'll leave for Visalia tomorrow," she said, and picked up the bunch of carnations and, cradling them like an infant in her arms, started toward the grave.

It made Alice's chest hurt to watch her. A deep-down hurt that spread across to her back and into her stomach and down her legs. She was weak and tired and old. And sadder than she had ever been in her life.

Chapter 17

*E*llie's front door was locked. Teo could have opened it. He probably had a key that would fit. It wasn't a dead bolt. It was an easy latch. He had a screwdriver in his pocket that would have broken it apart in two seconds.

Knowing how to break into a house was like riding a bicycle: you never forget how to do it. Ellie's house was easy, but there was a neighbor washing his car two driveways down and a woman pushing a baby carriage near the corner. Teo looked at his watch, made a show of pushing up his sleeve and really looking at it, as if he were late for an appointment. Then he took out his cell phone and rang Ellie's number and pretended to be talking to someone, nodding his head and moving his lips. Still holding the phone to his ear, he walked briskly around the side to the rear of the house, slipped a credit card between the jamb and the lock of the back door, gave it a tweak, pulled it through, turned the knob, and walked into the kitchen.

The last time Teo broke into a house without a warrant to search he was seventeen. It was a Thursday in the middle of his senior year at Santa Ana High School. Fog was rolling in that Thursday, and from the roof of the wood shop Saddleback Mountain looked insubstantial, fleeting, almost ghostlike. He could always tell the weather by Saddleback. On sunny days, with the sky clear, Saddleback was a gray knob of granite that seemed to float headless and riderless above the Irvine Ranch. Impending rain turned it brown and blurred the edges so that it looked as if a child had taken a crayon and drawn a mountain on one corner of the sky. A sunny day turned it weighty and dark, an indelible stain on the horizon. That Thursday it was foggy.

Teo finished sanding the chair he had made, told the teacher his mother was sick, then got on his bike and rode through the fog to a quiet street on the edge of Santa Ana near the Bowers Museum. Anglos lived in that part of Santa Ana in well-kept two-story Victorian houses that had been built when most of Santa Ana was orange groves and dirt roads. Land and labor were cheap then, and the houses were spacious and had enormous lawns and elegant sun porches.

The first house on the street had cypress trees ringing the property and hibiscus bushes that had grown up around the windows. He rode up the walk on his bike (he always rode or walked his bike to the front door; he always wore his track sweater; he always combed his hair neatly) and knocked on the door. There was no sound from inside, so he knocked again, and when a tall, gray-haired woman opened the door he told her he was looking for Harwood Street.

I'm supposed to do some yard work for a woman who lives on Harwood, and I'm all turned around. I've been up and down Grand looking for Harwood, and can't find it.

The woman came outside, smiling at him as she sauntered down the path, agreeable as she showed him by hand motions and finger pointing where Harwood Street was. She didn't go back in the house, but began pulling weeds out of the begonia beds along the walk, which meant he couldn't stop at any more houses on that street. He hopped on his bike and headed up the block, turned right, left, right again. The few cars on the street drove slowly, their amber lights burning holes in the fog. Teo pumped faster, stood on the pedals, chin up, drops of moisture settling on the top of his head and dampening his sweater.

He stopped at a house three blocks away. No cars in the driveway. The garage door was open a crack. No cars there either. An old motorcycle lying on its side, a wheelbarrow, a pile of used bricks. He walked his bike up the walk, tapped the lion's head knocker against the mahogany, waited, then rang the bell and waited some more. He tapped and rang a few more times and then went around to the side, propped his bike against the house, stood on the seat, pushed in the bathroom window screen, and crawled in.

The woman who lived there had been sewing on a noisy sewing machine and hadn't heard the tapping or the ringing. Teo came out of the bathroom just as she was about to come in. She screamed, and as he made a run for the front door he tripped on a throw rug and sprained his ankle. She stopped screaming and called the police.

There was a juvenile hearing. Ma and Pa dressed up as if they were going to church, Raul, who was in the army, showing up in his dress uniform. Mrs. Peters, the woman who had screamed, was wearing a saggy black suit (she had been in a faded bathrobe when he broke into her house) and she had wrinkles in her cheeks and brown spots on her hands like Ma did. That startled Teo, that he had broken into a house and the woman who lived in it looked like his mother.

Teo didn't have a lawyer. Raul was taking care of everything. He told Teo to wear the same thing he was wearing when he was arrested. Jeans and track sweater. No slacks and white shirt.

Look your age. Don't act too smart. Don't smile too much. Be serious, but not so serious you look as if you knew what you were doing.

Raul was the leader in the family. Even Pa listened to what he had to say. If Raul said how to do a thing, everyone, including Teo, did it that way.

The judge came in and told Teo to stand up. Then he read the charges. After that he asked Teo why he broke into Mrs. Peters' house.

I wanted to see if I could figure out how to get in and get out and no one would know I was there. I don't know why she screamed, because I didn't have a gun or a knife and I wouldn't have hurt her.

He didn't tell the judge that he had broken into houses lots of times, that sometimes he didn't even take anything, but would just go in and wander around and maybe eat something out of the refrigerator or turn on the television for a few minutes.

He's a good kid, Raul said, and talked the judge into letting Teo join the army instead of going to jail.

There was still coffee in the coffeemaker, but it was cold and sludgy looking. The junk drawer was open, the one some people kept jewelry in. He rummaged through it. A hammer, a ball of string, Scotch tape, out-of-ink pens, scraps of paper, rubber bands, carpet tacks. There was a piece of paper on the floor next to the drawer. He knelt down and picked it up. A plain piece of paper with nothing written on it. She had been in a hurry. Open drawer. Paper on the floor. Coffee turning to sludge.

She had left bottles of hair gel and shampoo in the cabinet in the bathroom. The water faucet hadn't been turned all the way off and was still pouring a thin stream of water into the sink.

Underwear was gone from the drawers in her bedroom. The pictures that had been on the bedside table weren't there. She hadn't taken all her clothes out of the closet, but then she probably didn't want to take more than what would fit into a single suitcase. She had left nothing personal behind, no letters, diaries, photo albums. Anyone could have lived in this house for all the evidence of herself she had left behind.

He sat down on the bed and stared at the open closet door. He felt so angry. The anger welled up in him, and stuck like a bitter knot in his throat. He stood up and kicked the closet door. He kicked it again. He kept kicking it. He wanted to break it down, wanted to see it splinter into a thousand pieces, but it was solid and didn't give and all he accomplished was to scuff it up, and so he pulled at it with his hands, yanked it, twisted it until he tore it off its hinges and it fell against him. He stood holding the closet door, breathing hard, and feeling overwhelmed and maybe even slightly crazed. He leaned the door up against the wall, ran his hand over the still smooth surface, then sat back down on the bed and breathed deeply, told himself to calm down, that it didn't matter, that he didn't need her, that she could go any damn place she wanted to and it wouldn't matter to him.

Teo had driven past San Onofre every time he went down to San Diego. This stretch of coast, except for the barracks and barbed wire of Camp Pendleton Marine Station, was dull and empty. Bare mountains, freeway, ocean, and then suddenly the cement igloos of the nuclear generating plant rising out of the dunes like giant molehills.

It was a brisk walk from security to the operations building where a guard handed Teo a hard hat and a badge and told him to wait for someone to take him through the explosion test gate.

"Empty your pockets. Feet inside the yellow outlines. Stand perfectly still. Try not to breathe. Wait for the light to turn green, then step out."

An alarm went off.

"You moved. Let's try it again."

He held his breath and stared at the row of guards on the other side, then at the one-way mirrors and the sun streaming in through the glass doors.

Another gate, this one a metal detector. He put his keys and watch on the conveyor and stood beneath a bank of flashing lights.

An alarm went off.

"Take off your belt."

Then through one revolving door, a few steps more, then another one.

"Destination?"

"Technical Support Center."

"I'll escort you."

He admired the operation, but he could have shown them where their weaknesses were. He would have told them to cut out some of the redundancies, get rid of some of the guards, some of the questions. He would have explained that if you load you operation with too much personnel trying their damnedest to dot every *i* and cross every *t*, real security can get lost. Between strokes. That's when a genuine, bona fide terrorist walks in.

The escort walked on Teo's left, his long red hair flowing into his long red beard, pens stuffed into the pocket of his shirt, rips in the knees of his jeans, dirt streaks on his running shoes. His ID badge said TIMOTHY DOOLEY, ENVIRONMENTAL ENGINEER.

"So you want to talk to Eric Holmgren about a police matter?"

"That's right."

"What did he do?"

"It's just routine."

"We went to school together. MIT. Good guy. A little opinionated, but I say if you can't have an opinion, what's the use? In here. I'll ring down to him."

They were in a narrow, darkened office, an observation room with thick glass windows overlooking the crescent well of the control room. Down below, men sat at desks in front of intersecting walls of monitors and stared unblinking at knobs and buttons and colored lights. The nerve center of the plant, Dooley was saying. A soundproof isolation booth. No one in, no one out. Ants in a bottle.

"If they so much as scratch their crotch or pick their nose, someone up on top can see it."

A sign tacked to the wall above a brown phone said, USE BROWN PHONE TO RING DOWN TO TEC. Dooley picked up the phone.

"Could you send Eric up?" he said.

Eric was a scratcher. He'd say a few words and then scratch some part of his body. His face, his scalp, his chest, his thigh. He once crossed his legs so he could scratch his ankle. And in between he looked at the clock on the wall of the cafeteria.

"Yeah, I heard Morty shot himself," he said. "Where's the mystery to that?" He was about Teo's age. Slim, smooth muscled, and pale. The belt on his jeans had an Indian turquoise buckle. His T-shirt said SAVE THE WHALES.

"I'm not saying there's a mystery," Teo said. "I'm just checking all the angles, tying up loose ends."

"How do you know Ellie?"

"Friends."

"Friends."

"Friends."

"It's Alice you're interested in, but you want to know where Ellie is."

"Something like that."

"Are you sleeping with her?"

"Come on."

He scratched his chin with his index finger. "So did Alice have something to do with it?"

"Maybe."

"I always thought Alice was pretty low key. You know what they say, the quiet ones are the ones you have to watch out for. Morty was a big talker, a loudmouth, always bragging about some deal or other. I could never figure the two of them together. I've seen pictures of Alice when she was young, and she wasn't bad looking, but you couldn't have an intelligent conversation with her. Morty was no Einstein either, but I guess he knew how to make money. Women like men who can make money. So what do you think of the plant? Antinuclear, or pro?"

"I don't have an opinion."

"Everyone has an opinion."

"I don't."

Eric looked up at the clock, unfolded his arms, and scratched harder at his chin.

"I've got to get back."

"When did you see Ellie last?"

"Last week. She said she was leaving town and wanted me to go out to the Valley and take care of Jamie's grave. Four hours round trip just to sweep the leaves off the marker and polish the granite. I said, 'You can take care of the grave when you get back,' and she told me she might not be coming back. I'm remarried, and I don't have time to drive out to the Valley just to polish a tombstone and rake a few leaves. I told her that. She sat right where you're sitting and started crying. She looks at life too narrowly, can't see the big picture. She tried for seven years to have a kid. She'd get pregnant and then miscarry. I told her to forget it, not everyone has to have kids, the world's overpopulated as it is, but she kept at it and kept at it. You know how salmon swim upstream? That was Ellie, swimming upstream. I have to hand it to her, though, she hung in there. And then Jamie was born. He was a great kid. Smart. Jesus, he was smart. And then he got sick and died and I was as bummed out about it as she was, but I didn't go around looking like I was going to die myself. I told her to buck up, look at the grand scheme of things, that we're just specks in the universe, what's our losing a kid compared to all the kids starving in Somalia? She couldn't see it."

"Where did she say she was going?"

"Visalia. Her folks had an artichoke ranch. It's not much of a ranch now. I told her lots of luck. Sixty-year-old pipes, leaky roof."

"Were you in Vietnam?"

"I was in graduate school. I registered for the draft. It never came to that. I never had to make a decision about whether to go or not. It was over before I finished grad school."

"Okay. I don't have to go as far as Somalia. While we're sitting here kids are getting beaten up in Newport Beach, and for sure three-point-four people will die on the freeway this afternoon, and you managed to stay out of Vietnam. You had homework to do. So I don't give a fuck. What I want to know is what happened that made her pick up and leave, probably in the middle of the night, without even calling her boss."

Eric inspected the spot on his arm he had just scratched.

"She said she had found out something that threw her for a loop. It had to do with her family, something that happened in Visalia. I asked her what it was and she said she couldn't tell me, just that something happened there and she just found out about it, and that was it, she was going to iron it out with Alice. I was busy, and it didn't really interest me that much. Your attitude, it really bothers me, you know that? I was in grad school, for chrissakes." He glanced up at the clock. "So where do you live?"

"Santa Ana."

"You're out of the disaster zone, twenty-five miles, but just barely. Some radioactive fallout if the wind's going that way."

"I work in Newport Beach."

"You won't know what hit you."

Chapter 18

"The plane's late," the agent at the gate said. "Weather delay. It's storming up north."

"Hard to believe," Alice said. "It's clear as a bell here." She had barely managed the walk from the parking lot into the terminal, had needed to sit down for a few minutes at every gate from 36 to 48, and was now holding on to the check-in counter for support.

"How late is it?" Ellie asked.

"Another hour at least. They're promising arrival in LAX by dark."

"She'll need a wheelchair," Ellie said.

"My heart," Alice said and went and sat down.

There was a bank of telephones next to the rest room. Still time for Ellie to call Teo. All day she'd been wanting to call him, to tell him she was leaving. He probably wouldn't care, anyway. Didn't he say something about cooling it, they were going too fast, he thought they should take a breather? And then not calling her? He probably thought he could jump in and out of her life anytime he wanted to. Well, calling him would be the worst thing she could do. Phone calls were dangerous. She said things on the telephone she would never have said otherwise. She let her guard down on the telephone. All that silence on the other end always tripped her up, led her to say too much, reveal too much. He'd think she was leaving because of him, when it had nothing to do with him.

She sat down across from Alice and stared out at the tar-colored sky. She tried to arrange her thoughts, to put them in some kind of order, but they skittered away before she could catch hold of them, just split into fragments and went whizzing by her head. She wasn't leaving because of Teo. It was because of Alice. A few words from Alice had turned Ellie's world upside down, and she didn't know how she was going to ever get it right again. Alice had pushed her off the precipice, and there was no end to the fall, no solid ground to land on.

"Rain in June," Alice said. "I don't remember the last time it rained in June. Storming in the north. I wonder if that means Visalia. I suppose it's possible, although it's probably more like a shower. Seems hard to believe a little shower would stop an airplane. People do get weird ideas about what a storm is. A storm is when the water level reaches the steps of the house."

"Would you like me to get you a cup of tea?" Ellie asked her.

"Would you? And a chocolate-glazed biscotto without nuts would be nice."

"Some more mashed potatoes, Bonnie?" Estella said.

"You're just trying to fatten me up," Bonnie replied, "make me lose my figure."

She laughed, and then Estella laughed and got up from the table and began wrapping leftovers.

"If you're going to throw the potatoes out, I'll eat 'em," Oscar said.

Oscar had moved in. Just came over one night in his police uniform, and when Teo went into the kitchen in the morning he was there eating scrambled eggs, Estella sitting across from him in her nightgown. That was two weeks ago, and the two of them were still there, sleeping in the oak bed in the big bedroom, the same bed and bedroom Ma and Pa had slept in. Estella and her family had taken over the house. Every day Angela drove Derek over after school and Estella cooked dinner. Angela and Derek usually stayed until around eight o'clock, but tonight she said she had an algebra test in the morning and she took Derek home right after dinner.

"I see where there might be another earthquake," Oscar said and finished up the rest of the mashed potatoes. He had read the newspaper all through dinner. Estella lifted the edge of it now to pick up the dish of pickled beets.

"Can they really predict earthquakes?" Estella remarked. She had bought a plastic wrap dispenser and Oscar had installed it under one of the sink cabinets. She held the plate of pickled beets under the dispenser, pulled a lever, and a sheet of plastic floated down.

"It has something to do with sunspots," Oscar said.

"Really?" Estella said, and put the beets in the refrigerator.

"Do you know that chickens in China know when there's going to be an earthquake?" Bonnie said. This was the third night in a row Estella had invited her over for dinner. She never helped with the dishes or cleared the table. Neither did Oscar. Teo got up now, slid the trash container from under the sink, and took it outside to the garbage can. Through the kitchen window he could see Bonnie lighting up a cigarette and hear the sound of a Brillo pad scrubbing against the sides of the roasting pan and then the drill of water on metal. Teo felt as if he had seen this all in some crystal ball, every bit of it. He turned and went back up the stairs.

"It's all farm animals, not just chickens," Oscar was saying. "Hogs. Cows. Ducks. They make a different noise when there's going to be an earthquake."

"I've never heard that," Bonnie said.

"No one can predict earthquakes," Teo said. He slid the empty trash container under the sink. "If they could predict earthquakes, they would. There'd be a warning system."

"They can predict them by sunspots," Oscar insisted. "The government is trying to keep it secret. It's like UFOs and cures for cancer, there are all these lobbies in Washington. They find a cure for cancer and the drug companies will lose money; they let out the secret of predicting earthquakes and the contractors won't get to build new houses and the morticians won't get as much business. It's all economics."

"Really?" Estella said again.

Estella wasn't herself. If she were herself, she'd have yelled at Oscar about reading the newspaper at the table and told him he didn't know what he was talking about—*Sunspots predicting earthquakes?* she'd have said and then laughed. *Drug companies preventing a cure for cancer?* she'd have said with a sneer. *Where's your brain, Oscar?* she would have asked him. But she was behaving like a newlywed nitwit. She didn't even make fun of the way he ate (he was a fast eater and a shoveler), and she hadn't mentioned the woman in Lakewood even once.

"I know someone who was killed in the last earthquake," Bonnie said.

"Who?" Estella said.

"A guy I know. He was in bed and the roof fell in on him."

"No!"

"I'm not kidding."

"At least we don't have tornadoes," Oscar said.

"I don't know what the difference is," Estella said. "Dead is dead, no matter how it happens, Oscar."

Oscar looked up at her.

"I don't mean that you're wrong, honey," she said quickly. "Tornadoes are probably a lot worse than earthquakes. And floods, that's got to be the worst of all. I've always had a fear of drowning. That and fire, getting trapped on the second floor of a house and downstairs the couch is burning and the—"

"I need to make a phone call," Bonnie said. She had been using her salad plate to flick her cigarette ashes in. She picked up the plate and her pack of cigarettes and went into the other room.

Estella began washing the dishes, swirling ribbons of green liquid soap into the sink.

"I always knew you and Bonnie belonged together, Teo," she said.

"We're not together, Estella," Teo told her.

"You will be."

"Estella wants everyone to be matched up and miserable," Oscar said.

She turned around, and Teo saw her mouth tighten, then suddenly relax. It was nothing short of miraculous the way Estella had learned to stop herself in midnastiness. She didn't even need to see Oscar's face go dark before she was backtracking. "You're not miserable, honey, are you?"

"Not as long as you keep your mouth shut, I'm not."

Bonnie came back into the kitchen.

"My landlord," she said. "I just told him I wouldn't pay this month's rent till he fixed the apartment."

"What's wrong with it?" Oscar asked.

"What isn't? The roof leaks, the pipes make noise, the garbage piles up in back until you can't see through the swarm of flies. It's disgusting."

"You poor thing," Estella said.

Oscar and Bonnie began talking about real estate. Oscar said apartments were a bad deal, that you couldn't deduct the rent from your income tax.

"I don't pay income tax," Bonnie said.

"Everyone pays income tax," Estella told her. "Haven't you ever been audited? Aren't you afraid of going to jail?"

"No. Should I be afraid?"

"You probably don't make enough to pay any, anyway," Teo said.

"I'd buy a condo if I were you," Oscar told her. "In a condo you don't have to depend on a landlord, you can handle things yourself, make your own repairs."

"Then she'd have to pay for everything," Estella said. "Don't you think she'd buy a condo if she had the money?"

"Who's having this conversation, you or me?" Oscar sniped. Estella began crying into the sink. Oscar put down the newspaper and got to his feet.

"I didn't mean it, honey, you know I didn't mean it." He started kissing Estella's neck. Bonnie stared at them. Teo tapped his foot against the table leg.

"Can I talk to you in private, just us," Bonnie finally said to Teo, "just for a few minutes?"

"Sure," Teo said.

They went into the living room. Estella had taken all the hundred-watt bulbs out of the lamps in the living room and put in forties because, she said, hundred-watt bulbs made women look old. Teo could have sworn that moving out of the bright kitchen into the murkiness of forty-watt bulbs took at least ten years off Bonnie's age, just erased the creases and shadows and smoothed out every single age line.

"Well, here's the deal," she said. "I think we ought to stop kidding around, because you know you want to fuck me, so why don't we just do it and get it over with, then that'll be out of the way and you'll stop trying to decide whether you want me back or not. And if you're worried about catching anything, I've had my AIDS test and it was negative, and I don't have herpes. I'm very picky who I sleep with. I'm like a little detective, Teo, you'd be proud of me, asking guys whether, you know, they're AC/DC. They're the ones you've got to watch out for, the AC/DC ones. They tell me they're AC/DC, I'm out of there."

She came closer, and he could smell cigarette smoke and roast beef on her breath.

"You always liked to fuck me, honey," she said. "Don't you remember all those times we did it and you said you couldn't think of anything you liked to do better, that you could do it all day if you had your way, do you remember that?"

"Dimly."

"Well, here I am, and I don't know if I can go all day, but I can give it a try."

She took his hand and kissed his fingers.

"You knew the first time you saw me in the church parking lot that this is what was going to happen," she said. She still had hold of his hand and was pulling him out of the living room, past the kitchen, and into his bedroom.

"I'm kind of lucky I didn't go to flab the way Estella did," she said, and began shedding clothing, throwing blouse and skirt and bra and panties on the floor. She had always looked better without clothes. Honey-toned skin, cherry nipples, flat blond patch of pubic hair. She still looked good, but if a body could be described as tired, hers looked exhausted.

"We can do it standing up, if you want, but the floor is out," she said.

He sat down on the bed and pulled off his shoes.

"The bed is fine."

"Do you want to be on top?"

"It doesn't matter."

She had a small scar above her pubic hair. A little lightning bolt of a scar. There was a time when he could have drawn a map of every freckle and mole on her body. He didn't remember the scar.

"Ectopic pregnancy," she said, following his gaze. "I nearly died. They had to yank everything out."

"I'm sorry."

"I'm not. It was such a pain every month wondering and worrying. No matter how careful a person is, you can still get caught. You really don't mind if I go on top, do you?"

"I don't mind."

"I developed a disk problem, and it's better for me if I'm on top. If I'm not on top I can get a spasm right in midfuck. It can be very embarrassing."

"I said it doesn't matter."

"Are you angry because I want to be on top?"

"Let's just do it, Bonnie."

They got in bed and she climbed up onto his stomach. It felt familiar, her warm weight pressing his spine into the mattress, the wiggly little movements she made to get comfortable, the way she kept clearing her throat as if she were about to sing.

"There it is," Bonnie exclaimed. "Look at it bounce up. Old dick, old Jack."

She fit the way she always did. Nut and bolt. Tongue and groove. She had her eyes closed, sort of gently floating, as if he were a lake and she a rowboat. He felt himself concentrating, trying not to lose it. He shut his eyes and thought of Ellie.

Afterward she got out of bed, walked into the living room (still naked), came back with her cigarettes, lit one, and stood at the window smoking and fanning the smoke into the window screen.

"So did you have a good time?" she said.

"When?"

"Teo, stop playing around. Now. Right now. Did you have a good time with me right now?"

"Sure."

"You don't have to sound so enthusiastic."

Estella and Oscar were sitting on the living room couch when Teo and Bonnie came out of the bedroom. Teo wondered if they had been sitting there when Bonnie walked naked into the living room to get her cigarettes.

"What have you two been up to?" Estella said, smiling.

"Guess," Bonnie said. She was still buttoning the front of her blouse. "Do you mind if I use the phone again?"

"You don't have to ask," Estella said.

Bonnie took the phone into the back porch.

"Like old times," Estella said. "All of us together again. It's fate, Teo."

"You always hated Bonnie," Teo said.

"I know, and I said terrible things about her. But I was wrong. You need her, just the way I need Oscar. You and Bonnie. Oscar and me."

Bonnie was arguing with someone on the phone, saying she didn't give a fuck, she wasn't paying.

"That must be the landlord," Oscar said.

"Must be," Estella agreed.

"Well!" Bonnie said. She came into the living room and sat down on Teo's lap. "That's that." She twirled a lock of Teo's hair. "He said he's going to have me evicted."

Teo could see the crest of the wave, feel the silvery foam washing over him.

"Because you're one month behind on the rent?" Estella said.

"Actually three."

"Oh."

"Well, it's all the same to me. I don't have the money for one or two or three. You know how once you get behind, you try to play catch-up but there's always something you have to spend that money on, and the place isn't that great, anyway."

"So what are you going to do?" Oscar asked her.

"Well, that's what I was going to talk to all of you about. If you let me move in here for a while it would save my life, I mean literally save my life." She kissed Teo's forehead. "You'll see how much I've changed. You really don't know how I've changed, Teo. You have to live with someone to know what they're really like, and I'm not the girl I was, I swear I'm not. I don't sleep around with just anyone. It's got to be special. I'm very particular now. I told you how particular I was, Teo, and if you let me stay here, I'll just be true to you, you'll see how true I can be. Just for a few months, just to help me out, save my life, keep me from sleeping in my car—and I did that, too, a few years ago, got thrown out of a place off of Fairview and couldn't get up the money for first and last on a new place, so I slept in my car. I'll tell you, Teo, it wasn't any fun. You remember how we used to sleep in the car sometimes when we were too drunk to find our way home? I sure do remember a lot about us, Teo."

"I can't believe it," Teo said.

"What can't you believe, honey?"

"You. I can't believe you're still the same. Forty-six and still the fucking goddamn same."

"I am not. I'm not the same at all. Why do you say I'm the same when you haven't even given me a chance?"

"I see a big difference in her, Teo," Estella said.

"Who's going to pay for the groceries?" Oscar said.

"I'll chip in my share," Bonnie replied.

"I could throw you all out, right now," Teo said.

"You don't eat that much," Estella said.

"But I want to be fair," Bonnie told her.

"I've been trying since the first day you moved in not to lose my fucking temper," Teo said.

"Are you talking about the house, Teo?" Estella asked him. "Are you talking about me living in this house?"

"He just likes to argue," Oscar said.

"It was never written down anywhere that the house was yours," Estella said. "We just all knew how crazy you were and that if we didn't give it to you you might take one of your guns and shoot us all. It's not written in stone that the house is yours, you know."

"I've lived in it for eight years. It's mine, Estella. And I've been trying to tell you that for a month now, but you won't listen. The fucking house isn't much, but it's my place. You have yours and this is mine, and any fucking thing I want to do in it or with it I want to do without you and Oscar."

"Take it easy, Teo," Oscar said. "Watch your mouth and calm down. I don't want to fight over this dump."

"This isn't a resort and you're not on your honeymoon," Teo said. "Let's see what you do when you're on your own, in your own place. Let's see if you're so fucking lovey-dovey then."

"Are you trying to pick a fight?" Oscar said. "Because if you are, I've got my black belt and I don't want to hurt you. I'm too close to my pension to break your neck, but I could, you know, big as you are, snap you like a twig."

"Save it. I'm not going to fight you."

"I was born in this house, too, Teo," Estella said. "You're not the only one. You think because you were in Vietnam that you can blame everything in your life on it, you can go on with that sad face of yours acting like the world owes you something, but I can tell you, Teo, it doesn't owe you anything more than it owes me or Oscar."

"Give it up, Estella. Take the plastic wrap dispenser and the new curtains and your husband and go on back to your kids."

"You're selfish. Do you know how selfish you are? A person could be dying right in front of you and you wouldn't lift a finger to help. You don't care about anyone but yourself, and you deserve to live in this house all alone and die in it and no one will come to your funeral and no one will cry over you, either." She was sobbing now. "I won't cry over you, Teo."

"I'll cry over you, honey," Bonnie said, and nuzzled Teo's cheek with her nose.

～　　～　　～

"Is that everything?" Teo said. It hadn't taken long to empty Bonnie's apartment.

"My cat," Bonnie said. "I'm not leaving without Baby."

He had loaded her possessions into his car, most of them still in the supermarket boxes they were in when she moved from her previous apartment. It was pitiful, the way she lived. A futon to sleep on. Her underwear in the kitchen drawers. A card table and a chair. No couch. No furniture. She did have an old Zenith black-and-white TV, and a book of her publicity photographs and a manual typewriter (she was writing a killer screenplay, she told Teo).

"Come on, Bonnie, let's go," Teo said. "I'm not going to spend all night looking for an alley cat."

"I won't leave without Baby," Bonnie said. "Here, Baby, here, Baby."

The cat, a brown-striped tabby, was shivering on the closet shelf. Bonnie scooped him up into her arms.

"You naughty boy," she said.

"We'll need a few things for the house," Ellie said, and stopped at a mini mart near the WELCOME TO VISALIA sign. "Do you want to come in?"

"I think I'll just sit in the car. Get a loaf of bread and some cheese, not the awful processed cheese that sticks to the roof of your mouth. Some Jarlsberg, but sliced thin. Oranges, if they're firm. Toilet paper. Soap."

Alice hadn't complained about being dizzy or having trouble breathing or her heart beating too fast on the airplane, but when they got to the airport in Fresno, she sat down every chance she got—while Ellie was getting their suitcases, while the car rental agent was filling out the rental agreement on the Oldsmobile, while they were waiting for the bus to take them to the lot where the Oldsmobile was parked.

"Did they have firewood?" Alice said when Ellie got back in the car.

"You didn't tell me to get firewood."

"I thought you'd know."

"It didn't occur to me."

"It wasn't a reproach. I just merely said . . ."

"Don't."

The town hadn't grown much. Ellie had expected to see new buildings, expected not to recognize the place. The artichoke fields were still
there, spreading out in every direction. Roadside stands still sold special
artichoke dip and homemade relish. The grammar school she attended
was still there, whitewashed and old-fashioned, broad steps leading up
to the single solid oak door. The wood-frame Valley Methodist Church.
Ellie had once disappeared out of that very church. She was five years
old, and she remembered the dress she was wearing, a blue silk with
gathers at the waist and tiny pearl buttons down the front. It was in
March, a not particularly cold evening, but it had been drizzling on and
off all day. Mom told Dad maybe they shouldn't go to the welcoming
party for the new minister because it was starting to rain harder. Dad
said the new minister would be insulted if they didn't. Dad was a deacon
at the church, part of the delegation that had gone up to Seattle to interview the minister for the job and the one who wrote the letter hiring
him. He said it wouldn't have looked right if on the minister's welcoming night Dad wasn't even there.

Mom baked a lemon meringue pie and squeezed herself into a dress
she had made the year before for Alice's wedding, a high-collared, long-
sleeved chiffon that made crinkly sounds when she walked or sat down or
reached out her arms. Dad wore his black suit.

There was no problem driving down the road from the ranch,
although Dad said there were flash flood warnings on the radio, and Ellie
asked him what a flash flood was, and Mom told her that Dad was driving
now and not to bother him with a lot of questions.

The church was in an old apple orchard right on the edge of Visalia,
and everyone parked their cars under the trees and then slogged through
the mud toward the yellow light shining through the open door.

An old man played the violin and a young girl with silver barrettes in
her hair sang, and when they were through the new minister asked Dad
to say a few words, but he said he couldn't think of anything to say,
except that he was glad there hadn't been any flooding on the way over.
Mom helped serve the refreshments (every woman in the congregation
had baked a pie or a cake) and Ellie got chocolate frosting on the front of

her blue silk dress. That was when she disappeared, when she went to the rest room in the building in back of the church to try and wash it off.

If someone had been in the rest room with her, she would have followed them back to the church, but she was the only one in there, and when she came out she was all turned around and it was raining hard. She started walking, sure that she'd see the yellow light of the church in a few minutes. Rain soaked her silk dress, her Mary Janes began to sink into mud up to her socks, and the trees made moaning sounds that scared her so much she started to run.

She didn't know how far she was from the church, or how long she had been running, but she finally came to what looked like the end of the orchard, and out before her stretched rows and rows of artichokes, glistening green in the light of a nearby house, and at first she thought she had run all the way home, but this house had no porch, just a few wooden steps made out of field boxes. The woman inside said, "What are you doing out in the rain?" and she took off Ellie's wet clothes and muddy shoes and wrapped her in a blanket and laid her down in a bed with one of her own children.

"Tell the policeman you're sorry, Ellie," Dad said when he found her in the morning.

Ellie said she was sorry (she didn't know what for) and then the policeman told the woman she should have called the police the minute Ellie came to the door, and Dad said, "How would you like it if one of your children disappeared?"

There was the bank. And the Pepper Tree Restaurant. Eric asked her to marry him at the Pepper Tree. She slowed down. Christmas of 1982 and they sat in a booth and had hamburgers and french fries and Eric said he had never met anyone like her and what did she think about the future of nuclear energy?

They had reached the access road to the ranch. The sign was gone. Instead of PETERSON'S QUALITY ARTICHOKES, there was a rain-bleached banner stapled to the wire fence. KEEP OUT. TRESPASSERS WILL BE PROSECUTED TO THE LIMIT OF THE LAW. Dad always talked about paving the access road. The ruts would fill up in the rainy season and then dry into a minefield of sinkholes and rocky mounds. It was nearly unpassable now. The Olds bumped along, the undercarriage banging into mounds, tires dropping into holes and shrieking as they climbed out again. Ellie couldn't remember how many times she had ridden down this road with Dad, violet-topped green plants radiating out from the road like spokes on a wheel, eucalyptus trees raining their silvery leaves over the hood of the car, Dad saying, *Hold on, Ellie, don't want you bouncing out the window.*

She used to string eucalyptus leaves into necklaces when she was seven or eight. She used to draw faces on eucalyptus leaves and pretend they were dollar bills. Mom would soak eucalyptus leaves in hot water and use the liquid for poultices when Dad sprained his back. The eucalyptus trees were still there, taproots going all the way to China probably, looking for water, but there were no violet-topped green plants, no rows and rows of tough green clumps, no sign of the beautiful geometry that Dad had made of his fields, just acres of dirt purpling in the late afternoon sun along with old cars and pieces of rusted machinery and shredded tires.

They drove past the cottage where Dad used to do his accounts and pay the laborers. Squatters had torn it up. There was no glass in the windows and most of the shingles were gone from the roof.

The house was at the end of the road. It startled Ellie to see it there, raw wood showing through the flaking paint.

She carried the suitcases onto the porch and unlocked the front door.

"I have to explain," Alice said. She had, with effort, made it to the top step.

"I don't want to hear it," Ellie told her.

"Then what's the point of coming here at all with me?"

"I don't know what the point is."

A cousin had run the farm after Dad died, but when the cousin died, his children didn't want any part of artichoke farming. No one had lived in the main house for at least ten years. It smelled of old kerosene rags and mold and dust.

"Open a window, Ellie, I can't breathe," Alice said. She sat down on one of the horsehair couches and a dusty plume sailed upward.

Most of the windows in the living room were stuck shut, glued down by years of sifting dirt and rain. Ellie managed to open one of them, and all she did was touch the parchment shade and it made a snapping noise and rolled up by itself.

The cousin's wife had tatted doilies for the horsehair furniture and laid down rag rugs on the plank floors and polished the ancient stove until the green enamel was nearly worn off. All of Mom's china was gone, along with her copper pots and the cabinet with the porcelain birds in it, but the painted scenes from the Bible that Dad had framed for her in tiger oak were still hanging on the kitchen walls. Moses in the bulrushes. David and Goliath. Samson and Delilah.

Alice said she had to go to the bathroom. Ellie handed her one of the rolls of toilet paper and then went out onto the back porch and looked out at the place she knew better than any other place in the world. It looked cold and forbidding to her now. There were no houses for a mile in either direction, just a suggestion of a city out in the distance, steepled roofs and brightly painted signs. She once had thought that someday she and Eric and Jamie would move out here and live, that they'd be farmers, live simply, grow their own food, that she'd open one of those roadside stands and sell her own artichoke dip and fresh peach pie and homemade raspberry jam.

"I'll make dinner," Ellie said when Alice came out of the bathroom. "It will have to be sandwiches."

"I'm not hungry. I think I'd better go to bed."

Ellie had arranged for the water and electricity to be turned on, but the only lightbulbs in the house were the one in the lamp in the living room and the overhead light in the kitchen. The long hall (like a train, Ma always said) was dark, and the flowered wallpaper had dried out and now hung in long stiff strips that stuck out from the wall like spiky tongues.

Bedsheets were in the same closet they had always been in, but threadbare and stained. Ellie took two out and made the bed in the bedroom at the end of the hall while Alice watched from the doorway.

"You'll have to do without a pillow," Ellie said.

She heard the bedsprings creak as Alice lay down, heard the rapid breathing. She didn't turn around.

Chapter 19

ᕙ

The beeping startled him awake.

"Your pager, honey," Bonnie murmured next to him.

The numbers on the pager glowed in the dark. Unfamiliar numbers.

He flipped on the light and dialed the number.

"Who is it?" Bonnie said.

"Line's busy."

He was up and out of bed and getting dressed. No one had paged him in the middle of the night since he went on medical leave. A page in the middle of the night had always meant bad news. Who had his pager number? What bad news?

"Throw me my cigs, hon, will you?" Bonnie said, and sat up in bed.

There were packs of cigarettes all over the house, all over the bedroom, on the dresser, on top of a heap of underwear, on the floor next to the remains of the pizza Bonnie bought on her way home from work the night before. Bonnie didn't have to walk more than two feet in any direction to find a cigarette. Teo tossed her the pack that had been on the dresser and dialed the number again. It was still busy.

"I was really good last night at karaoke," she said.

He pulled a sweater on over his head and grabbed his shoes from under the bed.

"Breath control is the secret to singing on key. I didn't drift once. Straight as an arrow. Everyone came up to me afterward and told me I was a natural." She took a drag of her cigarette. "I've got the hand gestures just right now, you know how Ella Fitzgerald did it, that elegant, quiet way, not too much, just enough."

Jeans. He had a pair somewhere. Bonnie's clothes were all over the bedroom, everything covered in cat hair, everything reeking of cigarettes.

"What did you do with my socks?" he said.

She had taken over the bureau, put all the junk in it that had been in the cardboard boxes, just jammed it all in there, stuffed each drawer to the top so that none of them closed.

So, how serious is this with your ex-wife? Aaron asked at Teo's last session.

Not serious, Teo replied. But he hadn't told Aaron that she had unpacked her cardboard boxes, that she was talking about quitting her job at the Monkey Bar, that her cat slept on the bed between them, that he couldn't find a spot to put his clothes, that there were always dirty dishes in the sink and hair balls on the floor, that he would go out for a walk and come back to find strange people sitting on the couch in the living room. One was a singing teacher, Bonnie said. He sang for the Palmdale Civic Opera, she said. Another one was someone she met at some producer's house who said her screenplay was a natural for Universal Studios. Teo didn't give a fuck who they were. The real issue was, what was the use of checking doors and windows when anyone could just walk into his house anytime they wanted to?

"Is it a woman?" she said now.

Baby had dragged Teo's clean socks through the litter box in the hall. They smelled of cat piss.

"I don't care if it is. My God, Teo, why would I care? Did I tell you what I sang last night? Did you hear me when I came in? I told you what I sang. I'll bet you don't even remember what I said."

Teo slid his bare feet into his shoes, put his wallet in his pocket, and picked up the phone.

"'What Kind of Fool Am I,'" Bonnie said.

"Don't get dramatic," Teo said and dialed the number again.

"That's what I sang, 'What Kind of Fool Am I?' So is it a woman? Is it *l-o-v-e*, baby?"

"Cut it out."

"Is she better looking than I am? Teo, I'm talking to you. Is it a fucking romance, or just one of those imaginary things where she's married and you can't have her, so you want her all the more? Is it one of those, Teo, or is it the fuckable kind? Because if it's the fuckable kind, I'll get out right this minute, I don't need a shove, you know."

"Hello." A man's voice, impatient, sharp. It stopped Teo for a moment. He thought he had dialed wrong.

"Theodore Domingos here, did you page me?"

"Theodore? Who the hell is Theodore?"

"Teo. Teo Domingos. You paged me. Talk."

"I'm a friend of Roxana's. Gordon. We've got trouble here."

A half-moon drifted in and out of billowy gray clouds, and by the time Teo reached the Temple Street exit it had begun to rain, handfuls of water splashing across the windshield as the wipers labored to keep up. Main Street. Not skid row yet, but close. The stock exchange had once been on this street. People now lived in the tall buildings, tended geraniums in cans on the windowsills, hung flimsy curtains. Whole families, whole neighborhoods camped out in deserted offices, their cooking stoves blackening the windows. It was four o'clock in the morning, and there were men in hooded jackets huddled in the rain on the corner of Ninth and Main. He knew without stopping, without looking, that they were dealing dope.

Gordon wouldn't tell him what the trouble was on the phone, said it was serious, though, and Teo had to come right now, and no, it couldn't wait until morning, it had to be right now, right this minute.

Probably another one of Roxana's schemes to get money for dope. Call your brother, he'll give you the money. Gordon sounded sober, not like the last doper Roxana lived with, who couldn't string two coherent words together. This one's an artist, Roxana told Teo at Easter, he's making some sculpture shit for the City Hall lawn.

Hill Street. The signs were all in Spanish. JOYERIA. PAPELES DE IMI-
GRACION. NOTARIO PUBLICO. ABOGADO. AGENCIA DE VIAJE. CREDITO, NO
PREGUNTAS.

There's a bridal shop on the corner, Gordon said. *They open at dawn. Their
real business is selling fake IDs. No one speaks English. Go around the side of the
bridal shop to the alley, park anywhere. Ring the bell where it says* Deliveries.

There it was. The building had the remains of gold stenciled lettering
on the windows. MONUMENT INVESTING. SWITZERLAND IMPORTS. MARINE
INSURANCE. Teo pulled into the alley behind the building and parked.

He rang the bell a few times. He was getting soaked, rain running
down the back of his sweater and into his shoes. He had run out of the
house so fast he hadn't thought to put on his police slicker. He should
have stopped and put it on. He rolled his shoulders forward, ducked his
head down, and waited.

The bell had started a freight elevator. It made a grinding noise as it
moved from floor to floor toward him. He looked up at the windows of
Monument Investing. More lights had come on.

The elevator door opened and he stepped in and pressed the button
for the sixth floor. Of course, he should have known it was Roxana. He
was the one she always called. *I'm in jail, Teo. I'm in the hospital, Teo. I'm in
San Diego and can't get home, Teo.* He had thought they were over that. She
had been with this Gordon guy for a year, she said, everything was going
great, he was this big fucking artist, she was happy, she wasn't using, no
trouble, smooth sailing. Shit.

The elevator stopped. The door opened and the whole sixth floor was
in front of him, like a gigantic warehouse, like an airplane hangar, like a
goddamned garden filled with what looked like swarms of giant
grasshoppers crouching on metallic lily pads.

He hadn't come armed. He should have. He thought of it now, and that
surprised him, that he hadn't thought of it before, that he could have been
so stupid as to forget to do his checklist before he walked out the door.

Someone was coming toward him now from behind one of the bent
metal creatures, out of a doorway that didn't have a door, merely two-by-

fours that had once framed a door. No bulge in the pocket. A short man, balding, with loose hairs hanging down his neck in a messy ponytail, shiny forehead, pockmarked cheeks. He was wearing overalls and scuffed leather slippers and eating a sandwich.

"Roxie said you were a policeman. I expected to see a uniform. I'm Gordon."

There was no one else that Teo could see.

"Sorry if I woke you up. Are you hungry?"

Teo shook his head.

"What time is it?" Gordon said.

"Four-twenty-three."

"I don't wear a watch. I tell time by the sun. When it's out, it's day-time, when it's not, it's night. It doesn't matter. When I'm working I lose track of time. I could be on the moon."

"Where's Roxana?"

"Gone. She said you're the man to call, that you can be counted on in an emergency."

"It's four in the morning."

"You said four-twenty-three."

"So you had your fun. I'm going home."

"She left her kid here."

"She'll be back for him."

"I don't think so. She's gone. Gone, gone. Bye-bye. He's in the back."

Gordon led the way to the living area, wallboard partitions on three sides. Desk. Drafting table. A sink and stove and refrigerator. Troy was sitting on an army cot wrapped in a blanket, leaning forward. Teo could hear his wheezing from fifteen feet away.

"Some guy came by, she said she was going to go buy groceries, so I gave her some money, she said don't forget to give Troy his medicine, and I haven't seen her since. I like the kid. I'm used to him. He doesn't talk, doesn't give me any trouble. I'd keep him, but—"

"When did she go out for groceries?"

"Two weeks ago. I don't even mind giving him his breathing treatments. Makes me feel useful. But he ran out of medicine and when she left she took the last of my money. Troy and I have been eating mayonnaise sandwiches."

Teo knelt down next to the cot. "How're you doing, Troy?"

Lips moved, but no sound came out.

"He's having an asthma attack. Worse than usual. That's why I called you. He needs a treatment and I don't have two cents to go buy the stuff he's supposed to get. I'll have money soon. A month or two at the most. I'm waiting for the rest of the money on the Pancho Villa piece I did for the Mexican ambassador and I've got three kids of my own scattered all over the place, I don't even see them, don't buy them medicine or worry about what they eat, so it doesn't make sense that I'd saddle myself with someone else's. She said to treat you with kid gloves, not to say anything about the Vietnam War, and I told her I was in Canada all through it, and I wasn't dumb enough to say anything to a vet about it. She said you always looked out for her, gave me your beeper number. It took me about four days to figure out where I put it."

"She just left, just like that?" Teo said.

"Told me to give him his breathing treatments and call you, kissed Troy, told him to be a good boy, and left. He's been like this all day, bent over, trying to breathe."

Teo knew fundamental first aid. CPR, Heimlich maneuver. He could deliver a baby if it wasn't breech. He had once, on Laguna Canyon Road in the middle of a mud slide with his partner holding a flashlight and Teo up to his elbows in blood, tied off an artery that had been severed by a skip loader. He didn't have the slightest idea what to do to help Troy get air into his lungs.

"You never know what's going to set it off," Gordon said. "Welding fumes can do it. So I open the windows to air out the place, and if it's too damp that makes it worse. Could be dust. There's plenty of that around here. Could be the mayonnaise sandwiches. I told Roxana to take him over to Children's, she didn't need money there, they'd do tests on him to find out exactly what was going on, but she never had any time. She slept all day and never had any time. I don't know what happened to her. She was great for a while, not using, took good care of Troy, was teaching him his ABCs, reading to him. She used to help me weld. I told her she had an artistic bent. She's not a dummy. I don't know why she left. I don't get it."

The Los Angeles County Hospital was the closest. Troy lay on his side on the front seat of the car, face twisted and lips turning blue. He was in pajamas. His glasses and hearing aid and an empty vial of medicine were in a plastic Baggie in Teo's jacket pocket, a toy truck and a few changes of clothes in the trunk.

Five minutes from downtown Los Angeles in good weather, ten in bad, with taillights of the cars in front weaving and darting all over the place, Teo skidding behind them, jockeying for an opening. He nearly missed State Street, but at the last minute saw the hospital's grimy white facade, did a wheelie, and sped up the hill.

Teo had been to Los Angeles County Hospital once, a suspected meningitis case, a sixteen-year-old boy whose frantic mother had flagged Teo down on Sunset Boulevard. The teenager was unconscious by the time they reached the hospital and died on a gurney in a dingy corridor while Teo was making out the forms. Teo took the back entrance now, the doctors' entrance, picked Troy up, and ran through a door that said NO ADMITTANCE.

"I think he's dying," he told the nurse who tried to stop him at the door.

She led him quickly past dark examining rooms, and like a relay race, a doctor, or someone in a white coat with a stethoscope around his neck, rounded a corner, took the child, and darted into a brightly lit room.

"Father?"

"Uncle."

A name tag on his chest. *Dr. Sherman.*

Troy's small body was lost in the hospital bed. "Pediatrics is too far," Dr. Sherman said as a small squadron of nurses and technicians surrounded the bed, leaned in, and began to work.

"Allergies?"

"I don't know."

Teo went out into the hall. He had hardly broken a sweat. He knew how to do this, how to react in an emergency, how not to think of what he was doing or what the result would be. But this was where he stopped, at the door to this room. This was where it ended. Troy was in good hands and Teo had done his duty. It was no different than showing up at the scene of a homicide, no different than a quick tussle to grab a perp's gun, fasten the handcuffs, and throw him in jail. Done. He'd hang around awhile, see if he was all right, then take off.

"There's a coffee machine downstairs." It was a nurse rushing by on her way into the room where Troy was being worked on. A slow night. Troy was the big attraction.

"Thanks."

Teo was perspiring now. Damn Roxana.

This was the part Aaron said was causing a problem, figuring out what he should have done about that corpse in Vietnam. Aaron said to forget about it, that he had done the right thing, that the whole company had done the right thing. But Teo couldn't forget about it, that last retreat when his company was bivouacked on the beach waiting to be evacuated, shells coming in and snipers everywhere, and that dead soldier out in the open.

"How are you paying?"

It was someone from the admitting office, looking solicitous, a black woman in high heels with a clipboard and pencil.

"He's not mine. My nephew."

"Cash, then?"

"What?"

"You'll be paying the bill in cash, then?"

"Jesus Christ, how do I know?"

She looked frightened, at something he said or the way he looked when he said it, and then was gone, around some corner, into some room, and he leaned back against the wall.

Soldiers are particular about how they handle the dead, Teo told Aaron.

Bodies are put in body bags and transported by truck to Graves Registration. Wounded are taken off by ship or helicopter. And no one wanted to put that body in a truck and take it back to Graves Registration. Instead, one by one, they'd run out, grab the corpse's feet, and drag it over to someone else's tent.

But it was a body, Aaron told him, *a dead body, and you were trying to stay alive.*

We didn't have to make a game of it, Teo snapped. *We didn't have to treat it like a dead cat, like a pile of shit.*

Dr. Sherman came out of the room.

"What's he been getting?"

Teo handed him the empty vial Gordon had given him.

It was a grim game waiting to see who got stuck with the corpse. By the time daylight came, the uniform was so muddy it was hard to tell whether it was a body or a supply bag. When dark came again the body was still there getting rained on. No one bothered to move it anymore, and it had sunk so far into the muck that it was no longer a body or even a corpse, but merely that thing lying out there waiting to get someone killed. It was still out in the open, unclaimed and untransported, when the helicopter arrived and everyone scrambled aboard. As the helicopter took off, it passed directly over the body. Arms and legs fluttered as though doing a flappy little dance, and the helmet tilted backward to reveal the soldier's face, a shiny gray in the cold dawn.

A nurse stuck her head out of the room. It was a farce, everyone thinking Teo cared that much about what happened to the kid, stopping whatever they were doing in there to report his status, to issue bulletins. The nurse was telling him to relax, it looked as if the boy was going to be all right.

"Well, that's great," Teo said. "Great."

The problem was no one wanted to admit that it was a retreat, no one wanted to call it that. Teo explained to Aaron that some people thought retreating was the same as cowardice and preferred to think of it as an advance, but in a different direction.

He felt like drinking coffee now. He was hungry. He'd go down to where they said the coffee was. Maybe there was a machine with peanuts or crackers. But first he'd make a phone call.

He caught Estella just about to go out the door. She was short with him, said she didn't have time to talk, she'd be late for work.

"I talked to you all I'm going to," she said. "Don't you remember what you said to me, Teo? I haven't. Neither has Oscar. You could have been diplomatic, you didn't have to say what you did the way you did. I promised Oscar I wouldn't talk to you until you apologized, and we're in agreement on this, Teo, just because you're my brother doesn't mean you can go stepping on my head any old time you want to, saying whatever comes into your mind, no matter how hurtful it is. Have I ever treated you other than with loving, sisterly kindness? Even coming over to the house, didn't I take good care of it, clean and cook and worry about you? How could you have talked to me the way you did? I'm so hurt, Teo. I didn't deserve it."

"Troy's in the hospital. Roxana left him."

"What are you talking about? Roxana did what?"

"She took off and left Troy with the guy she was living with, and I brought him to the hospital because he was about to stop breathing."

"Make sense, Teo. You're not making sense."

"It's as plain as I can make it. She took off two weeks ago, and Troy nearly died of an asthma attack, and now he's going to have to go somewhere and I'm not going to be the one to get stuck with him."

"Oh, my God, Teo, what in the world is wrong with that girl?"

"I'm not talking about Roxana now. I don't give a fuck about Roxana. I'm talking about the kid. I don't know him. I don't want to know him. I'm telling you, Estella, I'm leaving the hospital and I don't know what's going to happen to him."

"I don't understand how she could do this. I always recognized that strain in her, that willful selfishness she has. When it suits her she's a mother, when it doesn't, she leaves. It's beyond comprehension."

"You're missing the point. I don't know anything about kids. I haven't seen him more than three times since the day he was born."

"Is she back on drugs? Is that what happened?"

"Are you doing this on purpose? I'm telling you I've done all I'm going to do. I don't want him."

"She's never had the slightest bit of motherly instincts. I blame Ma for that. She always did everything for her, spoiled her rotten, made it so that she never had to lift a finger to take care of herself. All the rest of us had to take care of her. Watch out for Roxana. Roxana needs this, Roxana needs that. Roxana's delicate and fragile. And look at how she ended up. No regard for anyone. Makes a mess and walks away. No work ethic, absolutely none. No sense of responsibility. Do you know she doesn't vote? She isn't even registered. Do you know that she doesn't read the paper? She doesn't have a clue about what's going on in the world. I don't know how I could be related to her. She's a complete idiot. She has no feeling for family at all. I've seen this coming. It's not as if I didn't see it coming. If you had asked me what I thought was going to happen, this, this is what I thought was going to happen. And I'm in such a mess here, Teo. Angie is so mad at me, and Derek won't go to school. He's in the bathroom now with the door locked, and I have to leave. I just can't keep calling in and having subs take my classes. I'm only one person, and Oscar says to quit if I feel that way, but I don't want to quit, I don't want to stay home." She lowered her voice. "He's seeing someone. I'm not sure if it's the one in Lakewood or not. I can always tell when he's onto someone new, he gets so amorous, wants to fuck me all the time. To tell you the truth, Teo, sometimes I think it's all just not worth it."

Late in the afternoon someone came down to the cafeteria where Teo was drinking his tenth cup of coffee and said that Troy was stable and could go home.

Go home. Wrapped in a hospital blanket and put in a wheelchair with a box of medicines.

"He'll have to have a treatment every hour for a few days," Dr. Sherman said. "The instructions are in the box with the nebulizer. Mix the medicine, put the mask on him. Simple. Read the instructions."

Teo pulled the car up to the entrance so Troy wouldn't get rained on, but the nurse wheeled him out holding an umbrella over his head. Teo put him in the backseat and the nurse wrapped a blanket around him. It had cost Teo $545 to bail him out: $300 for the emergency room, $245 for medications and tests. Nothing for the blanket.

Troy slept on and off in the car. It seemed to Teo that he was breathing all right, except for a steady moist hum when he exhaled. When they got off the freeway, Teo pulled over to check on him. He opened his eyes, lifted his head, looked out the window, and said, "I want my mommy."

"Your mommy's a flake. Do you have to pee?"

"No."

"Are you hungry?"

"Uh-uh."

He slept the rest of the way. Teo tilted the rearview mirror so he could see his face. He didn't look familiar. He didn't have Roxana's perky features. Teo didn't feel any connection to him. None. Zero. Zip. The only thing he felt was trapped.

He hadn't left the front door open. There was no way he could have walked out of the house and not locked it. He remembered putting the key in the door. But there it was. Unlocked. He carried Troy inside.

Rita Brookner was sitting on the couch in the living room.

"The door was open, so I came in. No one was here, so I thought I'd wait. No one leaves a fucking door open if they're going to be gone long. You really need a decorator. This place is so nineteen forty."

Teo carried Troy down the hall toward the bedroom. Rita was behind him, holding her hand to Troy's head to keep it from hitting the wall. The phone was ringing.

"Do you want me to answer it?" she said.

"No."

It was Estella's voice on the answering machine.

"Teo, are you there, Teo? It's Estella. I think I lost my mind. Did you say you have Troy? I'm at school. Call me."

"I know some movie people who'd die to use this place in a movie. You don't see old houses like this. Of course, the furniture, darling, is so shitty."

Bonnie had thrown her dirty laundry on the bed. The cat was sleeping on one of the pillows.

"Definitely not in here," Rita said. "You do have another bed in this place, don't you?"

Teo picked the child up again, and Rita put her arm around both of them. They walked lopsidedly down the hall.

"It could be the most adorable house. Did you see *Misery?* This is the kind of house location people die for. Of course, it needs something. Have you ever thought of Mission style, you know Gustav Stickley? I have this connection in New York, he gets the most fuckingly beautiful Stickley pieces. Expensive. Nothing's cheap, you know, if you want a name. Of course, there are knockoffs, but if you're going to spend good money for knockoffs, why not go for the real thing? Investmentwise, you can't go wrong."

There was cat hair in the big bedroom that Estella and Oscar had occupied, a tight, fine, furry sheen on the quilt.

"What fucking idiot lets a cat live in a house with an asthmatic child?" Rita pulled the quilt off and shoved it into the closet. "Philip was asthmatic, but he grew out of it. A fucking disease. Do you know that people die of asthma? Their hearts give out? You don't have to be old, either. Shouldn't he have some medication?"

"It's in the car."

"Go on. I'll stay with him."

He went out to the car and carried the box of equipment into the house and set it on the dresser.

"There, there, sweetie." Rita was on the bed holding Troy's head against her bosom. "We'll have you fixed up in a second."

The mask was on, steamed medicine pouring through the plastic hose.

"You have to wait for it to work," she said. "I see you haven't done this before. Whose kid is he? Don't tell me. I'm not going to get involved in your fucking life, I didn't come here to get involved. Does he have a mother? Oh, not that one, the one who wanted to be a movie star. Don't tell me that. I don't want to hear that. There are prostitutes and then there are prostitutes. She was the worst kind, the very worst. Well, it doesn't matter now. He's your child and you're stuck with him, and he's sick. They grow out of it. I told you that. I've had a lot of experience with asthma. I can spot an asthmatic four blocks away. I worked at Cedars as a volunteer with parents of asthmatic children. They gave me an award."

"It doesn't look as if it's working," Teo said.

"It will. You have to have patience. Everything with patience."

"What do you want?"

"What do I want?" What do you mean, what do I want?"

"Jesus."

"You mean why the fuck did I come into your house and sit down on your couch and now I'm holding your kid's head so he can breathe? Is that what you mean?"

"I mean, what do you want?"

"Okay. What do I want? Okay. I want you to promise me that you're not thinking about my Philip in any way whatsoever connected to Morty Miller, because I took care of the whole situation. And it wasn't as if I hadn't taken care of it before, because when I found out what he was doing in the beginning, I told him that blackmail was not something you fool with. But he was stubborn and I had absolutely no control over him, which happens when they're sick and you just let them do whatever they want because you feel so sorry that they're sick. When he found out Morty was his father, I told him to stay away from him. I said it wouldn't work out, that he couldn't fix his life just by finding his father, that they didn't know each other, and biology is just biology, and he had a father, his real one, the one who raised him, and be grateful. I can't see his eyes. Is he asleep?"

"No."

"But it was something in him that just wouldn't quit until he had made trouble for everyone. But I've settled it now. I told him the police were after him. I told him you knew everything."

Teo looked up at her. "Knew what?"

"I told him that you'd put him in jail, that you were manufacturing evidence that he was the one who killed Morty, that he had better forget all about Alice and trying to get anything out of her, that it wasn't important, that I was going to make sure that he couldn't get any more money out of her, and so I did. He's asleep. I can always tell. There's a relaxation in the body that's different from being awake. You should get some help in to clean up this shit hole, you know, dust and dust mites and cat hair and tobacco and I don't know what the fuck else is deadly for a kid like this."

She eased Troy back against the pillows and stood up.

"He's not very cute, is he?" she said. "I mean, for such a good-looking mother—"

"Bonnie isn't his mother."

"Well, it's none of my business, anyway."

Chapter 20

ᵏ↜

There was supposed to be an officer at the desk who wouldn't let anyone into the records depot without signing in and signing out, and then someone was supposed to eyeball you while you sorted through evidence bins and file folders to see that you didn't palm any readouts, didn't slip them into your jacket pocket or wad them up and stick them up your sleeve. But no one was at the desk and Teo just walked in.

A square room, steel shelving, brown linoleum floor. Active cases to the right (one full wall), then an alcove to the rear (boxes toppling sideways and blocking the aisles) where the dead records were warehoused. Morty Miller had to be in the active section. George said he was working on it the last time Teo called him. Interviewing people who knew Morty, doing background checks, George said. Or did he just tell Teo that to get him off his back?

Fluorescent lights overhead lit the paper labels on the sides of cardboard boxes. Everything was alphabetized, or supposed to be, but there were some *M*s where the *R*s were, and *B*s mixed in with the *D*s. Running down the rows he saw a Mahler, a Mayer, a Mueller. No Miller. That didn't necessarily mean it wasn't there. Sometimes on lab results the deceased's first name was used instead of the last, or the name was left off entirely and just the date of the homicide was recorded. Or the date of the homicide was missing and the victim's name was misspelled. Or any one of a half dozen other ways it could have been fucked up. There were quite a few labels with nothing but dates on them. He decided to pull out the boxes and go through every one that looked as if it might be mislabeled. But first he needed to stand up and shake out the soreness in his right arm. Troy didn't weigh much, but Teo had been carrying him around a lot, and the mangled muscle was acting up.

Troy was still asleep when Teo left the house. Bonnie was in the kitchen drinking a cup of coffee and smoking a cigarette.

Oh, sure, honey, I'll watch him, as long as I don't have to give him his medicine, it looks too complicated, I'll forget how much to mix and where it goes and how to do it. You know me with instructions, in one ear and out the other.

I told you no cigarettes in the house, Teo told her.

It went right straight out of my mind. I'll have to write myself a note or put a string around my finger. Or a rubber band on my wrist. They do that, you know, people who want to remember things. He isn't going to want me to read to him or anything like that, is he?

He's not going to ask you for anything. Just feed him breakfast and watch him till I get back.

An officer was at the desk now with a steaming cup of coffee and a newspaper. He might have seen Teo if he turned around. He might have heard him sliding boxes around on the shelves, but he had picked up the telephone and was intent on his call, serious faced, gesticulating with his free hand.

Bonnie could try a little harder with Troy. Teo didn't expect her to like him, but she didn't have to act as if he annoyed her. She acted as if Teo annoyed her, too. Which was pretty dumb of her considering he was giving her a place to stay. He used to think she was shrewd, that she had some smarts, maybe even traces of intelligence, that she just played dumb because it was easier if no one expected anything of her, because that way she could just keep stepping into shit holes and pretending she didn't know they were there. For a long time he had even counted on her waking up one day and paying attention to what was going on around her and maybe even realizing that her life was more than just trying to screw her way into the movies. All he counted on now was for her not to smoke in the house.

Morty Miller wasn't in the active files. Teo couldn't believe it. Had George filed it away already, just given up on it, when Teo told him he didn't like the way the hand was holding the gun, that it looked too stiff to have just been a reflex? He hadn't thought he'd have to go into the inactive section, hadn't planned on having to look through twenty years of homicide forensic records.

At least she had gotten rid of the cat. Teo told her he'd strangle it if she didn't. Other than that, he wasn't keeping track of what she did or where she went, wasn't sure whether she was even still working at the Monkey Bar. He was now sleeping in the big bedroom with Troy so he could hear him if he woke up. He didn't know what the hell Bonnie was doing. One thing he was glad of was that he had never had any children with her.

Boxes in the alcove had yellowed and cobwebs hung from shelf to shelf. He sat down on a step stool in the corner and began looking.

Bonnie had no maternal instincts. None. She was pregnant when Teo shipped out to Vietnam. She wrote and told him she had an abortion because she didn't think he'd ever marry her. Teo thought about that baby once in a while. Mostly out of curiosity. Wondered if it would have looked like him. He didn't even know if it was a boy or a girl. He never asked. He didn't want to know. Bonnie would have told him the details if he had pressed her on it, but he didn't care enough to pin her to the wall, make her sweat. It was over, done with, and didn't matter.

Paper labels had dried up and fallen on the floor. Teo had a pile of them at his feet. It wasn't enough that there was no logic to the filing system in here, now he had to match each shriveled label to its yellowed box. And it was hot. No air-conditioning. Which was probably why the labels had fallen off.

Trying to pawn Troy off on someone else was turning out to be a problem. Teo had a short list of people who might take him. His sister Luci and his brother Jose. He called Jose first. Jose was a bleeding heart, had picketed grapes with Cesar Chavez, had even gone on hunger fasts with him. Gave up making money as a dentist, for chrissakes, to devote his life to farmworkers. He should jump at the chance to take Troy.

Jesus, Teo, Roxana's gone? Jose said. *Was Troy sick when she left?*

He's been sick since the day he was born.

Have you tried to find her?

I don't see the point. What do I do if I find her?

You ask her why she left. No one just leaves their kid because they want to. The last time I talked to her she was going to go to real estate school.

She's always going to do something.

She could be sick, could be in need of help, could be in some shelter somewhere. People are more complicated than you think, Teo. Roxana's not all bad. There's goodness in her. How about if I run her name through Catholic Charities and see what I come up with?

Roxana's not going to the church to get help, Jose.

She wanted to be a nun, and anyone who thinks about entering a convent never loses that feeling of communion.

She was thirteen when she wanted to be a nun.

Almost an adult. You don't lose that sense of vocation just because you decide not to do it. And remember not to judge, lest you be judged. She probably has her reasons. We all have our reasons, Teo.

So can you take him?

An asthmatic kid? With all the pesticides around here? All the TB? I'm living in a migrant shack with no heat or running water. Fuck it, man, you put me in a hell of a spot. I want to do it, but if you send him up here it'll kill him.

When he got through talking to Jose, he called Luci in Oregon. She had three kids. What was one more?

If there was any way in the world to do it, I would, she said, *but this is a really bad time for me, Teo. Julie is being confirmed next month, and Kenny is trying to remodel the kitchen on his days off. The place is just a madhouse, and you know how Kenny gets when the house is a mess.*

I don't know how Kenny gets.

He gets mean, Teo. Right now we're having a difficult time, an especially difficult time. We've been going for counseling. Kenny's mother wants us to move up to Quebec, and we've been fighting about that. I can't see taking the kids out of the United States. They won't know what they are, Canadians or Americans. And his family speaks French, Teo. I can't speak French. "Hello" and "good-bye" is all I know.

Kenny says his mother is getting old and his father is senile, and I told him that's all the more reason we shouldn't go, I'll be the one ending up cleaning bedpans. I didn't exactly say that to him. You don't exactly talk that way to Kenny. But I did remind him that Jerry was dyslexic and would probably never learn to speak French, and that Julie and Harlan don't want to go. They don't understand a word Kenny's mother says to them when she calls on the phone. And she blames me. She told Kenny I've turned the kids against her. I'm fighting just to keep my sanity. How are you feeling?

I've been better.

I heard about a naturopath in Portland who gets rid of posttraumatic stress with herbs and acupuncture. Honestly, Teo, you ought to come up and try it. Alternative medicine is all the thing up here now. Hardly anyone goes to a doctor anymore. I heard Estella and Oscar were getting divorced. Is it true?

I don't know. Who'd you hear it from?

Her girlfriend Marge. You know Marge. The heavyset brunette with four kids, two of them twins? Well, anyway, she divorced her husband. She met someone on the Internet who lives here, and she came up to see him and stopped by to tell me about Estella. Can you imagine falling in love with someone on the Internet? What is the world coming to, Teo? He could have been a serial murderer. We have them up here, you know, hiding in the woods, leftovers from the sixties. Not that all hippies ended up as serial murderers, but you know what I mean. Marge really looked happy. I've never seen anyone so happy. Especially when she was telling me about Estella and Oscar getting a divorce. She couldn't believe that I didn't know. I said, how would I know? Estella's been mad at me since I won the music scholarship to Reed and she had to work her way through Columbia. It doesn't even matter that I dropped out and she got a degree. Families are so fractured, Teo. I hardly know of a single one where everyone is speaking. My God, you should have seen Marge's eyes gleam when she was giving me the dirt on Estella. I can't say that I'm happy about it, no matter how awful a sister Estella's been. Anyway, this naturopath guarantees his results. It's been in all the papers up here. I will say, though, it serves Estella right. Always telling everyone else how to live their lives. So, how sick is he?

Not too sick. He's actually getting better, hasn't had an attack for three days. He doesn't complain when he does. He's not that much trouble, hardly talks at all. Most of the time I don't know he's around.

That sounds abnormal to me. Children have to talk and jump around and make noise.

I don't know what's normal and what's not. I just need to find someplace to put him.

Have you tried to find Roxana?

I wouldn't know where to look.

I think you ought to call Raul. He probably knows where she is. Raul always knows where Roxana is.

I'm not calling Raul.

Honestly, Teo, it's way past time that you two got over this. Twenty-four years of not speaking to your own brother.

Twenty-six.

Do you know how much it hurt Ma to see you standing there at Pa's funeral and acting like Raul wasn't even there? She told me over and over how much it hurt her.

I'm not calling Raul.

I don't know why you have to be so stubborn. You're trying to do something for Troy, you want to find Roxana, I'd think you would call Raul, it just makes sense to me, that's all I'm trying to say. And now don't get mad at me, but you don't always do things that make sense, like holding a grudge against a brother who loves you as much as Raul does.

Then you can't take Troy, is that it?

I would, you know I would if I could. So do you think you can come up for Julie's confirmation? We've decided to do Mexican food at the party. It was Kenny's idea. He says the kids don't know a thing about their heritage.

Is food going to do it?

There's no reason to be nasty. Just because I can't take Troy. Just because you're mad at Roxana. You ought to know Roxana by now. She never did stick to anything, never really had a sense of family. I always had the feeling that she wasn't even my blood sister. I never said this to anyone before, Teo, but I used to think she might have been left on our doorstep, you know, some girl got in trouble and didn't know what to do, and she knew Ma had a big heart, and so she put Roxana in a basket—you know, like Moses—and Ma found her and . . .

She wasn't left on the doorstep, Luci, and don't start crying.
It's just that I wish I could help you, but Kenny—
Sure. Kenny.

MORTY MILLER, DECEASED. The box was mostly empty. A property receipt for the gun and bullet. No notation as to where they were. A test for gunpowder residue. Positive. He scanned the page. Positive where? Residue where? On his face, or on the hand holding the gun? Miller's body had been cremated, the bullet and gun probably sent to disposal and melted down, and some lab tech forgot to specify whether there were powder burns on Morty's fingers. So, was that it? End of murder theory? End of story?

Teo leaned back against the cardboard boxes. He had dreamt about Vietnam the night before, about that last evacuation, hearing voices in his head yelling out in the dark, *Are you all right? Are you all right?* It was an old dream, hollowed out over the years until there was nothing left but outlines and echoes. He stared at the mess on the floor. Each scrap of paper was a piece of someone's life, and as hard as he tried and as much as he wanted to he couldn't put the pieces together to make a whole. He didn't know what had happened to Morty Miller or to that mud-spattered body in Vietnam. He didn't know why Ellie ran away. He didn't know how to erase what had happened between him and Raul. A shudder went through him and tears, salty and bitter, rolled slowly down his cheeks, for all the things he didn't know and couldn't figure out.

Troy was asleep on the floor at the front door, wrapped in blankets, the television a few feet behind him tuned to cartoons. Teo nearly stepped on him when he opened the door. For a split second he thought it was a bag of laundry or a pile of pillows. Then he saw Troy's bare foot and the blue of his pajama bottom. He didn't even bother going through the house to see if Bonnie was there. He knew she wasn't.

Troy hadn't had breakfast. He said he woke up and got out of bed and no one was there. He didn't cry when he said it. He said it as if he had expected it, as if it happened all the time.

He ate his cereal slowly.

"Do you like this kind of cereal, or should I buy something else when I go to the store?" Teo said.

"I like it."

He didn't ask for things, didn't say, well, Uncle Teo, I'd prefer Kix or Charms. He never said anything like that. He didn't have any preferences. At least he didn't say that he did or show that he did. He had probably never in his whole life had anyone ask him what he wanted to eat, or if he wanted anything at all, or how he felt, or if he needed anything. He didn't even ask Teo to help him get dressed. He couldn't always get the buttons in the right buttonholes, but he could put on his underwear and jeans and shoes and socks. He could even comb his own hair.

He'd be easier to like if he cried once in a while. He didn't know how to get sympathy, how to make you feel sorry for him. He would probably have gotten further with Bonnie, who was a sucker for sentimentality, if he knew how to pour on the juice, let the teardrops roll.

"So what if you get dressed and we do something, go somewhere?"

"With you?"

"Of course with me. What do you think I'm talking about, sending you with someone else, for chrissakes?"

Troy blinked a few times, and then stared into his cereal.

"I don't want any more."

The problem wasn't Troy. He was blameless. He couldn't help it if his mother took off, and he certainly couldn't help it that he had asthma and weak eyes and poor hearing and couldn't cry. The problem was Teo. He didn't like the feeling that he had to do this, had to take care of him, that there was no way out, no one who would take him off his hands.

"Hey, I'm sorry. Did you hear me? I said I'm sorry."

Knowing what to do with him all day was another problem. Not that he ever said he was bored. He'd sit on the couch for hours and not move if you told him not to.

"Get dressed and we'll go have some fun," Teo said.

Gordon had brought over the rest of Troy's clothes. Teo expected Troy to cry when he saw Gordon, to ask about Roxana, especially when Gordon gave him a hug and told him he missed him. But he didn't.

So have you heard from her? Teo said.

Nope. She went out for groceries and stepped into the void, was the way Gordon put it.

There was an amusement park on Bristol that had rides. Small rides, nothing fast or scary. A little train going around a track at two miles an hour, a small Ferris wheel, a miniature roller-coaster.

"So what do you want to ride on first?" Teo said. He had bought $10 worth of ride tickets.

"The train."

They waited in line for the train to stop. It was a weekday, and only a few mothers with their kids. A gray day, misty and unappetizing. A birthday party had been set up on the benches in the pavilion next to the video arcade. The guests hadn't arrived yet, but the helium balloons were flying, party hats and noisemakers lined up on the table, empty paper plates catching the breeze, piling onto one another and then sliding one by one off the table onto the concrete floor.

The ride attendant had his hand out to help Troy up into the train.

"I'm afraid," Troy said.

"Afraid of what?" Teo said. "This little train? I could pick it up with one hand. Do you want to see me?"

Troy shook his head.

"They get that way sometimes," the attendant said. A little girl walked around Troy and climbed into the caboose.

"So what if I get on the train with you?" Teo said.

They took the last car. Teo put his arm around him and could feel him trembling. He wanted to talk to him like a drill sergeant, wanted to tell him that there were lots of scary things in life and this was nothing compared to some of them. He wanted to shake him and say, Listen to me, you can ride this train. I tell you you can, and you can. Or something like that.

They went on the Ferris wheel, but Troy kept his eyes closed the whole time. The roller-coaster was out.

They stopped at McDonald's before they went home. Troy said he wanted a hamburger, but he ate two bites and then played with the plastic dinosaur. He positioned the dinosaur so its back legs were even with the table edge, then tore a straw into tiny pieces and lined the pieces up in front of the dinosaur, then a napkin in front of that, and the remains of the hamburger in front of that. Teo had bought him some toy airplanes, and when he played with them he did the same thing, lined them up in a row, precisely, neatly. He didn't make machine gun noises or fly them with his hand. He just lined them up.

When they got home at five-thirty Bonnie was there.

"Can't talk," she said. "I'm in a hurry. What do you think of a cocktail dress for a house party in Holmby Hills? Do you think everyone will be in jeans, underdressed, or do you think it's one of those butler, catered-dinner, tents-out-in-the-backyard kinds of party? I don't know why I'm asking you, anyway. I'll bet you've never been to a real party."

She went into the bedroom.

Teo brought out the box of airplanes, watched Troy begin lining them up on the carpet, then turned the television on and the sound up high and went into the bedroom.

"You left him alone. You said you'd watch him and you walked out and left a four-year-old kid alone in the house."

"I knew he'd be all right. He never does anything. He never says anything. I knew he wasn't going anywhere. I had an unexpected invitation, and I wasn't going to turn it down. Life doesn't work that way, Teo, that people just turn down invitations to suit you."

He sat down on the bed. She was pulling dresses out of the closet, holding them up to her chest, and then tossing them on the bed next to him.

"I didn't tell you I was going to be a baby-sitter, did I? Did I ever tell you that, Teo? Did I ever say, when you brought him home, that I was going to help you watch him?"

"You left him here alone. You didn't give him breakfast. Anything could have happened. He could have had an asthma attack. The house could have caught on fire."

"You always expect the worst. I always expect the best. That's why I couldn't live with you, Teo. You dragged me down. I like to feel the sun on me, get out, see people, enjoy life. You're half dead in this house, and now you've got him weighing you down, and you expect me to stay here and rot with you. Well, I'm not going to do it. You can't make me do it. I asked for a place to stay. I didn't say I wanted to be in jail. And this is a jail, you know. You can call it a house if you want to. Does this blue match my eyes?"

"I don't know how you can be so far off."

"There are all shades of blue, you know."

"I'm talking about your head, Bonnie, your screwed-up head."

"Look who's talking."

She picked out a red dress and hung it over the foot of the bed.

"Estella said you were pining away for me, waiting for me to come back. Well, here I am, and I don't like it any better this time than I did eight years ago. I don't know if you're crazy or not, but as soon as I can swing it, I'm leaving. Right now I'm going to put on that red dress and go to a party in Holmby Hills, and don't ask me to baby-sit that kid again, because I won't do it."

He watched her step into the red dress and adjust the shoulder pads and smooth the skirt down over her hips. She had soft skin, slender arms, and eyes the blue of the delphiniums that once grew in the yard.

"I think you'd better leave now," he said. "There's no use waiting. I'll give you some money to rent a place."

"The one guy I've been trying to get to for three years calls me on the phone and says he wants me to read for a part in a commercial, and I go, and I was only gone a few lousy hours, and nothing happened to your precious nephew, and now you tell me to get out. You know damn well you'd leave the kid alone, too, if you had something important to do."

"You don't even know that what you did today was stupid and dumb and selfish, do you?" he said.

She stuck out her chin.

"You didn't think I was stupid and dumb and selfish when we were still fucking."

"Don't bother taking your stuff. I'll pack it up for you and you call me and tell me where you want it sent."

She was standing at the mirror, adjusting the collar of the red dress, her eyes looking back at him.

"Estella's right, no one's going to cry over you, Teo, especially not me. I did you a favor coming back, you didn't do me one." She turned around. "I'll bet you want to hit me really bad right now, don't you?"

"You've been watching too many soap operas."

"If you so much as touch me I'll file a restraining order on you."

Whatever had happened between them when they were married, he had never hit her, and wouldn't have, no matter what, even when she cut up two of his police uniforms because he told her the sorriest day of his life was the day he met her.

"When you get settled, call me and let me know where you want your mail sent."

"That kid's not going to appreciate what you're doing, you know. You think there's a book in heaven where they write down all your good deeds and that'll make up for all the lousy things you've done. Well, there isn't."

"Just pack your things up, Bonnie."

"You think you're a saint and I'm just a slut. One thing I know for sure, I may be a slut, but you're no saint. We've all got urges, we're all human, and you used to be a lot of fun, and now you're dead as a door-nail, just a dead, dead piece of shit."

"If you need me for anything—"

"I don't need you, period."

Chapter 21

⤝

"We'll have to turn off the water in the kitchen till we see where the leak's coming from," Tony said. He was the plumber recommended by Jeff, the owner of Tuffy Hardware in downtown Visalia. "I wouldn't count on doing any cooking in there tonight. Why don't you two ladies take a drive into town, do some shopping, take your time coming back? Say about eight o'clock. We should be out of here by then."

"I'll get my sweater," Alice said.

"Maybe you'd better shut the windows in the bedrooms before you leave," Tony said. "It looks like it's going to rain again."

Ellie asked Alice if she wanted her to close the windows, and Alice said no, she wasn't so delicate that she couldn't shut a few windows.

"Then I'll be in the car," Ellie said.

The roofer (he had been recommended by the plumber) waved at her as she walked down the steps. She waved back and got into the car.

Workmen were tearing the house apart. The old kitchen cabinets were down, walls a pristine white where the cabinets had been and a grimy gray everywhere else. Dishes and pots and pans were stacked in a corner next to the old Kelvinator refrigerator, waiting for the new cabinets to go up. The floor man had already yanked out the cracked linoleum and laid down gold-speckled ceramic tile. The big window in the living room was gone (the exterminator found termites in the wooden frame), a sheet of plastic that looked like someone's old shower curtain covering the empty space. The carpenter (he had been recommended by the roofer) was under the house checking the floor beams for rot.

She sat sideways on the car seat and watched the roofer work. There was an art to everything, even to ripping off shingles. He strolled sure-footed up and down the peaked roof, kneeling, standing up, taking a few steps, then kneeling again, as if he had no idea that he might step where the beams had turned spongy and fall through or lean too far toward the ground and roll off.

A waste of money, remodeling. The whole place should have been leveled. The only original thing left in the house (besides the iron tub with the claw feet in the big bathroom) was the fieldstone fireplace. The stonemason said the fireplace was a honey, that you could look for a hundred years and not find stones like those, that the stones they had nowadays were man-made and looked cold and artificial, and that it was a shame some of the gesso lion heads had fallen off the mantel, no one made lion heads like those nowadays, some antique dealer up in Fresno probably had pickers down here stealing lion heads off mantels, and that if he had time he'd go up to Fresno and look around and see if he could buy them back.

Alice could have built a new house with the money it was costing to remodel the old one. Well, it was her money, and Ellie wasn't going to be in Visalia that much longer, anyway. She hadn't told Alice that yet. As far as Ellie was concerned, the trip back to Visalia had been a mistake. Alice said they would talk things out once they got to the farm, where every-thing was familiar and there'd be no one sticking their nose in where it didn't belong, they'd get matters settled between them. But they hadn't. They couldn't talk about that thing that lay between them and was in the air they breathed and in the looks they gave each other. They just couldn't. They edged up to discussing it, but never got down and did it. Alice's doctor appointments were about all they discussed, what day they were and the time. Dr. Freed in downtown Visalia was taking care of her, and all Alice had to do was call up, make the appointment, and Ellie would drive her over there, sit in the waiting room, read a magazine until she came out, then take her home. They didn't go anywhere else. The market. The drugstore. That was about it. Alice said she was too tired to go running around, and Ellie didn't want to bump into anyone she had gone to high school with, didn't want to get involved in one of those conversations that people are bound and determined to have with you when you've been away for a long time. Like:

My God, what's happened to you since you left Visalia? Weren't you going to go to medical school?

I was going to, but I never got further than two years premed.

That's too bad. What happened?

I met a man on a raft on the Colorado River. I fell overboard and he saved my life; so I quit school and married him.

That's the most romantic thing I've ever heard.

Well, yes, but after sixteen years I divorced him. And, oh, yes, my eight-year-old son, Jamie, died last year. And, oh, yes, I just found out my sister is really my mother.

The weather had turned cold and dreary. She should have told Alice to get a coat instead of a sweater. Tony was right, it looked like rain again. Most of Ellie's memories of Visalia were of summer, butterflies on shafts of sun, dust devils rising up out of the heated fields and coating everything with a thin, gritty film, sprinklers on the lawn making lazy arcs as she ran through them on sticky afternoons.

At least with all the workmen going in and out all day, the house didn't feel dead and desolate the way it had before they started, Alice staying in her part of the house and Ellie staying in hers, Alice getting up in the morning and making her own breakfast, then Ellie getting up and making hers, both of them cooking dinner together, but not saying much more than, *Do you want your potatoes mashed, or baked?*

Alice had started sewing again, stitching away on Mom's old treadle machine, making drapes for the living room and curtains for the kitchen. Ellie read and took walks and sat on the front porch and watched the workmen come and go. Men talking sports and telling jokes and yelling out the doors and windows at one another relieved the gloom. Tony carried a portable radio from room to room tuned to talk shows where most of the callers claimed to have been abducted by extraterrestrials. *I was standing in my field and saw this humongous spaceship, and I didn't tell any-one before because I didn't want anyone to say I was crazy, but . . .* Even nuts sounded reasonable on the radio.

"It's so damp, I forgot how damp it was in Visalia," Alice said as she got in the car.

The carpenter's truck was blocking the drive. Ellie honked the horn and he came out from under the house.

"I'll have to buy a car," Alice said, looking out the window as the car-penter maneuvered his truck off the drive and into the gravel strip that bordered the utility road. "I can't keep renting this one." She shivered in her gray cable-stitch sweater. "The weatherman didn't say it was going to be this cold."

"I've decided to go up north, maybe to Seattle," Ellie said. The truck was out of the way. She backed up and turned left.

"When?"

"As soon as you can drive yourself to the doctor."

"Oh."

The fields had lost their gold cover of dry grass since the rainy season started and were now a weedy, clumpy green. Lately Ellie had been look-ing at the fields as if she had never seen them before. Rows and rows of weeds swallowing the rainwater out of drainage ditches. Peach trees, leaves whipped off by the rain, sprouting new branches.

"I knew you'd never forgive me," Alice said.

They were on the main road now. The freeway was to the right, but there was no reason to get on it. Ellie decided to drive until it got dark, and then turn around and drive back. The water should be turned on by then.

"I was just seventeen," Alice said. "I didn't even really know how babies were made."

They passed the grammar school. The first week in October and the front door was already decorated for Halloween. Cotton cobwebs draped from hinges to doorknob. A paper skeleton was hanging from the flagpole.

The pumpkin lot was open on the main road, piles of pumpkins on the cold ground, a rain-spattered scarecrow lying comatose atop a bale of hay.

"We need some milk," Ellie said.

She stopped at the mini mart across from the library.

"I went to high school with you," the clerk said when Ellie brought the milk up to the counter.

Dollar bills wouldn't come out of the wallet. Driver's license and coins went skittering along the floor.

"I suppose you don't remember me. Terry. It was Terry Sampson in high school. It's Adams now."

"Terry. Sure. I remember you." She bent down and picked up what had fallen. "All the boys were in love with you."

"I wouldn't go so far as to say that."

Terry was a cheerleader in high school, rah-rah-rah, with long slim legs and permed hair. She used to put her makeup on in home room. Max Factor pancake that she smeared on with a little sponge. And red lipstick, a moist, glossy goo she applied with a brush and then licked to a shine with her tongue. Now she had chunky arms and a thick waist and her legs somehow seemed shorter than they had been in high school. She wasn't wearing any makeup. No Max Factor pancake or gooey lipstick. Just a tired, washed-out, plain-looking face.

"We all called you the brain," Terry said. "I'll bet you didn't know that, that we called you the brain, did you?"

"I didn't know that."

"Weren't you going to be a doctor?"

"I was going to, but I didn't."

"I'll bet you did something important."

"Bookkeeping."

Terry looked disappointed.

It had started to rain. Ellie said she wanted to stay and talk some more, but she was in a hurry to get home and get into bed, she thought she was coming down with something, a cold probably, she was feeling a little light-headed, and it was really nice seeing someone from high school, really nice, and one of these days they'd get together and have coffee and talk over old times.

Terry carried the milk out to the car and waited until Ellie got in, and then handed it to her.

"Cold-Eze," she said and stood in the rain, peering into the car. "It does wonders when you're catching cold. We don't carry it, but you can get some at the drugstore."

She kept staring at Alice.

"My—umm—my—this is Alice," Ellie said.

"Hi," Terry said and Alice smiled at her.

Terry went back into the store, and for a long while Ellie just sat behind the wheel without turning the key.

"I wonder if she knows," she said finally.

"No one knew."

"I'll bet some of them guessed."

"Oh, honey."

Ellie started the car.

"Everyone's been waiting for rain," she said. "And now it won't stop."

"You don't have to go away. You don't know anyone in Seattle."

"Staying here isn't going to work."

There was no traffic. Some RVs heading for Sequoia, bicycles and lawn chairs tied to their roofs, thick tires bulldozing their way through flooded intersections.

"I guess we'd better eat dinner somewhere," Ellie said.

"The milk will spoil."

"It's too cold for the milk to spoil."

Neither of them was hungry, but Ellie said they had to eat, and if the water wasn't turned on in the kitchen when they got back, how were they going to cook anything? It was raining hard now, a blowing rain that shoved at the right side of the car and dripped down the windows as if looking for a way to get in.

"What you need is some hot soup," Alice said. "The Cottage Inn isn't far. We ought to be able to get some soup there."

They used to eat at the Cottage Inn on Sundays after church. Café curtains at the front windows, dried wreaths and Danish plates on the walls. A man named Munson owned it, and there was always lots of cold-country food on the menu. Pork loin stuffed with prunes and apples, Danish meat patties, sautéed flounder, raspberry pudding with almonds and light cream. Their specialty was yellow pea soup that had ham and chunks of pork fat in it.

A bell on the front door jingled as they walked in.

"Rainy out," the waitress said. She had braces on her teeth, pimples on her forehead, and the knee socks she was wearing with her black sneakers had flowers on them that were the same color pink as her uniform.

"Very," said Ellie.

"Too wet for me," Alice added.

They sat at a table near the back wall, a wreath of fir branches and pine cones and red-and-blue plaid ribbons above their heads. The place had changed hands. The menu said Jim and Jean Castle owned it now, both of them graduates of the Cordon Bleu in France. They had left the decor the way it was except for a huge ficus tree in the middle of the restaurant where the iron stove had been. The tree was strung with tiny lights that blinked on and off like summer sparklers. A middle-aged man and a younger woman were seated next to the wall of blue plates, and a plump woman with her little girl were at a table under the arching branches of the electrified ficus tree. The other five tables were empty.

"Take off your sweater," Ellie said. "It's wet."

"It's all right with me if my sweater's wet."

The waitress brought them some water, then took a small white notepad out of the pocket of her pink uniform.

"You guys ready to order?"

"What happened to the pea soup?" Alice said. "It's not on the menu."

"The onion soup is pretty good. If you like onions and cheese in your soup. I never tasted it myself, but lots of people order it. They like it. They come in special to order it." She kept glancing out the window while she was talking. "It's, you know, French."

"I'll have a bowl," Ellie said.

"I suppose I will, too," Alice said.

The waitress put the notepad in her pocket, refilled the water glasses at the other two tables, and then stood at the window peering out into the rain.

There were cellophane-wrapped saltines on the table. Alice unwrapped a packet and the cracker fell into pieces on the tablecloth.

"If you're going to go away, you at least have to let me tell you what happened," she said.

"You don't have to tell me anything, it's all past and I'm getting used to the idea, and it doesn't matter, anyway, what was done was done, and you telling me about it won't undo it."

"That's not the point, undoing the past, who said I wanted to undo the past? Because if I could do that, then you wouldn't be here, and I'm not sorry about that, not sorry one bit, it was the best thing I ever did, having you, and I'm not about to explain that away, and I don't want you to think for one second that I want to explain it away, but I want you to know how it happened. I want you to understand. And I wish you wouldn't look at me as if you hated me."

"I don't hate you."

"Then what is it?"

"Everyone lied to me. And then you—you know, Morty"—she lowered her voice—"the gun and Morty. What I hate is that no one told the truth and now I'm having to deal with you being—you, you know, being—well, I have to deal with that and with Morty being killed because of me, and—"

"Because of you? What gave you the idea it was because of you? It wasn't because of you. It was because he was waving a gun at me and I thought he was going to kill me."

"But it wouldn't have happened if it hadn't been—oh, what's the use?"

"How did I know Morty would tell his son about you, and that he'd want money, and that it would go on and on until Morty decided he didn't want to pay Philip anymore?"

"You see, that's what I mean. You were fighting about me."

"He didn't want to give Philip any more money, he wanted to tell you. I said no, I didn't want him to. We were fighting about money, we weren't fighting about you. I knew you wouldn't understand."

There was no food coming out of the kitchen. Everyone had water and napkins and silverware in front of them, but no food. And Alice was reciting dates and years now, beginning when she was in grammar school, describing what it was like living on an artichoke farm with the nearest neighbor four miles away, and then suddenly turning pretty when she was fifteen and winning the Miss Artichoke contest when she was sixteen, and then the Miss Visalia contest six months later, and then going to San Francisco for the Miss California contest, and then . . .

As far as Ellie was concerned, she had heard enough the night Alice came home from the hospital in a taxi, looking pale and upset and saying she had to come home, she couldn't wait for the doctor to discharge her, there was something important she had to tell Ellie, and before she could say what it was, Rita Brookner appearing at the door. As if it weren't the middle of the night. As if she were an old friend and could barge in anytime she wanted to. She didn't stay long, didn't bother with niceties, didn't say, It's a bitch having to be the bearer of bad news, or, This hurts me as much as it does you. She just came in and sat down, without asking if she could, and lit up a cigarette, without asking if they minded if she smoked, and then she looked Ellie straight in the eye and said it.

Alice isn't your sister, she's your mother. I don't know why the fuck she's been keeping it a secret, but there it is, and Philip won't bother you again.

Then she left, and Alice, without saying a word, went to bed. Ellie couldn't get up off the green velour chair she was sitting in, couldn't raise her arms, couldn't move her feet. Actually couldn't speak. She sat there in the same spot without moving or speaking all night. She tried to arrange her thoughts, but they wouldn't stay arranged. *She's not your sister, she's your mother.* It was like a song. Catchy. Alice came out of the bedroom about four in the morning and tried to explain about Philip wanting more money, about Morty saying he was fed up with the whole thing and was going to tell Ellie the truth. It all sounded like Chinese.

"Dad didn't want me to go to San Francisco for the Miss California pageant," Alice was saying now, "but Mom said there were going to be chaperons, and that I had a good head on my shoulders, and she wasn't worried. Even if Dad had money for a compartment on the train, there weren't any left. There was a war on in Korea. I didn't know anything about it. It was too far away for me to care. Dad managed to get one of the last coach seats for me. It was the first time I had been away from home by myself and I didn't even have a suitcase. I put two changes of underwear, a nightgown, and a sweater in Mom's knitting bag. I had been on a train once in my life before, when Mom and I went to Fresno to visit Aunt Celia. I was five years old. I remember I carried a doll on the train and looked out the window at the telephone poles passing by."

The waitress came away from the window long enough to say she was sure their food would be coming up soon. It was, she murmured, the rain and all that was doing (something mumbly) and did they want some more crackers? Alice said she thought someone had sat on the crackers, they were awful, they were falling apart, and the waitress looked as if she were going to cry, and then she hurried back to the window and stood staring out into the rain again.

"I felt so grown-up in my blue suit and black-and-white spectator pumps," Alice said. "It was dark out, and through the train window, signs and house lights and signals and streetlamps looked like lit matches, lined up, blown out, passed by, and I was so excited, honey, I just couldn't sit still, couldn't concentrate on the magazine I was reading. I decided to go to the club car and get something to eat, but the aisles were so crowded, lots of young boys in uniform sleeping in the aisles or playing cards, that I couldn't make my way through and finally just had to stop. A young marine offered me his seat."

Alice wasn't eating the crackers, merely mashing them with the bowl of her spoon, the way she would if she were going to make a cracker shell for a fruit pie, mashing, then piling up the crumbs and mashing some more.

"The pageant was in the St. Francis, and there weren't enough rooms for all the girls, so we had to split up. I stayed in a hotel on Market Street. It was next door to an all-night movie, twenty dollars a day. I remember every single thing about that room. It had a lamp, a mirrored dresser, and an iron double bed. Neon lights blinked against the window, and there was nowhere to sit except on the bed, which was two steps away from the bathroom. It was a terrible room, with chipped tile around the sink and brown mold growing in the shower. But I thought it was a beautiful room, I thought it was wonderful.

"I didn't win. I didn't even come in third. The marine I met on the train was stationed at Treasure Island. His name was Allen and he was twenty years old. We spent three days together, most of it in that hotel room, in that bed, and I didn't care about anything. I couldn't imagine the future. I couldn't imagine what the next month or the next year would be, and so I lied to Dad, told him I was staying with some girls I had met, that we were having fun sightseeing and riding the cable cars. And I think back and I know I would do it again. I'd do it over and over again, honey. You're here because of it, and I wouldn't change a thing."

The waitress was back. "Umm, gee, umm, you know, I—well, I guess the rain is worse than I thought, you can look outside and see for yourself how bad it is, and, well, umm, the problem is that Jim and Jean aren't here."

"Who are Jim and Jean?" Ellie said.

"Jim and Jean Castle. They're on the menu? They own the place? Well, they do the cooking and they're not here. They went home after lunch and were supposed to be back when we opened again for dinner, but they aren't. They live out near the river, and I keep thinking they might be stuck in a flood somewhere or they would have called."

She was really, really sorry, she said, and really, really embarrassed, especially after taking their order, but it wasn't like Jim and Jean not to show up, all the money they had was in the Cottage Inn, and she supposed they'd have to be drowned because there was no other way to explain it, and she was really, really sorry and was going to tell the other customers how sorry she was and that they'd have to eat somewhere else.

Alice wouldn't hear of it. She said she'd go in the kitchen and cook. She didn't even ask if Ellie wanted to help her, she just got up and told the waitress to come with her. Ellie sat at the table and watched them walk away. Alice had her hand on the waitress's back and was talking soothingly to her, probably telling her it would be all right, everything would be all right, just the same gesture and the same words she used when Jamie died. *It will be all right, honey, everything will be all right.*

And now this. What did Alice expect her to say? That now that she had supplied the details, given a name to the boy, described the hotel room they made love in, Ellie was no longer hurt by all the lies, by having the truth dumped on her by a strange woman, by being made to feel like a fool, like an idiot for not knowing?

The dining room was quiet, a few people waiting to eat, rain splashing the windows, the streetlamps shining on the wet streets and turning them into dark, gleaming pools. Alice had no business saying she'd fill in for the absent owners. She could have a problem with the pacemaker. She could lift a heavy pot and dislodge the wires. She could faint. Ellie got up from the table and went into the kitchen.

Alice looked fine. The waitress was showing her the pantry, the freezer, the vegetables bins, the boxes of fruit, the mixers and graters, the choppers and dicers.

"I won't need too many things," Alice said. "I'm not going to get that fancy. It'll be something quick and easy. What's your name, honey?"

"Dixie. This is really freaky. I don't know what Jim and Jean would say about it."

"They'd say everyone's hungry, so feed them."

Ellie opened the refrigerator. "There's a beef roast."

"Cooked, or raw?" Alice said.

"Cooked."

"Then it's roast beef sandwiches and french fries."

"That isn't what they ordered," Dixie said.

"That's what they're getting," Alice said. "So go out and tell them that."

Ellie poured oil into the pot, turned the burner up high, and began peeling potatoes while Alice sliced the roast.

"She looks too young to be a waitress," Alice said. "Unfinished and gangly. A Cordon Bleu restaurant? I don't think so."

"The lies are what bother me the most," Ellie said. "And Morty, of course. I just can't forget about Morty."

"I hardly remember who I was when I was her age. When I think of what I didn't know it scares me to death."

The waitress was back. "The couple near the wall can't eat french fries."

"What else have we got, Ellie?" Alice said.

Ellie had the pantry doors open.

"Pasta. I can boil up some pasta."

"Olive oil?" Alice said.

"Olive oil," Ellie said, "and garlic."

"I'll tell them," Dixie said, and went out again.

Ellie browned some olive oil and then tossed in some minced garlic. Alice had found some cheese in the refrigerator and a grater.

"All along I knew it was wrong not telling you," Alice said, "but it had started out wrong and there was nothing to do about it but keep going in that wrong direction. Mom thought it was for the best and Dad wouldn't have it any other way. This is the best for the child, he said, and there was no arguing with him when he made up his mind about something. I didn't mean to hurt you. I meant to protect you."

"You meant to protect yourself."

Alice put the bowl of grated cheese on the worktable and began whipping olive oil and egg yolks together.

"You don't have time for fresh mayonnaise," Ellie said.

"I have time. I don't have time for coq au vin, but I have time for fresh mayonnaise."

Dixie stuck her head in the kitchen door, said, "Thank you," in a shivery, relieved little voice, and was gone again.

"The bread is a little on the hard side," Ellie said.

"Try browning it in olive oil," Alice told her.

"It was my life and everyone knew but me."

"I always wanted to tell you, but it was a different time we lived in, and everyone was so ashamed, and there were lies from the beginning to the end, so what were a few more? I went to Fresno and stayed with Aunt Celia, and I had lectures every day for the whole nine months, and I was so alone I thought sometimes I'd die of aloneness and sadness. Is there any lettuce?"

Ellie opened the refrigerator. "I don't see any." She brought out two large tomatoes. "I know what I would have done. I would have stayed. I wouldn't have run away and married the first man who asked me."

"You can say that because this is nineteen ninety-eight."

"The tomatoes look mushy."

"They'll have to do. We can't give them a bare sandwich. It has to have something else besides meat on it."

The bread slices were browning nicely. Ellie turned them over and the oil bubbled on the edges of the crust. She slipped them onto a platter and turned the pasta out of the boiling water into a colander.

"I walk through the house now, and I can't imagine who I was when I lived there, who you were, who Dad and Mom were," Ellie said. "I've lost my bearings. This morning I went out onto the porch and watched the sun come up, and I thought to myself that I was different now that I knew, I'm not the same person I was. I've crossed some sort of line I didn't know existed. Logic tells me it shouldn't matter. But it does. It matters. How could you do it? Your own child? How could you leave me to be raised by grandparents and not know you, not know that you were my mother? How could you have done that to me?"

She opened the pantry again and took out a jar of relish. The pasta was in the skillet, coated with cheese and olive oil and garlic. She pulled the basket of fries up out of the oil and salted them.

"But I always came back to see you," Alice said, "and I knew you were well taken care of. What difference does it make anymore what happened in the past, what I did, what Mom and Dad did, what anyone said or thought? We all loved you."

The ranch road was passable, although every once in a while the car would hit a flooded spot that threw water up over the hood of the car. Ellie drove slowly. Alice had her window open and was watching out for debris that had washed down from the highway.

They had stayed at the Cottage Inn until ten-thirty. A few more customers came in once the rain let up, but at nine-thirty Ellie told Dixie to put the CLOSED sign on the window and she'd help her clean the kitchen and load the dishwasher. At ten o'clock Jim and Jean Castle arrived on the big red fire truck that had pulled them out of their car in a flooded wash near the Kaweah River. They were wrapped in blankets and had lost their shoes. The newspaper reporter wouldn't let them come in out of the rain until he took a picture of them sitting on the back of the fire truck.

The house was dark, locked up. The workmen were neat. Tony said he wouldn't work with any crew that didn't clean up as they went along. The water was on in the kitchen. Alice sat down at the table while Ellie brought her a glass of water and her medicine.

"I think you overdid it tonight, standing on your feet, rushing around."

"I enjoyed it," Alice said.

The light fixture in the hall was gone, the new one hadn't been put in yet. Ellie held Alice's hand and they groped their way toward Alice's bedroom. She wanted to give Ellie something, she said.

It was a small metal box with leather straps. Inside were a silver bracelet, a lipstick with a mirror on one side, a silk scarf, a bottle of perfume that had never been opened, a pair of earrings with blue stones in them, a packet of letters tied with a white grosgrain ribbon, and three photographs, two of them of Alice and a dark-haired man standing next to a cable car and one of the same dark-haired man alone, sitting on a lawn somewhere, his knees up, arms resting on them, his curly hair mussed up as if he had been lying on the grass asleep and sat up to have his picture taken. Ellie turned the photograph over. *March, 1953. Allen.*

"I *am* tired," Alice said. She took off her shoes and got under the covers.

That was where the dimple came from. From Allen. Ellie put her finger to the indentation in her cheek. And her deep-set eyes.

"He was very handsome," she said, and carefully put everything back in the box.

"Yes, he was."

"Are you cold?"

"A little."

The air-conditioning and heating man hadn't finished the ductwork yet, and the stonemason said not to use the fireplace until he repaired the flue. Alice had a portable heater in her room. Ellie turned it on and then sat down on the bed and rubbed Alice's feet.

"You are my sweetheart, you know," Alice said.

Ellie brought the quilt up around Alice's shoulders and turned off the bedside lamp and lay down beside her. It was raining hard again, the house sighing and creaking as if it were trying to break free.

"Why didn't you marry him?"

"He was killed in Korea a few days before the cease-fire. You were born two months later."

Ellie knew Alice's smell, of talc and ivory soap. She put her arms around her and lay her head in the spot between Alice's collarbone and soft bosom.

"I've always thought of you as my daughter," Alice said, "even if I never said it."

Chapter 22

Troy usually slept until at least seven, but here he was in the kitchen at six o'clock in his bare feet, rubbing sleep from his eyes. It was October and although the days were still bright and sunny, there was a chill in the house in the early morning.

"Where are your slippers?" Teo said. They were alligator slippers, green rabbit fur with blue button eyes and cloth teeth.

"I can't find them."

"Did you look under your bed?"

"It's dark under my bed." He was wearing Mickey Mouse pajamas. Teo had wanted to buy him plain pajamas in a solid color, but they didn't make pajamas in solid colors for four-year-olds. And Teo shouldn't have listened to the clerk, who said she thought Troy looked like a size four. The size four pajamas were too big, the arms hanging over his fingers and the legs drooping over his bare feet and puddling on the floor.

"We'll look for them after breakfast."

Teo had been up since five. He had dreamed of Ellie and it woke him up, and then he couldn't remember what the dream was, so he came into the kitchen, made a pot of coffee, and sat at the table and waited for the sun to come up.

"They're gone."

"They're not gone. They're probably in your closet."

Teo had taken Troy to Mervyn's in Santa Ana and bought the slippers along with three pairs of the size four Mickey Mouse pajamas and five pairs of size four jeans (not only too long in the leg, but so wide in the waist that Troy couldn't keep them up; Teo took them over to the cleaners on First Street and had the waists taken in and the legs shortened), and six T-shirts (they drooped off his thin shoulders and looked as if they were meant for a ten-year-old), and a jacket (so bulky that when it was buttoned up the woolly collar covered his chin and most of his nose, so that all you saw were his eyes), and a pair of sneakers (they were the only item Troy tried on in the store, and they fit), and ankle socks that came up to his knees.

"I lost them." He held his right hand to his mouth. He had been doing that lately, holding his mouth when he was about to cry. He had started crying the past few weeks, crying for hardly any reason at all, like not being able to find his slippers.

"You didn't lose them. They're in the house somewhere. And it doesn't matter if they aren't. They're just slippers. Okay? I don't care if you lost them. I'll buy you another pair. Now sit down and I'll make you some breakfast. No crying. Come on. You'll be wheezing if you keep that up."

Troy cried without noise. It was unnerving how he did that, just tears rolling down his face and no sound.

"Okay, let's look for the slippers. Get the flashlight out of the drawer."

They went through the house, in and out of every room, opening drawers and looking under beds and into closets, Troy holding the flashlight in both hands and aiming it out in front of him. The slippers were in the back bathroom next to the tub.

"I told you they were in the house," Teo said, and he sat Troy down on the sink and rolled up his pajama legs and put on his slippers and then carried him into the kitchen.

"You have to ask yourself some questions when you can't find something," Teo said.

He poured some Cheerios into a bowl and added milk.

"Do you want a banana?"

"Uh-uh."

"The way a policeman does it, he asks himself if he took the slippers anywhere."

Troy nodded his head.

"You weren't outside, were you?"

"No."

"Then they couldn't be outside, could they?"

"Uh-uh."

"So then you have to ask yourself where you were the last time you saw the slippers."

"In the bathroom," Troy said and smiled.

"In the bathroom," Teo said. Troy was playing with the cereal, poking at the floating Cheerios with his spoon and occasionally putting a spoonful in his mouth. "Another mystery solved."

There wasn't going to be much sun today. The trees in the backyard had lost their leaves, and skeletal limbs swayed in the wind, their sharp tips snagging the kitchen window and tracing spidery lines in the glass. Teo hadn't torn any months off the wall calendar next to the sink since August. It was a Police Association calendar, and August had a policeman and policewoman in full uniform, including caps and badges, sitting under an umbrella on a tropical beach.

"Eat your breakfast," Teo said, and went into the living room and dialed Estella's number.

"I have to talk to you, it's important," he said.

"You read my mind," she said. "I want to talk to you, too. Where have you been, anyway? I've been trying to reach you all week and all I get is the machine, and you don't call me back, it's really frustrating, Teo, it really is. What are you doing that's so important you can't call me back when I leave messages? I must have left fourteen. Twelve, anyway."

"Troy's had doctor appointments all week. Asthma doctor, eye doctor, hearing doctor."

"Are you trying to make me feel guilty?"

"I'm not trying to do anything. You asked me a question and I answered you."

"Don't snap."

"I'm not snapping."

"I know when you're snapping and when you're not snapping. I'm not in the mood for any snapping, Teo. I'm nearly destroyed, is what I am. Can you come by the school this afternoon? I've got a half hour free between two and two-thirty. Derek's seeing a psychotherapist and I've got a four o'clock appointment. I have to pick him up at his school and there might be traffic, and I just don't have the time to drive all the way to Santa Ana. Oh God, Teo, I could write a book about everything's that happened, but no one would believe it. They'd say I made it up. Two o'clock, at the school, I'll meet you downstairs and I'll tell you everything, that is, if I can do it without breaking apart, because it's so shattering, so embarrassing, so humiliating I don't even know where I'll begin."

The Briar Middle School was twenty minutes from Santa Ana, on the other side of the barrio, at the edge of a brand-new pink-roofed housing development. Troy looked anxiously out the car window the whole way and when they got there he took hold of Teo's pants leg and wouldn't give Estella a hug, even though she was kneeling down next to him and telling him how happy she was to see him, in a voice two tones higher than she usually used.

"He gets this way," Teo said and picked him up. The boy's straight, soft hair brushed back and forth against Teo's neck. "It's nothing personal."

They walked up the school stairs to the teachers' lounge, Teo carrying Troy, Estella discoursing on the shyness study she had just read in *National Teacher* that concluded that shyness was biological, innate, had nothing to do with parenting, and how could that be true when anyone with half a brain could see that Roxana was the reason Troy was the way he was, you didn't need a study to figure that one out.

The teachers' lounge was a brightly lit rectangular room crammed with old Formica tables and vinyl chairs. Student artwork and pictures of dead presidents hung on the white walls, and in a corner near the window a refrigerator hummed between the steel sink and a card table littered with used paper cups and empty sugar packets. Troy tightened his arms around Teo's neck.

"There's orange juice in the refrigerator," Estella said. "Would you like some juice, Troy?"

"Uh-uh."

"He likes to draw," Teo said.

Estella found a sheet of poster paper and colored chalk in the utility closet. She put it on a table across the room, and Teo carried Troy over there and sat him down and promised he wasn't going to leave, he'd be right over near the door; all Troy had to do was look up and he could see him.

"I don't think it's shyness at all," Estella said. "I think he's scared to death."

"Maybe he is," Teo said.

Teo poured himself a cup of coffee and Estella asked him if he wanted a doughnut to go with it; she had brought a box of doughnuts to school that morning and there were still four or five left of the kind he liked, didn't he always like jelly doughnuts, and Teo said it had been years since he had had a jelly doughnut, that the coffee (which tasted bitter and had an oily film floating on top) was good enough, he wasn't hungry, and he sat down across from her at one of the Formica tables.

"I didn't know you were going to bring him, I had no idea you'd bring him."

"What did you want me to do with him?"

"I just didn't think you'd bring him. He looks so sickly."

"He's not sickly. He's got problems."

"But he doesn't talk at all."

"He doesn't have anything to say."

"That isn't funny."

"I didn't mean it to be funny."

In the bright light of the room she looked haggard, and now her eyes were dripping tears.

Teo put his hand on her shoulder. "Come on, Estella, don't do that."

"It's so awful, Teo."

The door swung open and a woman in a long peasant skirt and baggy sweater came in and poured herself a cup of coffee. Estella put a paper napkin to her face as if she were going to blow her nose and kept it there until the woman left.

"Look, he's okay, he's all right, stop crying," Teo said.

Estella shook her head. "It's not him. I'm not crying over him. Oscar's gone."

Teo leaned back in the chair. It was solid wood, built for rough handling, with legs that were too short for someone as tall as he was. Troy was engrossed in what he was drawing, his left ear (the one with the hearing aid in it) nearly touching the paper, right arm flat on the table, just the hand holding the crayon moving back and forth.

"I'm absolutely in a living hell, Teo. You just don't understand how it is. My life is shit. I was thinking back this morning about when we were all at home. Remember the dog Raul picked up off the street?"

"The one that ate the lawn furniture?"

"He didn't eat it. He just gnawed at it a little bit, and Pa got mad and took him out to South Gate and left him there. I feel just like that dog, like Oscar's taken me out to South Gate the way Pa took that dog."

"When did he leave?"

"Last week. I tried to call you. Fourteen times I left messages."

"You said twelve."

"Don't be so literal."

"You're better off."

"You can say that because you don't know how much I love him. Not that I want him back. I don't. It's just that you don't shut off love the way you do a faucet. It won't shut off. With all he's done, I still love him. And he gives me plenty of reason to hate him. You don't know the awful thing he's done, Teo. It's horrible, just horrible."

"So can I leave Troy with you while I go up to Visalia?" he said when she paused for breath.

"Just horrible," she said again. "You have no idea what I'm going through, Teo. Oscar and I are definitely finished."

"He'll apologize next week and you'll take him back. Meanwhile I need a favor."

"You're wrong. There's nothing he could do or say that would make me take him back, not after what he's done, not after what he said to me. The machinery's in motion, Teo, I'm not turning back, not this time. I've been running to banks and accountants and attorneys all week, you'd be proud of me the way I'm taking care of things, being efficient, being calm, just doing what I have to do. You'd think there were millions involved instead of just a house and a few mutual funds and fifteen hundred dollars in a savings account. I felt terrible taking the money out, like a thief, but my attorney says that's the way it's done, the first one to the bank gets the money, and Oscar would have taken it if he had a chance, I just got there first." She blew her nose into the napkin. "I don't think I've been happy since the day I got married. Were you ever happy with Bonnie? I mean really, truly happy?"

"It was too long ago. Sure. Maybe. So can you do me a favor and watch Troy while I go up to Visalia for a few days?"

"Visalia? What are you going to do up there? Why can't you take him with you?"

"Because I don't want to. Because it's personal business. I want to see someone there. A woman I met."

"You met someone? You never go anywhere. How could you meet someone? Is she Mexican? She isn't another one like Bonnie, is she? Anglos don't understand us, Teo. You have to be careful. Everyone says there's no tension, but there is. I feel it everywhere, even here with the other teachers. It's just oil and water, Teo, and you know how that goes."

"Oscar's Mexican, and you two have been at each other's throats since the day of the wedding."

"That isn't what I'm talking about. Culture and lifestyle are what I'm talking about. You know exactly what I mean."

"Bonnie's a whore. It has nothing to do with culture. So can you take him?"

"Weren't you listening to what I told you about all the things I have to do and places I have to go to take care of myself, to make sure Oscar doesn't get everything?"

"I heard every word."

"Then how can you ask me to take on another problem?"

"Jesus, Estella, what has Oscar got to do with you taking care of Troy for a few days? I'll leave on Friday night and be back Sunday."

"I don't know how many ways I can tell you what a mess I'm in, it takes all my energy to keep myself from falling apart, to concentrate on getting up in the morning. I know you don't want to hear about it, how I don't sleep nights. Look at my hand." She held her hand out in front of her. She had thin fingers and a flat hand that didn't curve or dip the way most hands did. The tips of the fingers, nails filed straight across, made little fluttery stabs at the air. "And Derek is acting out, punishing me for Oscar leaving, as if I could have stopped him. He goes around locking doors. He locked me out of the house last night. I had to climb in a window. I'm afraid he'll do something terrible. How could I bring a sick little boy home when Derek is so full of hostility that I don't know what he's going to do? And Angie is sleeping with her boyfriend, and I'm so afraid she'll get pregnant. I asked her if she's using protection, and she said she didn't have to tell me about her personal life. Her personal life, Teo. Her personal life. I struggled so hard to keep her from making the same mistakes I made, and she tells me it's her personal life. She won't tell me where she goes at night, and she blames me for everything, that her teeth are crooked after four years of braces and that her hair is curly instead of straight and that she's not good in math. But that's not the worst thing. You can't imagine what's happened, something awful, Teo, something terrible."

"She's not sick, is she?"

"Angie? I'm not talking about Angie." She took a few deep breaths and pressed her thin flat hand against her forehead. "I'm girding myself, because I'm having a hard time dealing with it, and I have to tell you, because you ought to know, and I don't think you should go up to Visalia to see any woman about anything when you're just getting over your wife leaving you, because it's so complicated, and maybe you'll change your mind after I tell you."

"Jesus, Estella, Bonnie isn't my wife. And if she told you she wants to come back, forget it. It's not going to happen."

"I don't know how you can be so flip over someone you once loved when I'm so upset over Oscar I can't even think straight. I've been crying nonstop all week. I keep reliving what Oscar said to me. I don't even want to tell you about it, it's too terrible, too emotionally draining."

"Then don't tell me. If you don't want to, I don't want to hear it. I just want to know if you'll take care of Troy for the weekend."

"I can't. I'm an emotional wreck. I can hardly keep myself together, and Oscar did the worst thing, Teo, I didn't think he could do any worse than he's done already, but he has, and it's disgusting, with his own sister-in-law, and it wasn't the first time. He told me when you two were first married that he and Bonnie—"

"Oscar and Bonnie?" Teo said.

"Oscar and Bonnie."

He dropped his head back and laughed out loud. "That's the funniest fucking thing I've ever heard."

"Don't you care? Your own wife and my husband?"

"She's not my wife, Estella. And no, I don't care. I've got a kid on my hands I'm trying to get rid of, and no one wants him."

"Don't say that."

"It's the truth."

"And I don't know how you can laugh at me when I'm in such pain."

"Because it's crazy, that's why. It's like we're in a funhouse somewhere, wandering around, bumping into walls trying to find our way out, and all we get is a bloody nose for our efforts. And don't tell me Oscar's going to put her in the movies."

"He says he loves her, that he didn't realize all these years that that's why he was so miserable, was because he loved Bonnie."

"Jesus."

"She called up one night and I answered the phone. She said she had a flat tire on Harbor Boulevard and needed Oscar to change it. I should have hung up on her, told her to call the Triple A, told her Oscar was taking a shower, that he had a cold, that he had pneumonia. I've thought about all the things I should have said or done to keep him from driving up to Harbor Boulevard. But I didn't do anything, because I was stupid and didn't understand what was happening. Two days later he told me he was moving in with her. Just like that. He said he'd never been so happy with anyone in his whole life. I said what about me, what were all these years about, putting up with you, and he said they were just years, that I didn't give him what he needed, I had no passion, didn't let him breathe, that I was too serious about life and didn't know how to lighten up, didn't know how to kick back and let myself go. I said I've got enough passion for three women and hit him in the face. He hit me back. It was the first time he ever did that. I couldn't believe it. Then he called me a cunt, and I called him a bastard, and those were the last words we said to each other. Bonnie was in the car waiting for him when he walked out the door."

"Your husband is a fuck-off, always was, always will be," Teo said.

Estella told him not to say things like that, that Oscar had his good points, he wasn't all bad, he was a good father to Angie, and she wasn't even his, and it wasn't his fault that Derek took after Oscar's cousin, who had to take Ritalin every day and wouldn't have shot the policeman if he had been normal, and he was upset when he said what he said to her, who wouldn't be, he was just trying to hide his humiliation at running off with his sister-in-law.

"She's not his sister-in-law anymore, Estella, and I'm not surprised about the two of them hooking up. It fits. It's so logical that if I had cared enough to sit down and give it some thought, that's the way I would have figured it."

That shut her up. She was silent. Thinking. Or maybe just in a trance. Biting her lip and staring at the refrigerator. Then suddenly she was on her feet, saying she was late, she had a staff meeting, said she'd certainly take Troy if she didn't have Derek to worry about, she was picking him up from school at three and taking him to his therapist's appointment, because the lawyer said she'd better be pro active if she wanted custody, and Derek may be a handful but she wasn't going to let him go off with

Oscar and Bonnie, no way would she let him be raised by Bonnie, not that Oscar and Bonnie would stay together, there was no chance of that.

"Don't be stubborn, call Raul," Luci said on the phone. "If you explain what's happened, I'm sure he'll take Troy for a while. He might even keep him. I think this thing between the two of you has gone on long enough. He's your brother, Teo, where's your Christian charity?"

"I'm fresh out," Teo told her.

"Give Raul a call," Jose said on the phone. "What happened between you should be buried. It's over, Teo. Forget it."

Easy for Jose to say. He was only ten during the Vietnam War. He hadn't done two tours like Teo did and then have to come back and see Raul's picture in the paper every day protesting the war, leading marches on Washington, parading down Pennsylvania Avenue in tattered uniform and combat boots, shouting antiwar slogans, his hair as long as a girl's, looking like a goddamn hippie, like a goddamn traitor. And then that flag burning in 1971 on the steps of the Jefferson Memorial. Looking back later, Teo realized he had been set up, that the *Times* wanted a story about two soldier brothers, one for the war and one against, so they flew Teo up to Washington to confront Raul, and he confronted him all right. Maybe if he had gotten there when the flag had already burned to ashes instead of seeing it flame and curl and shrivel up when Raul touched the cigarette lighter to one corner of it, he wouldn't have gone crazy the way he did. But he had to watch it burn and he just lost it. Ma saw the picture in the paper the next day of Teo trying to strangle his brother on the steps of the Jefferson Memorial and had her first heart attack.

Teo looked at the phone a long time before he dialed the number, and when he did it was in a rush, his finger punching the number out so fast he hoped he'd get it wrong and someone else's brother would answer. Then the phone was ringing, and he could have hung up then, but he thought maybe he'd be lucky and Raul's wife, Cindy, would answer. He wouldn't have to say much. I'm thinking of putting Troy into foster care, he'd tell her. That is, unless you and Raul will take him off my hands.

Raul answered. Voices don't age as much as faces. They deepen, turn mellow but less fine. Tones wander, spread apart, words sometimes fall between breaths and are lost. But you can always recognize them. Raul's voice hadn't aged at all. His "hello" still had the same youthful liveliness, the same anticipation as it did the last time Teo talked to him twenty-six years before.

"Who is this?" A clock was ticking somewhere in the background and Raul's mouth was so close to the receiver Teo could hear the whoosh of air as he breathed in and out.

"Who is this?" Raul said again, impatiently this time.

"It's me," Teo told him.

Chapter 23
🦢

Teo recognized the flat landscape of Texas below the plane. And then they were on the ground and the stewardess was asking how Troy was feeling, if he was all right, if he wanted some more 7UP before he got off the plane, or how about a few packages of crackers to take with him?

"We have loads of crackers left," she said.

"No, that's okay," Teo told her.

About an hour out of Los Angeles Troy had vomited in the aisle next to his seat, just leaned over without saying he was going to or that he felt sick, and let it go, and you'd think he had deposited a pile of gold on the airplane carpet the way the stewardesses fussed over him afterward, bringing him 7UP and crackers and ice and a cold wet towel, and now the head stewardess had come over and was kneeling down in the aisle (the older one, with the thirty-year button on her lapel), giving Troy a hug and telling him to have a good time in Texas and to be sure and tell his daddy to keep flying United.

Raul was waiting in the airport lounge. He came out of the crush of people and for a moment Teo thought it was Pa coming toward him. He was taller than Pa had been, and thinner, but his face was Pa's, right down to the stubborn chin and wiry gray hair.

"There are complications," Raul said as he picked up the bag that had Troy's clothes and medicine in it. "How did he do on the plane?"

"He vomited," Teo said. "What do you mean, complications?"

"I'll explain on the way."

Teo could have said hey, wait, what the hell are you doing, going back on what you said, thinking because I came here that everything was all right between us, everything forgiven and forgotten, and you can push me around the way you did when I was a kid? But he didn't. Just the idea of saying it tired him out.

Raul drove a pickup. Teo never would have pictured Raul in a pickup. Pickups were for farmers hauling feed sacks and fertilizer, for militiamen who mounted their rifles in the rear windows and chained their monstrous no-breed dogs to their citizen band antennas. Raul's last car when he was still living at home was a Firebird bought from L.A. Wrecking that Raul and Teo rebuilt in the alley behind the house in Santa Ana, a mustard-colored Firebird with wire wheels and a sleek, sloping nose that Raul covered with a horse blanket at night and wiped off every morning.

"The editor of the daily paper in Guatemala City is crossing the Rio Grande today with his wife," Raul said and threw Troy's bag into the bed of the pickup. "I was stopped in the airport before I picked you up. This INS guy asks me where I'm going, who I'm meeting, all that shit, so I can't take Troy after all. The editor called from Matamoros this morning, panicked, thinking I wasn't coming, that I'd just leave him sucking his thumb in Mexico, because he heard I was under surveillance, and I told him to sit tight, I hadn't forgotten him. Anyway, it's pretty complicated. I live from crisis to crisis. Immigration watches my house. I don't think Troy ought to be here."

They were out of the airport circle now, on the expressway. Raul drove fast, his elbow sticking out the open window and his fingers resting lightly on the steering wheel. He had been a drag racer in his teens, took his souped-up car out to the California desert and opened it up to 110, won some races, never had an accident, and then one day said he wasn't interested in cars anymore and said he thought he'd go into the priesthood. Instead he joined the army.

"You said you'd take him."

"It wouldn't be smart right now."

"I was depending on it. I should have known better."

"Maybe you should have questioned me more closely, asked me what I was doing, whether it was really a good idea to bring him here."

"You shouldn't have said you would."

"I wanted to see you. It's been a long time. Maybe I thought I could help you. I wanted to help you. You look good. Healthy. Luci said you're still on disability."

"Yeah. Well, Troy's wheezing, so stop the car."

Raul made a U-turn and pulled into a gas station.

"Five minutes," he said.

The restroom was locked. The attendant came out of the booth and unlocked it.

"I don't want to stay in Texas," Troy said as Teo sat him down on the lip of the sink.

The medicine was flowing into the mask. No talking now, just medicated mist and Troy's face relaxing. Someone had bled in here. There were bloody wadded-up paper towels on the cement floor. Teo felt like punching something.

"Feeling better?"

Troy nodded his head.

"Then we better go."

Raul had gassed up the pickup and started the engine.

"The situation in Guatemala sucks. The editor was shot at in his office putting out his newspaper. Who can wait for amnesty hearings when people are shooting at you?"

They were in downtown Brownsville now and Troy had fallen asleep on the seat between them.

"I don't think Roxana's ever going to come for him," Raul said. He glanced at Teo often while he was driving, as if he didn't need to look out the windshield to know where he was going. "You'd better not depend on her turning up and wanting him back. She called me from Alaska."

"She called you?"

"The connection was bad. I couldn't hear anything she said. The operator asked if I'd take a collect call from my sister in Alaska, and I said yes. After that all I got was static."

"You know, you haven't changed. You make promises, you say you're going to do something, and then you fuck off, you've got an excuse, it's not convenient, I should have asked you this and asked you that. Jesus."

"You're never going to stop fighting the war, are you?"

"You didn't have to march in your uniform. You didn't have to burn the flag."

"I didn't do it to spite you. I was making a point. I could have wiped my ass with the flag. Instead I decided to burn it. It got in the paper, and that's all I wanted to do was something outrageous enough to get in the newspapers. It was just a piece of cloth."

"Yeah, and I saw coffins with shit smeared on them in San Francisco. They were just wood with bits of flesh inside."

"You think I wasn't spat on coming home? One day I'm hip deep in mud in the jungle, and the next day I'm in the San Francisco airport getting spat on and cursed. So what? The trouble with you is you've never really taken a stand on anything. I'm waiting for that day, when you make up your mind you really want something, really want to do it, and then go ahead without thinking about what it's going to mean, what you're risking, what you might lose, and just do it. You let me push you into joining the army and you didn't waver when you got out, you didn't question, you just stuck. Well, I didn't."

Raul pulled into a grove of trees and parked a few yards away from the river, a sluggish-at-its-borders, churned-up-in-the-center stripe of mud-colored water. People were wading across from Matamoros, some of them in slacks and clean white shirts, some with bundles on their heads and children in their arms, stepping carefully, calling to one another in Spanish, voices echoing from one side of the river to the other. *Watch out, the middle is deep, it can trick you, it can catch you, it can pull you down, hold the children high, watch your feet, don't fall, keep going, it's close, we're almost there.* Some were floating across in inner tubes, arms and legs looped over half-inflated rubber. The air was moist with droplets of stinking river water, both banks slick and slimy. Not even flotillas of inner tubes could turn it into a pretty stream. It was an industrial ditch, a polluted hole, an odorous germ-filled pit to be swum over, under, and through, to be outmaneuvered and outwitted. And yet people kept coming, innocent faces, smiling, thinking it wasn't that far, they could cross in two minutes. *You hold the package, I'll hold the baby.* As if they were on a picnic, as if this sump of a river were a sylvan lake and on a whim they had decided to test its depths. Or as if they had a sudden urge to wade into deep water, on a lark, as a game, for the fun of it, as if it were a hot day in August instead of a chilly one in October, as if *la migra* weren't watching from downstream and wouldn't chase them and arrest them and send them back across.

"There he is, the editor, over there," Raul said.

The editor was in a suit and tie and his wife had on a white silk dress with a string of pearls around her neck.

"Wait here." Raul got out of the pickup and headed toward the river.

The editor had stepped into the brown water, and it was comical, watching his tie float up in front of his face. He had hold of his wife's hand, urging her in Spanish to come in.

"Just do it, just start, it's easy, look at me, there's nothing to it."

"My shoes will get wet."

"Take them off."

She took off her shoes (black high-heeled pumps) and held them in her hand.

"It's not deep, is it?" she said. The skirt of her white dress swirled up around her waist and flared out on the surface of the water like a silken parachute.

"My shoes, I dropped my shoes." She pawed at the water, dug at it with her manicured fingers, made circular sweeps in it that rippled out around her.

"I'll buy you new shoes, *querida,* just come, we'll walk across together. I can feel the bottom here. It's shallow. Take my hand."

There was a glare on the water, a mirror shine that blinded Teo for a moment, and then he saw her fall. And then her husband fell, and the water gathered them in and, like a sated beast, turned placid again. It was as if the editor and his wife had never been there, had never stepped into the water in their stocking feet.

The border patrol bus had come upriver and stopped along the muddy bank. Every seat in it was full and there were people with dirt-stained faces leaning out of the open windows. The border patrol agent got off the bus. Raul was already swimming.

How long had it been? Ten seconds? A minute?

Raul had the editor by his necktie and was towing him toward shore, and the border patrol agent had his cell phone out and there was no sign of the woman.

How many laps did you do today? Pa would ask Teo when he came home from school. *Do you know I learned to swim crossing the river in Brownsville?*

Troy was still sleeping, curled up on the seat. Teo got out of the pickup, hesitated a moment, and then began running along the bank toward the spot he had seen the woman's head go under.

The water was cold and he couldn't find his way in the murk, and his eyes filled with grit, and he felt as if he were swimming in circles. He heard people shouting at him that she was over there, no, she was over here, no, not there, in the middle, no, near the bank, no, that's too far, she's over there, on that side, can't you see her, what's the matter with you, save her, you idiot, you dolt, you stupid. Then he felt a tangle of cloth, thicker than it had looked spread out on the water, and he dived down and tugged at it, felt his nostrils fill with mud as he tried to pull the cloth free, but it was caught on something sharp and sleek, and he tried to rip it away, but it wouldn't rip, it was made too well, the best silk, the sturdiest fabric. Raul was swimming alongside, trying to help, and then the border agent was in the water, and he had a knife that could cut through rope. When they finally brought the editor's wife up she wasn't breathing.

There was nowhere to go. Just stand outside the border station in his wet clothes, Troy in his arms, and wait for Raul. He was inside with the editor and a priest and a lawyer. The editor's wife was on a table in one of the inside offices, lying on her back, her hands clasped on her chest as if she were praying. Anyone passing the front door could look in and see her, could check the chipped fingernails and the mud-caked feet and the beads of sand glistening like tears on her eyelashes.

"Is she sleeping?" Troy said. His heart was beating fast against Teo's chest.

"Kind of sleeping."

Teo recognized her from somewhere, some Mexican television commercial advertising a face cream. *Look at my face, look at how the skin glows, how there are no wrinkles, no marks, no spots. Would you believe I'm forty-five?* Now her skin looked like crumpled dirty paper.

"Why is she sleeping?" Troy said.

"She's tired."

Troy was wheezing, stretching his neck the way he did when air was scarce. Teo rubbed his slender back, up and down against the small shoulder blades, then carried him away from the door so the editor's wife was no longer visible.

"But why is she sleeping on a table?" Troy said.

"Because she's very, very tried," Teo told him. "Look up in the sky, Troy, at the birds."

Screeching grackles were flying in a dark cloud over the river. Hundreds had already roosted in the live oak trees to the west of the border station. Trees shuddered and swayed under their weight. Teo put the boy down and watched him run after the birds. He was laughing, holding his hands out, his narrow feet awkwardly pounding the ground as he ran. He was not a perfect boy. There was no mistake about that. He was sick and nearsighted and hard of hearing, and maybe everything that had happened to him would stunt his growth and ruin his future. But there was also joy in him and life, and Teo was sick of death and dying. It didn't matter whether anyone else wanted him or not. Teo wanted him. It was as simple as that.

The editor's grief filled the pickup. He sat silently, tears rolling down his face onto his mud-caked trousers as Raul drove. The road to the ranch was dark, not a sign or a house for the past half hour, and then suddenly up ahead in the pickup's headlights was the ranch gate. Teo had been to the ranch once, right after his first tour of duty in Vietnam. Cindy's great-grandfather came from Germany in 1868 and bought the place from a Civil War vet, and by the time Cindy's father died the ranch was the biggest one in Harlingen, with a landing strip for small planes and a rodeo ring and a herd of longhorns roaming over six hundred acres. When Raul came out of the army and began protesting the war, Pa said it was because Cindy was a communist and had made Raul one. Ma always liked Cindy; she said she was gentle and kind and took the Ten Commandments seriously. A brainy girl, Estella said when Raul brought her home the very first time, and she's rich, but she's not very pretty and she isn't Mexican.

Cindy was waiting at the gate in a red Jeep.

"We got him an amnesty hearing," Raul told her. "But he wants to go to Canada."

Cindy had brought a blanket out of the Jeep. She draped it over the editor's shoulders.

"We could drive him to San Antonio tonight," she said. "There's a ten o'clock flight." She smiled at Troy. "Aren't you a good little boy?" she said. In the gate lights she looked middle-aged and heavy. She and Raul moved to the front of the pickup, stood in the beam of the headlights, talking.

"I'm sorry about your wife," Teo said to the editor.

"Yes," he said.

Something had been settled between Raul and Cindy, some arrangements, some plan. She came back to the driver's side and helped the editor out of the pickup and walked him to the Jeep. Raul came over to the side door and handed Teo his keys.

"Drive back to the airport. Park in the public parking lot and leave the keys under the seat. I'd have asked you to stay for a while, but you can see how it is. It just didn't work today. Sometimes no matter how hard you try it doesn't work. You couldn't save her. No one could save her, but I'm glad you were here."

Then he leaned into the cab of the pickup and kissed Teo's cheek and told him to take good care of Troy.

Chapter 24

✑

I t was the middle of the night when Roxana arrived. Teo heard a car door slam and voices (*That'll be eight ninety. Here's ten, keep the change*) and then footsteps on the walk. He opened the door as the cab drove away. Roxana was sitting on the steps, a small suitcase next to her, and she didn't make a move to come into the house, didn't even stand up or look as if she was going to.

"I'm as cold as I've ever been in my life," she said. "I'm really hot, but I feel cold. And I don't know what happened to my legs, Teo, but they gave out at the airport, just bam, and I was on the floor. And there I was being wheeled to a cab in a wheelchair, like an old lady. I can usually walk fine, there's nothing wrong with my walking. I guess I was just tired. I can walk as good as anyone."

He used to carry her around when she was a baby. *Back, back,* she'd say, and he'd put her on his back and pretend he was a horse, and she'd slap his neck with her baby hands and laugh and laugh. He picked her up now, easily, as if she were three years old, and carried her into the house and put her on the couch.

"Well, here I am," she said. She was wrapped in layers of clothing, a long wool skirt, sweater, jacket, coat. A turban that looked like a big powdered-sugar doughnut was pulled clear down to her ears, with only a few stray wisps of hair sticking out. She took off the jacket and coat and dropped them on the floor next to the couch, but didn't take off the turban.

"Same old house," she said. "Same old couch." She gave a delicate cough, her hand in front of her mouth. "Can you get my cigarettes out of my bag? You can't believe it, Teo, seven and a half hours on airplanes without a smoke. I puffed my last in Juneau. Raul told you I was in Alaska?"

"He told me."

She was thinner than Teo had ever seen her. Her face had lost its roundness, the soft chin gone, her cheekbones like two sharp shelves beneath eyes that seemed too large for her face.

"You can't fly straight through," she said. "I asked the steward in Ketchikan if we were going to ever take off again, if I could just have a smoke because we were on the ground and what harm would it do, and he said the FAA could smell the smoke. Like the FAA was a person or something." She lit a cigarette, took a deep drag, and snuggled into the sofa cushions. "Juneau to Ketchikan to Anchorage to L.A. Andy arranged it. He runs the Polar Bear Inn in Juneau, fourteen rooms and a bar. He drove me to the airport and said he'd be waiting by the window for me when I came back. Isn't that sweet, Teo, saying he'd be waiting by the window, like some old corny movie? He's fifty-eight and was never married, and he wants to marry me. I told him no. Can you imagine me marrying anyone? But we're as good as. You should see the way he looks at me, like he's never seen a girl before. We don't do much fucking. He's not all that interested in doing it, and I end up coughing in the middle, anyway. Can you make me some hot tea?"

He found an unopened box of tea bags in a drawer in the kitchen, along with glass stirrers and measuring spoons and nesting cups that Estella must have bought. The plant she had stuck on the windowsill and watered every morning before she went to work was dead and dropping dark brown leaves into the sink. Estella was gone and now here was Roxana, coming home because she was sick and because, no matter what kind of romantic story she told about the guy in Alaska, she needed a place to stay. Well, fine, no reason why she couldn't stay here till she was on her feet. And he wouldn't get on her case about disappearing or being a lousy mother. Although it wasn't the greatest idea in the world having Troy think she was back to stay when Teo knew that the minute she was feeling better she'd take off again. Well, anyway, she's here now. She could have the big bedroom. The sheets were clean on the bed. The last thing Estella did before she moved out was wash all the linens and towels in the house. But he'd have to dig up some more blankets, nights got cold, and the heater made more noise than heat. So he'd move Troy to the small room off the back porch, there was enough space in there for a bed and play table and shelves for his toys and books (he liked Dr. Seuss's *Green Eggs and Ham,* which Teo read to him every night before he went to sleep). What was he talking about? Eight people once lived in the house and no one complained. Estella and Oscar had moved in for a while, and aside from Estella driving Teo crazy with her neatness, and Teo never knowing whether she had locked the doors and windows when she went out, it had worked out all right. But he couldn't remember what Estella said she was going to do with the quilts she took out of Ma's old cedar chest. She talked so much he didn't listen to half of what she said. *I'm organizing, putting things where we can find them easily.* But where did she say that was? Maybe in one of the bedrooms in a drawer. Or in the closet next to the front door.

When he came back into the living room with the tea, Roxana had her suitcase open and was unzipping a side pocket.

"Time to take my pills," she said, and tossed three tablets into her mouth and sat back down on the couch (actually fell onto the couch, as if her legs had suddenly given out). "I'm almost through with chemo. I've had some problems, but I'm licking them, I'm getting better, getting really, really better. You should have seen me a couple of weeks ago, Andy had to put me on the toilet and hold me there, I was so weak. Well, I'm not going to go into all the bad stuff that's happened since I saw you last, you'll say no one could have that much bad luck. But believe me, I've been on a losing streak. It seems that everything I touch just turns to shit, Teo. I mean it. I think, oh, great, this is going to work out, and then, fuck, it falls into the toilet. And I know I shouldn't have left Troy with Gordon, but I didn't think I'd be gone long, I really didn't. I met this guy Franco at the gallery where Gordon had some of his shit, and he called me up and said he was going to Alaska, had I ever been, and it just hit me that I never had, and I thought to myself I had to see Alaska before I got a day older, and so I went with him. Just like that. It felt really, really good doing what I wanted, I was getting so bored with that whole downtown art shit scene." She started to cough, lightly at first, and then hard enough for the veins to stick out in her neck. When she was finally able to talk again, her voice was low and raspy.

"Franco had this really weird sense of humor. We're driving along, see, and he says he wants to take my picture sitting on the hood of the car, so he stops the car, and I get out and sit on the hood, he snaps my picture, he gets back in the car, and he drives a whole block with me hanging on to the windshield wipers. It was so funny, Teo, you had to be there to know how funny it was. But when we hit Juneau he said that was the end of the line and dropped me off in the middle of the street. I had no money and was starting to feel sick. Andy saved my life, Teo, I mean it. I was down to it, skimming the bottom, and he gave me a room in the Polar Bear and fed me and took me to the doctor. I never was so scared in my whole life. I never have been afraid of anything, but lately, I don't know, life is just piling in and piling in and all I want to do is stay in one place and not go anywhere, which is crazy, Teo, I mean, can you believe it? Me wanting to stay in one place? Andy says it's never too late to change. He's been really good for me, Teo, really good. Makes me sleep eight hours a night. Imagine, me sleeping. And he cooks and keeps a chart on what I eat, and goes to the doctor with me, and makes sure I take my medicine on time. He treats me like I'm his baby or something, it's so weird, because I never liked anyone hanging over me, you know, it scares the shit out of me, like I'm in jail. But I don't mind the way he does it, because all I have to do is say quit pushing me and he goes all right, all right, and backs off. And I know you're thinking that every time there's a new guy I say he's the one, and that I'm probably making this all up, but God's truth I'm not, this time it's the straight shit, no joke, Teo, this is for real, and I want to do something for him, you know, something real nice, to show how much I appreciate everything he's doing for me. That's what people are supposed to do, you know, is return favors, and you don't know the favors Andy's done for me, I can't even count them, so I said to myself what can I give him that he's never had, and pow! the idea hit me, hey, he's never had a kid, and I've got one in California."

She looked around the living room. "Jesus, I haven't been in this house in so long, I forgot how much I hated it. I can smell Ma's tamales, I swear I can. It's so depressing, I don't know how you can live here. It feels like the walls are scrunching my bones all up inside my skin. It's the same way I felt when I was fifteen and walked out the door, and now, I swear, Teo, it feels like I never moved a step, that Ma's going to come out of the kitchen and yell at me for ditching school and Pa's going to tell her to go easy on me, which he was wrong about, boy, was he ever, he should have sat on me, shouldn't have let me get away with anything. But I'm not complaining. I've had my fun, I sure have, you can't take that away from me. I've lived more than anyone has a right to."

She said she'd like some more tea. He went into the kitchen and stood at the sink waiting for the water to boil again. Troy's toy airplanes and trucks were lined up on the kitchen table next to his box of crayons. The front and sides of the refrigerator were covered with drawings of dinosaurs and trees in green and yellow, his favorite colors. Teo poured the hot water into the cup and ripped open another tea bag. So she had come to take Troy away.

He brought the tea into the living room.

"I called Estella because I didn't know where you were," she said, "and she told me you went to see Raul, and I said, you're kidding, Teo sure must be desperate to get rid of Troy if he went to see Raul. And then she told me about Bonnie and Oscar, and I could hardly believe it, not that Bonnie wouldn't take anything she could get from anyone, but that Oscar was stupid enough to think she wanted him for himself. Estella sounded really wrung out, I never heard her like that, and I told her to come up to Juneau, there are more men per square inch than she'll ever see in California. It just proves my point about marriage. Why do it? I personally like to move quick, make up my mind and go. Of course, now I'm settled down, just an old stay-at-home, but I'm glad I never got married, it's such a mess when it doesn't work." She held the cup in both hands and sipped the tea. "Estella said you were impossible to deal with lately, that she didn't know what had gotten into you, and I told her she just didn't have the touch, she didn't know how to handle you, that you're the sweetest bear in the world when you're treated right. Jeez, I'm really tired. Traveling is the worst, Teo. I never used to think that. Remember that van I had when I was with Doug, you remember Doug, the redhead, the one who played the bongos? I'd drive that van for twenty hours straight without sleeping and he'd play the bongos, and we'd pick up people along the way, and I never got tired, it was such a blast. So I thought I'd leave tomorrow early. Andy bought Troy's ticket, so that's taken care of. You can ship his stuff. Remind me to give you the address of the inn. You can come up and visit us. There's great fishing up there, and hunting. Andy can show you all the best places. I guess I can handle the nebulizer, that's not too heavy. Won't Troy be surprised to see me here when he wakes up? I meant to bring him a present, but I was in such a rush I didn't get a chance."

"You're not taking him with you."

"Of course I am. He's my baby. Shit, Teo, you're not going to get all noble on me now, are you? You're not going to start thinking you're going to save my baby by taking him away from me, are you?"

"You didn't give a damn about your baby when you left, and you don't give a damn about him now."

"How do you know?" she said, her voice shaking. "Are you a mind reader? Can you get inside my head? You think you're so smart, and everyone else is so stupid."

"Buy your boyfriend a shirt, he's not getting Troy."

"You can't even keep a job. No one wants you around. You fight with everyone, you push everyone around, you think you're God. Well, you're not God, Teo, not by a fucking long shot."

"You're not getting Troy. He's staying with me."

"I remember what Bonnie always said about you. Teo wants to rule the world, wants to arrange it and then glue it into place so he'll always know where everything is. Well, you're not going to glue me into any goddamn place, I can tell you that for fucking sure, because I'm going to take him with me whether you like it or not."

She lay back weakly against the cushions. "He's mine," she said.

"I never said he wasn't yours. I said you're not taking him."

"You just don't want me to be happy, that's all. You've always tried to tell me what to do, and I don't want to do what you want, I want something else, I want—I don't know what I want. I just know I want it."

He sat down on the couch and put his arm around her.

"I'm so tired," she said.

"I'd be tired, too, transferring from Juneau to Anchorage to—"

"Juneau to Ketchikan. You weren't listening."

"I heard every word."

"What if I die, Teo, what then?"

"We all die, Roxie."

"But I mean die young, you know, in a year or two. I don't want to stay in Juneau and be cold when I'm dead. They have to wait till spring to bury you. I want to come home if I die, where it's warm, and they put you in the ground right away. Andy says I'm fine, that everything is going the way the doctor said, but I don't think so, I don't think the pills are working. They make me sicker. It's a bitch. I hate it. I hate everything. I hate you. I hate Andy. I hate myself for being this way." She sighed and closed her eyes, and he thought she was asleep, but then she said, "I didn't think you'd care if I took him. You never liked children."

"Well, I like Troy," he told her.

Roxana sat down on the edge of Troy's bed. It was too dark to see her face, but Teo heard her whisper that she'd just sleep in here next to Troy, that all she needed was a blanket or two, and she'd be up early and make breakfast. Andy had taught her how to cook, she said, wouldn't Ma have been surprised at that, and he heard her blow him a kiss.

He went into the kitchen and sat looking at the clock on the stove. It was two in the morning, and he felt wide awake and jumpy, as if something terrible were happening right this minute, not next year or the year after that, but right now. At five o'clock he was still sitting in the kitchen when he heard Roxana walk down the hall into the living room. He could see her as she picked up her small suitcase, put on her sweater and jacket and coat, and walked out the door.

Chapter 25

⟶

Teo threw some clothes in a bag, put Troy and his nebulizer and medications into the car, and started driving. The weatherman said cool and damp through the weekend. If Troy's wheezing turned to gasping, Teo could have had the car stopped and the albuterol mixed and the nebulizer going in three minutes flat, he was getting that good at it.

It was a day's drive to Visalia from Santa Ana, if you didn't dawdle or stop and tramp through the fields of wildflowers along the road. Teo wouldn't even have stopped for lunch, he would have gassed up in Delano and kept on going, but Troy said he was hungry, so Teo pulled into a McDonald's. A quarter-pounder and a Happy Meal. Teo picked Troy up so he could reach the ketchup dispenser, and then held him there while Troy pressed the metal handle and carefully, slowly, and without spilling a drop filled four little paper cups with ketchup.

"Do you want to eat inside, or outside?"

"Outside."

There were some kids chasing one another through the plastic tubes in the outside eating area, flashes of flowered blouses and torn jeans flitting by the fogged-up windows.

"Eat your hamburger and then, if you want to, you can play awhile."

Troy hadn't taken anything out of his Happy Meal bag except the spaceship, which he was now rolling up and down the spotted table.

"Are we going to Texas again?"

"No more Texas. Eat your hamburger."

Troy put down the spaceship and took the hamburger out of the bag and unwrapped it. He laid the oily paper on the table, then the top half of the bun, then lifted the meat and looked under it, straightened the pickle, patted the lettuce flat, and as if rearranging it were as good as eating it, neatly reassembled the whole thing and put his thumb in his mouth.

"How about taking one bite?"

Troy took his thumb out of his mouth and said he didn't want to take a bite, he didn't want to eat, he wasn't hungry, he wanted to sit on Teo's lap.

There was a circle of sun baking the stucco wall at Teo's back, and he leaned against the warm wall with his arms around the child. It was comfortable, sitting in the sun, watching the girl at the take-out window hand out bags of hamburgers.

Troy was asleep, perspiration beading on his forehead and dampening his hair. What did he dream, lying against Teo's chest, his forehead creased and his eyelids fluttering? About Roxana? He didn't mention her. Teo didn't even know whether he had seen her that night. The only thing that was any different about him since then was that he had started sucking his thumb, and it struck Teo suddenly that Troy may not have been in a war, but that he might as well have been, he had so many wounds and battle scars.

He didn't sleep long. Teo bought him a yogurt (he licked it about five times and then gave it to Teo to finish) and by then it was midafternoon, and time to get going if they were going to get to Visalia before dark.

Eric had given Teo careful instructions. Watch for the access road and turn left. The road is bumpy and half torn up by old floods and roots of trees, but keep on it and after a while you'll see the house.

The sun was nearly gone, just a lavender halo skimming the tops of the trees, when Teo turned onto the access road. He couldn't remember when he had last felt this anxious about anything. Maybe the first time he saw combat, when he realized that someone was shooting at him, and it was real and final and there was no running away.

Ellie had just put a plate of coconut cookies on the porch steps for the tree cutters when she saw the car come up the access road. At first she thought it was the man who was going to fix the fireplace flue. Everyone else was working and accounted for. The landscapers were putting in the new lawn, Tony was paneling the dining room, nailing up honey-colored sheets of wood, while the plumber finished installing the new sink in the small bathroom off the back porch. The roof was finished, although there was a problem with the gutters, or maybe it was the eaves. Anyway, the roofer wasn't supposed to be back to fix whatever was wrong until the following Monday.

The car pulled in next to the plumber's truck in the field across the road and a man got out followed by a little boy, and for just a moment, in the lavender light Ellie thought it was Jamie, and her heart jumped. But for only a second. Of course, it wasn't Jamie. And then she realized that the man was Teo, striding across the dug-up yard, up the steps, and onto the porch, the little boy's hand in his. Alice came out of the house, and there was a flurry of conversation, unintelligible to Ellie, because her mind simply couldn't grasp why Teo was standing on the porch or who the little boy belonged to. Teo said something to her about wanting to talk to her, about having to talk to her, and Alice was saying something to Teo about weather, he was lucky he missed the storm, they had nearly been stranded, water all around, a lake of water, ditches full of water, he should have seen it, the worst in a hundred years, the paper said.

"Are you going to leave me here?" the little boy said.

Teo swung him up into his arms. "I told you I wasn't going to leave you anywhere."

"You can't just show up like this," Ellie said. "Do you think you can just show up, just decide you feel like taking a drive and show up, when I wrote you off, when I thought you didn't even like me? I never saw anyone with your nerve. What are you doing here, anyway?"

"I didn't know you had a son," Alice said. "He's a nice little boy. You never even mentioned being a father."

"Do you think you can jump in and out of my life anytime you want to?" Ellie said. "Did you think all I've been doing is praying you'd show up? That that's all I've had to do these past few months is wait and wonder what I did wrong? Well, I haven't. I don't think I've thought about you twice in the last month. If that. Maybe not even once."

"You disappeared," Teo replied. "I went to your house looking for you. You didn't say you were going anywhere. You didn't leave a note."

"I've always thought I could tell if someone had a child," Alice said, "that it showed on their face. I certainly never thought you fit the picture. You don't have that fatherly look, although I don't suppose that every man who's a father has it."

"What did you expect me to do, sit and wait for you to call me?" Ellie said. "And when I wasn't wondering what I did wrong, I was worrying about you, thinking you were sitting alone in your house and you might have done something crazy, because you were so depressed, and I've been so worried about that, about you doing something crazy."

"If you were so worried about me, why didn't you call me up and ask me how I was? You could have said, hey, Teo, how're you doing? You could have told me where you were going. That's all it would have taken and I'd have been here."

"How was I supposed to know that?"

Another car had pulled up behind where Teo was parked. It was Alvin, the real estate man Alice had been talking to about selling the farm.

"Beautiful day," Alvin said as he walked up the steps onto the porch. He was in his seventies, red faced and a little overweight, and wore flowered suspenders to hold up his trousers. He shook Teo's hand and introduced himself.

"Alvin Durham, real estate and tax appraiser. Are you interested in the house, or just the land? I can make you a deal on either one."

"I told you I'm not sure yet what I want to do," Alice said, "whether I want to sell or not. You're rushing me, Alvin, and I don't think it's working. I'm not one of those who can be rushed or talked into things."

"I practically threw myself at you," Ellie said, "and it didn't make any difference. I thought you knew how I felt. I certainly didn't hide it."

"I didn't even know there was anything going on," Alice said. "You never told me a thing. I thought he was just hounding me."

"I wouldn't call it hounding," Alvin said. "And I don't want you doing anything you don't want to do. Didn't I tell you that right from the first, that I'm just here to help you and if you decide for sure to sell I'll work my tail off trying to get you the best deal on the place?"

"I'm not talking to you," Alice said.

"There just might be a buyer for the fields," Alvin said. "I didn't tell you that before. I know you said you didn't want to break up the acreage, but what do you care once it's sold how many pieces there are and who's got what?" He sat down on the wicker bench and it creaked under his weight. "Just might be, don't get your hopes up, but I had some people this afternoon inquiring about available land to build an amusement park on, and they might just take the whole thing. But, of course, they'd want to knock the house down first."

"Knock the house down?" Alice said. "What are you talking about?"

"I'm talking about Disneyland and Mickey Mouse and Donald Duck. Real live amusement park people, right here on this farm."

Troy had gone down the steps and was walking back toward the car.

"He thinks I'm going to leave him here," Teo said. "I told him I wasn't going to leave him anywhere, but he doesn't believe me."

"An amusement park on an artichoke farm?" Alice said. "That's the fanciest story I've heard out of you yet. First it was developers wanting to build houses and now it's Mickey Mouse. And who said we were selling, anyway? I told you it was just a thought, that maybe we would, because of the—this personal problem—well, because—and you show up every day with another wild scheme."

"Not too many people want a hundred-year-old house," Alvin said, "no matter how much reworking has been done to it, especially when you have to drive two miles down a road that nearly flooded out in the last rain."

Ellie stood stiffly on the porch and watched Teo follow Troy out to the car. The landscapers had cut the trees down in front of the house, but the eucalyptus trees to the west were still standing, and beyond that the canyon, and beyond that the giant sequoias like inkblots against the darkening sky. And Alice was now offering Alvin a coconut cookie and asking him to stay for supper; they were having leg of lamb with parsley potatoes and watercress salad with sugared pecans, but she didn't want to hear any more about Disneyland or Mickey Mouse, and Ellie thought of Jamie and Eric and of regretting things she hadn't done or said that might have changed what happened, that if she had bent to Eric a little more or if she hadn't left Jamie at that hospital, and it all went through her head in a split second and then she was running down the steps and out the gate.

"Wait," she called out, and Teo turned around.

"I wasn't leaving," he said. "You'd have to try harder than you did to get rid of me."

Troy had found the old arbor, the one to the rear of the house that the landscaper wanted to tear down and that Alice told him she wanted just the way it was, that she could remember helping Mom sort peaches on the picnic table in the summertime, firm ones for pies, soft ones for preserves, rotten ones for the compost heap, and eating ripe peaches in between till she was sick to her stomach. The gazebo roof had fallen in and the floor was rotted, but the picnic table was still sturdy, and Troy was playing in the leaves, lifting handfuls and flinging them up into the air.

"Alice is really my mother," Ellie said. "It's been a big shock to me. I didn't know where I was for a while, but it's better now, I'm getting used to it. I don't know what to call her, so I call her Alice. We concentrate on other things, try not to talk about it that much. There's really no fixing some things. You just have to kind of step over them. I would like to call her Mother, but I had a mother, and it feels wrong somehow. She says she did the best she could and I believe her. Most of the time I think of her as my sister. You can't change a habit like that. It doesn't mean anything what you call someone, anyway." She looked over a Troy. "I didn't know you had a child."

"He's Roxana's, but she left him and I took him, and I guess he's mine now."

"I waited for you. I wouldn't have come here with Alice if you had just called me, just once."

The shade was deep here, and the sorrel a thick mat beneath their feet where the river had overflowed.

"Look, Ellie, I'm not going to lie to you. Bonnie came back and I let her. I could tell you she needed a place to stay and that's the way it happened, but I didn't have to let it happen, I could have said no, I know how to say no, but I didn't, and so she moved in. It was like when we were married. It was an easy groove to slip into. I knew her and she knew me, so why not? It didn't work out. After she left I had Troy to take care of. He's got asthma and needs a lot of attention. And I used one excuse after another not to come after you when the truth was I just couldn't make the move. My whole life's plan the past few months revolved around how I was going to come up here and find you. The trouble was it meant doing it, and I've never been very good at that. I've always kind of let things happen. And then Roxana showed up, sick and wanting Troy back. I told her no, and then everything turned clear, and I asked myself what the hell I was waiting for."

"You took Bonnie back? You mean you—the two of you—in your house, together?"

"In my house, together."

She took a deep breath. "That hurts me more than anything."

"I told you it didn't work out."

Troy had stirred up the eucalyptus leaves so that pungent clouds of dust now swirled in the air around them. He came and sat down on the bench between them, leaning forward, taking deep breaths, his small chest moving slowly up and down. Ellie put her hand on his back and could feel every quivery breath he took.

"Things bother him," Teo said.

"But will he—"

"He's stronger than he looks. Reminds me of some of the soldiers I knew in the army, the ones who looked scrawny and timid in basic and turned into little war-making machines in Vietnam, leaping through rice paddies, wading through swamps, existing on a cracker a day and a thimbleful of water. He'll be all right. And if you can't forget about Bonnie and me, if you think you're going to throw it up to me every chance you get, tell me now and I'll go away. I'll be miserable, but I'll live. But if you can forget about Bonnie, really forget it, then I think we can make a go of it. We can get married or live together, either way is okay with me. All you have to do is say yes, you want to be with me and Troy, or at least that you love me. That's a start."

"But his mother might—"

"His mother might. No guarantees that she won't."

She looked out across the eucalyptus grove to the yellowed fields.

"Take your time," he said.

The house was dark, everyone in bed. It had been a long day, a trying one, what with one revelation after another, one surprise following another, and now Alice was exhausted. She lay on top of the quilt and listened to her heartbeat. Watch out for microwave ovens and magnetic resonance imaging machines, and what else was it she was supposed to watch out for? Policemen coming up from Los Angeles to arrest her, but instead going into the bedroom with Ellie and doing God knows what in there, and coming out after a while, both of them looking flushed and happy? Or Teo coming into the kitchen where Alice was spooning the rum sauce over the baked apples and saying to her, "I know you shot him"? Right there, that should have been enough to make her heart stop.

"What makes you think I shot him?" she asked him, and he said he had figured it out, but he couldn't prove it because there was a mistake in some tests or the fingerprints were lost, or some such thing that she couldn't quite get through her head.

"I'm not going to do anything about it," he said. "I'm not going to mention it again. I just wanted you to know that I know, and that that's the end of it."

And then he went back into the half-paneled dining room and sat down at the table and didn't take his eyes off Ellie, and Alvin kept talking about real estate values in Visalia, as if anyone was listening. After supper Teo and Ellie went out on the porch and Alice could hear them laughing, a musical trill from Ellie and short, staccato bursts from Teo, while Alvin and Troy sat on the dining room floor and made houses out of the scraps of wood Tony had left in the cardboard carton under the dining room table. Alice just sat on the living room couch in a daze, thinking about what Teo had said to her. It was the most interesting thing she had ever heard anyone say. Mysterious. I know you did it and I'm going to leave you alone. Not that it made any difference to her. He could have arrested her right then and she wouldn't have minded. She had resigned herself to whatever might happen and was willing and ready to go to jail if she had to. But talk about twists. She had thought for sure he had come to take her back to Los Angeles, but it was Ellie he had come for. And all this time Alice thought she was the sole cause of Ellie's unhappiness, the reason she was so silent and moody, and then he drove up and the whole picture changed. The way Ellie looked at him, the way she stood and moved and talked, so animated, so emotional, fire in her eyes and red in her cheeks. And then running down the steps after him when she thought he was leaving. Well, all of it certainly was a relief and a surprise. She had thought Ellie would never forgive her, that there was no going back to the way they were before, that she had broken something that couldn't be mended, when all those yearning looks of Ellie's, all those sighs and melancholy gazes out the window, were nothing but lovesickness.

There was no going to sleep when you weren't sleepy. Alice got out of bed and opened the window. There was a smell here like no other. She could conjure up all sorts of memories just by taking a deep breath of air at her bedroom window.

Troy was asleep on the daybed in the sewing room. He wasn't cute the way Jamie was, and he looked so fragile, as if a little cold could put him in the hospital, but Ellie clearly liked him, she fussed over him at supper, cut his meat up for him and asked him what his favorite ice cream was. He said he liked vanilla, and he didn't want to eat the meat, that he wasn't hungry, and Ellie made him an ice cream sundae right in the middle of supper, before anyone had finished, and you'd have thought she was tasting every bite he took the way she looked at him.

Teo and Ellie were in the rear bedroom together now, and Alice could hear the sounds of their lovemaking, soft hushes of breath, bedsprings groaning. Alice wondered if Ellie had told him about her losing a sister and gaining a mother. If she told him, it hadn't made much of an impression on him. He probably thought it was a small thing, not worth getting upset about. Well, it might have been a small thing, but it had been big enough to ripple out and touch all their lives in one way or another.

What was it Ellie asked her just before she married Eric?

Is he the one, Alice? How can I tell if he's the one?

How was she supposed to answer that question when the wedding invitations had been mailed out?

Alice got back into bed. Life goes in directions you never could have dreamed it would. Like shooting Morty. She still couldn't believe she did it. Sometimes she thought maybe she didn't, maybe he really did shoot himself. But she knew she had and she remembered every single second of it, what he said and what she said and how he raised the gun and she screamed at him and he put it down and she picked it up and shot him. But where had that impulse come from, that urge to hurt him that went past reasonableness and straight to her hand? She couldn't re-create it in her mind, couldn't feel it. She tried over and over to bring it back, to see if she could work herself into the same state of mind, the same emotion she had been feeling at the moment she shot him, but she couldn't. It was as if there was a wall between her and those feelings. Oh, she remembered what she was thinking just before she did it, that she was afraid of him, she wished he would disappear, would go away, would leave her alone. She just couldn't put herself back there, couldn't reproduce that rush of adrenaline that made her lose her senses and pick up that gun. Not that Morty didn't deserve shooting. Not a week went by that he hadn't shoved her or pushed her or knocked her down or harmed her in some way. The doctor said he never saw anyone have as many accidents or fall down as much or get smacked in the face by swinging doors as often as Alice had.

Everyone said she should have stayed married to Jerome, her first husband, and she was too embarrassed to ever tell anyone why she didn't. When they had been married a month, he said he had made a mistake and wanted to become a priest. It took Alice one year to get the divorce, and Jerome two years to get a church annulment and then, instead of entering the priesthood, he and another man joined the Forest Service and disappeared into the wilds of some national park. Literally disappeared. Left their cabin one day and were never seen again.

Then there was Arthur, her second husband. He owned a restaurant in San Francisco and when they had been married for fourteen years he left her for one of his waitresses. He rarely came home when they were married, but she hadn't expected him to leave, and she cried more over her having been such a fool than she did over his leaving.

Allen was the one she couldn't forget. He was as vivid in her memory as if she had been with him yesterday. His face popped up at the strangest times, but mostly in dreams. *Where have you been?* she always asked him, and he would say, *Oh, here and there,* and smile at her. He always looked so healthy in her dreams, no holes in him, no mention of the war, no talk of how he had been killed in Korea.

She had been so young when she met Allen. She had no idea that he could actually die or that there would be time beyond those moments with him, or years to be lived and somehow gotten through, didn't know she'd marry three times and have no more children, didn't realize what hell there'd be to pay for lying about Ellie.

The sheets were smooth against her legs. They were fifty-year-old muslin sheets that Alice found in a cupboard, the same ordinary muslin sheets Mom had washed every week by hand in the tub in the yard and then put through the wringer and hung on the line, then brought into the house smelling of wild grass and river water. Mom wouldn't use the automatic machine Pop bought until the wringer machine broke down and there were no more parts to be found for it. Where had all those days gone? Going to church on Sundays, Pop pulling at his starched collar as he drove, Mom reminding Alice not to fidget when the minister was giving his sermon, that there was nothing like a fidgeting child to make a person lose his concentration.

Alice turned in bed, found the spot where the pacemaker wires didn't pinch her skin, and closed her eyes. All that rough washing and wringing had done something to the fabric in the sheets, had pulled it so hard and in so many directions that all the bumps and imperfections had been wrung out and smoothed away. It wasn't possible, of course, and no one would believe her, and it didn't matter whether they did or not, but she'd have sworn on her life that after all those years of being pulled through a wringer, the muslin had turned to silk.